CW00455406

THE NEANDERTHAL

PARADOX

Every Future Has A Past

Keith Argyle and Paul G White

Published, bound and printed by Shed Publications UK

Best wishes Keith Argyle

1

These four books in the Neanderthal Paradox series are dedicated to all writers' who try effortlessly to try and get their books published. Our message is, "never give in".

THE NEANDERTHAL PARADOX

Every Future Has a past

Chapter One

BACK HOME:

Ciara Branton stared at the Neanderthal in disbelief. Or-gon, resplendent in a brightly coloured tracksuit, sat quietly listening as Joe Laing related the story of his adventures in the Neanderthal past. Joe had just reached the part where he had entered the parallel timeline of Tarmis and Ciara's mind was balking at the concept of a multiverse of countless differing timelines.

"You mean to tell me," she demanded, "that this … friend of yours, shouldn't actually exist?"

"Not in *our* twenty-first century, no," Joe agreed, "but, as far as we can tell, he is the *only* survivor from *his* time. As far as we know, we cancelled out his entire timeline so that I could return to you. Anyway," he added, his voice heavy with emotion, "Tarmis was destroyed in a nuclear war, so there would have been nothing left for Or-gon if he had stayed."

Ciara's eyes clouded. "Timeline? Multiverse? *Nuclear war?*" she whispered. "Joe, I don't understand any of this. You're scaring me. You come back looking all different, dragging along someone you say shouldn't exist, and you expect me to understand … just like that, as if this sort of thing happened every day?" A note of hysteria crept into her voice.

Joe held his fiancée in a firm embrace. "Darling," he said quietly, "my friend has a name; it's Or-gon. He's a refugee in every sense you can imagine, and he deserves all the help and understanding we can give him."

Ciara sobbed. "Sorry, Joe! I'm being selfish, aren't I?"

"No, Sweetheart, I just think it's all been a bit too much for you. In your place, I suppose I'd find it difficult to accept."

Or-gon coughed and said in halting English, which owed much of its structure to the influence of a translator globe in Tarmis, "My apologies, mate of the Futa—" He realised just in time that he should not use his people's honorific for Joe in this timeline. "My apologies if my presence causes you discomfort. I would beg my

3

friend, Jo-lang to return me to the past, but I fear that my presence *there* would cause further disruptions in time. It hurts me to feel your distress at my presence, but I am a stranger in your strange world, with just one friend to provide a rock to cling to. I would be honoured if the mate of Jo-lang would be my friend also."

For the first time since Joe had arrived at the door with Or-gon, Ciara understood just how alone the Neanderthal must feel. His country had been obliterated in a nuclear war and, if she had understood correctly, his whole timeline had possibly been erased as if it had never existed. Yet, even in the midst of his loss, he retained a dignity that demanded understanding. She felt a surge of compassion for Joe's rugged-looking friend.

For no reason that she could readily explain, Ciara stepped around the coffee table and embraced Or-gon warmly. All her enmity and distrust was spent and she was left with an overwhelming need to comfort the Neanderthal. Or-gon's utter bafflement at the overt display of affection brought a smile to Joe's lips.

"Seems like you've made at least one more friend," he grinned, and the Neanderthal returned the smile, grateful that Ciara had finally accepted him.

Ciara gave Or-gon a final hug and said fussily, "We haven't even offered our friend a cup of tea. You do drink tea, don't you?" she asked as an afterthought.

The Neanderthal glanced first at Joe, then at Ciara. "Yes, mate of Jo-lang, I have experienced the beverage whilst awaiting the return of my friend with this garment." He fingered the polycotton material of the tracksuit. "I find tea strangely refreshing."

Ciara found Or-gon's reference to her as 'mate of Joe Laing' amusing and her laughter dispersed the last dregs of tension in the room. "If I'm to call you Or-gon, you'll have to start calling me Ciara. People will think it's funny if you keep calling me 'mate of Joe Laing'."

Or-gon smiled, "I will be honoured." He glanced at Joe, seeking approval, and Joe grinned.

With Or-gon's position clarified to everyone's satisfaction, it was now possible to continue the story to its conclusion, the telling punctuated intermittently by Ciara's questions. Eventually, the three sat around Joe's dining table, consuming bowls of spaghetti Bolognese and Ciara couldn't help noticing the way Or-gon tested every forkful by rolling the food around his palate.

"Is this much different from what you had at home?" Ciara enquired.

Or-gon replied with a question of his own. "Is this food from an animal?"

"The beef is from an animal," she indicated the mince on her plate, "but the pasta is from wheat."

"Then it is *very* different," came the reply. "We ate no animal products in Tarmis. We considered it barbaric."

"That's a far cry from your ancestors," Joe remarked. "The majority of their diet was meat from wild animals, which they killed by hunting them with spears."

"Now that you mention it," Ciara said, "if you lived with them for so long, what was it you did that changed the Neanderthal future?"

"Mostly I made their hunting methods more efficient, by showing them how to make throwing spears and bows and arrows. My biggest mistake was in talking to their shaman, Koo-ma. He was extremely bright, and everything we discussed made him want to know more. He would have done well in modern times, but for some strange reason, it needed my intervention to provide the spark back then. The Neanderthals, as a race, were really set in their ways."

Or-gon's curiosity was awakened by Joe's revelations. He had seen Joe's memories replayed before the Council of Tarmis, and he was intrigued to have Joe fill in the gaps. "It seems strange that my ancestors accepted one so different into their midst?"

Joe swirled his wine in the glass, then took a sip of the yellow liquid, savouring its delicate spiciness. The time had arrived to explain everything. He had intended to relate his total experience to Or-gon and his people in Tarmis, but the advent of Prua Landi and her sudden initiation of the nuclear attack, had prevented him from doing so. Now was his chance to explain to Or-gon and Ciara.

"At first," he began, "I watched the Neanderthals from the time tunnel, and studied their language over a period of weeks before I made contact. When I stepped through into the ceremonial cave they immediately called me 'Futama' and treated me as some kind of god. I tried to explain that I was just an ordinary man, but apparently there was an ancient legend amongst the Neanderthals that prophesied a great hunter would come to lead them, and they refused to believe that I wasn't the Futama. As it turned out, I really *was* the Futama of their legends – but don't ask me how that came about because I have absolutely no idea."

Or-gon was puzzled by Joe's explanation. "How then can you be so certain that you are truly the Futama, the one whose coming was prophesied amongst my people?"

"Because Koo-ma, the shaman, recognised me from the legend that had been handed down from generation to generation amongst the Neanderthal people. He was expecting someone who was not like them and, as time passed, everything I did seemed to fulfil some part of the prophecies. It was as if the Shaman knew what to expect from me – not the details, obviously, but the general picture." Joe took another sip of wine. "Anyway," he added, "it's probably all tied in with the fact that no one else but me can see the time tunnels or the hole in the cliff leading to them."

Or-gon stroked his chin. "That is true, Jo-lang. None of my people, in the distant past or in Tarmis could see or enter the tunnels. Is this so with the people of your world?"

"I can't say for certain," Joe answered, "but no one on the beach seems to pay any attention to the cleft when they're anywhere near it. I'm sure anyone could easily see through my camouflage from thirty metres, but no one ever does."

Ciara stared at each of the men in turn. Joe could see that she was about to ask a question and awaited her words expectantly.

"Joe," she said, "you have told me where Or-gon comes from, and how he came to be here; and how you were accepted by the Neanderthals as the Futama warrior. But how did all this begin in the first place?" Evidently Ciara would not be happy until she knew every detail.

Joe glanced at Or-gon, who was obviously anticipating his explanation. "Well," he began, "before Ciara and I got together, I had found a tiny fissure in the cliffs, which led through a narrow gorge onto a small secluded beach. I found a well-preserved flint axe-head. My curiosity got the better of me, so I started my own archaeological dig."

"But how did all this business with the Neanderthals begin?" Ciara asked impatiently.

"I'm coming to that," Joe smiled, winking at Or-gon as if to say, 'Aren't women impatient?' "One morning when I went to my dig, I saw what seemed to be an opening high in the cliffs, across from my tent. I thought it strange that I hadn't noticed it before, but it was probably revealed by a section of the cliff face collapsing. It wasn't easy, but I climbed up the cliff and explored the small cavern. The cave went back further than I could see without a torch, so I decided to return home for some equipment to explore further."

Ciara asked, "Why didn't you tell anyone else about your discovery?"

Joe didn't wish to appear selfish, or self-important. After a few moments' thought, he said, "Because of my experience with archaeological digs, and what happens when something interesting crops up, I didn't want anyone disturbing my find – or taking it over, for that matter. I decided to keep it to myself until I was sure exactly what I'd found."

Or-gon listened intently as Joe related his story; he smiled as Ciara interrupted with a seemingly constant stream of questions. Eventually Joe told how he lived with the Neanderthals, the knowledge and techniques he passed on to them, and the altered timeline leading to Tarmis and Or-gon's people.

When Joe reached the point about Prua Landi's murderous intervention in Tarmis, Ciara whispered nervously, "Joe, do you think Prua Landi is still around somewhere? Is it possible? Because she frightens me even though I've never met her."

Ciara's question made Joe wonder about the possibility; Or-gon's expression said he thought Joe's fiancée might have a point.

"Darling, if she is still around somewhere, I don't intend to go searching for her," he said, drawing a line under the subject of the tall time-traveller.

Joe finished his explanations and said, "I would love another cup of tea, how about you, Or-gon?"

The Neanderthal smiled. "Excellent! I am becoming accustomed to the flavour of this liquid." Joe and Ciara laughed at Or-gon's quaint pattern of speech.

As Ciara went through to the kitchen Joe was thinking of what she had said about Prua Landi. He had considered the same thing himself, but had deliberately kept his fears to himself in order not to alarm his fiancée.

While Ciara was making the tea, she ran through Joe's story in her mind: she felt certain he wouldn't invent such a story – but the whole thing was so incredible! She placed the fresh pot of tea on the table and sat down beside Joe.

"Joe," she commanded, "look at me for a moment, please!"

Obligingly, he turned and, to his horror, Ciara grasped his beard and gave a firm tug. A cry of pain escaped his lips and he demanded, "Why on earth did you do that?" Ruefully, he rubbed the offended area. "That hurt, you know!"

Ciara grinned mischievously. "Believe me Joe, if that beard had come off in my hand, you would have hurt a lot more – and in different places. At least I now know you're not winding me up with some kind of fairy tale." The gleam in her eye made it clear that she meant what she'd said.

"Okay, Darling," Joe answered, once again rubbing his chin, "I suppose I can forgive you if you thought that was necessary, but believe me, what I am telling you is the truth – and Or-gon's presence is vindication. How else could he be here?"

Ciara eyed Joe steadily. "There is only one part of your story that bothers me, Joe Laing," she said firmly.

Joe had a good idea what she was going to say, and allowed her to continue without interruption.

"You say this Lar-na women was attracted to you, and that she seduced you and eventually gave birth to your son?"

Joe nodded.

"Can you promise me that you didn't encourage her?"

He held Ciara's hands in a firm, yet gentle, grip. "I didn't," he explained. "I told her, right from the start, that I had a woman back in my time and that we could be no more than companions. I showed her your photo in the locket and explained that it contained a powerful magic to bind me to you. The photo scared her a little, because all she'd ever seen was a reflection in water and the photograph was so much clearer – and smaller. I thought she'd accepted the situation, and I promise you that what she eventually did was out of my control. I love you and only you, and I want you to be my wife."

She hugged Joe tightly, a relieved smile on her lips. Or-gon was a little nonplussed at the display of emotion. He remained silent as Ciara released Joe and sat back in her chair.

"Joe," Ciara said, "I believe you, but I had to be sure for my own sanity. I don't want to lose you to anyone, especially a woman thirty-thousand years old." She laughed nervously at her weak attempt at humour, allowing the tension to seep away.

At that moment, Joe remembered his video-recordings of the Neanderthals. He walked over to the small cabinet below the TV and selected the three DVDs he'd completed whilst observing Koo-ma and his people.

"I've just remembered," he informed them, "I made these when I was observing the activities and sign language of the Neanderthals. They're further proof I'm not lying. I'm sure Or-gon will find them interesting too, because I didn't have them with me when I found myself in Tarmis. Why don't you watch them together while I take a shower and change into fresh clothes? And," he added, "I reckon I'll get rid of this damned beard. It's caused me enough pain already."

He had to suppress a grin at the sheepish expression on Ciara's face as he mounted the stairs.

* * *

Refreshed and cleanly shaven, Joe rejoined his fiancée and Or-gon who, by this time, were in animated discussion about the primitive Neanderthals. Or-gon was kneeling beside the TV, pointing a thick index finger at one of the figures on the screen.

"Here is Lar-na," he said, his voice thick with emotion, "the mother of my people."

Ciara froze the image. "She was beautiful, wasn't she," she admitted. "I can see how any man would have found her attractive."

Or-gon nodded in agreement. "That is true," he admitted. "I saw her with the Na-futama, when I escaped with Jo-lang to the time of my ancestors. These images can only display the outward beauty—"

Joe coughed politely and Or-gon halted in mid-sentence. "I apologise, Jo-lang. I fear I am not helping Ciara to understand about Lar-na."

Ciara put her arms around Joe's neck and kissed him. "It's all right, Or-gon, I think I understand, and I trust my Joe – completely."

Unselfconsciously returning the kiss, Joe finally admonished Or-gon, "It's time you started calling me Joe, and not Jo-lang. We left that behind in Tarmis and people here will think it's a bit odd. And," he added, "we're going to have to give you another name that's more acceptable here. We want you to blend in, and we certainly don't want anybody asking awkward questions."

The name, 'Morgan' burst unexpectedly from Ciara's lips and Joe said, "What?"

"Or-gon sounds like Morgan, doesn't it?" Ciara replied defensively. "Or-gon doesn't talk like us, so why not pass him off as a Welsh cousin or something?"

"Sounds good to me," Joe agreed, "especially since Morgan can be a Christian name. Let's call him Morgan Griffiths. That should work, shouldn't it?"

Or-gon sat impassive as the names were bandied around. Finally, he said "Mor-gan," rolling the name around his tongue several times and accidentally producing a passable Welsh accent in the process. "I think I like my new name, Jo-lang," he admitted with a grin.

"Then that's settled," said Joe. "Let's hope every problem's as easy to solve, especially having you call me Joe."

The Neanderthal, smiled. "It is not so easy for me to call you by another name, because Jo-lang and Futama have been foremost in the history of my people for many thousands of years."

"Don't worry," Joe grinned, "it'll come. Now we have a name for you, we're going to need an identity that will stand up to close scrutiny. Unfortunately, I don't know the kind of people who can supply one."

"Leave that to me," said Ciara. "One of my ex-boyfriends knew some pretty dodgy people. I'm sure I can get him to come up with something, but it will probably be expensive."

"Go for it," Joe agreed enthusiastically. "I've got access to some funds and it will be worth it in the end."

With that settled for the moment, despite his improved fitness levels, a feeling of tiredness assailed Joe, and he yawned expansively. It was late, so Ciara immediately went upstairs to make up the bed in Or-gon's room. Joe explained all the facilities of the bathroom and bedroom to his Neanderthal friend then retired to bed. Minutes later, Ciara entered the bedroom to discover Joe deeply asleep and snoring gently.

"It's good to have you back, darling," she whispered ruefully, as she slid into bed beside him. Ciara kissed Joe's cheek as she snuggled close to him. "Let's see what surprises tomorrow brings," she told his sleeping form.

Chapter Two

OR-GON SETTLES IN:

Over a breakfast of cereal and toast Joe, Ciara and Or-gon discussed plans for the days ahead.

"It's important for Or-gon to meet my mum first," Ciara explained. "We'll have to tell her everything, won't we?"

Joe nodded in agreement. There would be little point in trying to convince Maeve Branton that Or-gon was a Welsh cousin – and, in any event, it would probably prove to be counterproductive. They needed to have Maeve's input, and Joe had already decided to ask Ciara's mother if Or-gon might stay with her, at least until the Neanderthal became more familiar with his new surroundings. Such an arrangement would doubtless prove to be more comfortable for Joe and Ciara. Two's company, et cetera, Joe thought.

"I'll go and get her, then," said Ciara, selecting another piece of toast from the rack. She scraped on some butter and rose from the table. "No time like the present," she added brightly.

Or-gon was experiencing a little difficulty with odd phrases, but he rose from the table and bowed to Ciara. "I look forward to your return," he said graciously, but Ciara was already halfway out of the door.

Moments later she returned, accompanied by Maeve Branton, still in her dressing gown. She was complaining, "I can't see what is so important at this time of day!" Maeve caught sight of Joe, and the surprise was evident as she remonstrated, "Joe? Sure, but we weren't expecting *you* back so soon!" Her gaze fixed on Or-gon, who had arisen from the table once more. "And, who is your friend?"

Before Joe could reply, the Neanderthal said, "I am Or-gon and I am honoured to meet the mother of Ciara."

The form of Or-gon's greeting took Maeve by surprise and she stared at him for a few moments with her mouth open.

Ciara giggled. "You should try closing your mouth, Mum. You resemble a goldfish."

Maeve obliged. With a mock curtsey, she said, "Sure, but you are . . . Or-gon. Anyway," she continued, "what sort of a name is Or-gon? Where are you from?"

Joe intervened before Or-gon could reply. "I think you'd better sit down, Maeve. It's a complicated story so I'll make a fresh pot of tea."

Reluctantly Maeve Branton made herself comfortable at the table, directly opposite the Neanderthal. Unselfconsciously, she eyed Or-gon, who remained impervious to her stare. She knew there was something strange happening, but she could not have imagined how strange.

Joe returned with the tea and four clean cups and Maeve demanded, "Right, now, which one of you will be telling me what this is all about?"

Joe cleared his throat. "Maeve," he said, "do you remember when you asked me if I'd found anything interesting on the beach?"

"Yes, I remember."

"Do you remember my reply?"

"Sure, but it wasn't long ago, after all. You said you had found a pound coin and a cave that might contain the bones of a sixth century hermit."

"Well, I did find a cave, but there were no skeletons in it. The people there were very much alive. In fact, they were Neanderthal tribesmen from thirty-five thousand years ago."

The import of what Joe had said raced around Maeve's mind and she immediately balked at the implications.

Joe waited expectantly.

"But you're not expecting me to believe that, are you?"

"*I* do," said Ciara, "*I* believe it. But you really need to hear the whole story, Mum. Then you'll be able to make up your own mind."

Maeve laughed nervously. "Sure, but you're pulling my leg. Tell me you are, Ciara."

"Just listen to Joe's story, Mum. Then we've got to ask you a favour."

With four fresh cups of tea on the table, Joe retold the tale of his exploits in the Neanderthal past. Maeve listened intently, and when the story moved on to the destruction of Tarmis and Or-gon's flight with Joe, Maeve's instinct was to believe, however incredible the story was.

Finally, she said, "And what will be the favour you need from me?"

Ciara, her cheeks turning pink, mumbled, "We wondered if you would . . . act as nursemaid for Or-gon – at least until he

12

becomes accustomed to our way of life. We—"
Uncharacteristically, she stumbled over her words. "J-Joe and I
wondered if Or-gon could lodge with you while I move in with Joe.
After all," she added defensively, "we are going to be married
soon."

Maeve stared at the others, her gaze finally fixing upon Or-
gon. "You're asking a lot for me to take in a complete stranger."

"*And* refugee," Joe added, "and we were wondering if you
could teach him how to read and write English. Or-gon's a scientist
and he's extremely intelligent, but he's only ever heard our language
spoken; he's never seen it handwritten or printed in books. He
needs to learn how to read, because he has some pretty spectacular
technology from his civilisation to pass on to us."

* * *

Over the following few weeks, Or-gon learned the intricacies of the
English language and was soon reading and writing fluently. His
speech quickly improved and Joe obtained for him a copy of every
computer magazine available. Ciara's ex-boyfriend obtained a false
identity in the name of Morgan Griffiths and Or-gon slid effortlessly
into the part. Maeve Branton formed a close bond with the
Neanderthal and, to her amazement – and Ciara's delight – found
that she was falling in love with him. Joe, Ciara and Maeve each
accompanied Or-gon from time to time as he familiarised himself
with the area and became known to the locals, amongst whom he
was readily accepted as Joe's Welsh cousin. Or-gon's assimilation
into the world paralleling his own was almost complete.

Joe converted his double garage into a workshop, and there
Or-gon commenced the development of twenty-first century
computer technology into the more sophisticated and advanced
technology he was accustomed to in Tarmis. Without the facilities
and backing of a huge laboratory, however, it would be impossible
to develop an organic AI or the complex interactions necessary to
produce an antigravity effect. They would follow later.
Nevertheless, there was considerable scope for the application of his
Tarmis-based science and Or-gon, with Maeve Branton's assistance,
commenced with a will.

The first thing they had to organise was funding for Or-gon's
inventions and requirements. Joe, Ciara, Or-gon and Maeve
discussed the problem around Joe's table over liberal amounts of
tea. It was finally agreed that Joe's small inheritance would be

enough to get things on the move, and they resolved to form a company so that Or-gon's inventions would be legitimate when they hit the commercial world.

Joe advised Or-gon that he should begin with inventions that people of the twenty-first century would accept without question; for example, better household appliances, improvements in computer technology, even the advanced hydroponics that had kept the people of Tarmis well fed.

Joe was concerned that if the Neanderthal produced some of the more advanced technology of Tarmis too soon, awkward questions would be asked for which they would be hard pressed to give a reasonable explanation. Anything too advanced they intended to keep to themselves until the time was right to release it.

This agreed, Or-gon firstly went to work on the most common household appliance, the vacuum cleaner. In the first few weeks they applied for patents for a vacuum cleaner that seemed certain to revolutionise home cleaning. Maeve tested the prototype and was delighted with the results. Soon, a manufacturer was commissioned to produce the vacuum cleaner and the machines were being sold in major retail stores within six months. Sales of the new appliance forged ahead and soon their fledgling design company was making a healthy profit. They were set for a prosperous future and it seemed that life in the twenty-first century was about to change in many ways.

Or-gon had established himself in his new persona, and although Maeve had eschewed the company of other men since the death of her husband, Peter, some years previously their relationship slowly blossomed.

* * *

Everything had been put onto the back burner in order to allow Or-gon to fully settle into the different timeline, but plans moved on for Joe and Ciara's wedding.

"Joe?" Ciara said tentatively. "You seem to be miles away tonight. Is something bothering you?"

"Not really." With all the events of the recent months, Joe had put the cave to the back of his mind. But it had begun stirring again in his thoughts.

"Come on Joe! That look tells me there's something going on. We're not going to have secrets are we?"

Joe smiled. "If you must know, I've been thinking about the tunnel to Koo-ma's people."

"Don't tell me that you want to go back to them?" she demanded, colour rising in her cheeks.

Gazing directly into his lover's eyes, Joe answered, "Not exactly. I was thinking of the tunnel with the abyss. I can't seem to get it out of my mind. It's got to lead to somewhere and I'd like to find out where,"

Ciara's expression became distant and Joe wondered what was going through her mind. He half expected her to insist that she didn't want him going off on another trip to the past.

However, to his amazement she said, "Well, if you go exploring again, I'm coming with you – and I won't take no for an answer." Ciara was making it quite clear she intended to accompany him and that he'd have to get used to the idea.

"Is this my Ciara who nearly went crazy when I told her of my exploits with the Neanderthals?" Joe gently teased.

Ciara smiled. "Yes Joe, this is the same Ciara who pulled your beard to make sure you weren't winding me up. And if you go off again, I'm coming with you, and that's final." Joe was in no doubt that she meant every word; and that trying to change her mind would be a waste of time.

* * *

Maeve discovered she possessed a flair for business and, whilst Or-gon produced new designs and inventions, she ran the company, which was prospering. There was nothing to keep Joe and Ciara from investigating the cave.

"Okay, darling," Joe agreed a little later that day, "you've made it abundantly clear that I'm not going without you. But, if we want to explore the tunnel, we'll first have to find a way to bridge the abyss."

Ciara disagreed. "No Joe," she insisted, "the first thing we do is get married. *Then* we can bridge the gap in the tunnel."

Joe wasn't going to argue; he knew the time had come for them to wed.

At that moment, Or-gon joined them, saying, "Good morning Joe and Ciara. I would like you look at the changes I've made to the computer we bought last week."

Joe and Ciara suspended their discussion about the time tunnels and followed Or-gon to the garage workshop, where it

15

transpired that Or-gon had modified a voice recognition program to Tarmis standards. The computer was now capable of following fairly complex instructions spoken in English.

"This is fantastic," Ciara agreed. "Have you shown it to mum yet? She'll be impressed."

At that very moment Maeve came into the workshop and hooked her arm around Or-gon, who smiled at her affectionately. "So, what has my genius being doing then?" she enquired.

Or-gon asked her to give the computer a complex command.

Slightly puzzled, Maeve obliged and the computer instantly complied. Maeve's eyes rounded in surprise.

"Pretty good eh, Mum?" Ciara said.

"'Tis brilliant," Maeve agreed, "but surely it can't make a cup of tea. Now *that* would truly be something." She burst into laughter and everyone joined in the joke.

Or-gon, not to be outdone, quickly replied, displaying signs of a gradually developing sense of humour, "Give me a month, Maeve, and that will probably come."

Before Maeve could riposte, Joe said with enthusiasm, "This will make writing my novel a damn sight easier and quicker. Well done, my friend! I should have the novel finished before the end of the month. I've just reached the part where I entered Tarmis."

"Will you be giving me a signed copy, Joe?" Maeve enquired.

Joe replied, mockingly, in a very bad Irish brogue, "To be sure you will have one, Maeve. To be sure."

Maeve gave Joe a hard stare and said, "I think it's time for a cup of tea. Who knows, it might cure your sad parody of my accent?"

"To be sure, Mum," Joe agreed, having already adopted Maeve as his mother-in-law.

* * *

Two months later, Maeve finally achieved her wish; Ciara and Joe were married. She was confident they would be happy together and, with the increasing success of their business venture, their financial future appeared to be pretty secure.

When their honeymoon was over, Ciara enquired, "Have you made any further plans in respect of the cave? I can tell you've been thinking about it lately. You've had that look in your eyes."

16

"I can't fool you for one minute can I?" Joe grinned. "Yes, I was thinking of having a chat with your mum and Or-gon. We need to discuss it with them."

"You haven't forgotten I'm coming with you?" Ciara said, reaffirming her intention to accompany him wherever the tunnels led.

"You won't let me forget, will you? I meant what I said, y'know. It could be extremely dangerous." Joe felt Ciara's body stiffen as she prepared for an argument. "We don't know what we might come across," he explained, "and there's always the possibility that we may not be able to get back home. How would you feel then?"

"It wouldn't matter to me," she replied, "as long as you are there with me. There's no way am I going to lose you – no way." As if to make her point, Ciara kissed Joe passionately.

Joe responded enthusiastically; he felt intense pride in his new bride, enhanced by the knowledge that she intended to accompany him wherever – and *whenever* – he went. He loved her even more for that, knowing she would go to hell and back with him, no questions asked.

Chapter Three

THE SECOND TUNNEL:

Or-gon continued to learn the intricacies of twenty-first century Mathematics and physics. Joe introduced him to the central library at Southampton, where Or-gon spent countless hours avidly studying the vast selection of books. Joe supplemented the library's volumes on the sciences with many that he borrowed from the university library. Or-gon had many ideas he wanted to explore and needed the extra knowledge to be able to create them in the twenty-first century.

Joe and Ciara were discussing their intended expedition into the tunnel with the abyss.

"So, how do you propose to bridge the abyss?" Ciara asked. "From what you've told me, it isn't going to be easy."

"I've got a few ideas," Joe replied, "but we will have to be careful when we take materials to the cave. We mustn't be seen and we don't want anyone following us to find out what we're doing."

"In that case, we need to take supplies late at night or early in the morning. Either way, it has to be when no one is around," Ciara agreed. "When I discussed it with Mum and Or-gon, Mum thought we were mad going there again. She didn't like the idea very much, especially when she knew I was going with you. I think she's worried we might meet that Prua Landi woman again if we go back there."

"I must admit I am too, but I feel I've just got to know what lies beyond that abyss, even if there's nothing at the other end." Joe carefully avoided voicing his suspicions that the tunnel would be unlikely to exist if it led nowhere.

"We can only find out by exploring, can't we? Has Or-gon got any ideas of how to get past the abyss? I know you asked him to come up with some ideas if he could."

After much discussion with Or-gon and Maeve, even though Maeve was completely against the idea, the best plan they devised was to use the two parts of an extending ladder, lashed side by side with planks attached to the top to create a walkway approximately sixty centimetres wide. This, they decided, was the safest method; so they carried the bridging components to the cave piece-by-piece, in the small hours, when no one was around, and then returned before the streets and beach became too busy.

Joe finished his novel about his exploits with the Neanderthals. Before they set a day to go into the cave, Joe submitted his novel to a Literary Agency. The hard part followed: waiting for the agent's decision as to whether or not they intended to include him in their list of authors. Whilst awaiting an answer from the agency, Or-gon, Joe and Ciara transferred the supplies they would need to the cave. They had successfully bridged the abyss and Joe was hoping to receive a reply before he and Ciara began their exploration of the new tunnel, though he still had serious doubts about her accompanying him.

It was on their return from the beach that Joe sensed Ciara was glaring at him as though she was about to explode. "I knew this was coming, Joe," she said loudly, "you don't really want me to come with you, do you? Go on, admit it." Her cheeks were flushed with anger and Joe was wishing he'd never agreed to Ciara's demands.

"I haven't said that, have I?" Joe protested.

"No, you haven't," Ciara agreed, "but you know it's true. I can tell by the way you talk about the danger."

In an attempt to appease her, Joe explained, "It isn't that … really. I admit I'm scared you could be in danger, and you know I would never forgive myself if you were injured – or worse."

"Now listen here, Joe Laing," Ciara ground out, still in the grip of her anger, "I married you for better or worse and, if you go down that tunnel, I'm right with you, okay?" She had made her feelings perfectly clear, and it was obvious she had no intention of discussing the matter further.

Joe gave a deep sigh and smiled as his wife glared at him. He grasped her hand and drew her towards the sofa beside him. Reluctantly, she acceded to his greater strength and her anger dissolved at the physical contact.

"You must concede that I had to try, but if you're so adamant about coming with me, then I won't argue anymore. You must promise me one thing, though," he added.

Finally calm, Ciara asked, "And what's that?"

"You must do exactly what I tell you without hesitation or argument," Joe said firmly. "Do you understand? It may mean our lives,"

Ciara smiled. "Yes, Joe. I'll do whatever you say." Leaning over the coffee table she poured out two cups of tea.

Snuggling close she kissed Joe tenderly. A rap at the door interrupted the couple. "Come in." Ciara called, assuming it would be Or-gon or Maeve – or both."

Or-gon and Maeve stepped into the room, their arms linked together. "We are sorry to disturb you," he said, "but we have been discussing your proposed exploration of the second tunnel."

Ciara had a feeling she knew what they had come to say, and interrupted Or-gon before he could continue. "Mum," she said firmly, "if you've come to try to change my mind about going with Joe, you're wasting your time. Joe and I have just been arguing about it and he couldn't change the way I feel. You've no hope of doing so either, if that is what you've come for."

Maeve gave a deep sigh and regarded Ciara in disappointment. Or-gon remained silent, sensing that Ciara's decision was final.

"Well, my girl," Maeve conceded, her eyes shining with unshed tears, "all I can say is, *please* be careful. Joe and Or-gon have told us about that Prua Landi woman, and they both think she may try again to kill Joe. If you go along, you could be mixed up in it too. You know I'm worried for you. I am your mum after all. And remember, you are still my little girl."

Ciara felt uncomfortable for remonstrating with her mum. She gave Maeve a loving hug. "Mum, I *will* be okay," she assured her, "I have promised to do everything Joe tells me – and I will. Don't worry! I'll be okay, I promise you."

Maeve broke the embrace and stared into her daughter's eyes. "Please be taking care, girl," she whispered, "for me?"

* * *

Joe and Or-gon set off to the tunnel to make a final check on the makeshift bridge over the abyss.

"How long do you think you'll be gone?" Or-gon asked.

Joe considered the question carefully. "It's not easy to say, old friend," he replied eventually. "I hope this time not to disturb the timeline, because I don't want to be responsible for another paradox. It really depends on what we find at the other end of the tunnel, but whatever happens, we shouldn't be returning hours after we set out as we did last time when we had to make adjustments."

Or-gon's craggy features mirrored his concern. He had personally experienced the perils Joe had faced in Tarmis with the advent of Prua Landi.

"You must promise that if things go wrong, you will seek my help – if possible," Or-gon urged.

Joe felt a surge of sympathy for his Neanderthal friend. Or-gon would remain behind developing his inventions, while Joe and Ciara were undertaking another adventure. "I promise you, my friend," he said reassuringly, "that if I need your help I'll try to return for you." Both men knew, however, that in such circumstances, an opportunity to return was unlikely to present itself.

Or-gon smiled. "Then I shall sleep in peace while you are away," he said, as they proceeded along the beach.

* * *

Three days before the date set for the expedition, Joe's post box clattered and a dull thud sounded as mail hit the carpet. Ciara was first to the front door and picked up the bunch of letters, which was predominantly composed of junk mail. She examined the various letters, shouting in excitement when one particular envelope caught her eye.

"Hey Joe, you have a letter from the literary agency." She carried the bundle of letters through to Joe. "I hope they haven't rejected your novel."

Joe stared at the envelope, hardly daring to open it. Finally, he ripped it open and read the letter inside. A broad smile lit up his face. "Guess what. The agent has agreed to represent me," he said jubilantly as he passed the letter to Ciara to read for herself.

"Oh, Joe!" Ciara cried, hugging him in excitement, "I'm so proud of you. Does this mean your novel will be published soon?"

"Not exactly. What it means is that the Agency will now try to find a publisher to take it on. The rest of the paperwork seems to be an agreement for me to sign and return." Joe was struggling to control his excitement.

Ciara gave him a congratulatory kiss. "Well done, my sweet. Let's tell Mum and Or-gon. They'll be over the moon."

* * *

It was the morning Joe and Ciara were to cross the abyss. Joe had taken a 'phone call from the agency the previous day to say they had

21

received the agreement and that they would be in touch with him later. He informed the agent that he would be on holiday for two weeks, which might extend to three, and to contact his mother-in-law, Maeve Branton should they have anything to report. Maeve, he explained, was empowered to act on his behalf.

It was five-thirty on a quiet Friday morning. Joe embraced Ciara. "Are you ready, Darling, because today we're going to find out whether there's anything at the other end of the tunnel?"

Ciara nodded, her freshly washed hair dancing with the movement of her head. The couple had taken a shower together and there was no certainty when the opportunity would present itself again.

"Yes, Joe," she answered, "I'm as ready as I'll ever be. And," she added, "I must admit I'm pretty excited."

They walked out onto the street and Joe locked the door behind them as quietly as possible. The streets were empty of people as they walked towards the sea front and the hidden gorge. Fifteen minutes later they were approaching the cleft leading to the hidden cove. Joe held Ciara's hand and the crevice appeared to her as if by magic. During the preparations for their expedition, Joe had discovered that the gorge was part of the tunnel complex that only he could see, which explained why no one else had stumbled upon his private beach.

At the cliff face, Joe experienced a strange, momentary sensation of vertigo as he was about to step into the crevice. His bones ached abominably and he felt a constriction in his chest as though some invisible force was crushing his rib cage. His lungs were on fire with the need for oxygen and his feet seemed to be encased in leaden boots. His hands were like claws as his fingers bent and stiffened. Through his pain, he heard Ciara groan beside him and he turned to comfort her. She had slipped free from his grasp and was leaning against the rock face, which formed the entrance to the crevice, her face white as the chalk of the cliff and her slim frame bent almost double in agony.

Joe fought to control the intense pain, suspecting that whatever he was experiencing, Ciara must be affected even more severely. An inner voice told him he had to reach the safety of the crevice and drag Ciara with him. As if moving through a lake of fiery oil, Joe manhandled Ciara into the crevice and collapsed heavily on top of her. Immediately the feeling began to dissipate, but Ciara remained in considerable distress as she lay supine on the rocky floor, her eyes clenched shut from the pain that seemed to fill her every cell. After a little more than a minute, her eyelids fluttered and she struggled into a sitting position, groaning in bewilderment and pain.

"W-what happened, Joe?" she demanded weakly.

Joe held her hand tightly, unwilling to break contact. "Something's happening out there." He nodded in the direction of the rocks around the entrance to the gorge.

Outside, on the margin of the sand and rocks, they could see the air shimmering, obscuring their view of the sea beyond. The disturbance quickly developed into a sandstorm several metres across, which twisted and spun as it gained strength. They watched in fascination as a blue light appeared at its centre, coruscating through several colours as it rapidly gained in intensity and brightness. Afraid of the unexpected phenomenon, Ciara held onto Joe tightly, and as they continued to watch the pulsating light, the form of a tall woman materialised at its centre.

Joe immediately recognised the unmistakable form of Prua Landi. "It didn't take her long to find me," he muttered.

"Who?" Ciara whispered.

"That, My Sweet, is Prua Landi." He gazed intently into Ciara's beautiful eyes. "You stay here and you should be safe. I'm going to find out what she wants."

"Oh no, Joe!" Ciara gasped. "Please don't go."

Joe was sympathetic with the emotions of his new bride and he kissed her and stroked her long, dark hair in an attempt to comfort her. Nevertheless, he said firmly, "Prua Landi must know I'm here, although I'm not certain if she can see me. Otherwise, there's no reason for her to be at this spot on the beach at this particular time. She's probably been trying to trace me ever since Tarmis and I reckon I ought to find out what she wants."

"J-Joe," whispered Ciara, "let's just get as far away from her as we can. I don't like what she did to us and I don't want it to happen again."

With a smile, Joe explained, "That wasn't Prua Landi deliberately trying to harm us. It must have been the energy produced by her movement through time. She didn't even appear until we were safely out of danger in the crevice."

"I still think we ought to go . . . now!"

Joe's voice assumed on a hard edge. "Look, Darling, this is *exactly* why I was reluctant to have you along with me on this trip.

23

You've agreed to do as I say and I want you to stay here while I see what she wants, okay?"

In a small voice, Ciara agreed, "Okay, but please be careful. I don't want to be trapped here without you, with no way of passing through the barrier to get back home."

"I'll be careful, I promise." With a final hug, Joe stepped through the barrier.

Prua Landi, who was staring at the cliff face, started in astonishment, but she quickly regained her composure.

"Ah, Jo-lang," she said jovially, "I thought I might find you here in this primitive time. Tell me," she added conversationally, "is this the true time of your origin, or is it merely a convenient base for your operations?"

Joe smiled and said nothing, turning over Prua Landi's question in his mind in an attempt to extract every morsel of information. Apparently, she was unaware – or wished him to believe she was unaware – that this was his natural timeline. Again, apparently, she seemed to believe that this might be a convenient place in time from which he might achieve something. But what?

Finally, Prua Landi gave a dismissive wave of her hand. "It matters little what you volunteer. You will reveal everything to me in time." She smiled at her own weak joke and, to Joe, the effect was ghastly. The severity of her features grew more pronounced until they were almost skull-like. Joe thought she probably wasn't accustomed to smiling.

As in Tarmis, Joe experienced the sliminess of Prua Landi's mental touch as she attempted to probe his mind, but this time he was able to brush off the insurgence with surprisingly little effort – and no discomfort at all. A second probe met with even less success and Joe demanded angrily, "Why are you doing this to me, and why are you following me?"

Prua Landi's reply would have been funny in any other circumstances. "I'm here to protect you."

"Protect me from what?"

"You are associating with criminals, who intend to harm you. I am here to remove you to a place where those criminals will be unable to find you."

Joe said nothing, although his mind was working feverishly in an attempt to make sense of Prua Landi's statement. He had never been linked with criminals of any sort – with the exception, of course, of Ciara's former boyfriend, who had obtained a false

24

identity for Or-gon. So, whom could she mean? The most obvious explanation for Prua Landi's presence would be that she had mistaken him for someone else, but that made little sense. He considered an alternative possibility. Whilst travelling in time, he had first encountered Prua Landi in an altered timeline that, as far as he knew, no longer existed and should never have existed. If she had been in Tarmis simply because Joe was there, then she must know of him from some other time or place, which suggested that she knew about events that would happen in his future. As he thought about it he liked the woman's involvement less and less.

"If you wish to protect me," Joe asked, "how come you sent your assassins to kill me in Tarmis?"

Prua Landi smiled once again, waving a long, slender hand dismissively. "A misunderstanding," she explained. "Their orders were to apprehend you and spirit you away to my boat in the harbour. Surely, Jo-lang, you can understand that I am on the side of the law. In fact, I *am* the law and I am here to save you from your own folly."

Joe couldn't help laughing at the bare-faced lie. "You could have fooled me," he told her. "Your henchmen had murder in their eyes in Tarmis. If I hadn't been able to handle myself, I wouldn't be here."

"As I said, a regrettable misunderstanding."

"And you expect me to believe that?"

"It matters little what you choose to believe, Jo-lang. I *will* succeed, and your criminal friends will all pay the price of their folly. Do you wish to die with them?"

Joe grinned. It was now clear that whatever system of law she represented, Prua Landi would have no more compunction in killing him that she would have of crushing a wasp in the sugar bowl.

"If it means anything to you, I have absolutely no idea what you're talking about," he said, "but I don't expect you to believe that. I've no doubt you'll keep following me, but not where I'm going now."

With a wave, he stepped backwards into the crevice and the whole world seemed to blaze with a blue-green light as Prua Landi focused a hand-held weapon on the entrance – just too late to catch Joe in its fire. From the safety of the time tunnel, Joe watched as the chalk of the cliff face turned through red to orange, then yellow to brilliant white as it was superheated under the beam of sun-hot

25

plasma. He felt no heat where he sheltered, which meant that the plasma fire was entirely restricted to the outside world. The tunnels, it seemed, did not exist for anyone or anything except those who were intended to use them. Which posed the question: how did he fit into the equation? And by what agency was he the only person, as far as he knew, who was able to pass through the time-gates?

Ciara gave a moan beside him. "Joe," she whispered, "What is that light outside?"

Joe was stunned. "You can see it?" he demanded urgently. "Tell me exactly what you can see!"

"I can see a sort of orangey red light waving about outside. It's brighter in the middle and it fades to the edges. What does it mean?"

"It means, Honey, that you're the only other person I know who can see through the tunnel entrance. For you, though, I think it must be a bit like looking through smoked glass, because it's a hell of a lot brighter than you say. I think Prua Landi is trying to burn her way into the tunnel by melting the rock of the cliff face."

Ciara's expression mirrored the terror she was experiencing. "Why is she doing it, Joe?"

"She obviously wants to kill me, but don't ask me why because I've no idea. I think it's tied up with something I'm going to do in the future. She says I'm associating with criminals and I reckon it must be something that hasn't happened yet. I just can't seem to get my head round it – but I will."

Ciara held Joe close and snuggled her face into his neck. "I'm frightened, Joe. Can we go home?"

"That's the last place we should go at the moment," he said decisively, "when we know that Prua Landi can't possibly harm us in here."

"Oh! So you think we should go on over the abyss?"

"We've nothing else to do, have we?"

As he held Ciara close to him, Joe sensed a lessening in the intensity of the light from Prua Landi's weapon and he glanced outside. The time traveller stood upon the rocks, her face a mask of hatred. Once again she had failed to either capture or kill Joe and it was apparent that she found the experience a source of deep irritation. She was shaking with anger as she slipped the plasma weapon into a sheath on her belt and, just as quickly, withdrew it and threw it onto the rocks. The muzzle must have been intensely hot from prolonged use and Joe laughed out loud at the woman's discomfort as he explained to Ciara what had happened. Prua Landi grasped the butt of the weapon and immersed its flared muzzle in the cooling water of a rock pool, sending wisps of steam into the air. Then, with the weapon safely stowed once more, Prua Landi touched a stud on a device on her wrist and disappeared in a whirlwind of sand and blue light.

The events of the past few minutes had shown Ciara exactly why Joe had been worried about having her along on his expedition beyond the abyss. He could have no idea what lay at the other end. As he had said, they may find nothing or they may find danger. Well, she thought, if the danger was to come from Prua Landi, then she owed it to her new husband to stand beside him and not whinge about it. If Joe was constantly worried about how she would react, he would probably be unable to function effectively. It was certain, from his adventures in the Neanderthal past and in Tarmis, that Joe could defend himself in tight situations, but Ciara now recognised she must not allow herself to influence his judgement to the detriment of their safety. She breathed deeply and exhaled a couple of times to calm herself.

"Joe?" she said.

Joe was still staring outside the crevice to see if there was any sign of Prua Landi returning. "Yes, my sweet?" he said absently.

"I'm all right now, and I promise you I won't complain again. I know I've got to trust you or it could make things difficult for us, and I promise I'll always do as you say." She grinned, showing signs of the real Ciara after her recent terrifying experience, "But just remember, once we're back home all bets are off!"

Hugging Ciara tightly to him, Joe kissed her tenderly. "I wouldn't have it any other way," he replied.

Ciara followed Joe to the secluded beach, where the tent remained undisturbed beneath the shelter of the cliffs in the tiny cove. Gone were her doubts about accompanying Joe, but she was still a little apprehensive after what had just happened. She thought about a recent foray with Joe through the original time tunnel, when he'd shown her Koo-ma's ceremonial cave, and she remembered the feeling of awe she had experienced when she had watched the shaman, Koo-ma meditating beside his fire.

Joe had explained to her that Koo-ma couldn't see them whilst they remained in the time tunnel, but he was certain that the canny shaman could sense their presence in some way. Ciara remembered the expression on Koo-ma's face as he stared at the blank wall, where the time barrier concealed their presence. A tingling sensation radiated from the nape of her neck to the small of her back as she thought about Koo-ma and his uncanny ability to 'see' through solid rock.

Joe shattered her reverie. "I think we should get an hour's sleep now we're safe from danger. We need to rest for a while before going into the cave." With a broad smile, he said, "I think you'll find the tent quite cosy."

It was plain that Joe wished to make love before entering the time tunnels, so Ciara kissed him passionately and led him towards the tiny tent. The early morning air was unseasonably warm, so they decided to make love under the vault of sky. Joe ducked inside and emerged immediately with a thick sleeping bag, which he laid as a mattress on the coarse marram grass. Afterwards, the lovers moved into the tent and slept soundly for a couple of hours.

* * *

The sun was a hand's breadth above the horizon as they awoke to a fresh sunny morning. Joe boiled some water on his stove and made two steaming mugs of tea. They fried bacon and eggs on the small stove and drank the tea whilst sitting on a large, flat rock facing out to sea. Over the rim of the tiny cove he saw dark clouds heading in their direction. They rinsed their utensils in spring water and returned them to the tent.

Joe put his arm around Ciara's shoulders and said encouragingly, "It's time to make a move up the cliff. I think it's going to rain and that could make the climb a bit awkward." He waved his hand in the direction of the dark clouds building in the sky.

"I'm ready. Let's do it," she agreed, resolving to enjoy the experience, whatever happened.

Joe climbed the rope and knelt ready to help Ciara over the edge of the overhang onto the ledge in front of the tunnel. Ciara climbed athletically up the knotted rope and Joe grasped her wrist to haul her over the final obstacle. At last, it was time to explore.

Chapter Four

INTO THE PAST:

Joe held Ciara's hand as they stepped onto the bridge that led to the other side of the abyss. "I'll go first," he said. "Hold tight to my hand and follow me, but be careful. It's a long way down."

"Okay, I'm right behind you," she replied, directing her torch at the planks which reinforced the makeshift bridge.

Safely across, they retrieved the rucksacks they had prepared some days previously, and set off resolutely into the unknown. Joe's powerful lantern lit up the tunnel before them, affording them a clear view of the way ahead. As with the original tunnel to the Neanderthal past, the thick layer of dust on the floor was undisturbed and they could detect no signs of footprints. There was no reason to suspect that it would be otherwise. The tunnel, however, seemed larger, with ample room for Joe and Ciara to walk side by side.

Joe cut into the silence that had prevailed since soon after they crossed the abyss. "How are you feeling now? You okay?"

"I'm fine. I was thinking, though. We seem to have come a long way."

"You're right," he agreed, "it's definitely longer than the original tunnel, and there doesn't seem to be any sign of the other end – if there is one." Joe was getting the feeling that the tunnel would end in an impenetrable wall of rock.

The tunnel ahead was silent; the only sounds they could hear were the rustling of their clothing and their breathing, accompanied by the soft, uneven rhythm of their footfalls in the two-centimetre deep layer of millennia-old dust.

Ciara tugged his jacket. "Can we stop for a moment? I need a drink."

"Of course, Darling. I'm sorry, I never thought about you being thirsty. I must admit that drink's the last thing on my mind at the moment."

They paused momentarily for Ciara to take a drink of the squash she had brought with her, and they rested for a few minutes. Joe was eager to move on, but had to consider his young wife. He was hoping they would soon encounter the end of the tunnel, when they would discover whether or not they had made a fruitless journey.

"Joe," Ciara asked, "do you really think we'll find anything?"

"I've given it a lot of thought, and it would make no sense at all if there was nothing at the other end but a wall of rock. This tunnel is no different from the first one in that it's man made, and if someone made it then it must have been for a reason. Any other explanation, it seems to me, would be senseless. Think about it, what's the point in a mile long tunnel to nowhere?"

"But have you any idea where it might lead?"

"I've thought about that, too," Joe answered. "There were tunnels leading off from the complex at the sacred cave in Too-ga's time. I suppose it's possible that this leads there eventually – although it would have to be several miles long to reach there."

Ciara persisted. "Do you think we've walked more than a mile already, because I do?"

"You're right," Joe agreed, "but the sacred cave was at least fifteen miles away from Too-ga's settlement."

Ciara was not happy about the prospect of walking fifteen miles with the heavy rucksack on her back, as it had already begun to chafe her shoulders. "Let's hope it doesn't lead there then," she grumbled as they resumed their trek.

Ahead, the tunnel curved to the left and Joe imagined he could detect faint luminescence ahead. He pressed the stud on his lantern and the tunnel was plunged into darkness.

Ciara gasped in surprise and Joe said urgently, "Don't switch on your torch, I need to be able to see if there's light ahead."

Moments later, he was certain. Jubilantly, he told Ciara, "There's not far to go now."

Ciara sighed with relief. At least she would soon be able to divest herself of the weighty rucksack. A short distance ahead, they saw a shimmering curtain across the width of the tunnel, resembling a heat haze rising from the tunnel floor. Apprehensively, the couple approached the phenomenon, which was utterly unlike the time-gate Joe had negotiated into the Neanderthal past.

"What are we going to do?" Ciara enquired. "Do you think it's safe?"

"Dunno," Joe replied absently, as he examined the barrier, "but we've come this far and it would be a pity not to go through."

He selected a small can of beans from Ciara's rucksack and weighed it in his hand. Then, with a flick of his wrist, he tossed it at the barrier. The object passed through as if through water, but there was no sound to indicate that it had hit the floor on the other side – or, indeed, if there was anything at all beyond the enigmatic curtain.

Joe squeezed Ciara's hand. "Well, this is what we came for. You know we've got to go through, don't you."

"Yes," Ciara replied in a small voice. Joe had experience of the technology of the tunnel builders, but Ciara had yet to come to trust it.

Hand in hand, they stepped up to the barrier and Joe reached out to touch the shimmering curtain. If he was going to be injured, he was determined that it would be no more than a fingertip. Delicately, he pushed his fingers toward the curtain until he finally, tentatively, made contact. A not unpleasant tingling passed from his fingers through his body and into Ciara, and with a vertigo-inducing wrench, they were deposited in a well-lit section of tunnel roughly a hundred metres long. Behind them, the curtain shimmered on, unchanged. A couple of metres away Joe saw the can of beans lying on its side in the centre of the tunnel. There was an absence of dust on the tunnel floor.

Joe tried to work out what had happened. He knew they had walked on the level for more than a mile from the little cove, which should have placed them roughly at a point about half a mile downriver of Too-ga's caves. But they were still in a tunnel below ground, which seemed to point to them having moved spatially between two points. As yet, there was no clue as to whether they had gone forward or backward in time.

He walked forward a few metres and glanced back over his shoulder. Ciara stood where he had left her, with stricken expression upon her face, so he quickly retraced his steps.

"Where did you go?" she demanded accusingly. "When you let go of my hand, this wall of rock suddenly appeared." She placed her hands flat against the rock and, to Joe she appeared to be pressing against a sheet of invisible glass.

Joe smiled in an effort to placate her. Until he had passed through the barrier, he had had no inkling that it was there. "Sorry, Sweet, but the barriers are invisible to me. Back there, you were able to see the bright light of Prua Landi's weapon, but this must be too dull for you to see through. Just hold my hand and I'll take you through."

They examined the ceiling and walls of the new tunnel. The illumination seemed to emanate from the rock itself, with no sign of light fittings of any kind. The soft yellow light was easy on the eyes, and allowed them to see into the distance down the tunnel. The technology employed by the tunnel makers was far in advance of the 21st century, even taking into account the innovations being introduced by Or-gon. Joe thought about the friezes on the walls throughout the sacred cave complex and remembered the advanced technology they portrayed. What he and Ciara were seeing must be the work of the same people who left the carvings in the sacred cave – and who also made the timestone. What was more intriguing, however, was the fact that there was no dust upon the floor. Everywhere appeared clean and new.

Ciara was following close behind Joe as he recorded with his camcorder the friezes covering the walls. The carvings appeared to be no more than a few months old, although, as in the sacred cave, they were covered by a transparent protective layer. Joe stopped, gesturing for Ciara to be quiet. In the ensuing silence they heard the distant sound of approaching footsteps.

"Quick, run for the time barrier. Take my hand!" he said urgently.

They ran through the barrier hand in hand and into the darkness of a tiny alcove carved into the wall of the tunnel near the shimmering curtain. With their hearts hammering in their chests, they prayed they had run far enough and that those who approached would be unable to see them.

It was too much to hope that the makers of the tunnels would be unable to see beyond the time barrier. Joe peered around the edge of the tiny alcove and, to his horror, he saw that he had dropped his small torch on the floor beyond the time-gate. It was out in the open and it seemed that whoever was approaching would be certain to find it.

He was cursing himself under his breath when Ciara whispered, "Can you see anyone yet?"

"Not yet, but I dropped my torch back there and I reckon they're sure to see it."

"They'll know someone has been in the tunnel," Ciara hissed.

"Quiet! I can see them."

Moments later Joe saw two extremely tall men striding down the tunnel towards them. He estimated that the men must have been almost seven feet tall. They reminded Joe of the figures carved into the tunnel walls of the sacred cave complex.

In the flesh, the figures so resembled Prua Landi that Joe had the worrying feeling she would be waiting for him at the end of the tunnel. Her presence would be disastrous. The men paused their long strides as one saw the torch lying in the middle of the empty corridor. He picked up the unfamiliar object and examined it closely, handing it to his companion to do likewise. They conversed for a few moments in an unfamiliar language, then one of the men placed the torch in a fold in his garment and continued walking.

The pair halted fifteen metres from Joe and Ciara, still apparently unaware of the presence of the intruders. Joe watched them from the tiny alcove, all the while gently stretching and loosening his muscles in preparation for a fight, should it become necessary. The men's heads were completely bald and they were naked from the waist upwards, displaying slender, but muscular bodies, with skin tanned a golden brown. They were devoid of body hair and they wore short, kilt-like garments, which fell to around mid-thigh. Their shoes were simple sandals with thin strapping, criss-crossing halfway up their calves. Around their necks they wore fan-shaped beaded necklets, approximately fifteen centimetres deep. The overall effect Joe found reminiscent of Egypt in the time of the pharaohs. On one wrist they each wore a broad metal band, inlaid with different coloured gemstones. Joe got the impression that the wristbands weren't just for decoration.

He watched as one of the men placed his hand in an indentation halfway up the wall. Soundlessly an opening appeared to a separate area of the tunnel system. The two passed through, and the wall became solid once again.

With a huge sigh, Joe told Ciara, "It's okay. They've gone through a door somewhere in the wall down here." He was already moving in the direction of the indentation in the tunnel wall. "They seemed curious about the torch, but didn't make a great fuss about it. I don't know what that means," he added, "but I don't like it. I'd have wanted to know how it got there, wouldn't you?"

"I think so. What shall we do now?"

Joe considered their next step. "I'm not sure, but I don't think we should go down the tunnel until those two have come out from that door and gone out the other end. If they appeared behind us we'd be trapped."

"Who do you think they are Joe?"

"I've no idea. I can only guess. Their dress is very much like ancient Egypt, but they are not Egyptians. Even though the Egyptians had the most advanced civilisation of their age, this technology is light years ahead of the 21st century, let alone the time of the Pharaohs."

Ciara abruptly changed the subject. "Let's have something to eat before they come back. I'm hungry."

Joe laughed. "That was the last thing I expected you to say, but it's a good idea."

Quickly, the pair delved in Ciara's rucksack and retrieved a poly bag filled with man-sized sandwiches, which Ciara had prepared early that morning before setting out for the beach. Making themselves comfortable half in, half out of the alcove, they each ate a couple of the sandwiches and washed the food down with bottled spring water, all the while listening for the return of the two men.

"At least they're human," Joe ventured, "and not something completely alien."

Ciara giggled nervously. "I would have been really terrified if they'd had six arms and three eyes or something like that."

Joe could see that, despite her nervousness, Ciara was enjoying her adventure; he, on the other hand, was unsure how he felt. Of course, it was good to have Ciara's company, but the downside was the unknown level of danger. He peered around the edge of the alcove just as the opening in the tunnel wall dilated and the same two men walked out. Without so much as a glance in the direction of the shimmering curtain, they turned and strode down the tunnel, leaving the doorway to close behind them like liquid stone.

As soon as the two men disappeared from sight, Joe said quietly, "Right, let's try again. I want to video more of the friezes. There are some I don't recognise, but I'm almost certain this is an extension of the tunnel Or-gon and I entered from the Sacred Cave."

"Okay, I'm right behind you. What can I do to help?"

"Just keep watch while I'm using the camcorder. I need to concentrate."

"Okay!"

With Ciara holding Joe's hand, they set off once again down the tunnel, and immediately Joe came across the frieze that told of Prua Landi. Nearby, there was a moving hologram inset into the tunnel wall, depicting a view from space, which showed, in fine detail, Pangaea before the supercontinents of Laurasia and Gondwanaland had begun to separate two-hundred and forty million years ago. The implication was that the builders of the tunnels had journeyed that far back in time. Joe wondered if he and Ciara could now be on the continent of Pangaea in the time before dinosaurs walked the Earth. In such an eventuality the British Isles would be a tiny, insignificant part of the vast landmass and would not have yet split from the continent. As they moved further down the tunnel, it was increasingly evident that this was indeed the complex at the sacred cave Joe had explored with Or-gon.

Eventually, Joe said, "Let's go back to the dark tunnel, darling. I want to examine what I've filmed and the light's too bright in here. Once we've made certain the recordings are okay, we can decide what we want to do next."

"I'm ready any time," Ciara murmured. "This place gives me the creeps."

They returned to the area beyond the time-gate, which was lit only by the shimmering curtain, and they immediately felt safer. Sitting down on his rucksack on the dusty floor, Joe rewound his camcorder, and they viewed what he had filmed so far. He saw the same tall people who had been in the tunnel, and again he saw Prua Landi. That she was a part of the lives of these people was significant, although in what rôle was unclear. Two alternatives came immediately to mind, the first being that Prua Landi was their leader – had she not boasted '*I am the law*'? The second was that she was their enemy – and they were the '*criminals*' she had warned Joe about.

"We'll have to make contact sometime," he mused as his thoughts spilled out into words.

"What? Are you sure?" Ciara asked.

"Not really. But whatever else we do, I want to explore the rest of the complex."

"Then let's hope we don't meet anyone else," Ciara replied, "I think I've had enough excitement for one day."

Joe pecked her on the cheek and, with Ciara in tow, stepped through the time-gate into the tunnel complex, leaving the shimmering curtain behind them.

As they walked along, Ciara said, "I've been thinking. We'll have to be careful, you know. The last thing we want to do is create another paradox."

"I'm with you there, and so long as we do nothing to change things around us, we should be okay."

Joe stopped and pulled the pistol from his rucksack, sliding the weapon into an inside pocket in his jacket after a cursory check. Ciara was aghast at the sight of the revolver, because Joe had at no *time* during their preparations suggested that he intended to bring *it* along on this foray into the tunnels.

Her voice filled with alarm, she demanded, "Why have you brought that—thing? This isn't the Wild West, you know."

"Don't worry," Joe said soothingly. I'll only use as a last resort. Just forget I have it, and pray I never have to use it."

"Okay," she reluctantly agreed, "but the fact you have it at all bothers me."

Walking along hand in hand, they came to a room that Joe found familiar. They peered into the large open area.

This is where I found the timestone," he confided.

Their attention was entirely focused upon the strange contents of the room before them and they were unaware of four tall figures approaching stealthily behind them.

Ciara saw a hint of movement and screamed, "Joe, look out!"

But, before Joe could drag out his pistol from its hiding place inside his coat, they were enveloped in a haze of static electricity and slid, unconscious, to the unyielding floor.

Chapter Five

CAPTIVE:

On awakening, Joe discovered he was in a circular room, whose smooth walls were a neutral, creamy white. From where he lay, bound to a flat, hard surface by means of strong elasticated webbing, the walls appeared to narrow towards the flat ceiling, from which light shone uniformly as in the tunnel where they had been captured. He twisted around as far as his bonds would permit to try to see if Ciara was in the same room, and was rewarded with a glimpse of her, lying unconscious and similarly bound upon a bench nearby. He watched Ciara's chest rise and fall a few times then resumed his examination of his surroundings. The walls he could see above the level of his bed were featureless and devoid of windows. Ciara gave a groan and stirred. Her eyes opened wide as she discovered she was tightly bound.

"You okay, Darling?" Joe enquired, and Ciara's head turned as quickly as the restraints would permit.

"I-I think so. I've got a headache, though. Where are we?"

"I don't know," Joe replied. "I don't think we're in the tunnels, though. I didn't see any round rooms there, did you?"

Ciara didn't answer immediately. She was trying to recall what had happened. Finally, she asked, her voice strangely calm, "How long have we been here, Joe?"

"No idea! If I could see my wrist I don't think it would help. I think they've taken my watch."

"What do you think they'll do with us?"

"Your guess is as good as mine," he replied, "but if they were going to harm us I reckon they would have done so already, don't you?"

"Probably," she giggled nervously. "I bet it came as a bit of a shock to find us in the tunnels. I mean, we're a bit different, aren't we?"

The sound of footsteps came to their ears, and two of their captors entered the room through a doorway, which flickered into existence in the featureless surface of the wall. One was male and the other female, though the woman was as tall as the man. She was beautiful, with a total absence of the severity of features that characterised Prua Landi. Unlike the man, her head was covered by luxuriant dark hair and, in contrast to the semi-nakedness of the men

37

they had seen so far, she wore a colourful one-piece suit, which covered her from neck to wrist and down to her ankles.

Two pairs of eyes examined Ciara closely for a few moments as she lay supine upon the hard surface. Then they transferred their attention to Joe. The woman spoke, the words flowing like liquid from a fountain.

"I don't understand," Joe protested, "you'll have to speak English. Anyway, you can't expect us to answer questions while we're tied up like this."

He strained against his bonds and they immediately fell away. The woman touched Ciara's restraints with the same result. They sat up together. The man touched his jewelled wristband, and began to speak. His voice faded into the background and Joe heard the words in English directly in his mind. A glance at Ciara told him that she was experiencing the same phenomenon. It was a translation device, but far in advance of the one controlled by the AI in Tarmis.

"Who are you," their captor enquired, "and what is your time of origin?"

Joe explained everything, with the exception of the timestone and his role as the Futama, and the tall people listened intently to his story. Eventually, he reached the part where they were captured in the tunnel.

"Describe anything which would enable us to pinpoint your time of origin," he was told.

"We come from the year two-thousand and twenty-three."

"How do you measure that?"

"From the birth of Jesus Christ."

Their captors were silent for a few moments and Joe gained the impression they were communicating telepathically. A few liquid words prompted a screen to appear in the curved surface of the wall, and the man fired off a rapid series of questions. The screen filled with symbols and the name of Jesus Christ issued from invisible speakers. They examined the text on the screen and, seemingly satisfied with the information, directed the screen to close. Instantly, there was no evidence that the computer terminal had ever existed.

"Did you find out what you wanted to know?" Joe enquired.

Yes came the reply in his mind. *It is clear that you come from a primitive era of violence and war. It is very disturbing to us.*

38

"You should tell that to the woman who's trying to kill us," Joe riposted. "Come to think of it she looks a lot like you."

An animated verbal discussion ensued between their captors so that Joe and Ciara would be unable to eavesdrop. Finally, the woman said, "You will be questioned shortly. Meanwhile, please be assured that no harm will come to you. We are not a violent people."

"Where are we anyway?" Joe demanded.

"In a small flying craft on a landing field outside the tunnel complex, but I believe you intended to ask *when* are we."

Joe nodded.

"I am permitted to tell you that we are in your past by some two-hundred and fifty-three thousand years."

Joe whistled through his teeth and Ciara gasped in astonishment. This was an era when the Neanderthals were beginning to split off as a separate race of humanity.

"Do you see many primitive humans around here?" he enquired.

"No," came the reply. "The population is scattered in small groups and they hide from us. We do not seek them out because there are many large predators roaming the land."

The woman's expression became distant for a moment, and she told them, "In the absence of Leiki, the base commander, who is at present on Mars, I am ordered to take you to the captain of this ship. Please follow me, and do not attempt to escape or you will be immobilised."

She led them along a curved corridor around the outside of the craft. Every three metres or so a small, oval window was inset into the wall, through which they could see a broad, grassy area containing a few buildings of plain, utilitarian appearance and two more flying craft. A high fence enclosed the area and occasionally the fence shimmered in the bright sunlight, producing a puff of dark smoke.

"Is that an electrified fence?" Joe enquired.

"No, it is more sophisticated than that. It is a force field with a physical barrier at its core. It is very effective in keeping out the predators."

"What was that smoke we saw?" Ciara asked.

"Unfortunately, we cannot prevent birds or other flying creatures from contacting the force field. It is regrettable, but we must protect ourselves. This is such a savage period." The woman sighed deeply.

Ciara felt immediate sympathy. "What's your name?" she asked. "Nobody asked us our names. I'm Ciara and this is Joe."

"My name is Romana," the woman smiled. "We have arrived. The captain will see us in this place, Ciara and Joe."

A doorway dilated and they followed Romana into a round room similar to the one in which they had regained consciousness, but far greater in size and with a domed ceiling. The room was split into quadrants with twenty seats in each sector separated by broad aisles. The seats resembled the best of twenty-first century recliner chairs, with a multitude of adjustments for the comfort of the user. In the centre of the room stood a low plinth from the centre of which arose a smooth, round column, topped by a geodesic globe approximately thirty centimetres in diameter. Joe received the impression that this was some kind of viewing room – perhaps even a futuristic cinema or planetarium. Romana indicated seats and they sat down, finding them extremely comfortable, despite the differences in their statures from those of the people for whom the chairs were designed.

Joe still carried his camcorder over his shoulder, and Romana explained that the device had been checked for weapons. In fact, everything they were carrying had been examined to determine whether or not it contained a threat. Joe patted his jacket; the pistol was still inside. Had Romana's people missed it, or did they not recognise it as a weapon? At least he and Ciara weren't entirely defenceless.

Ciara was feeling a certain empathy towards their guide. Conversationally, she asked, "Where are you from, Romana? I mean, what time period?"

"That will be for the captain to explain. Meanwhile, if you have other questions, I will answer as truthfully as I can."

"Okay," Joe said, "tell us about this flying machine. How fast is it? How far can it fly?"

Romana laughed. "I am just a medic but I can give you simple answers. You will have to speak to the captain or the engineers if you wish to know more. This craft is used to carry supplies to the Moon and I believe it is capable of reaching almost the speed of light – in outer space, of course."

Once more Joe whistled through his teeth. "But the Moon is barren," he protested.

"That is so," agreed Romana. "We have a base there, but our main base is on the fourth planet. To reach there we have a much larger ship, which transports us deep into Earth's primeval past before travelling, as you have referred to it, through space. I know little of the science involved, but I believe that to time travel in the emptiness between planets could result in the ship being lost in intergalactic space."

"How far do you go back?" Joe asked.

"Three-hundred million years – to a time when Mars was rich with water and life."

Joe turned over the information in his mind. *Three-hundred million years?* He and Ciara were already a quarter of a million years into the past, but he found it difficult to get his head around such a vast stretch of geological time as three-hundred million years.

"But Pangaea would not have begun to split up at that period," he protested.

Romana's reply was cut short by the arrival of the ship's captain. She immediately introduced Joe and Ciara.

Captain Marron conversed with Romana for a few moments before saying to Joe and Ciara, "We have determined the time of your origin, and we have your account of what has occurred so far in relation to the time tunnels. What you have been reluctant to tell us is the method or device, which enabled you to enter the time tunnels."

Joe sensed an aura of hostility underlying the Captain's statement. "I'd have told you if I'd known," he stated defensively, "but it just happens I have absolutely no idea."

Marron smiled thinly. "Let me explain. The whole system of time tunnels was designed so that it cannot exist for anyone, save those who are intended to use it. The technology is far in advance of that by which our enemy, Prua Landi and her army of murderers traverse time. Even I, a ship's captain, hold a position insufficiently exalted to be told how it works. Only the members of the Council of Elders are permitted a glimpse of the principles. And yet, here you are, having used not one, but two of these 'non-existent' time portals accompanied by a female whom you inform us, you towed through the time portals by holding her hand."

He paused and Joe felt that some kind of reply was expected. A little angry at Marron's belligerent attitude, he said, "I don't know anything about why no one else can see the time tunnels, but I walked on the beach one day and I could—see them that is. If you know how it happened, be my guest and tell me."

"If you will not disclose the method—" Marron said icily.

"Can't you comprehend?" Joe cut in, finding it increasingly difficult to maintain an even temper in the face of the captain's aggressive questioning. "I've absolutely no idea how I do it. Which part of that don't you understand?"

Ignoring Joe's reply, Marron continued, "If you will not cooperate, we will be forced to stun you in order to carry out a medical examination. Then we shall discover how you manage to achieve the seemingly impossible."

Romana, who had remained silent during Marron's interrogation, immediately protested, "But Captain, what you propose is contrary to the whole basis of our belief in personal freedom. I must protest, as Medical Officer, that I am reluctant to carry out such an invasive procedure without the permission of our guests."

Marron's eyes glinted. "You would refuse to obey your captain?" he demanded coldly.

Romana faced him, her eyes aflame with defiance. "I would . . . if you were to continue in this way. I am the medical officer of this vessel, and in matters of medical ethics and procedures, I outrank you, Captain Marron. However, I will bring your *request* to the attention of the Council of Elders on Mars, and you will be given an opportunity to argue your case. Until then, Joe and Ciara are our guests, and are under our protection."

Marron could see that Romana was unlikely to be swayed in her opinion, so continued on a different line, "I am informed that you have been approached by Prua Landi," he said to Joe.

"Yes, she tried to kill me on two separate occasions."

"Did you converse with her at any time?"

"Only briefly."

The captain's eyes gleamed. "Do you recall anything she said to you?"

"She accused me of associating with criminals. Are you criminals?"

Marron laughed mirthlessly. "Our only crime, if crime it is," he said, "is to belong to the Faithful – to be the Faithful."

"If you're not criminals, then I've no idea why Prua Landi is hell bent on killing me."

Marron changed tack swiftly. Aggressively, he demanded, "Are you one of Prua Landi's assassins?"

Joe immediately sensed that an attempt was being made by the captain to probe his mind. The clandestine effort to enter his thoughts reminded Joe of the slimy mental touch of Prua Landi. He had no cause to believe that there was a connection between the two people; nevertheless, he resolved to maintain his guard whilst around the tall officer.

"If you think that, you've got to be mad," he riposted.

Immediately following the unsuccessful probe Marron said briskly, as if nothing untoward had occurred, "This interrogation is at an end and the subject is closed. I understand you have questions Romana was unable to answer?"

"Romana told us that you would explain about the time you come from," Ciara ventured.

Marron nodded. "Very well," he said, "Please recline your seats and everything will be made clear to you."

The lights dimmed and immediately a three-dimensional image of a vast explosion blossomed from the centre of the domed ceiling. As the gases fled from the source of the detonation, they began to condense into galaxies and individual stars. Soon, the volume of the dome was filled with a multitude of galaxies, all slowly fleeing outwards from the centre. It was the Big Bang of modern cosmological theory. Eventually, a spiral galaxy approached until it filled all the available space, continuing to expand until it was replaced by an image of a disc of dark gas and interstellar debris around a proto-star. The proto-star blazed into life and the debris slowly condensed into a retinue of planets, of which the third became prominent, passing through various stages in its evolution until it shone with all the vibrant colours of the life with which it had become endowed.

Joe was astounded. "Is this the real thing?" he demanded and the display paused.

"It is."

"Then, how the hell did you do it?" Joe enquired. He was struggling to imagine the immense gulf of time since the birth of the Universe.

"We dispatched a series of unmanned time probes to record the event throughout time and, although we lost many of the probes, we obtained sufficient data to build up the sequence of events you have just witnessed."

Joe could think of nothing to say. Ciara reclined in her chair with an expression of rapture upon her beautiful features.

"Continue!" ordered Marron, and the show resumed.

They saw all the landmasses of Earth forming one supercontinent, until the sea began to gradually intrude as fissures appeared, due to the movement of the continental plates. The continents eventually passed through a short phase in which they were recognisable to Joe and Ciara, and then the Earth seemed to explode as a planetoid, more than two-thousand kilometres in diameter struck Asia, vaporising the world's oceans and sending vast streams of magma into space. They watched the magma cool to form a multitude of tiny moonlets, spinning rapidly around the crippled and lifeless planet.

Joe tried to sit up in his chair but Ciara held him down with surprising strength. "Is this what is going to happen?" he gasped, tears blurring his vision.

Romana, her tone full of sympathy, told him, "Yes, but the population of Earth will escape in a fleet of starships." The image morphed into a vast fleet of immense starships hanging in space above Mars, whose surface was a patchwork of green continents adrift on dark, deep oceans. The display faded out and the lights came on once again. The chairs came upright automatically.

"When will they terraform Mars?" Joe asked.

"The process was begun—" Marron spat a series of questions at the now inert projection globe, and continued, "in the year of 2147 by your reckoning of time, and took a little over two-hundred years to complete."

"But where do your people come into the equation?"

"We are from almost seven-hundred thousand years in your future. The destruction of the Earth will occur less than one-hundred thousand years beyond that."

Joe whistled. In the overall scheme of things, the Earth did not have long to live.

"Why are you people here in this time?" Ciara enquired. "That's something no one's seen fit to tell us."

Romana glanced at Marron, her eyes misting with emotion. Marron waved his approval for her to explain. "We are the Faithful," she said slowly, "and we have been dispossessed of our birthright by a regime, which cannot – and will not – concede our right to freedom of thought and belief." She wiped a tear from her eye and continued. "We have been forced to abandon our natural

44

time, and to flee into exile in the past to live free in our faith. Our faith is based upon a prophesy that one will come to set us free from the oppression of Prua Landi's regime."

Half-joking, Joe said, "But if you are time travellers, surely you can check whether the prophesy will be fulfilled?"

Marron considered whether or not to answer. Finally he said, "The truth or falsehood of the prophecy has been tested, but the leaders of our people have decreed that only they may know the truth, otherwise the course of our history in this past may resonate catastrophically into our future."

The captain stood. It was plain the interview was at an end. "You will remain with Romana, who is free to act as your guide throughout this craft and the whole base, until we leave eventually for the Moon and Mars."

When Marron had exited, Ciara asked, more casually than she felt, "Did the captain say *we*— " she gestured to encompass Joe and herself, "—are going to the Moon and Mars?"

"Eventually, yes."

"What if we don't want to go?"

Romana sighed and said apologetically, "Please understand, that although we would not wish to limit your freedom in any way, it may be vital for the survival of the Faithful that you meet with the Council of Elders on Mars. You will accept that, for some unknown reason, Joe is able to pass through the time tunnels?"

Joe and Ciara nodded in unison.

"It may be argued that where one can go, others will follow. We have to be certain that no one else, such as Prua Landi or her assassins, can do what you have done." Romana shuddered uncontrollably at the vision of Prua Landi's hordes pouring through the time tunnels, and Ciara felt immediate sympathy towards the tall young woman.

"We'll come with you, won't we Joe?"

Joe nodded. "Of course we will," he affirmed. "Anyway, however else are we going to go to Mars?"

"Indeed!" agreed Romana.

Chapter Six

THE LEGEND BEGINS:

An hour later, they had completed a tour of the ship, with Joe firing off a series of questions at Romana, most of which she was able to answer without the necessity of contacting her colleagues. Joe was most interested in the capabilities of the craft in space. He knew that journeys to the planets in the twenty-first century spanned months, even years, and wished to be assured that they had not let themselves in for such long periods in space. Romana informed him that control of gravity within the vessels, made acceleration to almost light speed possible in a very short period of time. The journey to Mars would take approximately four and a half hours, depending upon the planets' relative positions in their orbits around the Sun.

The three stepped out into the bright sunlight of the compound, intending to visit the various buildings, but they never made it beyond the ramp of the spacecraft. A commotion flared up outside the compound, near to the force field. Two huge bull mammoths had begun sparring with their enormous, curved tusks, in an effort to determine ownership of a harem of around fifteen females. As the humans watched, the struggle surged first one way and then the other, as one bull gained the upper hand, only to lose his advantage as his adversary fought back tenaciously. The clashing of the ivory tusks echoed and re-echoed around the drab, rectangular buildings and it was impossible to imagine that either of the two gigantic beasts could escape serious injury. With a resounding crack, one bull lost half a tusk as the titans locked together, and each twisted their heads in a mighty effort to break the other's neck.

Trumpeting with rage and pain, the injured mammoth drew back several paces and charged. He impaled his adversary in the shoulder with the two-metre stump of his shattered tusk, and drove him sideways into the force-field. In a blinding blaze of energy, the force-field evaporated and the battling behemoths surged through the physical barrier that had lain at the force-field's core. The mammoths' flesh was charred almost to the bone in places, but their primitive instincts drove them on through the pain of their injuries. Still fighting, they stumbled and stamped across the compound and

46

Joe hustled the two women rapidly back inside the craft, out of harm's way.

This instantly proved to be the wrong decision as the path of the continuing battle veered suddenly in their direction. Within a few seconds, the craft shuddered as more than sixteen tonnes of bone and muscle and ivory cannoned into the landing gear. With a screech of tortured metal and a hiss of escaping hydraulic fluid, the struts holding the landing gear parted company with the underside of the craft. For a few moments, the disc-shaped vessel teetered precariously on its two remaining legs. Eventually, the ship canted sideways, buckling its undercarriage, and its considerable weight fell heavily onto the unfortunate creatures. Nothing of flesh and blood could have survived the trauma of such a weighty craft falling upon it, and all movement and sounds of battle ceased instantly. An eerie stillness pervaded the corridor where Joe and the two women had been pitched onto the floor by the violence of the mammoth's collision with the craft's landing gear.

"Is everybody okay?" Joe asked, tentatively rubbing his elbow where he had contacted the hard, metallic surface of the wall.

Ciara sat up and groaned, "My head hurts. In fact," she checked herself thoroughly, "I reckon I hurt all over."

Joe slid down the canted surface of the floor towards her and held her tenderly in his arms. "You're a medical officer," he said to Romana, "is there anything you can do?"

Romana smiled encouragingly and pressed a stud on the wall. A section of the smooth, curved surface dilated, revealing a recess filled with everything necessary to cope with a medical emergency. She selected a smooth, flat ovoid with a colourful illuminated display and pressed it to Ciara's temple, noting the reading before moving to her shoulders and on to her arms. When she applied the instrument to Ciara's abdomen, Romana gasped in astonishment.

"What's the matter?" Joe demanded anxiously.

"I am receiving two life readings," Romana replied, unable to conceal the wonder in her tone.

"Are you sure?" Joe and Ciara said together.

Romana reset the diagnostic and applied it once more to Ciara's abdomen. "The diagnostic is extremely reliable, there *are* *two* life forces."

Joe and Ciara met each other's eyes for a few moments, then whooped with joy.

"A baby!" Joe cried, kissing his wife passionately. "We're going to have a baby."

It was Romana's turn to be amazed. "Does this mean that you will carry the developing embryo inside you until it is ready to be released into the world?"

"You make it sound as if it's not natural," Ciara said defensively.

"Is it?" replied Romana. "Women have been free of the burden of childbirth since— " she struggled for the correct description, "—since the dark times of prehistory. The whole process is so . . . animal, so . . . primitive."

"You mean your women don't know what it's like to give birth?"

"The whole process is completed in carefully controlled conditions," Romana explained, "from donation of the egg and sperm through to adulthood. That way, genetic problems have been eliminated and we grow to adulthood, healthy in body and mind."

"I'm not sure I'd like that kind of arrangement," mused Ciara. "I mean, it all seems so impersonal."

"Sorry to interrupt your cosy chat," Joe interjected, "but this changes everything. You know you have to go back home without delay, don't you, Darling?"

Ciara turned to face Joe, her eyes aflame and her cheeks rapidly colouring up with anger. "I thought we'd settled this, Joe. I'm here, and I'm staying. I'm just as excited as you are about a trip to the Moon and to Mars, and I won't let anything stop me from going, do you hear?"

"I hear you," Joe admitted, "but no matter how disappointed it makes you, I still *can't* let you come along any further."

"You—can't—let—me—come—along?" Ciara spat out the words disdainfully.

Joe cupped his wife's face in his hands and stared steadily into her beautiful eyes. "*Won't* let you come along, if you like. You've just experienced a small sample of what might happen. Despite all their technology, Romana's people were unable to prevent those two mammoths from wreaking havoc on this ship, and I bet if you asked any one of them, they'd tell you that what just happened here was considered impossible."

Romana nodded.

"Remember, Darling, you promised that you would accept every decision I made on the grounds of our safety?" Joe continued.

48

Ciara shook her head, vehemently. "I didn't mean *this*."

"Well, *I* did. Remember, I've seen what can happen. Not just something accidental such as this, but something intentional when Prua Landi's around. I won't have my—" he choked on the unfamiliar emotion, "—my wife and unborn child placed in any kind of danger that can be avoided." Joe caressed Ciara's cheek, then leaned forward and kissed her lips, quickly withdrawing as he sensed her reticence. "Talk to Romana if you won't listen to me. Ask her what kind of medical facilities they have for dealing with pregnancies. Ask her what sort of effect space travel has on developing foetuses. Go on, ask her!"

Ciara's shoulders slumped and her defiant gaze lost all its intensity. She knew she must accept defeat, but how it hurt to acknowledge that her adventure had come to a premature end. She kissed Joe, gently at first, then with rising passion as Joe responded.

Romana coughed quietly and the couple parted in embarrassment. "I am thinking that we have been presented with a major problem," she said, "because I believe that Captain Marron will be unwilling to permit you to return home."

"Damn the man," Joe replied angrily, "but it's not his decision to make. It's my wife and my baby. My decision."

Romana smiled encouragingly. "I am your ally, Joe and Ciara. I will do everything in my power to help you to return home."

Joe regarded the tall woman. "Won't you get into trouble?" he asked, "I mean, with the captain?"

"He cannot discipline me without the approval of the Council of Elders and I am willing, even eager, to stand before the supreme council in exchange for the opportunity to witness the miracle of birth."

"But I can't be more than three months pregnant," protested Ciara, "you are in for a long wait. Won't they miss you if you stay in our time for six months?"

Romana's beautiful features clouded for a moment, then brightened. "With Joe Laing, I will return to you at the appropriate time." She made a series of keystrokes into her wrist computer and added, "The date is set in my schedule and nothing will prevent me from accomplishing my goal. But first," she continued, "we must devise a plan to return you to your home."

* * *

49

The exit ramp and doorway had been rendered completely impassable by the bodies of the two mammoths, whose charred flesh completely blocked the opening. Halting footsteps signalled the approach of other crewmembers as they made their way along the curved corridor. The interior of the ship was canted at a steep angle, making walking difficult.

Romana hailed the two men as they came into view. "Ah Trione, Analy, are there any casualties?"

"We have seen none so far," Trione, a thin-faced individual informed her, "but more than half of the ship still remains unsearched. The incident has damaged the ship's sensory systems, and we are unable to trace the whereabouts of every crewmember by their life readings."

A communicator on his wrist gave a series of tiny beeps and Analy held the instrument to his ear. "Everyone should sit wherever they can make themselves comfortable," he informed them. "The captain intends to raise the ship off the carcasses of the beasts beneath us and set it down on level ground, so that everyone may safely use the main escape hatch. Because of the ship's present attitude it would be too dangerous to use the escape hatch at the moment. Captain Marron is a superb pilot and he should accomplish the manoeuvre with the minimum discomfort for those on board."

He sat on the sloping floor with his back firmly pressed against the wall, gesturing for everyone else to follow suit. Joe helped Ciara get comfortable and then joined her. Romana followed suit and Trione was last to comply.

The ship shuddered and slowly righted itself; the sloping wall pushed inexorably at their backs until they were upright and more comfortable. Moments later, the landing field drifted past the windows as the ship slid silently on antigravity towards three stone pillars a hundred metres away. Marron, as if to confirm Analy's assessment of his piloting skills, set the huge disc down atop the pillars without the slightest indication to those on board that the ship had docked.

A hideous grating noise reverberated through the hull of the vessel as Marron attempted to lower the primary loading ramp, despite the damage it had suffered during the impact by the mammoths. The groaning noise continued for almost a minute, setting everyone's teeth so much on edge that, when it suddenly ended, the silence was almost oppressive.

50

"What the hell was that?" Joe demanded.

"I believe the main loading ramp has been deployed," Trione explained, "but it may not completely reach the ground as the docking pillars are taller than the ship's landing gear."

He closed his eyes and touched one long finger to his temple. "Whilst this craft is being repaired," he explained, "we must transfer to one of the three remaining vessels. We will be safe there until the damaged force-field is reactivated. Until that time, there may be danger from the predatory beasts inhabiting this primitive land."

"I suppose the smell of burned mammoth in the air might bring a few carnivores to the compound. Are you going to move the carcases?" Joe said, half jokingly.

"Engineers are already working to address the problem," Trione informed him. He moved to the nearest window and pointed obliquely across the grassy compound, to where one of the smaller craft hovered above the bloody and charred mess that had once been two furiously battling mammoths. Joe watched in fascination as ropes descended from the underside of the disc and were attached to the leg of one of the mammoths. Immediately the ropes were secure, the craft dragged the carcase towards the gap in the force-field, where the pilot skilfully negotiated the breach before dumping the russet-coloured mammoth a hundred metres away beyond the force-field. Two men swiftly released the ropes while two armed men maintained a wary watch for the denizens of the forest. All four attached themselves to the ropes and the ship rose above the force-field and returned to the remaining carcase, where the process was repeated. The whole procedure lasted no more than twenty minutes, but by the time the second body had been deposited beyond the barrier, Joe noticed furtive movement at the forest's edge.

Two hominids, bearing several characteristics of the Neanderthals of Too-ga's time, were hungrily eying the mound of mammoth flesh. But they seemed reluctant to leave the relative safety of the forest to avail themselves of the unexpected bounty. They watched the activity around the flying machines and the compound, and they were understandably wary. As Joe observed the early Neanderthals, it quickly became apparent that none of his companions had noticed them at the forest margin. Perhaps, he thought, the lives of the primitive people held nothing of consequence to the Faithful and so they eschewed contact with their neighbours in this time.

The evacuation of the damaged ship began and the party descended the battered ramp. Joe leapt the last metre or so from where the ramp fell short of the ground, and immediately helped Ciara to negotiate the gap, mindful of her newly diagnosed pregnancy. Once on the ground, he gave his attention to the hominids, who were still half hidden by the trees. Furtive movement caught his eye and he saw the dun-coloured form of a crouching sabretooth, slinking stealthily through the cover afforded by the forest edge.

A feeling of déjà vu assailed him as he recalled the incidents in the Neanderthal past of Too-ga's people, when he had used his pistol to kill both a lion and a bear. Without a thought for the danger, he raced over to where the four men were disengaging their harness from the ropes beneath the flying craft. Snatching the weapon from the nearest member of the protection squad, he raced pell-mell towards the gap in the force-field, fervently praying that the weapon had not been deactivated.

In the distance, he could hear Ciara's anguished cries as he sped to cut off the approach of the sabretooth. At a distance of more than two-hundred metres, he stopped, and breathed deeply to calm himself. On one knee, he levelled the rifle-like weapon at the big cat and pulled the trigger. A cone of blue-green energy flared from the muzzle, charring the grass no more than thirty metres away and producing a thunderous sound from the superheated air. Quickly Joe examined the weapon, finding a series of three pictograms, illustrating how to set short, medium and long-range fire. By this time, the cat was moving forward once more and was rapidly gathering pace. Sliding the control to long range, he once again aimed the weapon and depressed the firing stud, moving the ensuing needle-fine beam in an arc from left to right.

The big cat ran into the concentrated stream of energy and was instantly decapitated, its separate parts disappearing into the long grass. Behind the cat, two mighty trees in the line of fire were severed just above root level and began to topple, slowly at first, but with ever-increasing momentum until, with a mighty crash, they fell onto the smoking remains of the sabretooth. Joe was stunned. He could barely believe the ferocity of the energy from this weapon of the future. Little wonder, he thought, that their captors had thought his pistol so inconsequential and unworthy of consideration as a weapon. He could not imagine the temperature required to slice flesh so effortlessly when the animal was moving at speed.

The thunder from the superheated air around the energy beam reverberated from the cliffs of the sacred cave, which formed one boundary of the compound, whilst Joe stood, silently scanning the undergrowth for signs of more sabretooths. Fortunately there were no other predators in the immediate vicinity, so he warily made his way in the direction of the mass of mammoth flesh and the two hominids, who had fled for the safety of the trees at the sight of the giant predator. At the edge of the forest, he halted and scanned the upper branches of the massive trees. A discreet movement caught his eye and he peered upwards, through the leafy canopy, at the two frightened hominids. They were cowering against the trunk of the mighty oak, and Joe couldn't blame them. They had just had a narrow escape from the sabretooth and had witnessed Joe make thunder and lightning with his own hands. The problem was how to coax them down from their place of refuge.

Joe heard the sound of excited voices behind him and turned to see Ciara and Romana approaching, escorted by two men carrying similar weapons to the one he had just employed on the sabretooth. He held up his hand and they halted some fifty metres away.

"Go back into the compound," he ordered. "I want to talk to these people and they won't come down from the tree while there are so many people around."

Romana touched Ciara's shoulder to get her attention and demanded, "How can Joe talk to these primitive creatures when, as far as we are aware, they have no language and their brains are undeveloped?"

"I'd like to know the answer to that one, myself," Ciara replied, "but he must know what he's doing." After a moment's thought, she called, "Can I stay, Joe—please?"

"Sorry, Darling," he replied, "but it's going to be difficult enough if I'm alone. They'll never come down from their perch if there are others around. Go back with Romana and the others, please. I won't be long … and I'll be all right. You've seen what this can do," he said, patting the warm barrel of the weapon in his hands.

With a sigh of resignation, Ciara nodded.

Romana conversed with the guards for a few moments and then everyone trooped back to the compound to watch the events as they unfolded. The armed guards remained alert just outside the compound, prepared to act in the event of danger from predators.

Now Joe was alone, he had to decide how to entice the two proto-Neanderthals from their refuge in the tree. He was aware that the time available would be limited. It would be foolish to imagine that predators would not catch the scent of the two mammoth carcases and the longer he remained here, the greater the chance of further sabretooths or heavy-jawed scavengers arriving at the scene. He stood, unmoving for ten minutes staring at nothing in particular and eventually, he caught the sound of movement in the tree above. Patiently, he waited until he saw the two Neanderthals slide down the last few feet of trunk and settle lithely onto the mossy grass at its roots.   This could conceivably be his only opportunity to communicate with the primitive people, and he could afford to make no mistakes.   Slowly, he lowered his weapon to the ground, balancing it across the bridge of his foot. If they were attacked he could – theoretically, at least – flip it up into his hands in an instant.

Carefully, he made the sign of welcome employed by Too-ga's people, far into the future of these early Neanderthals. Archaeological evidence pointed to the Neanderthals being an unambitious and uninventive branch of the human race and Joe was relying on that assumption being correct. He knew that the design of Neanderthal tools had changed very slowly over the millennia and he hoped that the same was true of their sign language. Certainly, the Neanderthals of Too-ga's time used a sophisticated system of signs, but Joe was hoping that the basic signs had survived intact throughout Neanderthal history.   Joe's gesture produced an immediate reaction, and he followed it with the sign 'approach me'.

Reluctantly, the two hominids brushed their way through the undergrowth and stood five metres from Joe, eying him warily. One was male and one was female and they were completely naked. From his experience of Too-ga's people Joe estimated their ages as late teens. They were both of the heavy build characterising their race throughout its quarter of a million years' tenure on Earth; they had prominent brow ridges, but their noses were considerably smaller than those of their descendants. The male was covered with coarse, dark brown body hair and, atop his head, was an untidy mass of matted hair. The young female sported a less extensive covering upon her body but the hair on her head resembled an unruly bush. Their teeth, despite their youth, were snaggled and broken, which, Joe supposed, was due to chewing bones to extract the nutritious marrow.

Hesitantly, the young male signed 'who are you?'

Joe replied that he was the spirit of their people and they would come to know him as their Futama. The complicated signs he employed were far beyond the simple vocabulary of the primitive Neanderthals, but Joe persisted. 'You must always remember me in your stories around your fires. I am your Futama. As Joe's hands formed the signs, he mouthed the word 'Futama' and enunciated the name several times.

* * *

In the compound, Ciara and the others watched in amazement as Joe communicated with the primitive humans.

Romana could barely believe what she was seeing. "How is it possible that Joe Laing is able to speak with these people?" she asked Ciara.

"It must just come naturally to him," replied Ciara, not wishing to give even a hint about Joe's jaunt into the late Neanderthal era.

"Your man," replied Romana enigmatically, "has a number of unusual talents. He seems to delight in achieving the seemingly impossible."

Ciara suspected the tall woman was referring to Joe's ability to penetrate the system of time tunnels. "I suppose so," she agreed, non-committally. But she couldn't help nurturing a certain pride that Joe was *her* man and no one else's.

* * *

Joe knew that there was little he could achieve on this occasion save lay the foundation for another meeting with the two Neanderthals – and any others of their kin they could persuade to accompany them. He also knew that somehow he must begin the legend of the Futama, so that the story would survive through to Too-ga's times, when he would be welcomed as the Futama by Koo-ma the shaman and live with the Neanderthals for many months. Although that particular episode had been expunged from the history of the Neanderthals, Joe *had* lived through it and it remained in his own past.

He signed for the pair to approach closer, and despite the strangeness of the man before them, they obeyed. Joe made a fist and lightly touched the young man's chest in the sign of acceptance used by the later Neanderthals and all signs of fear seemed to drain out of the two youngsters. Hesitantly, the youth returned the gesture and Joe repeated the ceremony with the young female.

'I will return,' he signed. 'Tell your people of the Futama.' He placed the flat of his hand on his chest and repeated the unfamiliar sign for the Futama, saying, "Futama," with every repetition.

The young man grinned, showing his snaggle-teeth, and accurately replicated the complicated sign. With the ground successfully prepared for a future meeting, Joe flipped up the weapon with his foot and caught it one-handed before striding back towards the compound. The two youngsters watched until Joe entered the compound through the breach in the force-field, and then melted into the trees at the forest's edge.

Ciara ran to Joe and leapt into his arms, raining kisses on his unresisting lips. "Joe," she admonished as she finally pushed him away to arms' length, "I was so worried when you raced off after that lion or whatever it was."

"Sabretooth," Joe corrected. "It is—*was* a tiger."

Ciara was determined to remonstrate with her husband for placing himself in danger. "I don't care what the damned thing was, it was dangerous and yet you still had to act the hero. Anyway, what if you've changed the future by saving those two people?"

Unabashed by Ciara's tirade, Joe pressed his lips to hers once again and halted her protest. When he finally released her from his embrace, he said, "I had to do it, you know. I couldn't let that sabretooth make a meal out of them because they might have been my only opportunity to meet with the Neanderthals in this time."

"But why would you want to do that?"

"It's complicated," Joe replied. "I'll explain later."

"You'd better," Ciara muttered ominously, "because I don't like the idea of you keeping secrets from me."

"There won't be any secrets," Joe laughed, "I wouldn't be able to stand up against the third degree." He had to dodge a blow to his ribs, but at least Ciara's anger had swiftly turned to amusement.

Romana waited patiently for the interaction between Joe and Ciara to end, then ushered them towards another craft. In the excitement, the tour of the base's facilities was forgotten.

* * *

56

Prua Landi prowled amongst the scientists and technicians in the time laboratory, her austere face dark with anger. Above a dais in the centre of the busy lab a moving holographic image displayed a badly out of focus scene of carnage as two giant beasts gave battle, *their long tusks entwined as they surged back and forth in a death dance.* The holograph flared blue-green as the two beasts encountered a force-field and then caromed against the landing gear of a spacecraft, bringing the bulk of the massive ship crashing fatally down upon themselves.

"Give me a clearer image," Prua Landi grated through jaws knotted by her foul mood, "or there will be reprisals. You," she spat at those in the room, "claim to have the best minds available, yet you still remain mere children in the face of the technology available to the Faithful." The last word was dripping with contempt.

A technician hurried to the holographic projector and made a few minor adjustments and the scene came into slightly clearer focus. The ship lifted from its position atop the carcases of the dead animals and drifted towards three docking pillars, where it settled lightly as thistledown several metres above the ground. The image clearly showed the massive damage inflicted on the landing gear by the doomed beasts. They watched in fascination as several people disembarked from a ramp beneath the craft and Prua Landi became instantly alert. Two of the figures stood out amongst the tall people due to their lack of stature.

"Bring the group closer," she demanded. "There is something familiar about the two smaller figures."

The image rippled and faded before regaining strength and clarity, but not before Prua Landi had lashed a neural whip across the naked back of the unfortunate technician. The man collapsed, writhing upon the edge of the dais, his upper body partially obscuring the holographic projector and breaking up the image.

"Get that pathetic creature out of my sight," Prua Landi screamed, waving the neural whip menacingly, "or others will suffer the same punishment."

Three technicians scurried forward and dragged the unfortunate man away towards a side room, leaving the laboratory suffused with a cloying aura of fear. The scientists and technicians were accustomed to outbursts of rage from the tyrannical dictatrix, but today's tantrum was proving particularly psychotic and violent.

The image moved on, following Joe as he grabbed the weapon and sped towards the breach in the force-field. Prua Landi's features wore a mask of hate as she watched the events unfold. There was no doubt in her mind that the person depicted in the holograph was Jo-lang, the very one she had failed to destroy in the altered timeline of Tarmis, and later on the beach when she had failed to persuade him to become her ally. Her thoughts were in turmoil. By what means, she wondered, was such an apparently insignificant primitive traversing the eons of time? The more logic she applied to the conundrum, the more inclined she was to believe that here, depicted in the holographic image before her, was the fabled Futama, the prophesied 'saviour' of the damnable Faithful sect, with the infinitely superior time-travel technology she coveted so passionately.

As the events in the past unfurled, Prua Landi demanded, "What era is this?"

A voice reluctantly offered the information that the events were taking place nine-hundred and sixty-one thousand years in the past.

"Are you certain?" she enquired, her voice assuming an ominous calm.

"Yes, My Lady, the data have been verified many times."

"Come before me," she ordered and the one who had volunteered the information stepped forward. It was Perdon, one of the team of scientists who had developed the remote viewing technology, at present being employed to spy upon Joe in the distant Neanderthal past.

Prua Landi exuded an aura of menace as she said in a quiet, carefully controlled tone, "If this remote viewing device is effective to almost one million years into the past, I am inclined to ask why the range of my time-travel is limited to a little over seven-hundred thousand years. Think before you give me your answer," she added, caressing the neural whip almost sensuously with her long fingers.

Perdon planted his feet firmly before the dictatrix. Whatever explanation he offered, he still might be the victim of Prua Landi's anger. In a firm voice he explained, "There is but one explanation, My Lady. The images we are receiving are at the extreme limit of our range, which is evidenced by their poor quality. If we attempt to see further into the past, the signals degrade to a level where we can extract no useful image. Physical time travel is even more problematical. Without the more sophisticated technology

58

developed by the scientists of the Faithful, we can travel no further back in time than seven-hundred and ten thousand years. We believe the time-travellers we have dispatched beyond that time, have each disassembled irretrievably into their component atoms."

Prua Landi nodded. "What do you intend to do about this deficiency in our technology?"

"My Lady, we are working ceaselessly to refine and improve our knowledge, but as yet the solution evades us. We nevertheless anticipate a breakthrough in one of several promising lines of research."

Prua Landi stared long and hard at the scientist until he visibly withered under her unrelenting gaze. "You say your name is Perdon?"

"Yes, My Lady."

"What is your rank?"

"Third assistant to the director," Perdon offered warily.

"Then you shall take over the research," Prua Landi informed him. "Out of this assemblage of spineless creatures," she added, gesturing to encompass everyone in the huge laboratory, "only you had the courage to stand before me. I am inclined to admire boldness in my subjects, but remember well: I will not tolerate disappointment."

Chapter Seven

THE RETURN HOME:

Once on board, Romana led Joe and Ciara to a refectory. The room was airy, with comfortable seating for up to twenty people. Along one side stood an array of gleaming, stainless cabinets, which she explained were the source of all the food consumed in the refectory; and along the curved outer wall, a long screen showed an ever-changing panorama of forest and hills, occasionally interspersed with views from space. There were two other pairs of diners present.

Romana's long fingers danced on a keypad inset into one of the cabinets and immediately it disgorged a bowl of steaming stew. Seconds later another bowl appeared, and then a third, which she handed to Joe and Ciara. A separate cabinet dispensed three round loaves and soon the trio were digging their spoons into the tasty stew.

"Compliments to the chef," Joe mumbled around a mouthful of bread. "This isn't bad at all."

Romana laughed for the first time since Joe and Ciara had encountered her. "The *chef* as you call it would probably experience a minor power surge at the compliment. All food production and preparation is fully automated under the guidance of a specialised artificial intelligence. No people are involved at any stage."

"The only AI that I ever met would have graciously accepted the compliment," Joe said.

Romana immediately showed interest. "You have artificial intelligences in your time?"

Joe realised that he had spoken without thought. He couldn't divulge the results of his meddling with the lives of the Neanderthals. "Only experimental ones," he explained hastily, "but they are improving all the time and my friend hopes to make a major breakthrough in the near future." He laughed at the incongruity of his reply. "What I meant is in the near future of our own time."

Romana returned to her stew, apparently satisfied with Joe's explanation and Joe knew that he would need to watch his tongue in future. Although Romana had indicated a willingness to help Ciara to return home, her attitude could conceivably change if Joe let slip details about Tarmis.

Lowering his voice, Joe asked their tall companion, "Can we talk in here without being overheard? I mean, without someone eavesdropping telepathically?"

The expression upon Romana's beautiful face reflected her horror at Joe's question. "It is, amongst my people," she said, "an unforgivable act to eavesdrop, as you call it, upon the mind of another. It would be so uncivilised – and strictly against the law."

"Then why did Marron try to enter my thoughts without my permission," Joe asked, "when he first interrogated me?"

Romana was utterly horrified. "That cannot be so!" she protested. "It is just too horrible to contemplate."

"I'm not lying," Joe insisted. "You have my permission to dip into my mind if you wish. Although," he added, "I don't know if you'll manage it because Marron met with as much success as Prua Landi did."

Romana's eyes had a steely glint when she said, "I am compelled to believe what you say, Joe Laing, and I assure you the Elders shall hear of Captain Marron's disregard of your rights the moment we reach Mars. Meanwhile, we must find a way to return Ciara to her home and her time."

"I've been thinking about that," Joe said. "Can you tell me what Marron meant when he said that even he didn't know how the time-gates worked? Did he mean that he can't use them?"

"No, he cannot pass through the time-gates. Nor can I or anyone else on this base. We must use the temporal displacer on the Master of Time to travel backward and forward through time. How does that help?"

Joe had a triumphant gleam in his eye. "All you have to do is get us to the tunnels and I'll do the rest. Once we reach the first time-gate, I'll get us through and no one will be able to follow us."

"The three of us, together?" Romana enquired.

"Probably two at a time," Joe replied, "so let's hope we're not disturbed."

* * *

Romana's status enabled her to escort Joe and Ciara into the tunnel complex unchallenged, and they reached the time-gate without incident. Ciara was walking in front, and Romana, carrying a medical kit over her shoulder in case of accidents, strode alongside Joe, holding his hand. The tunnel walls still glowed with omnipresent light, which cast no shadows, and their footfalls made

61

little sound on the smooth floor. Ciara walked on until she came in sight of the shimmering curtain. She halted suddenly in mid-stride and shuddered, though the temperature in the tunnel complex was a constant twenty-two degrees Celsius.

"Hell's bells!" she exclaimed, "I think someone just walked over my grave!"

Holding Romana by the hand, Joe strode forward to where Ciara stood trembling and gently urged her forward a couple of paces. The trembling ceased and Ciara gave a sigh of relief.

"What happened, Joe?" she demanded.

"You've just passed through the time-gate unaided," Joe explained. "I've never really seen or felt anything when I've passed through on my own. Obviously you felt something but did you see anything at all?"

Ciara was baffled and edgy. "Nothing," she said, "except the curtain over there."

"This means that you can now use the time tunnels just like me—but don't ask me how. I don't suppose Romana knows?"

Romana shook her head. "I have no knowledge of the time-gates," she admitted, "but the ability seems to have passed between you. Perhaps even your unborn child will possess the gift."

Ciara absently rubbed her abdomen. "Does this mean I might become a target for Prua Landi?"

"I don't think so," Joe assured her, "at least not when I'm in the past. It's me she seems to want, and we now know it's because of my ability to use the time tunnels. While she's interested in me, she'll leave you alone."

Ciara was worried. "But what if she tries to take the information from my mind?"

Joe wanted to reassure his wife, but how? Suddenly, the method became clear. "Darling, will you let Romana try to probe your mind?"

"What?"

"If she can't do it," he explained, "it means that Prua Landi can't either."

"And if she can?"

Joe shrugged. "Let's think positively for the moment, shall we? Will you let Romana try?"

Ciara sighed. This whole adventure had taken a severe twist in the direction of weird. Now she was about to be probed telepathically. "Okay," she said, "but I hope it doesn't hurt."

Romana had followed their conversation with increasing astonishment. "This is highly irregular," she said. "It is not, however, immoral or illegal, so I will comply with your wishes. I will be as gentle as I can be."

She frowned momentarily in concentration and Ciara felt feather light tendrils caressing her mind. The mind probe sought out dark places and crevices in which to obtain a finger hold, but met with failure at every turn. Ciara's mind was closed to probes from outside agencies just as tightly as Joe's. After a minute, Romana accepted defeat.

"You are safe from Prua Landi," she conceded, "but I am at a loss to understand how."

"Great!" Joe said. "Let's worry about *how* another time. It's time for Ciara to go home. He indicated the shimmering curtain. "Let's go."

The three stepped through the curtain hand in hand, with Romana in the middle, and with the familiar twist in their guts, arrived in the tunnel where Joe had left a small rucksack containing a spare torch and a few sandwiches. They began the mile or so trek to the cove and Joe couldn't help noticing the proximity of the top of Romana's luxuriant hair to the ceiling. He suggested that their tall companion walk down the centre of the tunnel to gain the maximum headroom.

Romana had to be coaxed across the makeshift bridge over the abyss but, eventually, they made it and continued their journey to the outside world of the twenty-first century.

The descent down the cliff face went smoothly, for although night had fallen, the stars cast a wan light over the tiny cove. The waves whispered onto the beach and the breeze, heavy with the scents of late evening, sighed as it caressed their faces. There was an aura of calm, at odds with the primal violence of the distant past.

Joe descended first and held the rope taut for the others, giving words of encouragement as they climbed down. Soon they were exiting the cleft onto the main beach. Romana was suffused with a sense of suppressed excitement. This was a new time period for her, and she was experiencing it illicitly. The time would come when it would be necessary to admit to her actions – but that would be in the future or, rather, the primeval past. Joe was glad that their return was taking place under the cover of darkness – explaining the presence of someone of Romana's stature and appearance could have proved problematical.

The lights were still glowing in Maeve Branton's home as the threesome arrived at Joe's front door. Swiftly, Joe turned the key and entered, followed by the others. He indicated a seat for Romana and entered the kitchen to make a pot of tea.

Ciara said, "I'll just go round to tell Mum we're back. She's sure to be pleased."

Joe called his acknowledgement from the kitchen. Less than two minutes later, Ciara returned, her face flushed, tears welling from her eyes.

"Oh, Joe," she sobbed, "it's Or-gon, he's really ill. Mum says he's in a bad way."

Romana glided instantly to her feet. "Take me to him," she ordered briskly, and the trio headed next door, where Maeve Branton was about to get a considerable surprise. Maeve let them in, her eyebrows rising as she appraised Romana's height.

"He started with a cold, this morning," she explained, "and it's worsened throughout the day. He's very weak," she sobbed, as she fought unsuccessfully to hold back the tears.

Ciara hugged her, whispering words of comfort and stroking her mother's corona of flaming hair. "Romana will fix Or-gon, Mum. She's from the future and she's a doctor. If anyone can help him, she can."

Maeve continued to sob quietly as Joe led Romana upstairs to where the stricken Or-gon lay, drifting in and out of consciousness, his massive Neanderthal frame shivering and drenched with perspiration. Dark, damp stains on the sheets told the story of just how much moisture Or-gon was losing through his skin.

Romana opened her medikit and selected an instrument similar to the one she had used upon Ciara. Swiftly, but thoroughly, she examined the Neanderthal, rechecking the reading each time an anomaly was displayed. Eventually, she reached into the medikit and drew out a shiny instrument, shaped like a pistol. Selecting a large ampoule of opaque liquid, she inserted it into the dispenser as expertly as a soldier fitting a fresh magazine into an automatic weapon, and pressed the instrument to Or-gon's neck. With a sustained hiss, the ampoule emptied and Romana stowed the instrument once more within the medikit.

"Now, we shall wait," she sighed, "one hundredth of a day. Meanwhile, I think I would like to experience a cup of tea."

"I'll bet there's one already poured," Joe said, glancing at his stricken friend as he exited the bedroom. Maybe it was his

64

imagination, but it seemed to Joe that Or-gon's cheeks were a little less flushed.

Romana preceded Joe down the stairs, bent almost double to negotiate the low ceiling. Ciara met her at the bottom, accompanied by a still sobbing Maeve.

"Will he be all right?" Ciara asked, thrusting a cup of tea into Romana's oversized hand.

Romana tentatively sipped the hot beverage. "By the time I have consumed this, um, tea, the nanomedics will have multiplied to fill Or-gon's bloodstream and will be eliminating the cause of his illness. They will then continue their work to ensure that all inimical life forms are exterminated."

"C-can we have that in English?" Maeve sobbed. "Or Irish, at least."

"Your companion will recover and, unless he is unfortunate enough to suffer massive injury, his body now has the capability to repair itself."

A series of muffled creaks from upstairs told them that Or-gon was moving in his bed, something he had been too weak to accomplish over the past few hours. Maeve listened for a few moments before moving towards the stairs. Romana gripped her arm with strong fingers and restrained her.

"Please allow a little more time for the nanomedics to perform their task. He will soon be strong enough to descend the stairs without help."

"Are you sure?" Maeve demanded.

The medic nodded. "Yes, I am certain. Listen to the movement above us. I believe your companion has arisen from his bed."

Joe placed his arm reassuringly around his mother-in-law's shoulder and urged her towards an easy chair. "Just wait, Maeve. You can trust Romana."

"If you insist, Joe, I'll wait a few minutes," Maeve conceded, "but I'd like to know exactly who it is you're asking me to trust."

Joe grinned at his mother-in-law. "I suppose we should tell you what's happened so far."

"Sure, but that would be a good idea," Maeve suggested.

"To begin with," Joe began, "Romana is the medical officer of the place where we ended up when we crossed over the abyss in the time tunnel. I think someone mentioned it's more than a quarter of a million years into our past."

"That's a long, long time ago," Maeve agreed.

"But that's not all," Joe continued, "Romana is actually from our distant future. Her people have fled to the past to escape persecution in their own time." He paused, deciding how much information Maeve could handle at this stage. "There was an incident with two mammoths and I—" he glanced over to Ciara for support, and she gave a slight nod. "—we decided that it was too dangerous for Ciara to stay there, especially when we found out—"

"That I'm pregnant," Ciara finished.

"What?" Maeve exclaimed in astonishment. "You're pregnant, you say?"

Ciara nodded enthusiastically. "I think we made the right decision, don't you Mum, especially with Or-gon being so ill?"

"Are you sure?" Maeve demanded. "About the pregnancy, I mean."

"Romana examined me after we'd all been shaken up in the incident with the mammoths." Her gaze flicked to Or-gon, who was silently descending the staircase, clad in a dressing gown and slippers. "If Romana can cure Or-gon the way she has, I think we can trust that she knows what she's doing."

Maeve's eyes opened wide at the sight of Or-gon so obviously well again, and she leapt to her feet to embrace him. Joe and Ciara exchanged glances. Ciara had long hoped that her mother would eventually find someone with whom she could form a relationship, and she had to admit to feeling delight that the big Neanderthal was a candidate to step into her dad's shoes. Somehow, the odd couple seemed to fit together.

Joe watched the interaction between Or-gon and Maeve with amusement. He would never have believed that the scientist could have so easily shed the reserve that was an ingrained character trait of all the people of Tarmis. Yet, here he was, affectionately embracing his landlady, Joe's mother-in-law.

"Are you feeling all right, old friend?" he asked.

Or-gon released Maeve and embraced Joe. "It is good to see you again, Joe. Yes, I am well. In fact," he added, "I feel better than at any time since I arrived here from—"

"Joe whispered in his friend's ear, "Don't mention Tarmis, please."

"—Wales," Or-gon finished. He approached Romana, who towered over him, and grasped her long, slim hand in his beefy Neanderthal fist. "I heard a little of what you were saying as I came

66

downstairs, and I believe I owe you my life," he said, brushing Romana's hand with his lips. Graciously, he added, "Thank you, lady of the future."

"The nanomedics technology is ancient and reliable," Romana assured him, "and will ensure your good health for many years."

This was the first time the scientist had heard of the nanomedics and his interest was immediately alerted. "Nanomedics?" he queried. "Please explain."

Romana was painfully aware of her responsibilities toward the future and the past. She must do nothing to change the path of this timeline. But yet, she had injected this man with nanomedics, technology of the future, in order to save his life and she had no knowledge of how her action might affect this timeline.

"My apologies, Or-gon, but I have already interfered with the course of time by injecting you in order to save your life, and I cannot exacerbate the effect by explaining to you what little I know of the technology. I have no doubt that you will research the subject and I hope that what you achieve does not affect this timeline."

"Perhaps your action will not affect this timeline as much as you fear," Or-gon informed Romana. "Scientists are already attempting to produce nanomachinery. Although," he added, "the research is at a very early stage."

After a few moments' introspection Romana said, "I have searched my memory and I understand that in the past of my people, nanotechnology began in this era. It is possible, therefore, that all my actions thus far were predestined and will not affect the course of time at all. However, if I remain here for too long, it is certain that anomalies will begin to appear, with the possibility of catastrophic effects on your future and my past."

Joe was quick to take the hint. "I'll bet they're missing us at the compound," he said, "and I reckon we ought to be making our way back."

Ciara was caught off-guard by the change of direction of the conversation. "So soon?" she exclaimed.

"Sorry, Darling," he soothed, "but we don't want Romana to get into more trouble than necessary."

"I was hoping you'd be able to stay a while," Ciara protested, "but I can see your point."

Joe embraced his wife and gazed intently into her beautiful eyes. "Look, Sweetheart, I want you to look after yourself. Don't do anything silly—and remember to take your mum's advice."

"I'm not an invalid, you know," Ciara protested, "I'm only pregnant."

"I know, but I don't want to be worrying about you while I'm gone. You know what I mean."

Ciara kissed Joe passionately, and when she released him from her embrace she said, "All right, Joe, but I want you to do something for me in return."

"Okay, tell me."

"I want you to remember you're going to be a dad. So don't go off trying to save every poor soul who's in trouble, and don't forget what you're leaving here. And one last thing," she added with a grin, "make sure you video everything, because I want to know exactly what the Moon and Mars are like. If I can't go there myself, I want to at the very least see what you see."

Joe returned the smile. "Will do," he agreed.

"And don't forget this: if you're gone too long, I'll come looking for you."

That, thought Joe, as he exited with Romana, is as certain as death and taxes.

Chapter Eight

LEGEND OF THE FUTAMA:

When Romana and Joe returned to the past of the early Neanderthals the compound was experiencing a major upheaval, as numerous pairs of armed men and women combed the tunnel complex and the buildings and craft in the compound, seeking the missing trio. As fate would have it they encountered Analy and Trione, who greeted them with raised weapons.

"Halt," Analy called from several metres away.

Trione wore an expression of concentration upon his long features, and it was clear that he was transmitting telepathic news of their discovery.

"Where have you been," Analy called. "We have searched the base from end to end." He seemed to notice for the first time that there was one person missing. "Where is the woman?" he demanded.

"I will explain in good time," Romana replied icily. "Meanwhile, please lower your weapons."

Analy and Trione maintained their stance and their weapons did not waver. "We have orders to escort you to Captain Marron," Trione stated, motioning with the barrel of the plasma rifle.

At the mention of Captain Marron, Joe whispered urgently to his companion, "Don't forget what I told you about Marron and his attempt to probe my mind."

Romana smiled grimly. "I have not forgotten, Joe Laing." To the armed pair she said, with all the authority she could muster, "I have asked you to lower your weapons, now I am ordering you to do so. I am not inclined to be in the presence of Captain Marron for any reason. So, unless you are prepared to kill us, you had better obey my command."

Analy and Trione glanced at each other, placed off-guard by the unexpected development. Finally, Trione shrugged and lowered his weapon and Analy quickly followed suit.

"We are your friends, Romana," Trione said, "but we must obey orders. The captain was most insistent."

"Captain Marron has such authority on his ship, but not in this complex. I demand that you take us to Leiki, the commander of this base, if he has returned from Mars. "

"Yes, but the captain—"

His words of protest were stifled by Romana's icy stare and he decided to accept the inevitable. "Leiki it is, then," he said as the four set off in search of the base commander.

* * *

Leiki proved to be an affable man, who seemed so wrapped up in his work that much of the simple, day-to-day activity around the base tended to escape his notice. He could not, however, have failed to hear about the arrival and subsequent disappearance of Joe and Ciara and of Joe's interaction with the primitive Neanderthals beyond the perimeter of the compound. He was filling in an official looking form as they entered his office.

"So this is our intruder," he commented, twiddling a pen in his long fingers. "Obviously not one of us!" he added drily, scrutinising Joe with a pair of piercing amber eyes. "Would you say he was dangerous?" he asked, subjecting Romana and the others to the same stare.

"I do not believe so," Romana replied, "though he has proved his ability to use a plasma rifle very effectively."

Leiki's face dissolved into a sunny smile that lit up his features and seemed to take twenty years off his age. "I heard about that," he beamed. "Rumour says that he killed several large predators and felled half the trees on the edge of the forest. Would anyone like to explain what actually happened so that I can enter an accurate version in this report?" He indicated the partially completed form on his desk and Joe couldn't help wondering why an advanced race should employ such a primitive mode of record keeping.

Leiki fixed Joe with his amber gaze. "It is an eccentricity of mine," he said.

"What is?"

"This ancient method of recording, using pen and paper."

"I didn't say anything," Joe protested, "and I thought you weren't allowed to read minds without the owner's permission."

Leiki laughed, a joyous expression of mirth. "I believe everyone on the base would have been subjected to your thoughts, such was their strength. I think some kind of training is indicated, Romana, or none of us will be able to sleep for the noise."

Joe found he was warming to the base director's sunny personality. So far, everyone he had met, including Romana, had proved to be reserved and serious, but Leiki seemed to delight in his

70

eccentricity, finding humour in almost everything. He laughed at Leiki's attempt at humour. But there was a darker side. If he was broadcasting his surface thoughts so loudly, the wrong person might be able to pick up information. In worried tones, he informed, Leiki, *"I hope not, because I don't want just anybody knowing what I'm thinking."*

Romana smiled. "I think you should tell Joe Laing the truth, Director. Otherwise—"

Leiki chuckled once more, all the time subjecting Joe to his piercing amber stare. "Of course," he began, his laughter subsiding, "we must remember that our guest is unaccustomed to the intricacies of telepathic communication. You need not fear, Joe Laing," he continued, "that your thoughts may be open to us. I merely read your body language – another of my eccentricities – and extrapolated what you *might* be thinking." His straight face melted once more into a smile. "From your reaction, I believe I was fairly accurate in my assessment?"

"Spot on," Joe admitted ruefully. "I must admit you had me going there for a minute."

Romana cut into the conversation. "Director, you should be made aware of the reason Joe Laing does not wish his thoughts to be made public."

Leiki raised his eyebrows. "Please continue."

Romana glanced at Analy and Trione and the director said briskly to the two men, "Lower your guards!"

Instantly, there ensued a rapid telepathic exchange of information between the three men, and Leiki finally told Analy and Trione, "You may remain." To Romana, he said, "Please continue."

Romana detailed Marron's attempt to pry into Joe's thoughts and the captain's barely concealed hostility towards Joe and Ciara. Leiki and the other two men were aghast at Marron's flagrant breach of the laws of propriety that were so fundamental to the ideals of the Faithful. She told of the general orders to bring Joe and Ciara before Marron as and when their hiding place was discovered.

Joe added that the only other times he had been subjected to such an intrusion were Prua Landi's failed attempts to enter his thoughts.

Leiki listened without comment before saying, "Analy and Trione will provide security for our guest whilst he is on this base and on the journeys to the Moon and to Mars. Now," he added, his smile returning to transform his long features, "will someone please tell me what happened to trigger the rumours so that I may complete my report?"

From their differing perspectives, the four gave an account of the events on the base from Joe and Ciara's arrival, to the point where they and Romana disappeared, precipitating the search of the tunnel complex and the outer compound. From that point onwards, Romana continued the story, detailing their return to the twenty-first century. The relating of the tale was accompanied by the furious scratching of Leiki's pen as he compiled his report. Eventually Romana reached the point where she had injected the nanomedics into Or-gon and the director's expression mirrored his surprise at her actions.

"Please lower your guard, Romana," he ordered, and there was, once again, the virtually instant, telepathic transference of information between the two. Eventually, he gave a satisfied nod and Romana smiled.

Joe experienced a feeling of exclusion as the two communicated telepathically. "What's happening?" he demanded.

Leiki smiled sympathetically. "I apologise, Joe Laing. Telepathy must be a strange experience for you. I have just given Romana a lesson concerning the history of nanomedics. As a student of history – another of my eccentricities – I am aware that this intervention had already occurred in your time, and it was, therefore, necessary for the cycle of events to be completed – though records of that period give no clue as to the circumstances, or to the identity of the person who provided the future technology.

Joe was making an heroic attempt to wrap his mind around the concept of a past where events were preordained once they had taken place. He recognised the parallel with his attempt to instigate the legend of the Futama so deep in the past of Too-ga's Neanderthals. And, he thought, with a growing sense of vindication, he must have been predestined to bring Or-gon from the doomed timeline of Tarmis to his own twenty-first century. Once one accepted the weird logic of time travel, it all seemed to fit.

Leiki continued filling in the report, ending with a flourish and folding the sheet a number of times. He was handing the paper to Romana for her to carry on her person to the Council of Elders on Mars, when the door dilated and Marron burst in, his face ablaze with anger. Trione and Analy brought their weapons instantly to bear on him, before slowly lowering them.

72

A swift glance at the weapons, so readily trained upon him, warned Marron of the heightened level of security. "What is the meaning of this?" he blustered, in an attempt to wrest some kind of advantage from the situation, "why were my orders ignored?" He glared balefully at Analy and Trione.

Leiki, no longer the easygoing director, content to let events unfold with the minimum of personal involvement, said sternly, "Your orders were rescinded by Romana and I have accepted her explanation of her actions. The matter is now closed, and you will restrict your involvement to the command of your ship. It may seem," he added, "that I exert very little control over the day-to-day running of this base, but must I remind you that I am the director, and that all such responsibility rests with me?"

Marron, in all his previous encounters with Leiki, had never experienced this steely aspect of the director's character. The anger drained from him as he fought to attain a measure of control over his emotions, and he finally inclined his head in a suggestion of a bow. "No, Director Leiki," he murmured, "but you must understand, my actions stem from my distrust of this ... primitive." He eyed Joe with an expression of unconcealed contempt.

Joe's fingernails dug into his palms at Marron's description of him as 'primitive' and the muscles in his jaw tensed.

Leiki's practised eye caught the slight movement and he swiftly intervened. The last thing he wanted was violent confrontation within the confines of his office. "Captain Marron," he said authoritatively, "you may return to your ship and supervise the repairs. I'm sure you will find enough tasks to occupy yourself. You are dismissed."

Marron, his ego in tatters at his summary dismissal by the director of the base, turned on his heel and strode out of the room, almost catching the controls of the dilating doorway unawares in his haste to escape.

Joe eyed the director and grinned, "Thanks," he said. "I don't know if Marron realises how close he came to getting thumped, but somebody ought to tell him I'm not a primitive."

Leiki's sunny smile returned. "He will be informed," he agreed, "and I must admit that for a 'primitive', you showed considerable restraint."

Joe couldn't help liking Leiki's impish sense of humour, and he found the director's comment amusing. "I don't normally fight unless I'm forced to," Joe admitted, "but Marron has been rubbing me up the wrong way since soon after Ciara and I arrived here."

"Do you fight often, Joe Laing?"

"Only when I have to," Joe countered, "in self-defence, or to protect my friends."

Leiki nodded. "When you killed the predator, was that an example of your fighting skills?"

Joe laughed. "No, I'm trained to use my bare hands."

The director wasn't the only one whose interest was aroused by Joe's comment. Analy and Trione paid even more attention to the conversation; Romana regarded Joe as if seeing him for the first time.

Leiki pressed on with his questions, intending to extract every piece of information possible from Joe, whilst he was in a cooperative mood. "Are you a soldier?"

Joe laughed at the question. "No, I'm not a soldier. I can use weapons, though. There's no use me denying it because your people saw me use one of those." Joe indicated the plasma rifles held loosely by Analy and Trione. "If I thought about it, those things would scare the hell right out of me. In my time our weapons fire projectiles, not energy."

"Such as the 'primitive' weapon we allowed you to retain on your person?"

"Yes, in varying forms; some more powerful, some less so." Joe was astonished at the casual revelation that his pistol had been recognised for what it was, yet he had still been allowed to keep it.

"Why did you not threaten Marron with the weapon when he tried, so unethically, to enter your mind?" Leiki enquired.

"Why would I do that?" Joe replied. "Ciara and I didn't come here to cause trouble. We only wanted to see what was at the end of the time tunnel. In our time, only a handful of men have set foot on the Moon, and Mars is a distant dream. Your people promised us a trip to the Moon and to Mars, so why would we want to jeopardise that? Due to the incident with the mammoths and Ciara being pregnant, Romana agreed to help me take Ciara home. Although," he added, his tone hardening, "you might have found out what I can do if anyone had tried to prevent it."

Leiki selected another piece of paper and commenced writing. "What can you do? Please give an example." His amber eyes fixed unwaveringly upon Joe. Gone for the moment was the former jollity; this was serious. "Could you, for example, disarm Analy or Trione?"

"Without killing them, you mean?" Joe asked casually.

Leiki nodded, smiling. "That would be preferable. After all, they are not your enemies."

Both men stiffened. They were trained to fight with the energy weapons, but the concept of hand-to-hand fighting, with death a distinct possibility, was alien to them. The plasma rifles had very severe limitations to their use at close-quarters, because no one was likely to survive on either side.

Joe considered his reply. He didn't wish to give too much away in case he needed the element of surprise in his favour but, thus far, the director had treated him with the utmost respect, almost as an honoured guest. "Yes," he said, "so long as they were so near that they couldn't use their weapons without fear of killing themselves and everyone else in the room."

"Would you be prepared to give us a demonstr—?"

Before the director could complete his request Joe leapt into action to utilise the element of surprise. He chopped Trione's wrist with the edge of his hand and the plasma rifle clattered to the floor. With seemingly the same movement, he grasped Analy's wrist and twisted it downwards, bringing intense pain to the radial nerve, and forcing the weapon from his grip. Then, with a reverse action, he brought Analy's arm upwards, putting him in a very painful arm lock. Analy's arm was completely immobilised by the hold, for Joe knew from experience that the slightest movement would initiate searing pain to his adversary's arm and shoulder. Joe explained that, from this position, he could break Analy's arm, throw him to the floor, or render him immobile for as long as he wished.

Leiki made his way back to the seat he had swiftly vacated at the onset of the demonstration and commenced making notes. Romana stood regarding Joe, her eyes wide in amazement, as he released Analy from the arm lock and handed the weapon back to him. Analy ruefully rubbed his wrist and shoulder, stunned by Joe's demonstration of lightning reflexes and technique. Joe retrieved the weapon that had clattered to the floor and presented it to Trione, who was also rubbing his abused wrist, a smile on his lips.

Leiki shot one more question at Joe. "Could you use these skills to kill an enemy?"

"Easily." The reply was made more chilling by the confident way it was delivered.

The director's chair rolled away behind him as he rose to his feet and bowed deeply, his forehead almost touching the surface of his desk. "Then welcome, Futama," he said, his voice choking with emotion. "Welcome to the world of your exiled Faithful."

Joe was thunderstruck by the sudden turn of events as Romana, Trione and Analy prostrated themselves before him. He had taken great care never to mention the name, Futama in the presence of any of these people and he was trying heroically to understand what was happening. "Get up!" he ordered, unable to keep the irritation from his voice. "I don't want that kind of attention from anybody. I might have expected it from primitive Neanderthals, but not from people who are from my distant future. I'm just a man for goodness sake, not some kind of superman."

Everyone rose to their feet and stood erect, towering over Joe, their eyes fixed avidly upon him. "How did you know about the Futama thing," he demanded, "because I haven't told anybody about it?"

"Everything will be made clear shortly," Leiki said, "but first, everyone present must be sworn to silence. Nothing that has occurred here must be heard beyond the walls of this room." He stared at Analy and Trione. "Swear it," he ordered, "and swear to protect the Futama – with your lives, if necessary."

The two bowed low to Joe once again.

"I swear it," said Analy.

"You have my oath," voiced Trione.

Romana had not been included in the director's order to protect Joe. Nevertheless, she added a passionate codicil to the others' vows. "I am a medic, charged with saving lives, but I will gladly shed the blood of any man or woman who would harm the Futama."

Joe eyed the tall doctor. Her beautiful eyes were ablaze with passion and he wondered where had the fervour sprung from so suddenly? Leiki, having received the assurances he required from the others, retrieved his chair and offered the seat to Joe, who sat down heavily. There were two other chairs in the room, so Trione stepped outside to locate two more.

Within minutes all five were seated around the director's desk and Leiki began, "You know me as director of this base, but what you do not – could not – know, is that I am also a member of the Council of Elders." Joe's three companions somehow managed to bow slightly at the revelation, despite being seated.

"Should I be joining them?" Joe enquired.

"You are the Futama," Leiki advised seriously, "and the Futama bows to no one. We are the Faithful and we have awaited your coming throughout all the eons of time. You are the reason for our exile and the one hope of our return to our true birthright."

Joe heard the director's words, echoing and re-echoing through his mind, but however he examined and evaluated the statement, he couldn't get them to make any kind of sense. Scenes from his adventure in the time of Too-ga and Koo-ma and Lar-na flitted across his memory and he once again heard the tones of reverence with which they had addressed him. His viewpoint turned to Tarmis and the reactions of the leaders of the doomed nation when they discovered he was the Futama. The scenes faded to be replaced by Leiki's words and Joe still failed to grasp their full import.

"I think you'd better explain that again from a different angle, so that I can understand," he said, "because I'm afraid you're not making any sense at all."

Leiki's smile returned and he was once again the jovial, friendly director Joe had seen earlier. "As you command, Futama," he said deferentially.

"Cut that out!" Joe ordered. "You know what I said about being just a man. I don't want any special treatment."

The director chuckled, "Very well," he agreed, "but still you are our Futama."

"If you don't stop calling me Futama, it won't be long before everybody knows who I am."

"That is true," Leiki agreed, "and we can never be certain whether Prua Landi's agents have infiltrated our ranks." He glanced at each of the others in turn. "You have eagerly awaited the coming of the Futama, but now I must ask you to keep the knowledge close to your hearts." He fixed his attention on Joe. "Futama, how may we address you?"

"Just call me Joe and I'll be happy. Now," he added, "how about that explanation?"

"The Faithful," began Leiki, with an exaggerated sigh, "are from almost a million years into the future of this era. For our belief in the coming of the Futama, we have been persecuted, mind-wiped and indiscriminately murdered. Fortunately for us our scientists developed technology, which enabled us to move through time and to escape. We fled to the distant past, where we built the system of

77

time tunnels and living accommodation. Fortunately, this technology is far in advance of that available to Prua Landi and her foul regime, and whilst we are here, we are out of reach of her vengeance."

"Is this why Prua Landi has tried to kill me on two or three occasions?"

"I believe that Prua Landi may suspect that you are an associate of the Futama, yes. But Prua Landi, and everyone on this base, may have difficulty in reconciling your appearance and primitive time of origin with the legend. Eventually, she will come to realise that you are the one she seeks, and then she will not limit herself to hand weapons."

"I can see what you mean," Joe commented. "She's already tried to kill me by starting a nuclear war. I only just managed to reach the time tunnel before the first bombs went off."

"In Tarmis?"

"How did you know about that?" Joe demanded. "I thought I'd wiped out the timeline altogether."

"The Council of Elders has maintained a discreet surveillance on your activities since you first entered the time tunnels, and I have been given the task of smoothing the path of the Futama in this time."

"So, how come your people didn't recognise me as the Futama the moment I arrived here? How come your bosses didn't post a description of me on your noticeboards or whatever you use?"

"Even though I am a member of the Council of Elders on Mars, my rank is too lowly to be privileged with that information. If I were allowed to guess, I would say that it is a means of ensuring the Futama's safety until he reaches our sanctuary on Mars. Then, everyone will know who has come amongst us."

"Okay," said Joe, "if I accept what you've just told me, my next question is why? I mean, why go to all this trouble for someone like me?"

Leiki shook his head slowly. "My apologies, Futama—"

"It's Joe from now on, right?"

"My apologies, Joe, but I fear I may already have exceeded my authority. The elders will tell you anything you wish to know on Mars."

"As Futama, I can't order you to tell me?" Joe said with a grin.

Leiki shook his head, "No, Joe, you may not."

78

Analy, Trione and Romana had listened to the discussion with rising astonishment. That they had now become an integral part of the legend of the Futama had not escaped their notice.

Trione suggested that it be made known he and Analy were to guard Joe, to prevent him escaping a second time. That way, they would be able to give him maximum protection and no one would suspect that he was, in reality, not their prisoner.

Leiki agreed with Trione's logic. "You will both travel to the Moon with the Futama," he ordered, "and, as Captain Marron's vessel is under repair, you will travel with Captain Terpin and his crew on the Master of Time."

Joe felt a sense of relief that he would avoid contact with Marron for a while. He was uncertain whether he would be able to maintain control over his temper if the captain continued to rub him up the wrong way. He had no idea of the punishment for violence upon the person of a ship's captain and he had no wish to find out. It was prudent, therefore, that they remain apart, at least for a while.

Chapter Nine

LUNAR INCIDENT:

The Master of Time proved to be a much larger vessel than the one damaged by the mammoths. She had arrived from the Moon during the short period when Joe and Romana had been escorting Ciara home and was, at present, provisioning for her return. Joe estimated the vessel to be in excess of seventy metres across, standing on huge tubular legs more than six metres high. The design was very similar to Marron's vessel, with the exception of a sizeable dark blister beneath the centre of the craft, from which a lattice of curved metallic rods projected to a point just above ground level and six flat-topped mounds on the upper surface forming a hexagon.

Joe was busily recording everything around the compound with his camcorder. "What's that?" he asked, indicating the strange array beneath the craft.

"As its name suggests, the vessel is able to travel through time as well as space," explained Trione, "unlike the smaller craft. The blister holds the time transference equipment and the metallic array is a fine-tuning device, without which it would be impossible to move such vast tonnages through time without building up serious displacement errors."

"I think I understand. Tell me, what are those mounds on top?" Joe zoomed in on the upper surface of the ship with the camcorder's telephoto lens.

"The Master of Time is our only vessel capable of time travel. We cannot build ships in this era, so we had to steal a number of vessels from Prua Landi's fleet. A smaller ship can be sealed magnetically to the Master of Time by means of those attachments and thus travel with her through time."

Joe's curiosity was aroused. "Was it easy to steal the ships?"

Trione's eyes clouded for a moment. "There are still members of the Faithful who remain incognito in our time, awaiting the day when the Futama will come to set them free. At great personal risk, they infiltrated many aspects of Prua Landi's government, and it is those brave people who made it possible to steal ships and other necessary supplies."

Joe could detect the pain in Trione's voice. "Have you left someone back there?"

"My wife," said the tall man, "remains at Prua Landi's mercy, along with a great many others. Still," his expression brightened, "the Futama—" He halted in mid-sentence and glanced furtively around to assure himself that he had not been overheard, "—you are here, Joe, and soon we shall be reunited."

They mounted the broad ramp and stepped upwards into the interior of the huge craft. A soft glow emanated from every surface, lighting the vast cargo area, in which Joe could see neat rows of boxes held to the floor by means of broad retaining straps. The centre of the cargo hold was occupied by the bulk of the time transference device and, to the right, there stood a vehicle approximately three metres wide and six metres long, resembling a tunnelling machine without the drilling attachments. It stood on dull grey caterpillar tracks devoid of driving wheels, and Joe supposed that it must use some kind of advanced motive power to drive the tracks.

The foursome, comprising Joe, Analy, Trione and Romana, stepped together onto a round plate inset into the smooth floor of the hold, and were whisked up to the accommodation deck. The deck was divided into eight sectors, each with eighteen cabins arrayed around the central power plant, which protruded from the floor below. A series of concentric corridors gave access to all areas of the accommodation deck. The next level proved to be the most interesting for Joe. It contained a spacious octagonal recreation room and refectory in the centre, and the rest of the deck was given over to laboratories, computer suites, a huge electronic library and planetarium. Around the outer rim was a broad corridor with huge, curved observation windows every ten metres. The upper deck contained the ship's bridge and the captain's accommodation. Joe asked to be shown around the bridge, but Analy informed him that it was not possible. As the Futama, he could go anywhere he wished on the ship, but as they must maintain the charade that he was under guard, his presence on the bridge of the Master of Time would raise too many awkward questions.

"In that case," Joe commented, "I wouldn't mind a bite to eat." He switched off his camcorder and stowed it in its case. Ciara wouldn't be very happy if the only record of his journey to the Moon and Mars proved to be of the compound and the interior of the Master of Time.

It seemed his three companions were also hungry and Romana swiftly obtained a selection of foods and drinks for everyone from the automatic dispensers. As the refectory was empty at this time, they discussed the events of the day in low tones as they ate.

"Are you the— " Analy lowered his voice to a whisper, "— Futama, in your world?"

Joe laughed, as he had done when asked the same question in Tarmis. "No, I most certainly am not. As I've told you before, I'm just an ordinary guy. The only thing special about me is that I can enter the time tunnels when no one, not even Prua Landi, can even see them."

Analy grinned at the others. "It is fortunate for the Faithful that you are such an *ordinary* man," he commented.

Trione added his own question. "Joe," he said, obviously struggling with having to use the name instead of the honorific to which all the Faithful had become accustomed, "what was it like to encounter Prua Landi?"

"The first word that comes to mind is 'horrible'. Anyone who can start a nuclear war to target one person, namely me, has got to be an evil bitch. She tried to get into my mind and failed for some reason I can't explain. Afterwards, she almost destroyed the sanity of Hotep to try to pry information from him about me. When all that failed, she pressed the nuclear button and I barely managed to escape through the time tunnel."

"Please tell us about Tarmis," Romana added.

"It was a beautiful land, where there was no hunger and no greed and no oppression. If I hadn't left Ciara behind, or met Prua Landi, I could easily have chosen to live there. But it was a false timeline for me, and when I escaped with Or-gon, I had to end it all to restore my own timeline, in order to return to Ciara."

He recounted the tale of his adventures with Too-ga's people; Koo-ma, the shaman's intensely enquiring intelligence; his hand-to-hand encounter with Mantoo, the giant Neanderthal, who was probably twice his weight; he omitted to mention the occasion when Lar-na drugged him to enable her to sleep with him. He continued on to Tarmis, ending with his flight home with Or-gon and their subsequent search for a means of returning to his own timeline. All the while, he carefully avoided even the slightest reference to the timestone. Finally, he told of his encounter with Prua Landi on the beach, and her unsuccessful attempt to once again enter his mind, culminating in her futile attack with an energy weapon upon the entrance to the time tunnel.

The trio listened intently, absorbing Joe's every word. Finally, Analy said ruefully, "I have heard of no one who could resist the power of Prua Landi's mind. You must be extraordinarily powerful yourself, Joe."

"If you say so, but I don't know how."

A number of people were filtering into the refectory, so the conversation turned away from the subject of Prua Landi and Tarmis and onto the journey to the Moon. The others had completed the journey many times and, to them, the experience had become mundane. But it was to be Joe's first time and he was alive with excitement at the prospect of standing upon the Moon's surface, something that few humans of his time had been privileged to do.

"How long before we take off?" he asked.

Analy touched a computer inset into the tabletop and said casually, "We are already leaving the atmosphere."

"I didn't feel any movement," Joe said in surprise, "or any acceleration for that matter."

"All our craft are fitted with devices to cancel the effects of gravity, which allows them to maintain high acceleration without fear of injury to their passengers. We are now in space," Analy added, "would you like to see?"

"You bet," Joe answered, enthusiastically unslinging his camcorder from his shoulder. Ciara wouldn't wish him to miss recording this part of the journey.

Analy led Joe down one of the radial corridors to the outer rim, where the multicoloured globe of the Earth filled the whole of the viewing port. The familiar continental mass of Europe disappeared below the ship, and Africa hove into view. Joe was astounded to see that a luxuriant patchwork of grassland and forest covered the whole of northern Africa; nowhere could he see the pale orangey hues of the Sahara Desert, which was such a distinctive feature of the Africa of the twenty-first century. Directing his camcorder at the unfamiliar sight, he was amazed to see the image in his viewfinder recede so rapidly that it produced an effect comparable to zooming out. The vessel was accelerating at a phenomenal rate and would complete the relatively short journey to the Earth's satellite within minutes, a vastly different scenario than Joe was accustomed to in his own time.

The globe of the Earth swung out of sight and the Sun came into view; the crystal of the viewing port instantly darkened to prevent eye damage, and returned to clarity the moment the light from the star no longer fell upon it. Millions of bright pinpoints of light filled the huge oval viewing port as the soft light of the Milky Way replaced the harshness of the Sun's glare. The half phase Moon appeared around the edge of the window and grew rapidly larger. Joe consulted his watch; so far the journey had taken less than three minutes.

Romana was observing Joe's reactions to the sights through the view port. "You seem to find wonder in everything you see, "she commented. "Yet, what you see is unchanging. Once you have experienced the journey, you will have seen everything there is to see."

"Sorry, Romana," Joe said, "but I have to disagree. In my world, space exploration is still an adventure. A few men have walked on the Moon's surface, but ordinary people have to experience space travel second-hand through newspaper and TV reports. We can't go into space ourselves, not yet, anyway, so this is like the fulfilment of a dream for me."

"Your pardon, Joe," Romana apologised, "but long ago space travel between the planets became so mundane that we have allowed our sense of wonder at the beauty of the universe to be eroded. Perhaps we should perceive the universe through your eyes to discover what we have lost?" She stared out of the view port in an attempt to appreciate the austere beauty of the Moon's surface, seeing nothing more than a dead world of mountains, craters and vast plains of dark basalt and grey dust. She was unable to hide her sadness as she enquired, "Have we lost so much?"

"Just look out there," Joe told her, "it's like a masterpiece ... better even. I don't think I'd ever tire of seeing it."

"I am beginning to envy you," Romana said finally.

Trione broke into their conversation. I am informed that there is congestion at the landing area, so Captain Terpin has decided to orbit the Moon to allow the docking facility to clear."

"That's great," Joe responded enthusiastically. "Does this mean I'll get to see the other side of the Moon?"

"You will, but I must warn you that there is nothing there but more craters."

"I know that, but don't you see, I'll be seeing them myself, first-hand. That's what I find so exciting."

* * *

84

The Master of Time floated down towards the surface of the Moon like a soap bubble on a still autumn day. Below, the broad, flat expanse of the Mare Serenitatis expanded to fill the view ports all around the huge craft as she slowly descended towards the northern extremity of the Haemus Mountains, which lay on the terminator between harsh sunlight and black, impenetrable shadow. The jagged peaks of the mountain range stood like white sentinels, guarding the pass between the Mare Serenitatis and the Mare Imbrium, where the walls of the two giant craters met. The ship floated lower and lower towards the eastern edge of the mountains, until Joe could see the entrance to a vast hangar, carved at ground level into the sloping rock face.

With the tiniest of vibrations, the landing gear touched down onto a broad, circular platform, which immediately propelled the ship into the maw of the man-made cavern. Two giant doors slid together behind the Master of Time to seal the entrance, and lights came on to bathe the area with a soft luminescence. After several minutes, the forward movement ceased, to be replaced almost instantly by the sensation of falling.

Joe's curiosity was aroused. "Why are we going so far underground?"

"To protect the base from meteors," Trione replied.

Couldn't you build on the surface and protect the base with a force-field?"

Trione smiled. "A force-field is very effective for protecting the compound on Earth," he explained, "but even so, two giant beasts managed to break through. Even a meteorite so big—" he indicated his thumbnail, "moving at planetary speeds, has many times their inertia and would pass through our most powerful force-field as if it were nonexistent."

"Surely there aren't too many of those," Joe protested.

"On Earth, most burn up in the upper atmosphere, but here, on the Moon, every meteorite reaches the surface unimpeded. When the Moon passes through the tail of a comet, the activity is increased a thousandfold, and the danger of destruction of the base would be very real indeed."

"What about huge meteorites, you know, the kind that make the big craters?"

Trione considered his reply carefully. "Most of the large craters were made when the Earth and the Moon were very young. It is very rare for a giant meteorite to strike the Earth or the Moon, but it still happens every hundred million years or so. On Earth the impact usually results in mass extinctions. For a base on the Moon's surface, the tiny meteors present a danger sufficiently grave to force us to build well beneath the surface. Another consideration is our need to remain hidden from Prua Landi, should her scientists develop a more efficient mode of travel through time. Nor would it be wise to leave evidence for later generations that we were ever here. Such evidence could produce its own disturbances to this timeline."

"I see what you mean," Joe grinned, "especially the bit about Prua Landi. But won't this base still exist in my time?"

"It will exist in our true time, beyond the Earth's destruction in the far future, but the entrance is so well disguised that Prua Landi's agents will never find it. When we leave, we shall activate the same technology that camouflages the time tunnels on Earth." He smiled and continued respectfully, "The camouflage that does not seem to exist for you."

* * *

All downward movement ceased and Romana informed Joe that that the ship would soon be parked in one of eight unloading bays radiating from the central shaft. Joe could sense conflicting vibrations through the hull as the huge craft slid slowly into place, and he knew they had finally arrived when all sensation of movement ceased. They were enveloped in profound silence as the ship's power shut down.

Through the view port, Joe could see several figures moving around unencumbered by spacesuits, indicating that the vast cavern contained a warm, breathable atmosphere.

As he and his companions made their way through the ship to the unloading ramp, Joe experienced an unaccustomed lack of coordination due to the reduced gravity. He momentarily lost his balance, and overcompensated, cannoning into Trione, who grasped his arm and steadied him.

"Thanks," he said ruefully, "I saw film of the first astronauts leaping about on the Moon's surface, but I never expected it to feel like this."

"Don't worry," Romana assured him, "your body will soon adjust to the Moon's gravity, and you will find the experience invigorating."

"I hope so," Joe muttered, "I don't like staggering about like a newborn foal."

Joe inspected the area around the bottom of the exit ramp: they were in a vast, brightly-lit cavern, the size of which dwarfed the considerable bulk of the Master of Time. In the distance Joe could see four smaller ships parked around the edge of the cavern, and he was experiencing difficulty in absorbing the enormous scale of the moonbase. All around the outer walls of the cavern, living accommodation, workrooms and warehouses climbed upwards to the ceiling, some distance from the central shaft, down which the Master of Time had descended. A circular platform, with six antigravity generators evenly spaced on its underside around its circumference, was swiftly rising in a shaft of shimmering pale green light towards an opening in the centre of the dome's ceiling.

They stepped onto a gravsled, which Romana piloted towards a reception hall on the far side of the cavern more than half a kilometre away. There Romana, Trione and Analy were warmly welcomed, but Joe's reception was cool, almost frosty. Personnel on the base had been informed by Leiki that Joe was an interloper, who had been transported to the Moon under guard, until such time as he could be brought before the Council of Elders on Mars. As he had previously escaped from the compound on Earth, Leiki considered it necessary to confine him in a place where escape would prove impossible. Wherever Joe went, his three guards were to accompany him.

They were ushered into a gravity shaft and whisked upwards to the office of Orina, the base commander, who bore a remarkable likeness to Romana. In Joe's opinion, the two were sufficiently alike to be sisters.

Orina welcomed Trione and Analy into her office and treated Romana to a warm hug, which Joe's companion returned enthusiastically. The commander stared coolly at Joe for several seconds, appraising his lack of stature, full head of hair and unconventional attire.

She raised one eyebrow and said quietly to Romana, Analy and Trione, "Now I have seen the prisoner, I must admit to being puzzled. Why is it necessary for Leiki to assign *three* guards, when appearances would suggest that *one* would be more than adequate? The obvious inference is that, in his case, appearances are deceptive. Tell me, who is he? Is he one of Prua Landi's agents? I believe that, as commander of this base, I have the right to know whom I am accommodating."

Romana's reply was unambiguous. "We have been ordered by Leiki to guard this man until he can be transferred to Mars. That is the full extent of our knowledge."

"Nevertheless, I am curious why a medic of your experience would be reduced to the status of a mere guard." It was obvious that something about the situation did not add up for the base commander.

Firmly, Romana replied, "I can only repeat the orders we were given."

Orina smiled thinly; even so, her beauty still shone through the austere expression. "I can see that I will learn nothing more, and I commend your eagerness to follow Leiki's orders so conscientiously."

"Thank you, Commander," Romana replied.

Joe listened whilst Orina questioned his presence on her base. "Commander Orina," he said, "please believe me, I won't be any trouble to you."

Orina stared penetratingly into Joe's eyes. "Should I believe the word of a prisoner?"

Trione spoke before Joe could reply. "You should, Commander. He has so far given us no reason to suspect that he would lie to us. In any case, we shall ensure that he does not disturb the smooth running of the base."

"Can I make a request?" Joe asked.

"Prisoners do not make requests," Orina replied coolly, "if, in fact, you are a prisoner."

"I just wanted to ask if I could go up onto the Moon's surface, because I'll probably never get another chance."

Orina was intrigued. "Why would anyone wish to willingly enter such a hostile environment?"

Romana answered for Joe. "Commander, Joe Laing finds wonder in almost everything he sees. He is from a primitive age when the exploration of space is in its infancy and few humans have walked upon the lunar surface. If you grant his wish, Analy, Trione and I will accompany him, as we have been ordered."

"I will grant his request," Orina informed her, "for no other reason than my belief that you are keeping information from me regarding the status of this man. However, I have a request of my own in return."

"What is it, Commander?"

88

"When you are permitted to divulge his true identity, you will tell me personally?"

"You have my word," Romana assured her, fairly certain in her own mind that Orina had already guessed Joe's identity.

*   *   *

There were several spacesuit lockers spread throughout the base, so that in the event of failure of the base's airlocks, no one would be more than a few paces from a suit. Romana opened the locker and offered Joe a cushion shaped sachet of soft, clear blue, gel-like material with a red stud inset into one corner.

"What's this?" Joe demanded.

"Your protection against the cold and vacuum," Romana informed him, amused by Joe's blank expression.

"What on Earth do I do," he grinned, "sit on it?"

"Do as I do," Romana ordered, holding the stud between the forefinger and thumb of one hand whilst placing the cushion of gel on the top of her head.

Joe placed his camcorder on a ledge and mimicked Romana's action.

"Now squeeze the stud and lower your hands to waist level in front of your body."

Puzzled, Joe complied and, accompanied by squelching noises like those produced when walking through deep, clinging mud, the sachet split open and its contents oozed downwards covering his face and body with a thin, flexible film.

"Please lift your feet in turn to allow complete coverage," Romana instructed, but Joe, whose face was now completely encased in the gel, was experiencing violent claustrophobia. All the life-giving air had seemingly been sucked from the room and he couldn't breathe.

Romana instantly sensed Joe's distress. "Breathe!" she commanded. "The suit will service all your bodily functions."

Joe fought against the cloying claustrophobia and drew a deep, ragged breath into his abused lungs. Gratefully, he steadied his breathing and, as Romana had instructed, lifted first one foot and then the other as the strange, almost living material, closed around the soles of his boots.

Romana, Analy and Trione donned their suits in exactly the same manner, but with none of the distress Joe had experienced as the gel closed over their mouths.

89

Joe flexed his fingers and felt nothing to restrict his movement. If this spacesuit actually works, he thought, people at NASA would probably be prepared to kill for the technology. But he could foresee a potential problem. How would they communicate in the vacuum of the lunar surface? He had to ask.

"Our apologies, Joe, but we had overlooked the fact that you cannot communicate telepathically, as we would do whilst suited up," Romana told him.

She reached into the locker and selected two tiny devices, one of which she pressed against Joe's ear and the other against his jaw. The two instruments instantly passed through the transparent film and the suit sealed itself once again. Each of Joe's companions followed suit and soon every member of the foursome had the facility to communicate in a vacuum.

"Are you comfortable, Joe?" Analy asked.

"More comfortable than I would be in a spacesuit in my own time, I reckon," he replied. "Shall we go?"

"Follow us," Romana ordered, heading for a personnel grav-lift nearby.

The compartment was tiny, holding just four persons. The space was so constricted that the plasma rifles carried by Analy and Trione dug painfully into their flesh and Joe's camcorder seemed to have gained more sharp corners than he thought possible. Once inside Trione keyed in their destination, and the plate accelerated upwards towards the surface. Seconds later, they arrived in an airlock chamber, where Romana immediately set the emptying cycle in motion. They stepped onto a moving walkway, which carried them half a kilometre to the outer airlock and the hostile lunar surface. The outer doorway slid aside and Joe followed the others out onto the dust-covered basalt plain. Immediately, the material of the suits turned an opaque white to protect the wearers from the harsh radiation of the Sun. Three hundred metres away the open maw of the hangar was almost invisible in the brilliant sunlight, but the dark metal of the landing platform stood out in stark contrast to the paleness of the lunar dust.

"A ship is coming in to land," Trione commented. "I see that the hangar is open."

Joe glanced upwards and saw, against the starry backdrop, the illuminated crescent of a slowly descending ship. Immediately, Joe brought his camcorder to bear on the craft, praying that it would still function in a vacuum. Light played upon the craft's sunward edge, giving the descending ship an insubstantial, almost surreal quality. As he followed the descending ship, Joe saw an actinic bright flash and a puff of white vapour as the tripodal landing gear was deployed beneath the craft. The ship shuddered like a dog shaking rainwater from its coat, then resumed its steady descent. A larger cloud of white vapour burst from the ship's belly and the craft plummeted suddenly towards the Moon's surface. To Joe's eyes its descent was unnaturally slow at first in the reduced gravity, but gradually it accelerated until, in eerie silence, the vessel pancaked violently onto the dusty terrain. One edge contacted the ground before the rest, and for a few drawn-out seconds, the craft wallowed like a spinning plate before coming finally to rest.

Eons old dust blossomed into the starry lunar sky from the violent impact, resettling symmetrically around the stricken craft with a silent, almost balletic grace. Joe could immediately see that the landing gear had punched through the upper surface of the ship, destroying the integrity of the hull, and it was clear that those inside had only minutes to live, providing they had not been caught in the area where the hull was breached. He suddenly realised that he was running, taking huge bounds over the flat terrain towards the crippled ship. His camcorder swung back and forth in slow loops as he ran.

His three companions followed close behind, aware of Leiki's orders to protect the Futama as much from his own impetuosity as threat from others. Romana called in vain to Joe to halt his rush, but he was rapidly covering the intervening ground, his breath sounding ragged in the earpiece of her suit. When Joe arrived, he could see that the damage was much worse than it had appeared from a distance. Two of the landing gear legs had torn substantial rents in the upper surface, just missing the central bridge. All over the skin of the ship white vapour was venting to vacuum, indicating that all sections of the vessel were gradually depressurising. Within a few minutes the interior would be as airless as the Moon, despite the automatic machinery's best efforts to maintain its internal pressure and temperature.

"Will all survivors be suited up by now?" he demanded.

"That is uncertain," replied Trione.

Joe's three friends telepathically scanned the vessel's interior, confirming that there were several casualties, some of whom were not yet in spacesuits.

"We've got to help them," Joe yelled, "because the atmosphere in the ship can't last much longer after so much damage to the hull."

"What can we do?" Trione demanded. "We need a fully-equipped rescue team from inside the base."

Snatching Trione's plasma rifle, Joe set the control to narrow beam. "Is there anyone in the outer corridor?"

"No," Romana assured him.

"Will each section have sealed itself?"

"Assuming the equipment was not damaged in the crash."

"Okay then, step back!" Joe pulled the trigger and inscribed a circle in one of the view ports. With a silent puff of tiny ice crystals, the plexiglass blew outward and Joe quickly clambered in, followed by the others.

Romana stopped to retrieve a medikit from a recess in the wall of the corridor, and then stepped up to the first of the radial corridors. Across its junction with the outer ring corridor, Joe could see what appeared to be a translucent film. Romana stepped through and the film sealed itself behind her. One by one, the others followed, heading towards the central hub. Romana, in the lead, encountered the unconscious form of a crewmember and quickly ran a diagnostic over him. His legs were shattered from the near vertical impact and the shock had transmitted through his skeletal structure, producing hairline fractures in many bones.

"Put him in a suit," she ordered Trione and Analy.

Trione searched the wall, locating an emergency locker, containing a supply of ten spacesuits. Selecting one, they immediately laid it on the chest of the unfortunate man and pressed the stud. The gel flowed over the prone form and Trione lifted first the head and then the feet to allow the suit to completely seal itself. When the final seal was complete, Romana ordered the suit to render its wearer immobile, and Joe saw the thin film tighten, forming a taut, semi-rigid cocoon around the casualty. Romana moved on swiftly to the next casualty, followed by Trione and Analy. Joe made himself useful by carrying the supply of suits. Within eight minutes the operation was complete. Every casualty in the outer corridors, most of whom had suffered broken legs and skeletal fractures, had been suited up and was ready for transfer to the moonbase. The only area remaining was the bridge.

Romana tried to iris the door but the heavy impact had jammed the mechanism. She met with the same response from the second door, so she mentally swept the room, finding no one conscious. Joe trained his weapon upon the door and cut a way inside. A scene of devastation met their eyes. The instrumentation of the bridge was scattered piecemeal around the room and several crewmembers had clearly been injured as much by flying debris as by the impact with the ground. Romana tended to injuries whilst Analy and Trione followed in her wake, inserting the casualties into spacesuits.

Joe received a shock when he saw that the captain of the ship was none other than Marron, who lay, bleeding profusely from a head wound. He was in a bad way; his forehead was horribly dented and extensive bruising was rapidly spreading around the wound. His right tibia protruded grotesquely through the flesh of his shin and his shattered form had the appearance of a broken and discarded doll. Marron groaned and his limbs twitched as if under the control of a demonic puppeteer. Joe laid the last of the spacesuits beside the stricken figure, ready for Analy and Trione to use upon the captain. Romana, kneeling beside Marron, hesitated for a moment before using the diagnostic

"Better be quick," Joe advised, "he's in a bad way."

Romana paused a moment longer before applying her skill to the badly injured Marron. She straightened the shattered limb and filled the indentation in the damaged skull with a blood-coloured paste before ordering her aides to apply the spacesuit to the unconscious form. Once she had attended Marron's injuries, a cursory glance told her there were no more casualties requiring her skill. The whole process, from the crash to Marron being suited up had taken eleven minutes.

Joe heard sounds resonating through the hull; it seemed the rescue team from the moonbase had arrived. Romana exited the bridge and strode to the point where Joe had breached the hull with the plasma rifle and the others followed close behind. Outside, several tall figures were hammering at the wreckage in an attempt to enlarge the hole in the plexiglass of the view port. Behind them a flotilla of gravsleds hung motionless a metre above the dusty surface, ready to transport the casualties to the base hospital.

Joe poked his head out of the hole and yelled, "Stand well back!" simultaneously gesturing with the plasma rifle. The men stood transfixed by the sight of the tiny man waving an energy weapon in their faces when they were trying to effect a rescue.

"Are they bloody stupid?" Joe demanded angrily.

"No," Romana assured him, restraining the arm brandishing the weapon with firm strength, "they cannot hear you." She tapped her earpiece to emphasise the point. *Go to the other side of the hull,* she telepathically commanded the rescue party, and they instantly moved to obey her.

Ruefully, Joe once more poked his head outside to ensure no one remained in the line of fire, then stood back and used his plasma rifle to enlarge the aperture considerably. Immediately the rescue party came into sight around the curve of the hull, and Joe and his companions stood aside to allow them to do their work.

Romana headed at once towards the personnel airlock. "I'm sorry, Joe, but we must end your walk on the lunar surface," she apologised, "as my medical skills will be required in the hospital. Perhaps when you run your fingers through the fertile soil of Mars, you will feel you have received a measure of compensation."

Joe tapped his camcorder. "If half the images come out, this will tell Ciara what the Moon's surface is really like and that's enough for the moment. Let's get back so you can help those people, because they certainly need it, especially Marron."

"You wish me to help Marron?" Romana asked in surprise.

"Of course I do," Joe replied. "Just because I don't like someone doesn't mean I'd deny them medical help. That would be barbaric."

"You may come from a primitive and violent era," Romana observed as they arrived at the entrance to the personnel airlock, "but you display the compassion that is deeply embedded within the psyche of the Faithful."

"Pity it's not present in Prua Landi," Joe commented as the airlock completed its cycle, allowing them to proceed along the moving way to the second airlock before descending into the moonbase.

As they exited the lift, Romana immediately mounted a gravsled and headed for the infirmary, which was situated on the far side of the vast cavern. Analy and Trione ushered Joe towards the recreation area and food hall, having decided that now would be an appropriate time for a substantial meal. Meals so far had consisted of little more than snacks and Joe realised that he was feeling rather hungry.

As they ate, Joe voiced his thoughts on the wrecking of Marron's ship. "When we left Earth," he observed, "Marron was overseeing the repairs to his ship. It would seem the damage was not just confined to the landing gear, but why would anyone risk their lives by not carrying out a thorough system check before embarking on a journey to the Moon?"

"The ship would have been checked thoroughly before it was allowed to take off," Analy informed him.

"Okay, let's approach the problem from a different angle. How often do these ships crash?"

"Never! They are completely reliable."

"That's my point," Joe informed the others. "Marron practically followed in our shadow to the Moon. So why would he risk the safety of his ship and his crew to get to the Moon so close behind us? It seems to me he must have been in too much of a hurry, and it begs the question, why?"

"I can see the point you are making," Analy agreed. "We shall pass on your observations to Leiki. It may be pure bad luck on Marron's part, but," he shrugged, "it may be carelessness brought about by the desire for haste."

With that topic exhausted, Joe broached the subject of their meeting with the commander of the moonbase. "You know," he said thoughtfully, "I reckon Orina has an idea who I am. Do you think she's likely to discuss it with anyone?"

Trione offered Joe something resembling a biscuit, which he accepted. "Orina understands the orders given to us by Leiki and will not speculate openly on your identity, though I agree that she probably suspects that you are, indeed, the Futama. She will respect Leiki's wishes, knowing that her daughter will honour the pledge she made."

Joe was surprised by the casual revelation that Romana and the base commander were related. "Her daughter?" he said. "But I thought babies in your time were all grown in artificial wombs."

"That is so," Trione assured him, "but many mothers, from the earliest moments, form a bond with their offspring, which lasts through to adulthood."

"That explains the resemblance," Joe commented, "and it makes me a bit more comfortable now that Marron is here on the Moon. By the way, I know a bit of first aid and I reckon Marron's skull was pretty badly injured. What are the chances of him surviving?"

"He will survive. Even now, the nanomedics in his system will be hard at work repairing all the damage to his body and his brain. Within a few days, it will be as if he had never been injured."

Joe was intrigued. "Do only the top people have the nanomedics?"

"No. Every one of our people is injected with nanos soon after they emerge from the artificial womb. The nanos multiply as the child grows to adulthood and remain effective throughout their lives."

Half-joking, Joe remarked, "If they're that effective, I reckon it would be a good idea for Romana to inject *me* with some nanos – and the sooner, the better."

"We must ask Romana when she has completed her duties in the infirmary," agreed Trione, not realising that Joe had been only half-serious.

Chapter Ten

THE VIEW IMPROVES:

Prua Landi swept into the laboratory, her cape swishing menacingly around her, supplementing, rather than masking, the power of her body language. Subconsciously, the technicians shrank away as she strode past, her features set in a mask of rage.

"Where is Perdon?" she demanded.

Perdon's voice issued from within a sizeable globular cubicle on one side of the room. "I am here, My Lady."

Prua Landi looked around in the direction of the cubicle. "Show yourself, Perdon. I have no wish to converse with you across the length of this laboratory."

Perdon emerged, red faced and sweating. "Yes, My Lady. How may I serve you?"

"By informing me of your progress. And," she added menacingly, "I will hear only of progress, or—" She let the sentence trail away and Perdon knew that the alternative to success could be very painful indeed.

"If you would accompany me, My Lady," he urged, "I can demonstrate a significant improvement in our remote viewing capability."

The dictatrix's thin eyebrows rose slightly, but otherwise, she gave no sign that her curiosity had been piqued.

Perdon led her into the globe, which held two simple seats and a control binnacle. He indicated one seat, which Prua Landi accepted, and he cautiously sat beside her. With his concentration at maximum – for he could ill afford to make mistakes in the presence of the tyrannical leader of his people – Perdon made minor adjustments to the controls and gave the command to view. Immediately, a one-hundred and eighty degree section of the globe's interior was filled with a holographic image of perfect clarity. At its centre stood the compound, the subject of the remote viewing some days previously, which had resulted in Perdon's promotion. In the foreground the two mammoths were once again reprising their titanic battle, culminating in the destruction of a section of the force-field and the collision with the landing gear of the flying craft.

Anticipating Prua Landi's command, Perdon focused upon the small group of figures issuing from the crippled craft, zooming in until their faces were easily recognisable.

The dictatrix immediately commented, "As I thought. It is the primitive and his woman. So, this is the fabled Futama, the one the simple-minded Faithful believe is their saviour." She laughed, the harsh sound being swallowed by the interior walls of the cubicle. "Would you not believe," she demanded, "that those idiots would have chosen a more impressive specimen in whom to place their hopes of salvation?"

The project director was uncertain whether or not a reply was required, so he remained tactfully silent.

They watched as Joe raced over and snatched the plasma rifle from the grasp of the guard and headed at breakneck pace towards the gap in the outer fence. Perdon rapidly vectored their viewpoint to follow Joe as he halted and discharged the weapon in the direction of a heavily-built feline predator with oversized teeth. A broad cone of fire resulted and Jo-lang immediately reset the weapon, producing a lethally concentrated pencil-beam of plasma fire, which decapitated the charging beast.

Joe's bravery was not lost on Prua Landi. Her eyes held a hint of grudging admiration. "It would appear that the primitive creature has an abundance of courage, a quality I find lacking in most of those who surround me."

As she was speaking, Joe stood still, staring at nothing in particular. Joe's still pose intrigued Prua Landi; she could imagine no reason why he would lay himself open to attack. "Move the viewpoint to the trees ... there!" she commanded, and Perdon rapidly adjusted the viewer.

Branches twitched and they watched as Joe coaxed two hominids from their hiding place in the forest. As the scene unfolded before them Prua Landi and Perdon observed Joe and the Neanderthals animatedly gesticulating to each other, and logic suggested they must be communicating in some way. Since the advent of rudimentary telepathy more than five-hundred thousand years ago, sign language had become obsolete and all knowledge of the skill had disappeared from the racial memory. It seemed that Jo-lang's association with this doomed branch of the human race was not restricted to the false timeline of Tarmis.

Prua Landi resolved to investigate ways in which she might turn that association to her advantage. But first it was necessary to extend the range of her time-travel device. Her eyes smouldered with malice. "Next time we meet," she vowed at Joe's image in the remote viewer, "I will spend no time on pleasantries." And with a note of triumph in her voice, she informed Perdon, "Jo-lang will never live to see the revolution his followers have, for so long, been promised."

As she swept out of the cubicle, with Perdon trailing at her heels, she informed him silkily, "Perdon, your success with the remote viewer has improved my appetite after a long period of disappointment. Come, you will dine with me in my chambers."

Chapter Eleven

NEANDERTHAL ENCOUNTER:

Joe enjoyed the return to Earth even better than the journey to the Moon. Word had soon circulated around the moonbase that he had taken a leading role in the rescue of Captain Marron and his crew, and he was treated more as a hero than the prisoner he was supposed to be. Analy and Trione, however, still accompanied him, fully armed, wherever he went. Captain Terpin insisted that Joe travel to Earth as his guest on the bridge of the Master of Time and Joe spent the whole of the journey in the observatory situated on the uppermost point of the ship, watching the globe of the Earth expanding as the mighty ship swiftly consumed the relatively short distance to the mother planet.

Joe's precious camcorder battery had given up the ghost after its exposure to the vacuum and intense heat of the lunar surface, but Captain Terpin instructed Heron, an engineer from the crew, to solve Joe's problem. This he had done by attaching a tiny power source to the camcorder, which fed current of the correct voltage and amperage through the battery into the camcorder. When Joe asked how long it would last, the engineer informed him that unless he subjected the power source to sufficient heat to melt its titanium casing, it should last more than twenty years.

Joe whistled through his teeth. "I bet Or-gon would love to get his hands on one of these," he said to himself.

"Or-gon?"

"Just someone I know," Joe informed him. "Tell me, what should I do if I want to attach this gizmo to another camcorder, because I can't see this particular video camera surviving for twenty years."

"Just detach it this way," explained Heron, twisting the tiny power source through ninety degrees and pulling it away from the camcorder. Attach it to another optical instrument this way," he said, reversing the process.

"Thanks," Joe told him, checking the camcorder display, which now informed him that his battery was fully charged, "Ciara would never forgive me if I failed to record these views of the Earth."

Heron waved away the expression of gratitude, saying, "As we journey through space and time we are constantly aware of the potential for disaster, such as that which occurred on the Moon. Captain Marron and his crew would not have survived without your intervention. By the time the rescue team from our moonbase arrived, everyone would have been either dead, or beyond the *capability of the nanomedics to repair the damage sustained by their* bodies, due to the vacuum and intense cold." As he descended from the observatory to the floor of the bridge, he said softly, "Everyone owes you a great debt, Joe-lang and I am happy that I was chosen by Captain Terpin to repay a small part of it."

Joe was aware of the emotion in the engineer's words, which doubtless stemmed from the close bonds tying each member of the Faithful to every other. There was little for him to say except, "You're welcome!"

* * *

Leiki listened intently as each of the four gave their own version of the events on the Moon, the scratching of his pen a constant accompaniment as he compiled a report. "Why did you insist on helping Marron, in the light of his animosity towards you?" he enquired.

"We've been through this before," Joe sighed. "I'd help anyone – even Prua Landi – if they needed it. Otherwise, I wouldn't be human, would I?"

"You embody all of the higher qualities your followers aspire to. When everyone learns your true identity, they will follow you through plasma fire."

"Let's hope that sort of thing won't be necessary," Joe declared. "And I've told you before, I'm only a man – admittedly less evolved than everyone here, but still a man."

"*And* you are the Futama."

Joe was quickly tiring of the subject; he felt a change of direction was needed. "When are we going to Mars," he enquired, "because before I go, I need to talk again to the Neanderthals who live in the area around this base. *And* I want to go home for a couple of days to check on how Ciara and the baby are doing. I'd like Romana to run her diagnostic over Ciara to make sure she's okay. If I'm going to be involved in a revolution in your time, I need to be able to put my affairs in order in case the worst happens."

Leiki immediately protested, "Futama, I cannot permit you to leave the compound. The larger predators are extremely dangerous

101

and the primitive humans are, at best, unpredictable. No, I dare not allow you to place yourself in unnecessary danger."

Joe felt the muscles in his jaw tighten. "You're telling me I can't go?" he ground out. "I'd just like to let you know that I've never been very good at taking orders. If you want to order Analy and Trione to stop me, you'd better be prepared to detail two more men to guard me because these two won't be in any condition to guard even themselves."

Joe's two bodyguards edged a little further away as he was speaking.

Romana soothingly placed her hand on Joe's arm to prevent him from erupting into violence. "Commander Leiki," she urged, "Joe must be free to do as he wishes and we must support and protect him. We three will accompany him to ensure that he comes to no harm."

Analy and Trione both nodded in agreement and the latter added, "If Joe believes he must go, then we must make it as easy as we can for him."

Joe, feeling embarrassment at having promised that he would attack his two friends, mumbled, "Thanks, all of you." To Leiki, he said, "I can sympathise with the idea that you need to keep me safe, but there are things I must do. I need to meet the primitive Neanderthals so that I can instil in them the legend of the Futama. Otherwise, when I visit them two-hundred thousand years into the future of this time, before their race vanishes forever from the face of the Earth, Koo-ma will not know of me and it's likely I will be killed before I can perpetuate the legend. I've already told you that Too-ga tried to kill me when he first caught sight of me, but as soon as Koo-ma convinced him I was the Futama he calmed down." He hesitated for a moment; what he had to say might not be what Leiki wanted to hear, but in Joe's view, it had to be said. "What effect that may have on your time, I've no idea, but if I die back then amongst Too-ga's people, I can't imagine there would ever be any of the Faithful."

Leiki gave Joe a penetrating amber stare. "You understand the intricacies of time far better than you realise. The Council of Elders had no knowledge of how the legend had begun, merely that you interacted with the Neanderthals thirty-five thousand years before the time of your birth. Interference of the nature you have described is sometimes necessary to smooth out inconsistencies in the flow of events."

"You may be right about that," said Joe, "because I had no idea that I would have to begin the legend until I found out what time period Ciara and I had landed in. Once I realised there were early Neanderthals in this time, it seemed the natural thing to do."

"Your instinctive defence of the two primitives has created the possibility of a meeting with the rest of their tribe," mused Leiki, "and I am now inclined to believe that it was preordained. If that is true, then you must follow your destiny to promote your legend. Logic dictates that I should not stand in your way, so you have my blessing."

Joe grinned. "Thanks, I'm glad we've got that sorted. Now we can get on with finding the rest of the Neanderthal tribe before I go home."

Leiki stood and pushed away his chair with the back of his knees. "You will take one of the six-man flyers," he said, "with sufficient supplies to last at least three days. If there is anything you require, please take it. I will give the necessary orders to remove any administrative obstacles from your pathway." He smiled at each in turn. "Good luck," he said, "and by the time you return, we shall have clothing for Analy and Trione, more suitable for the Futama's era."

"Good thinking," grinned Joe. "They'll stand out enough as it is, without walking about half-naked, like ancient Egyptians."

* * *

The flyer was little more than a gravsled, fitted with a plexiglass cover against the inconsistent weather. It was around six metres long and two-and-a-half metres wide, with a control binnacle and six fairly basic seats arranged in two rows of three. Behind the back seats there was a substantial load area, and at the rear there was a pod holding the antigravity and drive units. Its underside was flat, with three short, heavily sprung legs, allowing it to land almost anywhere. Three days' supplies were netted in the cargo compartment, and the expedition was ready to set off. Word had spread like wildfire around the small community and a crowd gathered around the four as they settled themselves in their seats, with Romana at the controls. Rumour was rife as to the reason for the expedition, but Leiki had steadfastly refused to divulge anything more than that Trione, Analy, Romana and Joe had been assigned to explore a broad area around the base.

Silently, the flyer rose from the grassy compound into a clear blue sky and headed eastward over the dense forest. Soon, the compound disappeared far behind and Romana activated the life-force scanner to enable them to see what lay beneath the thick forest canopy. Immediately, a number of blips appeared. Analy adjusted the sensitivity of the scanner and a small herd of deer filled the screen. Five human figures moved furtively towards the deer, herding them closer and closer together. Finally, in an explosion of action, the men isolated one of their prey and moved in for the kill. It was all over in seconds and they could see the events unfurl as two of the men grasped the unfortunate animal and held it immobile. A third man grasped the deer's antlers and savagely wrenched them around, snapping the unfortunate animal's neck.

Romana gasped at the primitive savagery of the hunt and the flyer slipped sideways as she lost her concentration for a moment. Recovering swiftly, she demanded, "Do you really wish to interact with these savages?"

"Yes. I know what we've just seen seems a bit bloodthirsty, but it's all a question of survival. These people need meat to feed the rest of the tribe and the deer provide it. You know, the Neanderthals aren't even at the top of the food chain like we are. There are a lot of other predators out there that would gladly make a snack of any human being they chanced across."

Romana shuddered. "I'll be glad when this expedition is over," she observed. "Let us hope that they have consumed their prey before we make contact."

Analy and Trione made no comment, but it was clear that the events they had witnessed by means of the remote scanner had unnerved them somewhat. Joe supposed they were unaccustomed to violence, despite the way they had been treated by Prua Landi's regime. Certainly, the sight of the deer being so graphically killed was outside their experience, but if Joe were to spend even a short time with the tribe, his three friends from the distant future would somehow have to come to terms with it. They were, after all, interlopers in an era of primal savagery.

Two of the hominids slung the carcase of the deer on a pole between them, and the five set out together through the forest, with three maintaining a constant lookout for hungry predators. Joe noticed they were heading for the river, whose turgid flow carried it between tree-covered banks, through the heart of the dense forest toward a broad estuary, visible in the distance from his vantage point above the forest canopy. In the time of Too-ga and Koo-ma, more than two-hundred thousand years into the future of these early Neanderthals, the river was bordered by broad, grassy meadows from its source in a glacial lake, down to the tidal reaches where it met the sea. Though the forest in this more primitive era afforded better cover for the Neanderthals, it also exuded a greater sense of menace. Game was more abundant, supporting a large and varied population of predators, amongst whom the early Neanderthals must pick out an uneasy and perilous existence.

At walking pace, above the treetops of the mixed coniferous and deciduous forest, the flyer followed the small hunting party, hovering silently when the men halted to change roles. Carrying the carcase of a deer would have proved tiring even for later Neanderthals, who were taller and more muscular than those below the craft, and Joe anticipated that the roles would change many more times before they reached their encampment. What was apparent, however, even at this early stage in their evolution, was the level of cooperation between the primitive people – a trait of immense importance to their survival and, ultimately, to the perpetuation of the legend of the Futama.

For six hours, the hunting party followed a barely discernable pathway beside the stream. From his airborne vantage point, Joe watched until they moved away from the river and began to climb. They skirted a jumble of rocks Joe found strangely familiar, before continuing upwards to where a chalk cliff, with grass and shrubs growing out of innumerable cracks and crevices, stood hidden amongst massive trees. Joe was fairly certain that below, in the cliff face, would be a cave, destined eventually to become home to Too-ga and his people.

Movement at the edge of the viewscreen signalled the presence of a giant bear and the onlookers in the aerial craft watched in fascination as the huge creature raced towards the two men carrying the deer, covering the intervening ground with an easy, loping stride. With no weapons to fight off the marauder, the Neanderthals dropped their precious burden and scattered in all directions, squealing and yelling in alarm. The bear grasped the deer in its jaws, then turned and ambled downhill towards the river, which at that point in its course was more than seventy metres across.

Several Neanderthals raced from the cave to the scene of the robbery, and with seemingly little regard for their personal safety, began hurling rocks at the retreating rear of the bear. A number of missiles found their mark. The bear dropped its booty, stood upon two massive legs, and stretched upwards to its full height, simultaneously giving vent to a hideous roar. The barrage of missiles intensified and the bear dropped onto all fours and lumbered towards its tormentors, who hastily withdrew. Nonchalantly, the massive creature scooped up its loot in powerful jaws and trotted downhill to be lost in the forest.

Joe's companions had watched, fascinated, as the drama unfolded. Romana asked Joe if he thought the primitive people would go hungry.

"Not if I can help it," Joe replied. "Look, I think I see a way to break down any barriers that might stand in the way of a meeting with the people down there."

"Please explain," Romana suggested.

"I just need to replace the food they've lost."

The others stared at him aghast. "You mean take the food from that . . . that monster?" Romana gasped.

"No, of course not," Joe laughed, "I just need to kill a deer myself."

"Is this *another* of the skills you possess?" asked Trione, remembering the way the three primitives had dispatched the deer.

"That's not necessary when you've got these." Joe tapped the butt of Trione's plasma rifle. "If I can manage to kill a deer without felling half the forest, that is."

"It seems such a waste of life," Romana commented, as she wheeled the flyer in the direction of a number of small blips, which had appeared at the edge of the screen. "Please do not take any risks, this is a savage land."

Trione set his plasma rifle to 'distance' and handed it to Joe. Romana piloted the flyer towards the blips, which turned out to be another small herd of deer.

"Does the canopy slide back, so that I can shoot from up here?" Joe queried, and immediately, he felt the breeze on his face as the cover vanished as if by magic.

Romana skilfully skimmed the treetops, almost touching the leaves with the smooth belly of the flyer, and as they followed the small herd, their prey entered a tiny clearing. Joe swiftly seized his opportunity, and a pencil beam of sun-hot plasma drilled a neat hole through the skull of one of the deer, cauterising the wound in the process. The unfortunate creature collapsed and the rest of the herd melted instantly into the forest, enabling Romana to drop the craft vertically to land beside the carcase. Joe's companions were reluctant to touch warm flesh that had so recently been alive, and it proved necessary for him to load the dead animal onto the flyer by himself. Once airborne, Romana headed the craft toward the exact spot where the bear had robbed the hunters of their prey.

When the flyer touched down, Joe knelt and slung the still warm carcase over his shoulder, standing erect once again with a grunt. "Follow me," he ordered Analy and Trione, "and be on your guard. Romana, lift off and hover over the trees out of sight of the cliff face and wait until you get the word that it's safe for you to land near the cliffs."

"As you wish, Joe," she replied. Before doing Joe's bidding, however, she cautioned the others, "Guard the Futama well."

Her companions nodded. Events would now depend upon the ability of their Futama to communicate with the primitive humans. Though they were from an age where both human beings and technology were far in advance of the twenty-first century, all three suspected that the gulf of knowledge and ability between them was not exactly in their favour whilst they were living in this savage era.

Joe's enhanced strength and fitness served him well as he strode up the slope to the cave, carrying the deer over the back of his neck, holding its legs in front of his chest. Analy and Trione padded silently behind, their plasma rifles primed and ready for instant use, and their telepathic senses fully alert. Whilst they would be unable to decipher the rudimentary thought images of the primitive hominids, they hoped their telepathic ability would provide them with information regarding the number and locality of the Neanderthals in the trees around them.

Breathing heavily from his exertions, Joe reached the flat area surrounding the entrance to the cave, where he saw a small group of five men and two women awaiting his arrival.

Analy whispered, "I sense more of the primitives high in the trees around us. A number of them are small children."

"Okay," Joe replied calmly, "I can see their point. They don't know yet that they can trust us."

He stepped forward and dropped the carcase of the deer onto the hard ground a few metres away from the waiting group of Neanderthals. He gave the sign of 'gift' and retreated immediately to stand between his companions.

One of the female Neanderthals, a leathery-skinned old crone, stepped warily forward, a short, crooked staff gripped firmly in her gnarled fist. Attached to the top of the pole was the polished skull of a large rodent – possibly a beaver. With the staff, she levered up the head of the dead animal and examined the neat hole in its skull. She prodded the carcase several times before pursing her lips and venting a piercing whistle. At once the rest of the group joined her and examined the beast in a similar fashion, communicating by means of an animated mixture of grunts, whistles and rudimentary signs.

From a few metres away, Joe was able to follow much of the signed communication. It seemed that over the vast stretch of time between the present era and the last days of the Neanderthal race, the signs had changed surprisingly little. After little more than a minute, the crone raised her staff and the whistling ceased. Ignoring Analy and Trione, she stared at Joe with deeply sunken eyes of unfathomable black, before beckoning him forward.

"Stay here!" he ordered. "But stay alert."

Joe's companions nodded in unison.

Joe stepped forward and the crone held her staff before her, halting him a metre or so away, making the sign for 'why?' and flicking her gaze at the carcase at their feet.

'A gift' Joe replied, repeating the sign he had made when he dropped the dead animal before the group. 'Friend' he added, indicating himself, before pointing to his companions behind him.

The woman regarded him once more before performing the complicated sign for 'Futama', that Joe had so patiently taught the two youngsters a few days before.

Joe signed that he was the Futama and the crone immediately gave a short whistle. There were tiny signs of movement in the trees and undergrowth and soon the remaining members of the clan were gathered around them. Joe counted seven adult males, five adult females and five youngsters, from toddlers to near adult. The two teenagers from his first encounter were standing unobtrusively at the back of the group.

Catching their eye, he signed for the pair to come forward and the witch doctor immediately reinforced the request; it was clear she intended to maintain command of the situation. Slowly, the pair approached and Joe praised them for preparing for the coming of the Futama.

108

The crone's staff twitched and a couple of women instantly grasped the feet of the dead animal, dragging the carcase away in the direction of the cave. Everyone else followed and Joe beckoned to Analy and Trione to bring up the rear. At the entrance to the cave, the two women began to skin the deer, using sharp slivers of flint, shaped into rudimentary knives. Even so, the process was remarkably quick and the carcase had soon been butchered into a number of pieces. The youngsters gathered around the scene of butchery, and each was handed a piece of raw meat, which they proceeded to devour with relish. Apparently the primitive Neanderthals did not have the ability to make fire.

Joe glanced at his two companions; their faces had turned a sickly shade of white beneath their bronze tans, and it was clear they were suffering considerable distress at the sight of the Neanderthals consuming raw flesh. He had to do something or the pair would be violently sick. Touching the shoulder of the old crone he directed her to follow him. Striding to the edge of the broad ledge surrounding the cave, he collected several dried branches blown from the trees and piled them in the middle of the hard ground. He signed for the two teenagers to collect a number of rocks, which he arranged in a circle to contain the fire. Using Analy's energy weapon, he sliced the branches into manageable pieces. Adjusting the rifle to its lowest setting he pressed the firing stud and the wood burst into flame. Within seconds, the fire was crackling in the makeshift hearth, sending sparks blossoming into the sky. Joe looked up to see that all the Neanderthals had retreated as far away from the fire as they could; a few peeked around the entrance to the cave, where they had hastily dived at the first signs of fire.

Ignoring the activity around him, Joe made a spit from green wood and set several small pieces of meat to broil over the flames. Once the meat was cooking, he formed a smaller fireplace with the remaining stones, with a pile of dry twigs beside it. Calling the two youngsters, Dar and Reed, to his side, he ordered them to accompany him. They stared fearfully at the plasma rifle on the ground beside Joe, so he called Analy over to retrieve it.

An area of the ledge had been used for centuries in the manufacture of flint tools, and there, Joe retrieved a few unused fist-sized lumps, struck from larger flint nodes. Back at the fireplace, Joe told the pair to squat down beside him and watch carefully. Using a sliver of flint, he scraped one of the dry logs to produce a small pile of tinder. Then he commenced striking the two lumps of flint together until he managed to direct a spark into the tinder, encouraging the resulting flames with gentle breaths of air, until he could build up the fire with larger twigs.

No longer afraid, Dar and Reed watched in fascination as the flames grew with every piece of dry wood added to the fire.

'You make fire' Joe signed, mimicking the building of the hearth, collection of wood and the striking of the flints.

The two youngsters grunted and whistled, and set off enthusiastically to gather the materials, while Joe checked the status of the broiling meat, at the same time adding more wood to the fire. When they had set off on their quest, Char, the tribal shaman, sidled up to Joe and tugged at his sleeve.

'Futama', she signed, 'why you bring fire from sky?'

Carefully, ensuring that every sign he made was perfect in every way, Joe replied, 'Because your people must always remember that I came among you. As shaman, *you* must ensure that I am remembered by your children and your children's children, forever. The fire will keep you warm in the winter and drive away animals that would prey upon you.'

The crone was thoughtful for a moment. 'Why burn meat of deer as fire from sky burn trees?' she signed.

'To improve it', Joe replied.

Joe lifted the spit and removed one of the small pieces of meat, offering it to Char. He signed that she should eat it, and she crammed the whole piece into her mouth. Instantly, she spat out the hot meat and it landed on the dusty ground. She glared at Joe as though he had personally burnt her mouth. Without delay, he retrieved another small portion of roasted meat and blew on it before taking a bite. He offered the rest to Char and she mimicked his action with stronger breaths than seemed possible from her slight, wizened frame. She bit off a mouthful and chewed the venison, an expression of delight on her wizened features.

Waving the meat in front of her face, she signed, 'Good to eat' before devouring the rest of it with gusto.

Joe collected two more pieces of venison and handed them to Analy and Trione, who had watched the interaction between Joe and the shaman with a growing sense of wonder. They were experiencing difficulty in coming to terms with the easy way the Futama had insinuated himself into the lives of the primitive people.

"You wish us to eat this flesh?" Trione enquired.

110

"Just try it," Joe encouraged, "and you might find you like it."

The ghastly pallor was creeping into their faces once again. "But Joe, we do not eat flesh. We eat only that which is prepared by our processing units."

Joe bit off a piece of meat and chewed it introspectively. There was no point in trying to force the issue. His two friends from the distant future were obviously averse to the concept of eating flesh, so he decided it would be best to drop the subject altogether.

Analy, his face a mask of mixed emotions, raised a morsel to his lips and bit into it. Joe half expected the tall man to be violently sick but, to his amazement and that of Trione, Analy began to chew, savouring the strong taste of the venison.

"This is unlike the food we are accustomed to," he admitted finally, "but it has more flavour." To Trione, he said, "You should try it and savour it as a memory of the time you spend with the Futama."

Trione, however, was unable to break the habit of a lifetime. "There is enough for me to remember, without eating the flesh of dead animals," he riposted, "however unusual its flavour."

Reed approached and nudged Joe's arm. 'Futama, we are ready,' she signed. Grasping his elbow, she urged Joe towards the place where she and Dar were preparing to make fire.

Joe told them to go ahead, and Dar struck the flints together, sending sparks showering in all directions. After a few strikes, a lucky spark landed in the tinder and Dar blew on it enthusiastically, producing a tiny glowing core. In minutes the fire was roaring and crackling in the rudimentary hearth and Dar and Reed leapt up and performed an impromptu dance of delight.

Dar's staff lay nearby and Joe decided to present the Neanderthals with one final survival aid. Selecting a piece of flint, he knapped a sharp edge and used the resulting tool to sharpen Dar's staff to a point. The fire was glowing strongly, so he hardened the spear point in the hot embers. The youngsters were showing interest, so Joe sketched the outline of a deer in the hard earth and stabbed it with the point of the spear. Dar immediately grasped the concept and repeated Joe's actions, first on the outline of the deer and then on an imaginary animal as he ran across the ledge. Joe could see that the youth had learned enough to pass on the technique to the rest of his clan.

The night was beginning to draw in and Joe remembered that Romana was still airborne in the flyer. He called his bodyguards over. "Can you summon Romana to join us?" he asked.

Trione nodded, saying it was done, and immediately the dark silhouette of the flyer hung against the evening sky in the gap between the forest and the cliff face. Once again the Neanderthals scurried for cover and Romana had the landing area completely free except for her three companions. She came down vertically, her powerful landing lights illuminating the shadowed ledge, and drifted the craft sideways beneath the cover of the giant trees. The flyer powered down with a sigh and the landing lights extinguished, leaving afterimages on the retinas of everyone who had watched the craft's descent too closely. With a hiss, the canopy slid back and a smiling Romana stepped out onto the hard packed earth.

"I was sceptical of your chances of integrating with these primitive people," she told Joe, "but it seems my doubts were unfounded. Analy and Trione kept me aware of your progress and the way you achieved it." She hesitated before continuing with a question. "May I caution the Futama?"

"Why, is there a problem?"

Romana had obviously been elected spokesperson for Joe's three friends from the future, and the responsibility was weighing on her. She was clearly worried about what reaction her words would elicit from Joe. "We are concerned that you may be at risk of changing the future of these people by teaching them new ways. We must not risk creating paradoxes and anomalies in this timeline."

"Don't worry," Joe assured her, "the simple skills I've passed on to them were—will be—known, and used, by their descendants, right through to the time when their race is almost extinct, more than two-hundred thousand years into the future of this era. I'm pretty certain that I was meant to do this to complete the circle. Anyway, I'm relying on a complete lack of inventiveness in these people for them to pass on the legend of the Futama unchanged for the next two-hundred or so millennia. Anything less would mean that, in all probability, I will be killed when I suddenly appear to them. And as I *wasn't* killed, I have to believe I *will* be successful here. Does that make sense?"

Romana considered Joe's explanation. There were aspects of it she could not verify, but having heard the story of Joe's jaunt into

112

the late Neanderthal past, she had to admit that it made an odd kind of sense. "You will teach them no more new skills?" she asked.

"No, I've done everything I wanted to do here, except strengthen my legend, and I'll finish that part off in a little while when we have a look inside their cave. There's something there I want to check on."

* * *

Spurning the use of technology of the future, Joe bound some dry leaves and twigs together with bark stripped from a green sapling and rubbed it with fat from the roasting meat. Armed with the rudimentary torch, he entered the cave, followed by Char, the medicine woman and his three companions. Dar and Reed waited until everyone was out of sight, and then stealthily followed. Inside, it was little different from when Joe was last there in the time of Too-ga and his tribe. The ceiling was much higher, because the build-up of mud and the general debris of human occupation were missing. The extent of the difference in levels was illustrated by the fact that the time tunnel entered the ceremonial cave more than three metres above the packed mud floor.

Joe held the torch above his head, spreading its meagre light to the furthest reaches of the cavern. The yellow luminescence flickered and danced, producing ghostly images as it played on the pale, chalky surfaces of the cavern walls. No one but Joe could see the black mouth of the tunnel in the rock face above their heads.

Handing the torch to Trione, Joe signed to Char, 'When I appear to your people again, I will come from the spirit world beyond the walls of this cave. You will relate tales of the Futama, the mighty hunter, as you warm yourselves beside your fires, and remember me every time you kill the wild beast with your spears. Tell your children's children of the one who struck down the big tooth with lightning he plucked from the skies. I am your Futama and you will remember me always."

Char stared first at the flickering torch in Trione's hand, then at Joe and his companions. 'It will be so,' she signed, 'forever.'

Joe's companions had watched the interplay with the medicine woman, completely unaware of what was being said. Quickly, Joe explained, and Romana raised one eyebrow quizzically.

"You will come from the spirit world beyond the walls of this cavern?" she queried.

In response, Joe held her wrist and, with a flick of his eyes, directed her to look upwards. Romana's eyes glinted in the guttering light of the torch and comprehension flitted across her beautiful features as she saw the dark outline of the time tunnel.

"From the spirit world," she grinned.

Char sensed that something important had passed between the Futama and the tall female. The medicine woman stared at the blank cavern wall for a long moment before she signed to Joe, 'We eat, then we sleep.'

Trione led the small party outside, preceded by the pattering of Dar and Reed's footsteps. Outside, it was almost completely dark and the fires had burnt down to embers. Joe grabbed Dar and explained that the fires wouldn't burn without fuel. The youngster immediately raced to the edge of the ledge to gather another supply of windblown debris. Within minutes the fires were once again sending fountains of sparks into the overhanging branches of the trees. Dar collected more wood in the fading light until Joe told him there was enough to last till morning.

The evening had taken on a chill and all the primitive Neanderthals wrapped themselves in furs before approaching the fires. A smell of decay pervaded the whole of the area around the fires and it was clear that the furs had been poorly scraped and cured. Joe thought about teaching Char and her people how to prepare their clothing so that it remained hygienic, but dismissed the idea immediately. In later times, the Neanderthals possessed those particular skills, so they must have learned them over the millennia, stretching through until the autumn years of their race.

From their expressions Joe's companions were also troubled by the foul odour, but they said nothing as quantities of roots and berries were brought forth from the cave to supplement the raw and roast venison. Many of the tribespeople wanted to sample the cooked meat, and soon the small amount was gone. Joe signed that if they wanted more, they would have to wait for it to roast properly, for inadequate cooking would give them a bellyache – perhaps even worse. His word was sufficient to stay their enthusiasm for the new taste, and it wasn't long before almost half the carcase had been consumed, mostly raw.

Joe and his three friends were eating nothing and Char demanded, "Why do you not eat?"

114

To which Joe replied, "The food is my gift to your people. We have food in our giant bird, which we shall eat shortly. We shall then sleep beside the fires."

The medicine woman, though a little put out, accepted Joe's explanation and returned to the fireside, while Romana slipped away to the flyer to collect some field rations. She returned carrying a box containing sufficient food for the four of them, plus four small, flat parcels.

"What are those?" Joe enquired.

"If the Futama insists that we stay here, surrounded by this foul stink," she replied, "we shall, at least, sleep in comfort, with a small measure of protection against predators. These are individual sleep environments."

In the flickering light from the fires, Joe's mouth formed an 'O' of surprise. It would be interesting to see what form the individual sleep environments took when they were deployed.

The rations were not as tasty as the meat Joe had broiled over the fire, but the food proved adequate to calm the hunger pangs, which had insidiously begun to make themselves felt. No doubt it contained all the nourishment necessary for his body to survive, but it could, at least, he thought, have been a little more appetising.

Romana finished her meal and selected one of the sleep environment packs. Laying it upon the ground, she tapped a code into a small keypad on its upper surface and it expanded to form a soft, rectangular mattress, approximately two-and-a-half metres by one metre.

"Looks comfy," Joe commented drily, but how will it protect you from creatures of the night?"

Romana peered all around, as if expecting to see a bear lurking in the darkness of the forest's edge. "When you lie upon it, the shield will become active," she explained.

"The shield?"

"The sleepzone generates a local force field around itself and I cannot imagine that even a large predator would persist in trying to break through."

"Oh, I see. But what if whoever's inside rolls out of bed? Won't they be toasted by the force field? Remember, I saw what it did to those two mammoths."

Romana's laughter was echoed by Analy and Trione's. "Don't worry. The field has an inner and an outer surface. If you touch it from inside, you will experience only a tingling sensation, but you will be unable to penetrate the field."

"What will happen if one of the Neanderthals touches it?" Joe enquired.

"The force field will keep them out, but it will not kill them," Romana assured him, "though it would be best to warn them not to come too close."

By the time Joe returned from warning Char and the rest of her clan not to approach his sleeping area, the other sleep environments had been deployed and his three companions were lying beneath their faintly luminescent canopies. He picked up a short branch and touched the hazy outline, shimmering around Trione's resting figure. Where it touched the force field, the wood was instantly enveloped in a violent electrical discharge, which crackled and spat alarmingly, illuminating dark branches overhead with its dazzling energy. He dropped the branch in alarm and it fell against the field, continuing to spark and spit like a blue-tinted firework.

The force field faded and Trione reached out to remove the offending object before settling down once more beneath the protective canopy.

"Sorry," Joe apologised, "but I had to see for myself."

* * *

The next morning dawned crisp and bright over the forest. Joe could see a sliver of sky between the cliff face and the trees over his head, its pearlescent blue tint heralding a fine day. He stretched in the comfort of his sleep environment and his fingers touched the inner surface of the force field, producing a not unpleasant tingling sensation through the upper half of his body. He had spent an extremely comfortable night, filled with dreams of Ciara, and had awoken with an intense longing to be in her company once again.

He sat up and the force field immediately faded away, allowing him to stand. His three companions were still soundly asleep, so Joe built up both of the fires from the store of wood laid in by Dar the previous evening. The pristine air was fresh in his nostrils, enticing him to stretch his legs before breakfast. With a last glance at the three occupied sleepzones, he set off at a brisk pace downslope into the forest, his senses on heightened alert for the presence of animals in the vicinity. A solitary birdsong decanted into the wine-like air, its liquid notes rippling through the silent forest.

As if in counterpoint to the melody, Joe heard the snuffling grunts of a beast in the undergrowth beside the path, some twenty metres ahead. He stopped, hardly breathing, and slipped his revolver from inside his jacket. Gently, he released the safety-catch, becoming one with his environment as he waited to find out what was ahead. He didn't have long to wait before a heavily proportioned wild bore emerged onto the path from beneath the trees. The beast spotted Joe in the half-light of the dense forest, and gave a grunt of surprise and annoyance. Joe remained immobile, waiting for the beast's next move. He didn't have to wait long; the beast lowered its head and charged, its curved tusks glinting menacingly in the gloom.

With his pistol held steady, Joe fired three rapid shots at the approaching boar, but the momentum of the beast's charge carried it onwards and he had to leap aside to avoid being impaled on the creature's tusks. Believing his shots had missed their mark, Joe quickly turned to meet the boar's next charge, but the beast staggered and fell, squealing in pain and outrage. The heavy animal made a mighty effort to rise, but it was badly wounded, and its struggles just caused its blood to flow more freely onto the forest floor. A bullet to the brain ended the boar's suffering.

Breathing heavily, Joe was aware of a riot of bird alarm in the forest around him. It seemed as if every bird in the whole world was vigorously protesting the noisy invasion of its territory. Joe's kill would soon be the centre of attraction for any predators in the vicinity and it was clear that he would have to move it to the Neanderthal encampment as soon as possible. He was setting out on the short walk back to the cave, when Analy and Trione came racing down the pathway, closely pursued by several of the Neanderthal men. Four of the Neanderthals immediately picked up the heavy carcase and set off up the slope towards the cave.

"Futama," Analy gasped, his chest heaving from the sprint, "we feared for your safety. Why did you leave the encampment alone?"

"Because I wanted to," Joe replied frostily. "I'm not a child, and I'll decide for myself what I can or can't do. I wanted to enjoy the surroundings on my own. I just happened to meet this boar and we had a disagreement. It's no big deal, okay?"

"But we must be permitted to protect the Futama, and we cannot do so if—"

"The Futama will not allow you to?" Joe finished off. "Well, my friend, let's just get one thing straight. I appreciate the fact that Leiki has made you my bodyguards, but you need to accept that I know this kind of environment a lot better than you do. I've dealt with these animals and people before and I'm aware of the danger all around us. I'm a man and you're just going to give me the chance to beat my chest occasionally."

Subdued, Analy glanced at Trione and replied, "You are the Futama and must have your freedom. Nevertheless, we must do our duty and protect you." The big man was utterly miserable.

Romana arrived and added her weight to Analy's argument. "Please, Joe, let us do our duty. It would be a catastrophe for our people if you should be killed or injured. Please think also of the ones you have left at home in your time."

The excitement of the encounter with the wild boar was fading as the level of adrenaline in Joe's system diminished. "Sorry!" he apologised. "I suppose I should have asked Analy or Trione to accompany me, shouldn't I. My peashooter is a bit ineffective compared to their plasma rifles, isn't it?"

Romana smiled in relief at the mellowing of Joe's attitude. "Shall we return to the flyer?" she urged. "It is time for us to say our goodbyes to these people."

118

Chapter Twelve

BACK HOME AGAIN:

Joe stared in consternation at the activity on the beach around the entrance to the time tunnel in the twenty-first century. Romana, Analy and Trione, all attired in clothing suitable for the period, stood waiting in the narrow confines of the cleft, their scalps almost brushing the roof. Outside, batteries of powerful lamps flooded the late autumn evening with intense white light, accompanied by the attendant throbbing of diesel-powered generators. He searched his memory in an attempt to find what had triggered the activity. The last time he had been here, Prua Landi had tried to kill him with her plasma pistol. He ran through the events in his mind, seeing the intense hatred in Prua Landi's eyes as she sprayed the plasma fire over the entrance to the cleft in a futile attempt to burn her way inside.

"How would a concentrated burst of plasma fire affect the chalk cliffs?" he asked Analy.

"The rock would melt," Analy informed him, "and flow like lava. Eventually, it would cool and set, forming a smooth crust."

"I see," Joe informed him. "Then that must be what *they* are investigating." He waved his hand in the direction of what appeared to the three future humans as a solid rock face.

Their puzzled expressions reminded Joe that the others were unable to see what he could see. "Place your hands on mine," he ordered, and instantly they saw the activity outside on the beach. "Prua Landi tried to burn her way through the rock to get at me, and all she succeeded in doing was melting the rock itself. I reckon somebody must have noticed it and the local council have brought somebody in to investigate." He smiled grimly, "I bet they're scratching their heads a bit, but we've got a problem too. How do we get past them?"

"It is a little unethical," Romana suggested, "but, together, we should be able to influence the thought processes of those people sufficiently for us to elude them. Do you wish us to try?"

"Yes, and it would be a good idea to provide them with a reasonable explanation for the melted rock, something that would persuade them to pack up their equipment and go home."

Still holding onto Joe's hand, the three linked their minds and projected information to the people on the beach. They implanted the suggestion that the melted area of the cliff face was due to a particularly potent incident of ball lightning. When they were satisfied that everyone had accepted the bogus theory, they telepathically misdirected the senses of their subjects so that they and Joe could pass unseen amongst them. Because he was in physical contact with Romana and the others, Joe caught the essence of what had transpired and his admiration for the ability his friends from the distant future increased considerably.

Joe stepped out of the cleft, closely linked to the others. Immediately, he was confronted by a bearded individual in an industrial helmet. The man was chipping off a piece of the glassy rock with a geologist's hammer. Joe halted but the man gazed straight through him as if he did not exist. So far, so good! The four wove a path between people, lights and equipment without challenge and stepped through the tape cordon placed around the area of the cleft. There was a small crowd of onlookers on the beach and Joe's companions found it necessary to repeat the telepathic hypnotism in order to convince everyone they had seen nothing.

Ten minutes later, Joe tapped quietly on his front door and, after a moment, Ciara opened it. With a whoop of joy, she threw her arms around his neck and rained kisses on him. When she finally pulled away from Joe's embrace, Ciara noticed the three tall figures standing in the pool of light spilling from the open door.

"Oh, hello, Romana," she said. Won't you come in? And that goes for your friends too."

With a quick thank you, Romana ducked inside the doorway, followed by Analy and lastly Trione, who did not stoop quite low enough and managed to contact the doorframe painfully with his head, to the amusement of his companions from the future.

Ciara bustled into the kitchen and returned with a pot of tea and five cups on a tray. The three tall people sat upon the settee, with their knees higher and their backsides lower than they were accustomed to whenever they used furniture more in keeping with their stature.

Romana broke the ice. "I would like to check your health and the health of your baby," she informed Ciara, "but this time, I will check you thoroughly. For Joe's sake I cannot risk the slightest mistake."

Romana's slightly odd statement puzzled Ciara. "Why not?" she asked.

"Because he is— " She glanced at Joe. "Because he is our Futama," she told Ciara defiantly.

"I thought you weren't going to mention that, Darling."

"I didn't say a thing," Joe protested. "They worked it out for themselves. It seems they've been waiting for a long time for me to turn up. When Romana's given you the once over, we'd better tell you the whole story. It's a bit complicated."

"I can't wait," Ciara agreed. "I hope this story involves you staying home for a while."

Joe's neutral expression informed her that she was incorrect in that assumption at least.

* * *

Romana glanced at the reading on her monitor. "The baby is developing well," she informed Ciara and Joe, resetting the instrument for a different scan. Seconds later, she reset the monitor once more, and took a further reading. In exasperation, she recalibrated the instrument and again applied it to Ciara's wrist. This time, there could be no disputing the data, although, to the tall medic, the implications were utterly bizarre.

"May I speak with you, Joe—alone?" she enquired.

"Let's go into the kitchen," he replied, "but Ciara comes too. There won't be any secrets between us."

Leaving Analy and Trione sipping their hot tea, the three entered the tiny kitchen and Joe closed the door behind them.

"What's this all about?" he demanded, holding his wife close to his side.

"I have discovered an anomaly," Romana said defensively, "one for which I cannot offer an explanation."

"OK," Joe ordered, "tell us and let's get it over with."

"Ciara," the tall medic asked gently, "how can it be that your body contains its own community of nanomedics?"

Joe heard someone say loudly, "WHAT?" and he realised belatedly that it was he. Slightly embarrassed, he asked, "How is that possible?"

"As I said, I cannot offer an explanation," Romana apologised, "but I believe that the Futama should undergo the same examination."

Without even thinking about it, Joe replied, "Feel free. If I've got them too, I'd like to know how it came about."

"As would I," Romana agreed, "but first I must run a complete diagnostic over you." She paused, seemingly embarrassed, glancing first at Joe and then at Ciara. "Would you please remove the clothing from your upper body?"

With a grin, Joe complied. "Two beautiful women after my body," he joked. Ciara glared at him and his grin faded. "Okay, Doc, fire away," he mumbled.

Romana ran the diagnostic over the whole of his upper body, pausing over his jugular vein whilst she read off a string of data. Finally, she said quietly, "The nanomedics are present in the Futama's system also, but they are far more powerful than those of the Futama's mate. If I were asked to give an opinion based upon the data I am able to gather with the simple instrument at my disposal, I would venture the theory that the nanos within Ciara's system are secondaries of those in the body of the Futama."

"Secondaries?" exclaimed Joe and Ciara together.

"Those within the Futama have spawned the secondaries within Ciara and must be a result of sexual intercourse."

"Does it mean that we have the same protection you gave to Or-gon?" Ciara asked.

"Certainly," came the reply, "but the nanos within you are most unusual. I cannot guess what other properties they may have."

"Can't you try?" Joe asked.

"Anything I tell you would be based upon guesswork," Romana informed him. "I need specialised equipment to analyse the nanomedics and their properties and such equipment and expertise are only available on Mars."

"What about my baby?" Ciara demanded. "I don't want these things running loose inside me if there's any danger to my baby."

Romana placed her arm around Ciara's shoulders and hugged her. "I am certain that you will have the healthiest baby on Earth in this era," she soothed. "His blood is already infused with its own nanos." She was thoughtful for a moment before continuing. "In my world, we do not inject nanomedics into foetuses, but computer models have shown that, to do so, would prove beneficial to the child as he grows towards adulthood. And remember," she added, "the nanos will keep you in good health until the end of your days."

Joe embraced his wife and kissed her tenderly. "Well, Darling, it looks as though we've struck lucky with these nanos. Let's just accept it for now and go back to our guests. Analy and

Trione must be wondering what's happening . . . that is unless Romana has been keeping them informed."

An expression of guilt flitting across Romana's beautiful features, informed him that he was not far from the mark. As Joe entered the lounge, the doorbell rang and he opened up to find Maeve and Or-gon standing there.

"We heard voices through the walls," Maeve explained, "and we thought Ciara must have guests." She couldn't miss the two giant men, who had arisen from their seats. She introduced herself and Or-gon to Analy and Trione.

"It is an honour to meet friends of the Futama," Trione intoned and Or-gon's attention was immediately piqued.

The Neanderthal stared penetratingly at the two men. "Joe is *your* Futama also?" he queried incredulously.

Trione, brooking no argument, stated emphatically, "Joe is *the* Futama, throughout *all* the ages of time."

Or-gon smiled at the revelation. Joe had always maintained that he was a mere man, but here was someone from the distant future asserting that his friend was known throughout all time as the Futama. "Tell me when the legend actually began," he demanded. "I have been to the time of my ancestors, thirty-five thousand years in the past, where Joe was the Futama. But the legend began long before that time."

Accepting Or-gon as a fellow believer, Trione informed him in reverent tones, "Less than two days ago, we three," he indicated Analy and Romana, "were honoured to be present as the Futama instilled his legend into the minds of a tribe of early Neanderthals."

Or-gon was on edge. "When?" he demanded. "In what era did this take place?"

"Two-hundred and fifty-three thousand years before this time," came the reply.

The scientist glanced at Joe and chuckled. "And Jo-lang still asserts that he is just a man?"

"You'd better believe it," Joe told him, "although it seems you're not the only one chock full of nanomedics. Do yours make you feel any different? Do they make you feel like a god?" Or-gon shook his head. "I thought not. And I still feel pretty ordinary, even if I'm in a bit of an unusual situation."

The understatement was not lost on those in the room and Maeve commented drily, "Sure, Joe, but you're the most ordinary son-in-law I have." Her intervention helped to lighten the mood in the room and she added, "I think another pot of tea is called for. Joe, will you help me?"

Puzzled, Joe followed his mother-in-law into the kitchen where she held the kettle under the cold water tap to fill it. "Okay, Maeve, what's on your mind?"

Maeve switched the kettle on, and with her back to Joe, said quietly, "You know that these people worship you, don't you Joe?"

"Yes, but I keep telling them I'm just an ordinary person like them."

"Don't you see, Joe, you're not ordinary? You might not wear a cloak like a superhero, but you *are* doing extraordinary things. You've created a new timeline – and destroyed it – and you have a legend built up around you. Not, I might add, just amongst primitive savages, but also amongst people from the future to whom we must be mere children. It's obvious you have a destiny to fulfil, which involves Romana and the others, but I want you to promise me something."

"What is it, Maeve?" Joe asked.

"Promise that you'll come back to your wife and child when it's all over, because they need you as much as everyone else seems to do."

"Don't worry, Maeve, I won't let anybody down," Joe vowed. "I intend to be around to watch my son grow up."

* * *

Prua Landi eyed the holographic display as Perdon struggled to clarify the image. Beads of perspiration glistened on the scientist's brow as the dictatrix glowered and fumed nearby. After several minutes, the holographic image flickered and strengthened into a clear picture of the activity around the cliff face in the twenty-first century. Perdon manipulated the point of view, focusing upon the smooth, glassy surface, where Prua Landi had directed a sustained burst of plasma fire. They could see people scurrying around, sampling here, measuring there, as if there was even the faintest chance of their discovering the true reason for the scorched rock face.

Prua Landi watched for a few moments. "Imbeciles!" she commented.

"The time-flux anomaly is due to occur very soon," Perdon informed her.

"You had better pay attention then, for things will not go well for you should you miss it," Prua Landi replied tartly.

As they watched, a figure emerged, seemingly from the solid rock, followed by another and then another, until four people stood inspecting the activity all around them. The group was made up of three tall people and one of much smaller stature, whom Prua Landi instantly recognised as Jo-lang. Slowly, they made their way through the cordoned off area and along the beach, through a straggle of spectators. Perdon skilfully followed with the remote viewer, and eventually the foursome halted at the door of a small dwelling. The door was opened manually by a female, the one who had accompanied Jo-lang at the cliffside, and everyone entered. Prua Landi derived a certain satisfaction from seeing one of the members of the Faithful sect crack his head painfully on the low doorway.

"Is my time travel control prepared?" she demanded.

"Yes, My Lady," Perdon informed her, "but I must caution you that the events depicted remain at the extreme limit of our ability to travel into the past."

"You will improve the range," Prua Landi informed him, "or you will suffer the fate of your predecessors."

"We are working tirelessly on it, My Lady."

Prua Landi pointed a long finger at the display. "I wish to be present at that exact point in time. Arrange it now!"

"Certainly, My Lady, but please remember, it will be possible for you to carry only the smallest of hand weapons."

"I am aware of that, but you will work harder to improve it, do you understand?"

"Yes, My Lady, I understand."

Prua Landi glared at the scientist, detecting a hint of insolence in his tone, but Perdon's bland expression was unfathomable.

"Are you ready, My Lady?"

The dictatrix nodded.

"Then please enter the cubicle."

Prua Landi checked her plasma pistol and complied. Moments later, a multi-hued flash of light signalled her transfer to the twenty-first century. Outside Joe's house, the roadway was illuminated by the echoing discharge as she arrived in a twisting vortex of energy.

"It's a bit early for fireworks," Joe commented, seeing the diffused flashes through his curtains.

Trione opened the curtains a touch and peered outside at the amber-lit street. Most of the evenly spaced trees along the avenue were still, but a localised whirlwind seemed to be stripping leaves from the tree across the road from Joe's front gate. The tall man nodded meaningfully at Analy and they proceeded to withdraw their plasma rifles from their protective cases.

Ciara's eyes widened in alarm. "What's going on?" she demanded. "Why have you got those guns?"

Ignoring her, Analy spoke to Joe. "Futama, I think we may have unwanted company. Please take everyone into the far side of the house for their protection."

"Okay," Joe agreed, hustling everyone through into the kitchen. "Stay here," he ordered, "I'm going with Analy and Trione."

Trione's huge hand met him in the middle of his chest at the kitchen door. "The Futama will remain *here*," the big man told him firmly, "and let us protect him as we have been ordered."

With a shrug, Joe accepted the situation. "Good luck!" he said. "I hope it turns out to be a false alarm."

Trione's expression informed Joe that the big man was under no such illusions. Opening the door a crack, Trione peeked out and, seeing nothing, stepped outside. Instantly, a cone of plasma fire speared out from beyond the trunk of the tree across the road. Mercifully, Trione was just out of range, but the intense heat shattered both gateposts, spraying globules of molten sandstone in all directions. Several of the white-hot globules struck Trione, setting his clothing on fire and knocking him backwards, unconscious, through the open doorway.

Analy leapt over his comrade's body and loosed a sustained burst of plasma fire in the direction of the tree. Set on middle distance, the weapon produced a metre wide bolt of plasma and its effect on the tree was instant and spectacular. All the liquid in the trunk of the tree evaporated in a cataclysmic explosion, and soon flaming pieces of the ruined tree began raining down upon all the houses in the street. In the aftermath of the explosion, there was no sign of Trione's attacker.

Inside the house, Romana tended to Trione's wounds, which were all superficial, with the exception of a broken arm, suffered as he fell backwards through the doorway. Joe joined Analy outside, searching for clues to the fate of whoever had attacked Trione. In the distance he could hear the sirens of the emergency services weaving through the streets, heading nearer with every passing minute. This was a catastrophe, and it was the last thing he needed if he wished to remain inconspicuous in his own time. The spectre of a police investigation plagued his worried mind, and he felt certain that Or-gon's fake identity would be investigated, with potentially disastrous consequences.

He asked himself over and over again, to the accompaniment of the approaching sirens, what he could tell the police about the incident, and every time the answer was nothing. Changing direction, he asked himself what he would do to change the events of the last few minutes, were it within his power to do so, and the answer hit him like a physical force. He could use the timestone!

Racing upstairs, he searched in the wardrobe where he had secreted the device in a shoebox along with a couple of flint axe heads. Grasping the timestone, he expertly twisted the controls, setting the time to ten minutes before the present moment. Then he reversed the twist and the sirens ceased their incessant wailing. Peering through his bedroom curtains, he saw no scene of devastation and no burning tree.

Descending the stairs, he met a puzzled Ciara, who asked him how he'd managed to get upstairs when she had just been talking to him in the lounge. "Me Futama," he declared with a grin, beating his chest.

Joe walked through into the lounge to be met by the enquiring stares of Romana, Analy and Trione, who seemed to have noticed a minor disturbance in the flow of time. Maeve and Or-gon were completely unaware that anything unusual had occurred.

With a smile, Maeve informed everyone that they were invited around to her house for supper. She winked at Joe and Ciara. "See you two in an hour?"

"Thanks, Mum," Ciara replied, "save some for us, won't you?"

* * *

The beach was deserted as Joe and his friends from the future plodded silently through the soft sand, towards the cordoned off area around the melted cliff face that was a source of interest for investigators and locals alike. They approached warily, and halted

127

before they reached the point where the light from a few lamps cast dappled patterns of brightness and shadow.

Romana whispered, "Make no sound. There is someone lurking in a flimsy shelter over there." Her long finger indicated a small tent, lit from the inside by a gas lamp."

A shadow temporarily eclipsed the glow from the lamp, and the unmistakeable sound of a zip being drawn reached their ears.

"Quick," Joe urged, "misdirect him or something."

With practised skill, the three used the same telepathic technique they had used on the investigating team and on the spectators on the beach, convincing the man there was no one around. A shadowy figure emerged from the tent and peered into the darkness surrounding him. Apparently satisfied that he was alone, he ambled away and emptied his bladder into the edge of the waves. His urge satisfied, he remained immobile, staring at the running lights of a yacht a couple of kilometres out to sea.

"Let's go," Joe whispered, "before he turns around."

"Don't worry," Romana assured him, "he will remain there for a little while, until he begins to feel the night chill."

As Joe ushered each of the others into the crevice, he looked around him at the reflections glistening on the glazed surface of the chalky cliff and the pools of illumination cast by the batteries of lamps, most of which had been switched off for the night. The steady thrub-thrub of the generator seemed to swell and recede in concert with the incoming waves. What a mess, he thought, hoping fervently that Romana's telepathic hypnotism proved potent enough to persuade the authorities to vacate the area completely. The interest amongst the local people was certain to remain at a high level for a while, and then would come along the cranks and conspiracy theorists promoting their own agendas. But, eventually, the interest would wane, and he hoped that would happen before he returned from Mars, because he couldn't risk anyone seeing him emerge from the 'solid rock' of the cliff face.

Once they reached the cove, Romana and the others waited for Joe at the tiny tent, their eyes clouded, their expressions neutral in the light of a camping lantern. Once again, it seemed that Romana had assumed the mantle of spokesperson.

"Futama," she began, her eyes lowered like a child, who was fearful that punishment was about to be meted out for misbehaviour.

"You'd better start calling me Joe again," he replied. "We don't want any mistakes, do we? Anyway, why are you looking so worried?"

Romana shook her head. "There must be no mistakes, which *is why we three are troubled.*"

Joe felt he knew what was coming. Still, he enquired, "What's the problem?"

The words came tumbling out. "Fut— Joe," she said, stumbling uncharacteristically over her words, "we *believe* that something strange occurred whilst we were at your home, something affecting time itself. We also believe that you are aware of the anomaly, perhaps even—" She paused, unsure whether to continue.

"Come on, Romana, spit it out!" Joe ordered tersely.

"We believe that you may have been responsible for the event." Romana stared at Joe defiantly, seeming to draw strength from having finally brought their suspicions out into the open.

"All right, I suppose you've got a right to know, but you won't like what you hear," Joe agreed.

Trione decided to join in the discussion. "Let us decide," he said.

Joe ducked into the tent and emerged with his tiny stove and tea making equipment. Firing up the stove, he put on the kettle. "This will take a little while, so you'd better make yourselves as comfortable as you can."

The three waited expectantly for Joe to begin, but he went through the process of building a campfire to ward of the encroaching chill, whilst arranging the events of the past few hours in his mind. The last thing he needed was for his friends to misinterpret his actions because he had failed to tell the story exactly as it had happened. The water on the camping stove was still some way from boiling as he began his tale. Trione's eyes opened wide when Joe reached the point where he had narrowly escaped being killed, and he absently rubbed his 'broken' arm, which for some unfathomable reason had begun to ache.

"But there was no scene of battle around your home," Analy protested, "and I remember nothing of firing on Prua Landi or whoever was out there."

"That's because I erased the incident," Joe told him, "so that it never happened. Only *I* knew . . . and now I'm telling you."

"Erased the incident?" Romana expostulated. "By what means?"

129

Her companions sat with stunned expressions on their bronzed features. They had witnessed one small facet of Joe's martial arts skills, and were in awe of his strange knowledge of the unspoken language of the primitive Neanderthal people. But this new, and unexpected, ability, which suggested a technology equal to the best of that of the Faithful, was a development they were unable to rationalise. In fact, it was impossible, from every viewpoint they could imagine.

Joe described how he had been subjected to an avalanche of data, when he had touched the frieze in the tunnel complex of thirty-five thousand years ago, long after it had been abandoned by the Faithful. He told how, buried amongst the information decanted into his memory, he had discovered a reference to a timestone, which had the capability of manipulating time itself. The information had contained a severe warning of the possible consequences of changing time, despite which, he had utilised the device to eradicate the timeline of the doomed Tarmis, enabling him to return to his own twenty-first century.

"And you used this timestone to 'correct' the damage from the battle with Prua Landi?" Romana enquired.

"Yes, because I thought it was necessary in order to avoid trouble for Ciara, Maeve and, particularly, Or-gon."

"You mention Or-gon," Romana probed. "If your interference with time has erased all knowledge of the battle and the ensuing damage, how can it be that Or-gon was not erased when you eliminated his timeline?" Deep in thought, she added, "And that he retains memory of the event?"

"I think I'll pass on that one," Joe answered. "All I can think of is that Or-gon was predestined to be a part of my timeline too."

"Perhaps," Romana conceded. "The sequence of events you have described – the timestone, the frieze, Tarmis and your return to your own time – seem to suggest that we are all part of a complex scheme to lead you to Mars. Since I discovered the nanomedics in your system, I have given much thought as to how you came to possess them. They are unlike those injected into every child in our time and I am inclined towards the theory that, in some way, they are the reason why you can see and use the time tunnels, whilst *we* cannot."

"I believe you should explain," Analy told her.

Romana searched her memories of events since Joe and Ciara first arrived at the tunnel complex. "You recall that Ciara has, over a period of days, gradually developed the ability to see and use the time tunnels?"

Everyone nodded.

"As far as we are aware, Joe has always been able to use the time tunnels, and it is my belief that Ciara's improving ability is the result of an increase in the numbers of the secondary nanomedics in her body. The nanomedics are the common factor between them."

Joe listened as Romana expounded her theory. "I'm not sure I've always had the nanomedics," he said, "but one day I spotted the cleft in the cliff face. At the time, it seemed a bit strange that I'd never noticed it before. Now you mention it, I reckon someone must have shot me full of the nanos when I was asleep. The question is who and when – and why?"

Romana answered, "We know the reason *why*. It was to enable you to live the legend of the Futama. *When* it happened is unimportant. *Who* was responsible is the burning question and I believe I may have an answer."

"Tell us," Trione said, "and we will examine your logic."

"In our natural time, we believe that the Futama will come to lead us to victory over Prua Landi's regime. Yet, it seems, the Futama was born in this primitive era of our past." She offered an apologetic glance in Joe's direction. "Though it has always been his destiny to become the Futama, nevertheless the path had to be cleared for him to walk. That, I believe, is the reason why he was able to discover and use the timestone. When we return to the complex, I propose that we examine the frieze, which educated Joe in the use of the timestone, and I suggest we will find that, for us, it will remain completely inert. I would also suggest, that in our lack of ability, we shall discover yet another facet of Joe's specialised nanos."

As they sipped their tea, they mulled over Romana's theory; it all made a strange kind of sense.

"In that case," Joe told his companions, "when we get to the complex, I'm going to ask Leiki what the hell's going on."

"I suspect," Romana ventured, "that our theories may prove educational even for our base commander, despite the fact that he is a member of the high council."

131

Chapter Thirteen

A PAINFUL SETBACK:

Lights shimmered and coruscated in the time cubicle, signalling Prua Landi's return. Perdon scurried to the pod and stood waiting impatiently for the process to reach its final phase. Eventually, in a flash of brilliance, the figure of Prua Landi materialised, but it was clear that something had gone horribly wrong. The dictatrix lay in a heap on the floor, covered in smouldering debris, a small amount of ragged clothing still clinging to her near naked body. Her badly burned flesh was patterned with hundreds of shards of tree bark, whose multiple impacts had been cauterised by the heat.

"Doctors!" Perdon screamed. "Doctors to the transport room immediately."

Seconds later, a medical team arrived, accompanied by Prua Landi's personal bodyguard, to begin the treatment of her injuries with the latest nanosalves and ointments. A screen was swiftly erected around the cubicle and the smouldering clothing was stripped away, leaving Prua Landi completely naked and defenceless. Perdon examined the time controlling device, stripped from Prua Landi's inert wrist. A sliver of wood was embedded between the bezel and the central stud, leading the scientist to the conclusion that the splinter had triggered her return. Prua Landi had been very fortunate indeed to survive.

Perdon heard the unmistakeable voice of his mistress scream, "Where is Perdon? Bring him to me!"

A guard immediately stepped up behind the scientist and prodded him with a plasma rifle. Meekly he called, "I am here, My Lady."

Prua Landi lay within the protective confines of a healing suit, her body smothered in nanosalves. Her eyes, which were closed as Perdon approached, flicked open, revealing the burnt stubble of eyelashes. "Tell me what happened," she ordered, refusing to allow the pain to influence her icy tones.

"My Lady, there has been insufficient time to investigate."

"Then do so now. And I would advise you to find an answer that I can accept."

Perdon knew that his life was probably hanging in the balance. "As you seem unable to remember, My Lady, I will return with the remote viewer to the exact time of your accident, and investigate."

"I remember something," Prua Landi gasped through the pain. "I was fired upon with a plasma rifle as I was concealed behind a tree. I suggest you view the time very carefully and report to me immediately. And," she added ominously, "you will prove that my trust in you is not misplaced."

Perdon bowed deeply. "My Lady," he replied.

A technician powered up the remote viewer at Perdon's command and the holographic image immediately returned to its last setting, which showed Trione's back as he ducked inside the doorway of the small dwelling. The image flickered and lost its sharpness for an instant and then strengthened once again. After a few hours, the four figures exited the building and made their way in the darkness to the beach, where Perdon witnessed them disappear, impossibly, into the apparently solid cliff face. There had been no sign of plasma fire, either by Prua Landi or directed against her. Yet she had returned to the cubicle, severely burned, and with a splinter of wood lodged in the control device on her wrist.

Perdon worked through the problem in his mind. There would be little point in presenting Prua Landi with anything less than an infallible theory to explain the events. Unless he had a death wish, he must work out exactly what occurred and let the dictatrix decide whether or not to believe him.

He returned with the viewer to the point where the last of the four had entered the house, and the image flickered once again, momentarily losing its clarity. Perdon watched the events several times, and every time there was the temporary loss of clarity, which seemed to eliminate a fault in the remote viewer. And if the glitch was not part of the viewer, then it must be a part of time itself. The answer came as a relief – although he feared Prua Landi would be murderously angry at the implications. Perdon experienced mixed emotions as he set off to tell her the news.

Prua Landi lay in a hospital bed, still confined within a healing suit. She was awake and, though the nanosalve had reduced the pain of her burns to a tolerable level, she was in a particularly vile temper. All around her bedside, doctors scurried about to ensure that everything possible was being done, all fearful of feeling the whip of her tongue. A guard met Perdon at the door, jabbing the muzzle of a plasma rifle painfully into the scientist's ribcage.

"State your business," the guard ordered tersely.

"I am Perdon," he replied, "and I am here to see My Lady."

"Nobody other than medics is permitted to enter," the guard informed him, prodding him once again with the muzzle of his weapon. "Get out of here, before my finger slips on the firing stud."

The scientist stood his ground. "My Lady is expecting me. Do you wish to be the one to tell her you have sent me away; or worse, that you have succumbed to a fit of stupidity and murdered me?"

Confused by Perdon's belligerent attitude, the guard considered the options for a few seconds, before telling him, "Wait here!"

Perdon waited. Moments later, the guard returned and ushered him inside.

Prua Landi stared balefully at him from the confines of her healing suit. "Well?" she demanded, her venomous tone indicative of her continuing foul mood.

Perdon, his feathers still ruffled from the treatment he had received at the hands of the guard, found himself snapping back, "You should inform your personal guards that I am in your confidence, My Lady. The idiot outside your door tried to send me away and then threatened to kill me. That, My Lady, is not the best way to maintain the loyalty I have always shown to you."

Prua Landi's hard gaze softened a little. "So, Perdon is not the meek little mouse his previous behaviour promised. Beneath the mild, accommodating exterior, there beats the heart of a . . . what? Tell me, Perdon, for I must confess I am both surprised and heartened that at least one of my subjects has the guts to stand up to me like a man."

Gaining courage from the fact that Prua Landi hadn't called in the guard to carry out his threat, Perdon replied, "The heart of your most loyal servant, My Lady."

The dictatrix nodded. "As you are proving to be," she told him. "Now, tell me what you have discovered about what happened to me."

"What I have discovered, is *absolutely nothing*, My Lady." Prua Landi's facial expression instantly mirrored the transition in her mood from almost friendly to potentially murderous. "But the *nothing* tells me a great deal."

"Explain, Perdon. And please believe me, I am in no mood for riddles."

The scientist knew that he had walked a dangerous line for the past few minutes, which had, due to a quirk of Prua Landi's character, succeeded in gaining him a small measure of kudos. To stretch the line would likely end in its breaking, with fatal results for him. "My Lady," he explained, "I searched the period before and after your projection into the past, and found nothing to suggest that you had ever been there."

The dictatrix fingered the burnt flesh of her face. "Does this tell you that I imagined being fired on with a plasma rifle?"

"No, My Lady. I watched the four figures enter the building as you personally must have done, and I followed them with the viewer as they left some hours later and returned to the beach."

The eyes regarding him from the confines of the healing suit became flinty. "And this is the *nothing* to which you refer?"

"It is. But there was also a tiny fluctuation in the image immediately after they entered the dwelling, which might easily have been due to a fault in the viewer. So I checked – a great many times – and the anomaly was present every time. Which indicated that the anomaly was part of the flow of time itself."

"And what did the anomaly tell you?"

"That someone erased the incident as though it never happened. I suspect that the only person in that particular time period who knows that you were ever there, is the one who manipulated time."

Prua Landi listened to Perdon's explanation with an increasing sense of frustration. The damnable Faithful sect possessed superior technology, enabling them to travel further, and more accurately, through time. Now, it seemed, they also possessed the ability to manipulate time itself, to expunge events at will. Why, she wondered, was she surrounded by incompetents who could neither emulate the technology of the rebels, nor provide her with the hope that they would ever do so?

"Is there a way for you to achieve such technology?" she demanded.

"At the moment, no, My Lady, because the Faithful are many years ahead of us in their science. But, if I might make a suggestion?"

"Go ahead."

Perdon, gaining in confidence, began, "Improving your ability to traverse time is not of primary importance. You should be

135

made aware that you are alive at this moment due to an outrageous stroke of good fortune."

Prua Landi was intrigued. "Explain!" she said.

"The tree, when subjected to plasma fire, exploded violently, projecting splinters of wood and bark all around. The heat of the plasma fire would pass through even the most violent explosion and should have instantly vaporised you. The reason why you are still here is that a tiny sliver of tree bark triggered your time control, returning you home before you felt the full effects of the plasma fire. You were, indeed, fortunate to survive, My Lady."

"So it would seem," Prua Landi commented drily. "Tell me, where is this story heading?"

"My first priority must be to provide you with a time control, which will instantly return you home if subjected to extreme heat or pressure. Only then will I feel I have done my best to protect you as you travel through time."

"I see," mused Prua Landi, her expression softening slightly. "Were it in my nature, I believe I might be touched by your concern for my safety."

Perdon said nothing for a few moments, surprised by the uncharacteristic mellowing in Prua Landi's attitude. Eventually, he said, "I am also working on the construction of a larger cubicle, capable of transporting up to three persons, so that you may be accompanied by two bodyguards. Unfortunately, I cannot find a way around the apparent limit on the size and potency of the energy weapons you are able to carry."

Prua Landi was immediately interested. "When?" she enquired.

"By the time My Lady regains her health," Perdon answered, the cubicle should be fully tested."

"I am pleased that someone is at last striving to give me the tools I need to seek out and eliminate the priesthood of the Faithful. Now, Perdon, before you leave me to the rest the medics insist that I need, there is a conundrum, which plagues me like an itch I cannot scratch." She glanced at her body and hands, immobile in the confines of the healing suit, and a smile touched her lips at the irony of her words.

"What is it, My Lady?"

"On several occasions, I have tried to enter the mind of the primitive, Jo-lang, who, I am inclined to believe, is the Futama to whom the Faithful pay homage. He has repelled my telepathic probes, although you are aware that no other is able to resist the power of my mind. Tell me, how can this be?"

Perdon's mind was in turmoil beneath his calm exterior. The legendary Futama was proving to be more than a legend. "I can give you an opinion, My Lady," he answered, "but that's all it is – opinion, as I have no data from which to form a theory. I can only imagine that his ability is due to a fault in his genetic make-up. Remember, he comes from a time before the advent of controlled fertilization, growth and nurture. He could be the result of nothing more sinister than a freak genetic accident."

"Nevertheless, he continues to thwart me," Prua Landi informed the scientist, "and, as you can see, it galls me." She stared hard at Perdon before subsiding into the comforting folds of the healing suit. "Keep me informed of your progress," she said, permitting a smile to soften the austere line of her mouth. "I will inform the captain of my guard that you must be permitted to see me at *all* times."

Smiling inwardly at the emphasis the dictatrix had placed upon the word, Perdon departed the medical facility and headed for the laboratory, his mind unexpectedly full of thoughts of the Futama.

Chapter Fourteen

AGENT:

The curtain shimmered behind them as Joe led the others through the time-gate into the tunnel complex. Romana had expressed her intention to test whether anyone, other than Joe, was attuned to the frieze but, as Joe was the only person, apart from Or-gon, who could identify the frieze in question, he led the way. Minutes later, they stood before the deeply-carved surface and Romana uncharacteristically hesitated.

"What's wrong?" Joe demanded.

"After your experience, I'm a little worried what might happen when we touch the frieze," she informed him.

"I wouldn't worry," Joe told her, "because I don't think it'll work for you. It didn't work for Or-gon, and it would be a bit strange if no one had accidentally touched the frieze in all the time since the complex was built."

Encouraged by Joe's words, Romana laid her hands on the carving and withdrew them moments later with a mixture of relief and disappointment. Analy and Trione followed suit with exactly the same result.

"Would the Futama agree to test the frieze?" Analy asked.

"Why not?" Joe agreed, stepping forward with his palms outstretched.

Romana's long fingers grasped his shoulder. "Would the Futama permit us to see what he sees?"

"If you think it'll work. By all means, grab hold of my mind and enjoy the ride," Joe told them, placing both palms firmly against the surface of the frieze.

Immediately, Joe's mind was assailed by a kaleidoscope of images and data as the frieze decanted more information into his memory. Its impact was like a physical force and Joe staggered backwards into the others. Strong hands held him upright as he lolled sideways like a puppet on loose strings. The omnipresent light in the ceiling and walls of the tunnel spun alarmingly around him as his brain attempted to rectify the trauma to his balance but, eventually, the spinning stopped to be replaced by the grandfather of all headaches. His legs felt as if someone had removed the bones, leaving just the soft marrow. As Trione and Analy held him upright,

Romana immediately applied her medical diagnostic to his trembling form, discovering nothing physically amiss.

"D-did you catch anything?" Joe gasped.

"Very little," Romana informed him soothingly. "All I saw was a few scattered images."

Analy and Trione admitted to much the same experience.

"Well, I reckon I've had the contents of a supercomputer dropped into my head," Joe complained, "and I'm not too sure I could take another experience like that."

"Did you learn anything new?" Romana asked.

"Probably," Joe told her, "but it'll take some time to get it sorted into some kind of order in my mind."

"We apologise for your discomfort," Romana told him, "but, as we anticipated, we have, indeed, learned of another facet of your specialised nanos. I believe," she added, "the time has come to report to our base commander. It has been an interesting twenty-four hours."

*　*　*

Leiki was just entering his office as they arrived. He greeted them warmly and ushered them inside. "Please sit down," he invited, offering them tall drinks of pale liquid from a dispenser in the corner of the room. The drink seemed to suffuse Joe with a sense of calm well-being.

"Well," the base commander queried genially, "how was the Futama's visit to his wife and unborn child?"

Romana, Analy and Trione glanced at each other almost guiltily, like children called upon to explain the aftermath of a prank that had gone wrong. As usual, Romana assumed responsibility for explaining.

"The Futama has returned safely," she began, "and is eagerly anticipating his journey to Mars to meet with the Supreme Council of Elders."

"And did everything go smoothly?" Leiki probed, a smile hovering on his lips.

Joe's companions looked thoroughly miserable. They had supported his need to return home, and now, on their return to the compound, they were realising the full implications had Prua Landi succeeded in killing him.

"We had a bit of trouble," Joe told Leiki. "Prua Landi took pot-shots at us outside my home, but my bodyguards," he stretched

139

to place his arms around the shoulders of Analy and Trione, "gave her more than she bargained for. We didn't find any trace of her afterwards, but those plasma rifles don't leave much behind, do they?"

Leiki shook his head and handed over a handwritten note. "You may find this interesting. I received this report shortly before your return. It is the work of one of our agents who is close to Prua Landi."

Joe intercepted the note as Leiki handed it to Romana. He scanned its contents and was astounded to discover that the swirls and curlicues of the script made sense to him. He realised instantly that his new-found ability must be connected to his recent encounter with the frieze. As he ran his eyes over the note, he groaned, "The lucky bitch. What were the chances of that happening?"

He handed the note over to Romana, who read it with increasing astonishment and passed it to Analy and Trione. The report told of Prua Landi's return to her own time, badly burned and incredibly fortunate to have survived the plasma fire. It mentioned Perdon's theory that a sliver of wood had triggered her return as the tree entered the first microseconds of its destruction.

Romana was deep in thought as Joe's two bodyguards read the note. Suddenly, she exclaimed, "How can the Futama have learned to read the commander's note?"

Four pairs of eyes fixed Joe with enquiring stares.

"It must have been that bloody frieze," Joe told them. "My head was filled with so much data that it's only just starting to sort itself out in my mind."

The mention of the frieze came as one more surprise to Leiki. "Perhaps someone had better start at the beginning," he suggested, looking Romana in the eye, "so that I may write a full report."

Romana told of their return to Joe's home and her discovery of Joe's advanced nanos, which now also inhabited the body of his wife, Ciara. She described the attack upon them by Prua Landi, hesitating for a moment before explaining about Joe's erasure of the event from the timeline by the agency of the timestone. Leiki's eyebrows rose at the mention of the timestone; even at his level within the hierarchy of the Faithful, he had never heard mention of such a device. His admiration for the high council grew with the realisation that the Futama's pathway had been planned in such intricate detail.

"Continue," he told Romana.

She explained her theory about the effects of the specialised nanos in Joe's system and Ciara's improving ability due to the increasing numbers of secondaries in her body.

When she had finished Leiki grinned broadly. "It seems that for someone from such a primitive age, the Futama has adjusted to our technology as easily as he adapted to the ways of the cavemen."

Joe accepted the accolade from the base commander with his usual modesty. "Whether you're in the distant past or the distant future, it's all a matter of common sense, isn't it?" he said. "I keep telling you, I'm just an ordinary guy who happens to be in an extraordinary situation. There's nothing special about me, except, I suppose, the fact that someone's shot me full of nanos so that I can tread a bit of a convoluted path through time."

Leiki could sense that Joe was becoming a little bored with the discussion. "You must be hungry," he told them. "Let us eat, because we leave for Mars in a few hours."

"You are coming too?" Romana enquired.

"It has been my duty to await the coming of the Futama, and now I must accompany him to Mars." Leiki informed her. "We five leave soon on the Master of Time. Once we reach Mars, the pretence will end and everyone will be told that their Futama is among them. Then, Joe will witness the extent and fervour of his following."

* * *

"You called for me, My Lady?" Perdon enquired.

Prua Landi sat in a comfortable chair, the healing suit no longer a necessity, although the skin of her face remained a patchwork where the nanosalve continued to rebuild the tissue. "I did," she said, almost genially. "Is there any news of progress?" she asked, although it was less than two days since her narrow escape from death.

"We have constructed a three-man unit, though it is still only capable of projection to the time of your, er . . . accident. The remote viewer can now focus a little more than four-hundred thousand years beyond that, but the Faithful are nowhere to be seen in that particular era." The scientist added wistfully, "Although we are making progress, it is pitifully slow, and it would be advantageous to have an agent amongst their ranks who could hand us exact details of the science behind their time travel devices. And then the damnable Faithful might feel the full strength of My Lady's wrath."

Prua Landi grimaced from the residual pain of her still-healing flesh, but still more from injured pride. The experience had focused her mind on her quest to destroy the Faithful and their Futama. It was proving propitious for her that Perdon had arisen from amongst the ranks of mediocre scientific advisors; he was someone she could almost admire but, most of all, he was someone she increasingly felt she could trust. And he was working tirelessly to give her the technology she craved. She beckoned the scientist closer and placed her scarred hand upon his wrist.

Perdon felt her warm, dry touch, unsure what was required of him. "My Lady?" he ventured.

The dictatrix grasped his hand firmly, although the action caused her considerable pain. "Perdon, you cannot imagine how lonely can be the lives of those who rule. One can never be certain whom to draw into one's circle of trust, but— " she treated Perdon to an imperious stare, "—you are proving to be a loyal friend."

The scientist was stunned at Prua Landi's unexpected admission. "Thank you," he said softly, "I'm honoured, My Lady."

Prua Landi, realising that she had permitted an unsuspected aspect of her nature to surface, quickly reverted to type. Her voice hardened. "There is such a one amongst the ranks of the Faithful."

"A spy?" Perdon demanded in astonishment.

"Yes, I have an agent who infiltrated the sect and escaped with them to the past. What galls me is that I have no way of knowing what he has discovered – or even if he is still alive." She caressed Perdon's wrist sensually. "Find a way to contact him and you will discover that my generosity knows no limits."

Perdon's mind was in turmoil. Whilst admitting that she had a spy within the ranks of the Faithful, Prua Landi had also offered him boundless reward: including, if he had read the signs correctly, herself. "I shall redouble my efforts on My Lady's behalf," he informed her, "beginning immediately."

Releasing his hand, Prua Landi waved him away. "See that you do," she said, "our future may depend on it."

* * *

Joe, accompanied by Leiki and the others, sat at a table in the refectory, consuming a surprisingly tasty meal. Analy paused from

142

eating to remark that the food was less appetising than the flesh of the dead animal.

Joe grinned. "I never thought I'd gain a convert to eating meat," he remarked.

Trione shuddered; he had already expressed his revulsion at the practice, and even discussing the concept filled him with overwhelming disgust. "Please change the subject," he told Analy tersely. "Let us talk about more civilised matters."

Even Leiki's usual affability had deserted him and Romana continued to eat in silence.

"In that case," Joe said, "when do we set off for Mars?"

"The Master of Time is almost ready," Leiki informed him, "and Captain Terpin is eager to have you aboard. He was most impressed by your rescue efforts, and he has expressed the desire to speak with you at greater length than was possible on your return from the Moon."

"That's okay with me," Joe replied, remembering the respect with which the captain had treated him.

A group entered the refectory, led by Marron, now apparently fully recovered from his injuries. Joe saw they were mostly crewmembers of the ill-fated ship. Marron glanced across the room and spotted Joe amongst the four tall figures. He strode over. "Commander Leiki, may I have your permission to speak with Jo-lang, alone?"

"You may speak with him here," Leiki told him.

"Very well!" Marron was displaying a degree of discomfort. "I'm glad," he said, "to have the opportunity to thank Jo-lang for saving my life and the lives of my crew. Commander Orina has informed me that, without his intervention, all my crew would have perished. For that, I will always be in his debt."

"You're welcome," Joe told him, "any time."

Marron shifted uncomfortably from one foot to the other; it was clear he wished to say something more to Joe, but felt unable to do so in the present company. At last, he said, "Thank you, once again," and left to rejoin his crew.

"Something's eating him," Joe commented, "and I've got a feeling it's about me."

Leiki smiled. "Perhaps it is because he owes you his life and has difficulty in reconciling the fact that he dislikes you."

"Dunno," Joe grinned, "but I wish I could be certain. I must admit I'm a bit uneasy whenever he's around."

"Then the feeling of unease should not last for long, because Marron will remain on this base when we leave for Mars. Which," he consulted a device on his wrist, "will be when we have finished our meal. Captain Terpin informs me that the Master of Time is now ready for take-off."

Joe was pleasantly surprised by the news, because he had expected to wait several more hours. He returned to his meal with renewed vigour and his plate was soon empty. His companions followed suit and Trione collected the tableware and pushed it all into a receptacle set into the wall. As they exited the refectory, Joe glanced over his shoulder to where Marron was eating with his crew, and he could have sworn that he saw an expression of alarm flit across Marron's face. Shaking his head in puzzlement, Joe followed the others out of the tunnel complex into the bright sunlight of the compound, where the Master of Time stood upon her tripod legs awaiting them. There was one other ship in the compound, the *Lunar Sunrise*, parked surprisingly close to the vast bulk of Captain Terpin's vessel, and Joe decided it must have been the one, which brought the shipless Marron and his crew from the Moon.

Moments after Joe's group left the refectory Captain Marron rose hurriedly from the table and followed them at a discreet distance.

Immediately they stepped from the top of the ramp into the vessel's interior, the ramp whined shut with a clang that reverberated through the hull. Terpin welcomed them aboard and ushered them to their seats, offering Joe a chair specially adapted to accommodate his smaller stature. Moments later, the whole ship resonated as her systems came alive. A plain, curved wall became a control panel as lights and screens appeared, as if by magic, in the smooth surface.

Two crewmembers rapidly scanned the multiple screens. Finally, the clear, feminine tones of the AI said, "I am ready, Captain."

"Initialise," Terpin commanded.

* * *

Marron stood at the entrance to the tunnel complex and watched the Master of Time preparing to make the transition to the primeval past. Cursing Joe for an interfering primitive, he turned on his heel and strode back into the tunnel towards the refectory. He had just rounded a corner when the pressure wave from a mighty explosion threw him violently against the tunnel wall. The rumbling of falling rock reverberated along the tunnel and a wall of choking dust swept over him as he lay, semiconscious, on the hard floor.

Minutes later, as consciousness slowly returned, he climbed to his feet and leaned on the wall to allow his head to clear. Hawking and spitting gobbets of dusty mucus from his throat, he staggered back towards the daylight, to discover that the tunnel entrance had been reshaped by the explosion. Its perfectly curved lines were now ragged and the opening was more than twice its original size. Clambering over the fallen rocks he saw that, to one side, the cliff face had collapsed, sending a cascade of rocky debris all the way across the compound, destroying more than half the perimeter fence.

A vast crater now occupied the place where the Lunar Sunrise had once stood beside the Master of Time, but there was no sign of either ship, not even the smallest piece of shrapnel. The area of the perimeter fence left untouched by the rock fall had succumbed to the power of the explosion. The powerful force-field no longer existed and the inner fence was now a series of ragged poles, half-buried in the shattered earthwork that had once proudly protected the compound from the predations of savage beasts. Trees as much as fifty metres inwards from the edge of the forest lay splintered and broken, their foliage ablaze from the intense heat generated by the blast.

With a satisfied shrug, Marron retreated into the tunnel to call for assistance from Commander Orina on the Moon. With the demise of Commander Leiki and the captains of both vessels, he was the highest-ranking officer, and it fell to him to organise defence of the base from the local predators until help arrived and the force-field could be rebuilt. An enquiry was certain to follow and Marron knew he had to get his account of the events of the preceding few minutes clear in his mind.

* * *

Captain Terpin's command to initialise the time transfer was accompanied by a blinding flash, which blanked out the screens before they could automatically dim, and Joe felt a painful wrench in his stomach, as though someone had reached inside his abdomen and tried to pull his spine through his navel. The ship lurched uncharacteristically sideways and all the computer screens winked

145

out. The interior of the ship was plunged into darkness and emergency systems came into operation, shedding a pale half-light over the bridge. Joe had been catapulted from his seat and was having difficulty in breathing due to a heavy body lying prone across his face. He had just managed to wriggle free, when he felt a hand grasp his wrist and haul him upright. It was Trione, who was now helping Romana to her feet. One by one Joe saw everyone pick themselves up and he heard Captain Terpin's voice crisply demanding a status report.

"Captain," the navigator answered worriedly, "the main drives are all functional but all time control systems are down. It is unclear which eon we are in."

Joe raced up to the observatory situated at the highest point of the hull, which afforded a three-hundred and sixty degree field of view of the terrain around the ship. The vessel was perched precariously on the edge of a low precipice above a fiery river of molten lava. All around him, the black, basaltic rocks contained dully-glowing pockets of heat. The ship seemed to have landed in the caldera of an active volcano. Even from the vantage point of the observatory, several metres above ground level, Joe was unable to see the rim in any direction, which suggested the volcano was immense. In every direction, he could see plumes of orange-tinted gases rising towards the black of the heavens – and that made no sense whatsoever, because he could also see the sun in the sky.

It took Joe several seconds to wrest an answer to the conundrum from his sluggish mind – the sky was black because there was only the barest traces of an atmosphere. He looked away from the sun, and the vault of the heavens sparkled with millions of points of light. But there was something dreadfully amiss: many of the point of light were moving about randomly in the darkness and *that* had to be impossible; for even in his confused state, Joe knew that stars and planets were too far away for their motion to be visible. He gazed in fascination at the mad dance of the tiny lights only to be brought out of his reverie by the spectacular impact of a meteor somewhere over the horizon.

A white-hot column of magma climbed rapidly towards space, quickly losing its heat as the rock solidified in the vacuum. Less than twenty seconds later, the ship bucked and tilted as a succession of seismic ripples from the impact flowed like glutinous sine waves through the barely solidified rock upon which the ship was standing. The ship trembled and her tripod legs sank two or

146

three metres, and Joe knew they were in very real peril of sinking through the thin crust into the lava below.

He raced back down to the bridge and called urgently to Terpin, "Captain, we've got to get out of here fast!"

Terpin reacted immediately to Joe's anxiety, because he was telepathically radiating alarm on a subconscious level. "What is it?" he demanded.

"I don't know how far back in time we are," Joe exclaimed, "but I think the Earth hasn't fully formed yet. That rocking of the ship was caused by seismic waves from a sizeable meteor impact just over the horizon. It's made us sink into the crust, but that's not the real problem. The impact blasted a huge amount of matter into space and what goes up, must come down. I don't think it'll be long before the first rain of debris strikes us."

Calmly, the captain assured him that the Master of Time's shields were fully functional, as was the antigravity system. Minor adjustments to the antigravity would ensure that the ship sank no lower into the crust, and the shield would, in all probability, prove effective against the larger debris because it would not be travelling at high speed."

"Are you certain?" Joe exclaimed, "because it was a pretty big meteor strike and I reckon all hell will be let loose when the rocks begin to rain down with no atmosphere to slow them down."

"Perhaps you're right," Terpin admitted. "Our shields have never been tested in such extreme conditions."

"Then we've got to get out of here before it hits us." Joe urged.

"Heron is working on the problem," Terpin informed him. "It seems that the AI was stunned by the violence of our transition, much as a human being would be if subjected to a blow to the head. The AI has regained consciousness and is in the process of resetting her atomic clocks. She will then be able to recalibrate the time displacement device and move the ship out of danger."

The computer screens caught Joe's attention as they suddenly flickered into life. Half of the screens portrayed the terrain outside the vessel, which was punctuated by a succession of increasingly violent impacts as the meteoritic debris rained down all around, blasting plumes of fiery matter back into the sky.

The AI's voice cut through the bridge, "Please be seated."

Joe rushed to his chair as he felt the familiar wrench in his gut, signifying that the ship had made a jump through time. The screens showed that the ship was standing upon a barren, rocky plain, with no indication that life had ever existed there. Water was pouring from the skies in a deluge the likes of which Joe had never before witnessed.

"We are now approximately two point five billion years in the past," the AI informed everyone. "The precipitation is extremely acidic," she continued, "and the atmosphere outside the ship is inimical to human life. I have sealed the ship completely, whilst I make final adjustments to my clocks. Only then will I be able to transfer to the Late Carboniferous era, which was our original destination."

"AI," Terpin interrupted, "I have decided to return to the compound, in order to investigate the reason behind this incident."

"I reckon you're right," Joe opined.

"Very well," the AI agreed primly, "I will inform you when we are ready for the transfer."

Joe grinned and commented, "She sounds like my old primary school teacher. *She* didn't like being told what to do either."

Joe's levity had the effect of raising spirits on The Master of Time. Everyone on board had his or her own thoughts on what might have happened, and everyone was expecting to discover that the compound had suffered some kind of disaster. Whilst they waited for the familiar wrench in their guts, signalling the jump through time, Joe wished aloud that he could have recorded the conditions outside the ship with his camcorder. With a tiny portion of her consciousness, the AI assured him that her memory contained a complete record of the event, which she could download into his camcorder providing that Captain Terpin agreed. Joe made a mental note to ask the captain at the first opportunity.

148

Chapter Fifteen

MARS:

As the compound shimmered into existence around the ship, it was clear that all was not well. Two small vessels from the Moon run were parked beside a vast crater in the middle of the compound, and teams of engineers toiled to erect a new force-field around the area. Supplies were stacked in the open, because the low storage buildings had disappeared as though they had never existed, an indicator of the terrible power of the catastrophe that had struck the compound.

Joe and his companions stepped from the ramp onto the hard earth, which had been scoured of grass by the explosion. They tried to assimilate the scene before them. To Joe, the cave entrance appeared to be pretty much as he remembered it in Too-ga's time, but he had a feeling that there was something else missing. He cast his mind back to the moment when he had boarded the Master of Time, picturing the relative positions of the ships within the compound. He had walked beneath the outer rim of the Lunar Sunrise to enable him to reach the boarding ramp of the time-ship, and he had the sudden realisation that the crater had taken the place of the shuttle ship. Which indicated that the Lunar Sunrise was at the epicentre of the explosion that had wrought such devastation to the compound. If the destruction of the Lunar Sunrise was responsible for the Master of Time's projection into the primeval past of almost four billion years ago, the question arose as to whether the explosion was caused deliberately. If so, it was almost certain that the murky fingerprints of Prua Landi would be upon it.

A voice, hailing from the entrance to the tunnel, brought Joe out of his reverie. It was Orina, commander of the Moon base. She strode over and embraced Leiki, and Romana's eyebrows rose in surprise at the unexpectedness of the emotional display.

"We feared the Master of Time and all aboard her had been lost," she told Leiki, "and it's good to know we were wrong."

"We had a lucky escape," Leiki advised her. "In fact we travelled almost to the time of the creation of our planet. But," his eyes lingered on the scene around him, his expression mirroring his pain, "it seems we were more fortunate than the crew of the Lunar Sunrise. I assume there were no survivors."

Orina's eyes filled with sadness. "None", she whispered.

149

"Have you begun an investigation?" Leiki asked

"Yes, and I have ordered the arrest of Captain Marron."

Leiki was intrigued. "Why Marron?"

"I have given the problem much thought," Orina explained, "and Captain Marron has a lot of explaining to do. Why, I wonder, did he pilot an unspaceworthy ship to the Moon, causing the only crash in living memory? His crewmembers have testified that he followed Jo-lang outside when he boarded the Master of Time. Why, then, was he virtually unhurt by the explosion? I have also been informed that Marron personally landed the Lunar Sunrise as near as possible to the Master of Time in order, he said, to demonstrate his skill as a pilot. There are also a few other unanswered questions, which we should discuss in your office."

Leiki thought back to the message he had received about a spy within the ranks of the Faithful, and he could see that Orina had a point. He nodded. "Perhaps we will find it more comfortable in the refectory," he told her.

Leiki, Orina, Joe and his three companions were seated in the refectory when Marron walked in, escorted by two guards. The base commander dismissed the two guards, who were immediately replaced by Analy and Trione. Orina glanced enquiringly at Leiki.

"What happens here must be restricted to those present," Leiki told her.

"Is this to be some kind of trial?" Marron sneered.

"No, merely an inquiry," Leiki replied coldly. "If a trial is necessary, it will take place on Mars, before the full Council of Elders. Meanwhile, are you prepared to answer questions?"

"Why not?" Marron replied. "I have done no wrong, except perhaps, to pilot an unsafe ship to the Moon. Which, I assure you, I was entirely unaware was unsafe. I was under the impression that all repairs had been completed to a satisfactory standard. The engineers who misinformed me will be made to pay for their incompetence in due course."

"I see," said Leiki, "then let us begin with your obvious enmity towards Jo-lang?"

"Are there not people amongst the Faithful whom you dislike?" Marron demanded. And before Leiki could answer, Marron continued, "And this primitive creature," he waved his hand airily in Joe's direction, "is not even one of our number."

Joe felt his hackles rise at the reference to him as a primitive creature. "That's not the first time you've called me primitive," he warned Marron, "so you'd better be careful. I might just forget I like a peaceful life."

From the vantage point of his extra thirty-five centimetres height, Marron stared disdainfully at the smaller man, whom he outweighed by a considerable amount. He snorted in amusement. "Your primitive ways do not impress me, Jo-lang," he sneered, but Joe had already risen angrily to his feet.

Analy and Trione immediately stepped forward to restrain Marron, but he threw off their hands and stepped towards Joe, who stood his ground like a latter-day David before Marron's Goliath. The guards stepped back and levelled their plasma rifles at Marron and Joe screamed, "No! You'll wipe out everybody in the room!"

They fell back uncertainly, unaccustomed to the concept of close-quarter combat, where weapons were inimical to friend and foe alike. Marron chose that moment to lunge forward, and grasp Joe by the throat with the long fingers of one hand, in an attempt to choke the life out of the smaller man. Joe reacted instinctively, grasping and twisting the big man's wrist, forcing his hand from its grip on his neck and into an arm lock, at the same instant slamming the outside edge of his boot into Marron's unprotected knee joint. With a sickening crack, the knee joint gave way and Marron collapsed onto the floor, screaming and writhing in agony. Joe released Marron's wrist and stepped back, breathing heavily from the rivers of adrenaline coursing through his veins.

He glowered at his disabled attacker. "Keep your insults to yourself in future, because next time—" He let the threat tail off as he fought to regain control over his emotions. "Next time things might get a bit nasty."

Analy and Trione stepped forward and dragged Marron, who was groaning in agony, across the large room, then stood patiently, with their plasma rifles trained upon the injured man. Romana tended to Marron, expertly straightening the fractured limb, in order to enable the nanomedics to complete the healing process without leaving him with a twisted leg. The nanomedics began their work by dulling the pain responses, and Marron was able to accept her ministrations with a little less discomfort.

As Romana bent over him, Marron hissed, "Why do you defer to this primitive creature?"

"Take care," she warned him, "because the Futama *will* keep his promise if you continue to hurl insults at him."

Marron's face turned an ashen shade beneath his bronze tan. "The Futama?" he whispered. "This insignificant primitive is the Futama?"

"He is."

"I was expecting a god," Marron confessed, "not this pale creature from our primeval past."

"You seem to forget that this 'pale creature', as you so derisively call him, has just snapped your leg like a dry twig," Romana reminded him. "Admittedly, he does not take the form of a god, but still, he is our Futama." Romana decided to make an impromptu attempt to trick Marron into a confession, whilst he was distracted by the pain of his injury. "Then the Futama was not your primary target when you destroyed the Lunar Sunrise?"

Marron laughed mirthlessly. "If I were to admit to causing the explosion, the Futama would not enter into the equation. If I were an agent of Prua Landi, I would try to break communications with Mars by destroying the Master of Time. But, as I am not an agent—" He let the words hang in the air, and Romana knew that a confession would not be forthcoming.

Across the room, Orina was still digesting the events of the preceding few minutes. She had experience of Joe's bravery during his Moon rescue, and now he had demonstrated that he could take care of himself in a fight against a much bigger man. She had nursed her suspicions about Joe's identity since that first encounter, and now she felt it was time to ask outright.

"Jo-lang," she asked, deferentially, "am I in the presence of the Futama?"

"You are," Joe told her, "but, for reasons of security, only those in this room know who I am and we'd like to keep it that way, at least until we get to Mars."

Romana rejoined them, saying, "Joe, I have foolishly informed Marron of your true identity in the hope that he might confess to the destruction of the Lunar Sunrise. Unfortunately, he admitted nothing."

"What did he say?" Joe asked.

Romana paraphrased Marron's hypothetical confession.

"Makes sense," Joe admitted. "Even if he didn't know who I was, it would be a good ploy to break the communications link with Mars. It would cut you off from the rest of your people, and that would be quite a coup for Prua Landi, wouldn't it?"

152

Leiki had been deep in thought since the confrontation between Joe and Marron. "I received warning of an agent of Prua Landi in our midst before we boarded the Master of Time, and I'm now certain the information was correct. The destruction of the Master of Time would have hurt our cause immeasurably, and the incidental death of the Futama would have destroyed us. Marron will travel with us to appear before the High Council, who will ascertain his guilt, or innocence, beyond all question of doubt."

"When do you intend to transfer to Mars," Orina asked, "because I would like to accompany the Futama on that momentous day."

Leiki smiled sadly. "Your place is here. We need you to supervise the rebuilding of the compound, in preparation for when the Futama returns with an army to defeat Prua Landi and re-establish our birthright."

"Then the sooner that is achieved, the better," Orina commented, "and we can all look forward to going home."

* * *

As the Master of Time transferred to the past, Joe experienced the usual constriction in his abdomen. But the sensation evaporated as swiftly as it had begun, even as his companions rose from their seats.

"Is something wrong?" he demanded.

"No, Jo-lang," Captain Terpin assured him, "we have merely completed the first part of our journey. We are now in the late Carboniferous era of a little more than three-hundred million years before your time."

"Really?" Joe exclaimed. "Can I experience what it's like outside?"

Terpin glanced enquiringly at Leiki, who nodded. "For a short while only, as we must soon resume our journey to Mars. Please take care. Some of the indigenous life forms are highly dangerous."

"Thanks," Joe told him, unslinging his camcorder from his shoulder and checking it out. He hadn't yet learned to trust the power pack Heron had provided on the journey back from the Moon; to Joe, a power source with the life-expectancy described by Heron, seemed too good to be true. However, all the correct lights came on, signalling that the camcorder was ready for action. He followed Analy and Trione down the ramp and out from beneath the shadow of the mighty ship. His spirits rose as he breathed the pristine air and he felt full of energy. Trione explained that his high spirits were due to the oxygen levels in this era being much higher than he was accustomed to.

He examined the area around him. The Master of Time was perched on top of a low hill, surrounded by mist-covered swamp, which vanished in the distance into the verdure of a forest. Clumps of clubmosses, tree ferns and horsetails clung tenaciously to tiny islands in the swampland, thrusting their emerald green topknots above the mist to catch the sunlight. Through the viewfinder, he saw a large insect heading towards Trione and he followed its movements as it zig-zagged along. When it was almost upon them, Joe realised it was a giant dragonfly, with a wingspan of at least sixty centimetres, hawking back and forth for its prey. The insect was a dazzling blend of iridescent blues and greens, sparkling in the sunlight above the low-lying mist.

As he made his way downhill toward the edge of the swamp, a movement in the low vegetation caught his eye, and he was astonished to see a two metre long, bright yellow millipede, with a seemingly inexhaustible supply of flame red legs, cross his path. As the creature re-entered the vegetation it was ambushed by a giant scorpion, which scurried forward and buried a ten-centimetre sting in its head. The millipede thrashed and twisted in a mighty effort to escape its attacker, but the scorpion held on until its venom sac was empty. By then the millipede was weakening and Joe watched with a sense of awe as it rapidly lost the unequal fight. He knew about millipedes and scorpions, but not on this enormous scale. He turned away to return to the ship, and discovered that his two bodyguards were standing on full alert, with their plasma weapons directed at the scorpion, which had settled down to consume its meal.

"If the many-legged creature had not crossed your path, you would have probably become the prey," Analy remarked sardonically. "Though your nanomedics would have eradicated the venom from your body, you would have suffered several hours of severe pain."

"It's happened before, then?" Joe queried.

"I fell victim myself," the tall man told him, "on my first trip. Since that time, I have always treated the creatures around this landing site with extreme caution."

"Thanks for the warning, anyway." Joe allowed himself a lingering look at the misty swamp and the distant forest, before walking the short distance to the ramp beneath the Master of Time, all the while wondering what twenty-first century adventurers would be prepared to give to be in his shoes. He had lived with Neanderthals at differing levels of their evolution; he had stepped onto the Moon and been part of a rescue mission there; he was presently breathing the oxygen-rich air of the late Carboniferous period on his journey to a fertile Mars, and he seemed destined to lead the Faithful on a quest to return to their own time in the distant future. All things considered, it was quite an adventure for an ordinary guy.

Leiki greeted him as he entered the bridge. "Have you satisfied your curiosity?" he enquired.

"For the time being," Joe grinned, "but I wouldn't mind coming back when this is all over. I don't mean just to this place. I mean, there's such a lot to see, such vast stretches of time I'd like to experience. You know, the age of the dinosaurs and even some of my . . . *our* early history."

The Master of Time rose smoothly from the surface of the low hill into the oxygen-rich air and headed for space at a rate of acceleration that would have astounded everyone at NASA in Joe's natural time. By the time she reached vacuum, she was travelling at more than thirty-five kilometres per second, with her speed rapidly increasing towards a maximum of more than two-hundred and ninety thousand kilometres every second – almost light speed. Mars was almost at conjunction and Captain Terpin informed everyone that, allowing for acceleration, deceleration and manoeuvring, the journey would take approximately three hours.

"Please make yourselves comfortable," he told his passengers. "You will find drinks and food and games in the refectory to while away the boring hours of your passage to Mars."

"Boring?" Joe exclaimed. "How can anyone find this boring? If you don't mind, Captain, I'd like to spend some time in the observatory. I've still got some tape left and I'd like to film our approach to Mars."

Terpin smiled indulgently. He and everyone else present had completed the trip too many times for the wonder of the event to retain its lustre. "As you wish, Jo-lang," he said. "By your courageous act on the Moon, you have earned the privilege. No one will disturb you, unless you find you need company." The captain accompanied Joe as he made his way towards the observatory with Romana and Trione a few steps behind. "May I speak with you

155

alone?" he enquired. "There are many questions I have wanted to ask you since you travelled from the Moon on my ship."

"Of course, you're the boss," Joe replied, flippantly

The captain favoured Joe with a penetrating stare. "Am I?"

Joe suddenly realised that he would be out of the protection of his bodyguards whilst he was alone with the captain. "Leiki insists that my guards must be with me at all times," he said. "You'll have to come to some sort of agreement with him."

"I have already done so," Terpin informed him, glancing at Romana and Trione, "and he has offered no objections." He halted and a doorway opened silently. "These are my quarters," he said, "we can talk here, in private."

Intrigued by the vaguely secretive nature of Terpin's actions, Joe preceded the captain into the comfortable, roomy cabin, where he accepted the offer of a seat in an oversized armchair.

As he settled in his seat, Joe said, "On second thoughts, I think I'd like Romana to be here, if it's okay with you, Captain Terpin."

"That is understandable," Terpin agreed, and he door immediately opened, allowing Romana to step inside. She accepted a seat beside Joe.

"Would you like to taste our wine?" Terpin asked in a friendly tone.

"Thanks, I will," Joe replied. "Now, what's all this about? If you have questions, ask away and I'll answer as truthfully as I can."

Terpin sat behind his large desk. He rested his elbows on the desk and steepled his long fingers under his chin. "My first question must be, 'Who are you?'"

Joe smiled ingenuously and replied. "Joe Laing. Why, who do you think I am?"

In a serious voice, the ship's captain replied, "I must confess, Jo-lang, that I am puzzled. You display the bravery and selflessness that we Faithful have learned to expect from the one who will come to restore our future. Though," he added, apologetically, "your physical attributes are significantly less impressive than the legend would suggest."

"So," Joe repeated his question, "who do *you* think I am?"

Terpin glanced at Romana but received no assistance from that quarter. He was left with little option but to voice his suspicions. "It is my belief that you are our Futama," he said, his voice tinged with emotion,

156

Joe glanced at Romana, who sipped her wine impassively. "Futama," he enquired, "who or what is a Futama?"

Terpin's face mirrored his disappointment. He was certain that he had interpreted the clues correctly, but Jo-lang was denying all knowledge of the Futama. He tried another angle. "You said that you would answer truthfully. And yet you answer my questions with questions. Please answer as truthfully as you can. Are you our Futama?"

Once again, Joe glanced at Romana, whose eyes held that distant look, which suggested she was communicating telepathically. He heard Leiki's disembodied voice say *You may tell the captain everything.*

The enormity of what he had just experienced hit Joe like a hammer blow. He had just overheard the tail end of Leiki's telepathic conversation with Romana and his mind was filled with wonder – and countless questions – at his newfound ability to read thoughts.

Romana nodded, and the gesture was accompanied by the echo of the words *You may tell him!* in Joe's mind.

Okay! he replied without speaking and the thought brought a look of stunned amazement to Romana's beautiful features.

The interchange had lasted scarcely a second and the echoes of Terpin's question still hung in the air as Joe replied, "In person."

The captain stared at Joe with a mixture of open incredulity and awe. "You are *truly* the Futama?" he whispered. "You would not jest about such matters?"

"I'm not joking," Joe told him, "and I'd like to apologise for not being open with you. It's been Leiki's belief that as few people as possible should know who I am until the High Council is ready to divulge the news. Until that time your silence would be appreciated."

"You have my oath, Futama," Terpin said reverently.

"And that's the first thing you need to do. Call me Joe until circumstances change, okay?"

Terpin nodded. "Am I permitted to ask the Futama other questions?"

"Fire away, and the same rules apply. I'll answer as truthfully as I can."

"When is you time of origin?"

"The twenty-first century, but I suppose you will know it better as the time of the dawn of technology. In my time, our civilisation is only a few thousand years old, and we have only just developed computers and harnessed the power of the atom."

"Ah . . . the time before the dawn of reason," Terpin commented.

"You might well call it that," Joe told him, "when I think of the depressing number of wars that have occurred over the centuries."

The captain stood up behind his desk and bowed. "I'm afraid that I must go to the bridge," he said. "You are welcome to stay here or visit the observatory. My ship is yours, for I am deeply honoured to have you aboard, Jo-lang."

* * *

With his camcorder at the ready, Joe repaired to the observatory to film the fast retreating globe of the Earth as the mighty ship accelerated in a shallow curve towards the fourth of the sun's retinue of planets. There would be no need for complicated slingshot manoeuvres around the Moon in order to gain speed: the Master of Time had pace in abundance, and by the time Joe reached the observation bubble on the upper surface of the craft, the blue green globe of the Earth was visibly smaller and receding at a rapidly increasing rate. Joe made himself comfortable and watched his home planet shrinking into the star-speckled blackness. Within half an hour all he could see was a bright, pea-sized disc, with its attendant white moon, hanging in the infinite darkness, which, a few minutes later, were just a couple of sparkling points to his unaided eye.

The realisation hit Joe that he was millions of miles *and* millions of years from Ciara and home, and he was suddenly overwhelmed by the gulf separating him from his loved ones. A sensation of loneliness and homesickness assailed him and he was unable to prevent unwanted tears from stinging his eyes. It had been many years since he had, at the age of thirteen, cried at his father's bedside as cancer finally claimed the still-young body, and Joe had resolved never to succumb to that kind of emotion again. He heard the sound of footsteps mounting the stairs up to the observation blister. It was Romana. Her soft eyes were full of sadness as she sat down beside him and stared through the plexiglass dome at the bright starfields of the Milky Way galaxy behind him.

"The Futama is full of sadness," she whispered. "He is radiating his pain throughout the ship, such that it is impossible for everyone not to share his despair."

Joe was momentarily stunned. "I thought your people didn't listen in," he protested, wiping the tears from his cheeks.

"We are *your* people," Romana reminded him gently, "and sometimes we are compelled to hear, without listening. Emotions, on a telepathic level, are often more powerful than thoughts."

As Joe stared into Romana's eyes, she moved closer and, with an unexpectedness that caught him completely unawares, the tall medical officer enfolded him in her arms, and embraced him with a tenderness that left him breathless.

"Futama," she soothed, "please let me use my skills to take way your hurt. As a doctor, and as your friend, I cannot stand idly by in your time of need."

Still quietly sobbing, Joe whispered, "I think I need something. Ciara just seems so terribly far away."

As Romana enfolded him within her thoughts and gently soothed his ravaged emotions, Joe felt his mind suffuse with warmth, melting away his despair and filling his heart with renewed hope.

* * *

Joe stared at the vast globe of Mars, which had swung into view as the Master of Time manoeuvred into an approach trajectory. He felt acutely embarrassed for allowing his homesickness to overcome him, but at the same time, he experienced overwhelming gratitude to Romana for her timely intervention.

"Thanks for what you did earlier," he told her. "I'm glad you came. You're a good friend, you know."

"It is an honour to help the Futama," she told him, "and I will be there whenever you need me." She grinned unexpectedly. "You will not feel I am helping if you miss *that*," she said, pointing at a huge, cratered lump of rock a couple of kilometres from the ship. "I am certain Ciara would like you to record such things."

Joe immediately zeroed in with his camcorder on the dark shape of Phobos and panned across to place the moon in context with the looming bulk of Mars. In the vacuum of space, the planetary surface and that of its major moon seemed close enough to touch. Immediately below the ship, Joe was astounded to see volcanic plumes climbing into the outer atmosphere over the immense mounds of Olympus Mons and Arsia Mons. A number of dormant volcanoes reached for the sky from the uplands of the Tharsis bulge, whose continental mass was surrounded by dark and expansive seas. The most exciting aspect of the planetary surface was the appearance of broad swathes of green over the continental landmasses. Mars was, indeed, a fertile world in this era deep into mankind's past.

As the ship swooped towards the surface, Joe sensed the almost inaudible whistling of air over its outer skin. Yet there was no evidence of overheating of the craft's outer surface due to friction with the atmosphere, which, to Joe's thinking, was a major bonus. Once again, he compared the technology of his friends from the future with that available to NASA in his own time. If the Space Administration had the ability to nullify the effects of gravity and friction, their efforts to explore the solar system would be certain to leap ahead. He wondered if Or-gon's research and knowledge would be sufficient to stretch those particular boundaries. Perhaps, he thought, in time.

The precipitous descent of the ship slowed as she lost height and Joe could see, over the rim of the craft, that they were approaching a large island continent in the middle of an indigo sea. As the island drew nearer, Joe could pick out details of dark reefs surrounding the ragged shoreline, and soon they were cruising high over a multi-hued jungle canopy, broken only by broad, meandering rivers.

The ship slowed further and a small town appeared in the distance. A few tall spires reached gracefully into the heavens, proclaiming the artistry of their creators and welcoming home the Master of Time. A broad, flat expanse beckoned and Terpin brought the ship to land beside a particularly stunning example of the architect's skill. If this is what the Faithful had achieved on Mars, Joe wondered what the Earth would be like in their natural time. He suspected that it would present a feast for the eyes, a gallery of the finest of mankind's artistic creations.

The craft settled with a sigh onto its tripod legs as the hydraulics accepted the strain of her massive bulk. In front of the building stood a welcoming party of several tall figures dressed in robes of varying shades. In the centre of the group two figures stood out from the crowd in robes of vibrant crimson. To one side, another small crowd waited, and Joe was surprised to see children amongst their numbers. Apparently, he was to be welcomed by

160

members of the High Council and he assumed that the small assembly was made up of families of the crew of the Master of Time.

Romana touched Joe's elbow. "Joe, we need to join Leiki and the captain."

"Of course, let's go."

They descended from the observatory and headed for the refectory, where Terpin was waiting for Commander Leiki to join him. The captain had donned his best white robes, which contrasted perfectly with his golden skin. Joe thought he looked splendid. Moments later Leiki joined them. He was wearing a robe of the same vibrant crimson hue as the two High Council members in the welcoming party.

Joe grinned. "I'm impressed," he told Leiki and the base commander beamed sunnily at the compliment.

"Thank you." He placed his arm around Joe's shoulder. "Shall we go?"

Chapter Sixteen

THE FUTAMA REVEALED:

Joe and Leiki walked side by side down the ramp beneath the discus shaped bulk of the Master of Time. The Earth base commander stood out in his crimson robes and Joe was attired in twentieth century outdoor clothes. With their differing statures and clothing, they made an odd pair as they approached the two red-robed members of the ruling council. Romana and Captain Terpin followed a few paces behind, and Marron, his wrists bound behind his back, trailed in a third group, flanked by Analy and Trione, their plasma rifles trained unflinchingly upon him.

Joe felt everyone's eyes on him as he strode along beside Leiki, hurrying to match the brisk pace set by the taller man's longer limbs. A number of council members waited before the entrance to the elegant building as Joe approached, their eyes filled with a light of expectancy. Leiki headed towards the two crimson-robed figures at the centre, and they separated from the rest as he approached.

"It has begun," Leiki said simply, "the Futama is now amongst us."

Joe could sense a feeling of suppressed joy amongst the welcoming high councillors. But, with his underdeveloped telepathic ability, Joe could also sense an underlying doubt in their thoughts. He smiled inwardly. There seemed to be a collective inability to reconcile his relatively tiny stature with one in whom the Faithful had invested what amounted to godhood.

* * *

Prua Landi was becoming impatient. Progress in forcing the limits of her time-travel was painfully slow, and Perdon knew that he must provide answers to her demands – and soon. He was making delicate adjustments to the remote viewer when the dictatrix swept into his laboratory. Her face bore none of the scars that had marred her flawless complexion following the unfortunate confrontation with Joe Laing's friends. But her improved health was not reflected in her temper, which was as venomous as ever. She strode over to the scientist. Perdon glanced up in surprise at the interruption to his train of thought.

"What news do you have, Perdon?" she demanded. "Remember, I am not renowned for my patience."

162

"My Lady," Perdon informed her, "we have worked tirelessly to push back the barriers, with little success. A technician, who wished only to please My Lady, volunteered to travel to the limits of our range. Unfortunately, his body was scattered into its component atoms and nothing recognisable returned through the cubicle. I fear that without radically new theories, we can travel no further into the past."

Prua Landi's features darkened with anger. "I have no desire to listen to what you *cannot* do," she grated, "only what you *can*. Remember, failure may prove to be a terminal affliction."

Perdon decided that the moment had come to play his trump card. "We have had some success," he informed her, "with the remote viewer. I was calibrating the instrument as you arrived."

"Explain!" Prua Landi ordered.

"We are now able to view much further into the past. And, as a bonus, we have a clearer view of the compound where the criminals have made their base.

Prua Landi's interest was pricked by the information. "And what have you discovered?"

"You should see for yourself, My Lady."

"Show me! And I had better find this interesting."

Perdon initiated the remote viewer and a holographic image of the compound shimmered in the air, attaining a level of clarity previously impossible. "You will, My Lady," he assured her.

They could clearly see the names inscribed on the flanks of the two ships, standing very close together in the grassy compound. Four tall figures and one much smaller left the confines of the tunnel in the cliff face, and made their way to the larger of the two vessels, which they boarded via the ramp below the hull.

Prua Landi's interest was instantly aroused at the sight of the smaller figure. "Is this all?" she demanded.

"Have patience, My Lady," Perdon soothed. "It's just getting interesting."

Prua Landi favoured the scientist with a sour look. "Take care," she advised acidly, "not to stretch the boundaries of familiarity."

"Of course, My Lady," Perdon agreed innocently. "Please watch the display."

Practically snarling, the dictatrix ordered him to continue. The ramp lifted and locked into place and, moments later, the ship shimmered towards invisibility. But, before the transition was

163

complete, the hologram blazed like the sun, forcing the two spectators to avert their eyes. As the intense light faded, Prua Landi gazed in fascination at the scene of utter devastation. A vast crater had replaced both ships and all the low buildings had vanished. The remote viewer panned around the compound, showing the havoc wrought upon the perimeter fence at the core of the force-field. Finally, the view encompassed the cave mouth, where the cliff face had collapsed catastrophically, fanning a vast rocky scree across the compound. Prua Landi's eyes were infused with a fanatical light of triumph. The event was made even more satisfying by the spectacle of Marron, staggering into the cave mouth, which had been altered forever by the massive explosion. Marron hawked and spat to clear his lungs, then re-entered the cave.

"I have dreamed of this moment," Prua Landi confessed to Perdon. "Tell me, is there more?"

"Just the chaos you see, My Lady. Do you wish to continue?"

"No," Prua Landi told him, her tone triumphant, "I have seen quite enough." Her gaze flicked around the laboratory before she told the scientist, "Perdon, you have done well and have earned a rest. You will be my guest at my summer retreat for as long as it pleases me. You have two days to wind up your affairs in this laboratory and then I will send an escort to bring you to me."

Perdon knew he had been given an ultimatum, wrapped up in silken trimmings. "I am deeply honoured, My Lady," he said, "and I am at your service."

"You are," Prua Landi agreed affably, "whilst it pleases me."

* * *

Romana and Leiki accompanied Joe as he followed the councillors into the tall building, Terpin having already joined his family, who were waiting in the crowd to greet him. In the broad corridors, it was possible to catch only fleeting glimpses of the tiny figure amongst the giants surrounding him, but everyone they passed craned their necks eagerly in an attempt to do so. The reverse was the case for Joe. He could see very little around him as he was hustled along, flanked by councillors in their flowing robes.

As he matched pace with his long-legged companions, Joe's mind flicked back to his visit to the Moon, where everyone adapted their gait to the much lighter gravity. As far as he could recall, Mars was much smaller than Earth, with correspondingly lesser gravity, yet he was experiencing no difficulty in adjusting to the difference in his weight.

He nudged Leiki and asked, "Is it just me, or is the gravity here heavier than it should be?"

"The Futama is very perceptive," Leiki told him with a smile. "The gravity is controlled within the confines of the city. Otherwise, despite the ministrations of their nanomedics, everyone would suffer the loss of bone and muscle during their exile here."

"I suppose I should have expected something like that, knowing how you control gravity in your ships." He thought for a moment about Leiki's words. "Are you saying that outside the city gravity is normal – for Mars, that is?"

The tall man laughed. "We would be hard pressed to adjust the gravity of a whole planet, even with the technology at our disposal. It is sufficient to know that we can live our lives in the city, much as we would do at home." The reference to their future home brought a wistful gleam to Leiki's eyes.

"You miss your home time, don't you?" Joe said gently.

"Every day we are away burns away a little of my heart and soul," Leiki replied. "But now the Futama has come to lead his people, the scars of separation will soon be gone as though they never existed."

Joe endured the rest of the short walk to the council chamber in silence; Leiki's expectations of him were doubtless shared by every one of the Faithful and, for the first time since he heard the name 'Futama' in the Neanderthal past, he felt the full weight of responsibility upon his slim shoulders.

He had no idea he was radiating his emotions until Romana stepped up beside him and placed her arm on his shoulder. "Futama," she comforted, "remember that I will always be here to share your burden, for as long as you need me."

Joe favoured the tall medic with a look of gratitude. "You're a good friend," he told her, "and I count myself lucky to have you around."

Romana withdrew to walk behind Joe once again, but not before he glimpsed an unfathomable expression flit cross her beautiful features.

The leading councillors halted so suddenly that Joe cannoned into the red-robed figure in front of him. The group parted and Joe saw that they had arrived at a broad door of dark wood, with a beautifully carved relief of the Earth in its upper panel and Mars in the lower. The door was set into an archway, around which the Sun and planets were carved into a single piece of wood. Joe tried to imagine the scale of the tree that had supplied the panel, deciding that even the giant sequoias of California would probably prove insubstantial beside such a monster.

The door opened and Leiki urged Joe forward. "The Supreme Councillor is waiting, Futama."

Romana stepped back; as the only person in the group who was not a councillor, her presence was not required. Joe grasped Romana's hand. "Come in with us," he urged. "You've been with me most of the way so far, and it's comforting to have you around."

"But the Supreme Councillor wishes to meet only with the Futama and the members of the Council," she protested.

"Then he's going to be disappointed," Joe commented. "I'm not a kid, and people are going to have to get used to it. I want you in there with me, so come on, indulge me . . . please."

Joe passed through the doorway, still holding Romana's hand, flanked by Leiki and the two red-robed councillors. The remainder of the councillors followed at a respectful distance. The walls of the council chamber were panelled with the same dark wood, which was just as richly carved, and the scenes were much the same as in the sacred cave complex on Earth, three-hundred million years into the future. Joe let his eyes rove over the panels as he walked towards the huge table at the centre of the chamber. How similar would they be? Would the carvings depict Prua Landi, just as they did on Earth?

Lost in thought, he was about to make a detour towards the friezes when he heard someone call out, "Futama!"

He jerked back into the present, to see a splendidly dressed figure arise from the head of the table and approach him. The man wore a robe of startlingly white material, held together at the neck by a palm-sized golden brooch in the likeness of Mars. He had the golden skin common to members of the Faithful but, unlike the rest, a thin covering of dark hair upon his scalp. The rest of the councillors moved aside to let him pass.

"Welcome, Futama," he intoned, "I am Gillane, and I am the Supreme Councillor of the Faithful." He stared pointedly at Romana and his eyebrows rose a little in query.

"She stays!" Joe told him firmly.

"As the Futama wishes," Gillane demurred. As far as he was concerned, any argument would be counterproductive and there

166

were important matters to discuss. He glanced at all the councillors standing expectantly around. "Everyone, please be seated," he said, and the seats filled so quickly it was clear that every councillor had his name engraved, figuratively speaking, on his own particular chair. Romana slipped into her place beside Joe, which deprived one councillor, Elian, of his usual position at the table. Elian shrugged and immediately selected one of two empty chairs at the point furthest from Gillane and Joe.

Gillane got to his feet, pushing away his chair with the back of his knees. He let his gaze travel around the table in a clockwise direction, pausing first at the two red-robed figures, Corowen and Dorn, who were next in rank below him, and continuing through Leiki via the rest of the council members, to where Romana and Joe sat expectantly. Romana, who had never been present at an assembly of the Supreme Council, sat stiffly erect, every muscle tense.

"Relax," Joe whispered, "they're not going to eat us. At least, I hope not," he added with a grin.

Romana smiled and relaxed, settling a little more comfortably into her seat.

"That's better. Now you can concentrate on what's being said."

Gillane allowed the interplay between the two to come to its natural conclusion before saying, "The Supreme council of the Faithful welcomes the Futama to this place of exile on Mars. It has been many months since the Futama first discovered he had the ability to travel through time. In that time, he will have seen many adventures, and experienced many dangers, some of which may have involved confrontation with Prua Landi."

A gasp of astonishment and awe rolled around the councillors at the table at the mention of the sworn enemy of their people.

Joe put up his hand, feeling akin to a small boy, wishing to interrupt the teacher.

"Does the Futama wish to address the Council?" Gillane enquired.

"I dunno," Joe replied, "it's just that you're talking as if you don't know for certain what's happened."

"That is so," Gillane admitted. "We *could* follow your path, but as every event produces a choice of possible timelines, such an undertaking is very complex. We find that plotting a course of greatest probability usually produces the best results. When I have completed my formal welcome we, the council, would be honoured to hear of the Futama's personal experience."

"I'll be glad to tell you everything so far," Joe conceded, "if you think it will help."

"It will fill in the pieces thus far missing from our history in exile," Gillane informed him, "and yes, it is of immense importance to us. But firstly," he added as he handed Joe a neatly folded garment, "the Supreme Council offers you this robe, which will show your people that you are their Futama."

Joe was going to ask if he didn't stand out enough already, but Gillane's serious expression told him that now was definitely not the time for levity. He slipped off his outdoor coat and donned the robe. It was magnificent! The robe was of the same, brilliant white silky material as Gillane's, but with a broad band of black, edged with gold, running diagonally from his left shoulder to his right hip. A gold-trimmed black obi around his slim waist completed the ceremonial attire. The garment fitted perfectly, evidence that the tailor had foreknowledge of his exact physical measurements.

Everyone around the table stood and bowed deeply and, for the first time, Joe felt that he really was the Futama, the one the Faithful had patiently awaited throughout their twenty-five year exile on Mars. Too-ga's people – and subsequently, Or-gon's – had revered him as the Futama; but, until now, he had never really believed. He had always harboured the suspicion that, somehow, someone had made a huge mistake, and he would eventually be exposed as a fraud. Now, all he had to do was to live up to their expectations.

Gillane's voice interrupted his thoughts. "Would the Futama care to relate his adventures to the council?"

Joe smiled at Gillane and rose from the table. "If it's all right with everyone, I'd feel a little more comfortable on my feet, because I might have to give a little demonstration from time to time."

Seventeen faces gazed expectantly at him. Romana and Leiki had heard it all before, but they knew there was a possibility they would learn new things. Joe began by relating his discovery of the time tunnels and went on to tell of the time spent with Too-ga's people. When he reached the point where he had done battle with Mantoo, Elian requested a demonstration.

"No problem," Joe told the junior councillor, "but I'll need help. Would you like to volunteer?"

Elian rose from his seat and stepped forward. "Now," Joe told him, "the shaman, Mantoo was this tall." He demonstrated by holding his hand level with Elian's nose. "But he was much heavier and more muscular because he was a Neanderthal."

Joe sensed an aura of scepticism amongst the councillors as they compared his size with that of the giant, Mantoo. Smiling, he asked the young councillor to attack him in the same manner as Mantoo; when he complied, Joe brushed him aside, urging Elian to the next stage of the fight. At the point where Joe had finally dealt the coup de grace to Mantoo, he halted and demonstrated in slow motion, explaining in graphic detail, the outcome of the deadly blow. Several of the councillors appeared slightly sick but Elian, who had enjoyed taking part in the demonstration, commented on Joe's lack of size when compared to his opponent. Joe told everyone unequivocally that size mattered little to exponents of the martial arts, but that skill, technique and speed were the key to victory.

Joe recounted the way he had foolishly given the primitive tribespeople technology they would never have achieved without his help, and how his meddling had changed the timeline when he tried to return home. He wept silently at the loss of Tarmis at the hands of Prua Landi and everyone present in the council chamber was engulfed by his grief.

Romana placed her hand on his wrist to comfort him, allowing his grief to ebb away.

"Thanks," he told her. The contact had lasted only a few seconds but its effect on the members of the council was electric.

Gillane smiled. "It is now clear why the Futama insisted upon Romana's company within this chamber," he said knowingly. "We should have anticipated their bond of friendship."

"That's all it is," Joe protested, "friendship. I've got my wife at home, you know."

Gillane was thunderstruck. "My apologies, Futama," he said, "but I would never be so coarse as to suggest otherwise."

"Right," Joe grinned, defusing Gillane's embarrassment, "now that's settled, shall I carry on?"

"Please do," the supreme councillor suggested, relief etched all over his handsome features.

Joe's story unfolded, encompassing Romana's discovery of the specialised nanomedics in both Joe and Ciara's bodies, and their journey to the Moon, which culminated in the destruction of

169

Marron's ship. Finally, he told of the near-disastrous episode in the time of the Earth's creation.

He glanced at all the faces staring at him from around the table. "Now that I've told you how I got here," he said, "I reckon it's time for me to get some answers. Firstly, how did I come to be shot full of nanos, and from what Romana tells me, pretty unusual ones at that?"

"The answer is simple" Gillane told him. "A few days before your discovery of the time-tunnels, Corowen and Dorn—" he gestured towards the two councillors; "—came to you in the night and injected the nanos into your blood. As Romana has suggested, the specialised nanos enabled you to see and use the tunnels. All your other experiences in the past then became possible."

"Fair enough," Joe conceded, "but why me? What made you so certain you'd picked the right man for the job?"

"Because you *are* the Futama, who is destined to lead us to victory over Prua Landi, and thus restore our birthright."

"But what makes *me* the Futama?" Joe pursued his enquiry like a dog worrying a particularly appetising bone. "What's so special about *me*?"

"The intricacies of time are too complex to explain in a few words. I can simply say that what is occurring now has already become an immutable episode of history before the time of your birth. Therefore, you must be given the opportunity to live this particular history. We gave you the nanos to make everything possible."

"I suppose I'll have to take your word for it, because I'm here, in the flesh, talking to all of you. But I still find myself asking *why me*? After all, there are numerous generals in my time and throughout history, who know about military campaigns and fighting wars. All I know is martial arts. I'm not a soldier."

Gillane was thoughtful for a moment before answering. "None of these others occur in this history, so it is almost certain that if we had chosen such a one, he would not have survived long enough to achieve success. You, however, in almost every timeline, will survive."

"In that case," Joe insisted, "why don't you investigate the future and see how we manage to defeat Prua Landi – if, in fact, that's what we do?"

"Because the intricate detail of that part of our future is unwritten for us," Gillane explained, "and is, therefore, subject to

170

the vagaries of chance. Victory for us will depend upon how you prepare your people for the forthcoming battle."

"Thanks," Joe told him ruefully, "I just needed that kind of responsibility."

"You are the Futama," Romana assured him, "and I am certain that you will lead your people to victory over Prua Landi's forces."

"Thanks," Joe told her, "you know just what to say when I need reassurance."

Romana smiled at the compliment.

Joe addressed Gillane once more. "One last thing," he said, "I know absolutely nothing about where you came from in the future. Somebody's going to have to fill me in, because we'll stand *no chance at all if I don't know the terrain and the people.*"

Gillane smiled and the austerity of his features evaporated. "All the knowledge you require is stored within the frieze containing the image of Prua Landi," he said. "It was with a sense of irony that the technician installed the data in that particular frieze, because it will eventually lead to the downfall of our enemy."

"I bet Prua Landi wouldn't appreciate the joke," Joe grinned.

"Perhaps not," the supreme councillor agreed.

"If Prua Landi hates you so much and is hell bent on your destruction, why do you include her in so many friezes?" Joe enquired.

"To remind us of what we shall regain when the Futama leads us to victory."

Gillane was about to bring the meeting to a close but Joe raised his hand once more and everyone in the chamber was silent, waiting for him to speak.

"Before we finish," Joe told them, "I've got a couple of questions that've been rumbling around in my mind waiting to get out ever since Romana told me my wife, Ciara had inherited a watered down version of my nanos through—" Joe hesitated momentarily before continuing, "—through sexual intercourse."

"Please ask your questions, and if we do not have the answer we will consult the AI," Gillane replied.

Joe nodded. "Thanks. What bothers me is this: when I was with the Neanderthals, I know Lar-na loved me more than life itself. If I passed my nanos onto Ciara, the same must have happened with Lar-na, and that means she would have been able to 'see' the time tunnel when her nanos were developed enough. I don't think anything alive would have been able to prevent her from following me to Tarmis, or wherever I went for that matter. And if she had the nanos, my son, the Na-futama would have had them too, and so would every one of my descendents up to the time of Tarmis. My friend – and incidentally one of those descendents – Or-gon, knew nothing of nanomedics, so I think it's safe to assume I didn't pass mine on."

"That is true," Gillane agreed.

"Would you like to explain? But make it simple because I know next to nothing about your technology."

Gillane smiled. "In that case it is fortunate that the explanation is, indeed, a simple one. In your time, geneticists extracted DNA from both Neanderthal and Cro-Magnon remains, and they discovered that Neanderthals and our branch of humanity were sufficiently different to be separate species. The nanos in your body are designed for our variant of the human line and would quickly perish in the body of a Neanderthal." He paused for a moment before adding, "The genetic differences account for the fact that mating between Neanderthals and humans could not produce offspring."

Joe was stunned. So the Neanderthals never interbred with Cro-Magnons. "Then how the hell did I manage to do it, and why were there so many Neanderthals with modern physical characteristics – modern as far as I'm concerned, anyway?"

"Again the answer is simple. Your nanomedics were able to restructure the relevant genetic codes in order to enable conception to take place. But that was at the limit of their capabilities and they would have soon died. As for the 'modern' as you say, appearance of some Neanderthals, that would most likely have been due to mutations in favour of living in a warmer climate."

Joe sat back in his chair, his curiosity satisfied. A smile touched his lips as he thought about what Gillane's revelations about interbreeding between Neanderthals and modern man might add to the arguments and counter-arguments currently raging on the subject in his own time; and he appreciated how fortunate he was to be privy to the truth.

Chapter Seventeen

PROCLAIMED BY THE PEOPLE:

Gillane passed his hands over the table and a monitor rose up from the polished wooden surface. He spoke a few words to the screen and it melted once more into the tabletop.

He surveyed the councillors seated around the huge table. "All citizens," he said, "have been called to assemble in the plaza before this council building. They will be given the opportunity to see their Futama for the first time. Every one of our people has eagerly awaited this day, knowing that the coming of the Futama will be the beginning of the end of their exile. Futama," he said to Joe, "there is still time for you to download the contents of the frieze into your memory, before everyone assembles outside. Although," he added with a smile, "everyone is certain to make the best possible speed to the plaza."

"Fine," Joe agreed, "but I hope it won't affect me like it did back on Earth."

"There would have been a sense of disorientation the first time you experienced a data download," Gillane assured him, "but your nanos should now have made all the necessary adjustments to your brain to eliminate any such problem."

"I hope so," Joe grumbled, "because it made me as sick as a dog."

"Nevertheless, the Futama survived?" Gillane grinned.

Joe couldn't help returning the smile. "I suppose I'm being a bit of a wimp," he confessed. "C'mon then, let's get it over with."

He placed his right hand on the carved image of Prua Landi and immediately his brain was filled with a torrent of images and text, scrolling through his mind like a computer monitor on fast forward. Instinctively, he withdrew his hand and the cascade of images instantly halted. Half expecting to have to vomit, Joe was pleasantly surprised to discover that there were no side effects whatsoever. So, with a rueful grin, he replaced his hand on the likeness of the dictatrix, Prua Landi. The download recommenced where it had left off and continued for some minutes until Joe wondered, somewhere in a detached portion of his consciousness, if the data would begin to overflow through his ears. The flow stopped as suddenly as it had begun, and Joe released his grip on the carving. He staggered sideways, swiftly regaining his balance.

"Wow!" he groaned. "How the hell am I going to be able to use any of that lot? There's far too much of it for anybody to understand."

"Your nanos have begun adjusting your memory to encompass the new information," Gillane informed him sympathetically, "and all the data will become available to you as new memories. The memories will be there for you to recall in every detail."

Joe was impressed. "Like a photographic memory?" he asked.

"You will recall everything and forget nothing."

"Will that apply to the whole of my memory, not just this new information?"

"Yes," Gillane assured him, "your memory processes will be considerably more efficient."

Joe whistled through his teeth. "That'll come in handy when I take my archaeology degree," he confided to the supreme councillor, realising immediately just how ridiculous that was, in the light of *where* and *when* he was at that very moment. A degree would be the last thing on his mind when he eventually returned to his old life – if, in fact, he ever managed to do so. He shrugged. "Now that's over," he said, "do you reckon it's time to meet the people?"

Gillane nodded. "I believe it is."

"Then let's go."

* * *

Gillane led Joe and the rest of the councillors out of the front doorway of the council building. They stood at the top of a series of concave steps, with Joe at the centre, Gillane to his right, Romana to his left and Leiki, Corowen and Dorn immediately behind. The remainder of the councillors were strung in an arc along the edge of the top step. In the plaza, with everyone gently jostling to obtain a better view, was assembled the total human population of Mars.

Joe could see a few who might have been military personnel,; a substantial number who, from their mode of dress, were probably farmers; and a great many more in casual clothing, who appeared to be off duty. Amongst the crowd there were many children, most of whom had been raised onto the shoulders of adults in order to afford a better view. He compared the size of the crowd to what he had seen at a football match and estimated that there were around five thousand souls in the plaza.

"Is this the whole population of Mars," he asked incredulously, "because there can't be more than five thousand?"

"Six thousand four hundred and twenty-two," Gillane informed him, "if everyone is here."

"Then how on earth do you expect to wage a war on Prua Landi with so few people? Assuming everyone is able-bodied, there can't be more than four thousand available to fight."

"In truth, less than three thousand," Gillane confirmed, "but that is our number here on Mars. In our true time, we are many hundred times that number, every one of whom is living a false existence under Prua Landi's regime. The time will soon come when the Futama will set them free from tyranny, and they will swell our numbers."

Gillane gazed at the crowd, which, by this time, was becoming a little restless. He touched a control on his wrist and addressed his people, his amplified voice booming out over the plaza. He rested his hand on Joe's shoulder. "The Futama is now amongst us," he told them, "and the end of our exile is near. We have awaited his coming for more than twelve of Mars' years. He will lead us to victory over the evil that is Prua Landi and restore us to our true time."

When Gillane's short address ceased, Joe heard a low growl begin in the throats of the throng. The sound rose in pitch and intensity and morphed into a repetitive chant of, "Futama, Futama," until it seemed the very ground under their feet would tremble from the sustained noise. A small section of the crowd began to jump up and down in time with the chant, and the movement was swiftly picked up by the rest and amplified a thousand times. Joe had seen reports of what happened at football matches when the crowds were out of control and he was aware that the same could happen here.

He raised both hands high above his head, and the swelling sound and writhing of the crowd stilled as if he had flicked a switch. He could feel more than six-thousand pairs of eyes upon him, six-thousand outpourings of joyful emotion.

The silence was disturbed by the thin, plaintive voice of a child at the front of the throng calling out, "Are you the Futama?"

Joe stepped down from his elevated position amongst the members of Mars' government, and approached the little girl. She shrank back a little in alarm as Joe squatted down before her to bring his eyes nearer to her level. His magnificent robe trailed on the pavement around him.

"Don't you think I look like the Futama?" he teased. "Do you think I should be a bit more . . . well . . . impressive?"

The little girl nodded, then shook her head, unsure whether or not to agree.

"Well," Joe confided, "I think so too. That's why they gave me these special robes, so that everybody will know who I am. You can touch them if you tell me your name."

Hesitantly, the little girl reached out and touched Joe's sleeve. "Lora," she said.

"Now, Lora, you can tell your friends you've actually spoken to the Futama," Joe informed her.

A section of the crowd nearest to Joe began to shuffle and several more children appeared around the legs of the adults. As soon as they reached the front, they stopped, filled with uncertainty. Adult hands reached down and held the little ones back, but Joe beckoned them all forward.

"It's okay," he said, "they've got to get used to me being around, so now is as good a time as any."

The children surged forward, each one touching Joe's robes before retreating into the crowd. For a few minutes their numbers were swelled by new arrivals from further back in the throng, but eventually, the last child, a bright-eyed boy of around three Mars years, completed the procession. Joe arose from his haunches, intending to mount the steps and rejoin Gillane and the other councillors, but the adults at the front of the crowd, surged forward, intent on claiming the same contact with the Futama as the children.

Joe glanced back over his shoulder at Gillane, who called down to him in amusement from the top of the steps, "Six-thousand four hundred and twenty-two, Futama." The supreme councillor entered the building, still chuckling to himself at the easy way Joe had integrated with his people.

Joe felt the light touch of many hands as he walked amongst the crowd. Through his embryonic telepathic ability, he was almost overwhelmed by a subconscious upwelling of emotion radiating from the six-thousand souls thronging around him in the plaza. He made for a statue in the centre of the square, and stepped up onto the sculpture's broad plinth, allowing everyone to touch his robes as they filed past. He was impressed by the gentleness of the people and the calm orderliness of their response to his presence once they

176

had been able to release their pent up joy in an initial noisy greeting. He climbed higher onto the stepped plinth until he could see over the heads of the tall people around him. The weak sunlight reflected from many bronzed and hairless heads.

"Now that everyone has seen me in the flesh," he began, "I think I should explain a few things about how I came to be here." He gazed over the many heads to the back of the crowd, and noticed that everyone seemed to be having little difficulty in hearing his words. (It would have surprised him to learn that he was subconsciously projecting his speech telepathically in parallel with his spoken words.) "By the puzzled expressions on some of your faces, I probably don't fit your idea of what your Futama should look like." Ignoring a low murmur rising in the crowd, Joe pressed on. "The fact is, I was nobody's Futama until a few months ago, when I discovered a means to enter a time thirty-five thousand years into my past. There, the primitive people called me their Futama and, since then, a lot has happened to make me realise that I really am the Futama; the person the Faithful believe will free them from the yoke of Prua Landi's regime. I've come into contact with Prua Landi on three occasions and every time she tried to kill me. As you can see, she failed." He paused to let a ripple of nervous laughter pulse through the crowd. "I'm just an ordinary man and I'm made of flesh and blood, just like you. What I can do, however, is teach our army how to fight at close quarters, without energy weapons. I intend to train you to be harder and swifter and more ferocious than the enemy, and how to use almost any part of your bodies to deadly effect. You will learn to trust these skills, and you'll come to believe in your invincibility in situations where energy weapons are too dangerous to use."

He scanned the faces of the crowd; all eyes were focused upon him. "The time is fast approaching when Prua Landi will learn, to her cost, that a worm will eventually turn, and that even the gentlest of people will rail against tyranny."

The crowd was silent for a few moments before everyone realised that Joe's speech was over. Then a murmur began to swell into a chant of "Futama, Futama!"

The little girl, Lora, had wormed her way through to the front of the crowd; her face was shining with joy. Joe leaped down from the plinth and winked at her. "Do I look like your Futama now?" he whispered.

177

Smiling, Lora nodded enthusiastically and Joe scooped her up onto his shoulders, carrying the child up to the top of the steps before the government building. "This child," he called out, "will be the symbol of the Faithful's uprising. When you look at her, you will never doubt that Prua Landi's days are numbered."

* * *

Prua Landi lay upon a silken bed, whose soft, broad expanse proclaimed privilege and opulence. She was draped in lingerie of the finest, most insubstantial gossamer, against which her recently regrown bronze skin was displayed to perfection. A light tap on the door to her chamber signalled the arrival of a visitor and she called, "Enter!" in a sultry mix of command and invitation.

Perdon stepped through the outer entrance. "My Lady?" he called uncertainly.

"Ah, it is you, Perdon," Prua Landi answered. "Come in . . . please."

The scientist padded through to where Prua Landi awaited him, the sound of his footfalls swallowed by the deep, luxurious pile of the carpet. He halted before the bed, unable to avert his eyes from the dictatrix's unaccustomed beauty. In all his time in her service, she had never permitted her mask of severity to slip. But now, in this state of complete relaxation, Prua Landi displayed an almost ethereal beauty, which drew Perdon to her like a sleepwalker in the thrall of a most persuasive dream.

Prua Landi patted the bed beside her. "Come, sit by me," she invited, seductively. "I find I have a need to celebrate the destruction of that abominable sect and their primitive leader," she purred, "and you will celebrate with me."

"I'm honoured, My Lady," Perdon answered, knowing he had received an offer that was akin to a command. Whether it was an offer or command, it was clear that he was in no position to refuse. He moved closer, reaching out to caress the vibrant new skin of Prua Landi's cheek with the back of his index finger. "I am your most obedient servant."

* * *

Gillane and his colleagues were awaiting Joe's arrival in the council chamber as Joe breezed in, still on a high from the success of his interaction with the populace in the square outside.

"Congratulations," he said, "I believe you have won everyone over. It was never going to be easy for your people to come to terms with your physical differences, but you overcame their preconceptions like a true leader of men."

"Excuse me," Joe complained, "but everyone in here was out of earshot. How come you know what I said?"

Romana touched his arm, saying, "You have not yet learned to control your thoughts. Every one of your words produced an echoing thought for all to hear. Even for those," she added, "within this chamber." She glanced at Gillane for permission to continue and he waved her on. "As a medic, I shall take the Futama in hand and teach him how to control his mind to prevent the unwitting release of vital information."

"Before we start, though," Joe proclaimed, "I'd like a tour of the city and the countryside around. I've met the people. Now I'd like to get an idea of the lie of the land."

"Romana will be your guide as she will be your mentor," Gillane announced, "commencing immediately. This meeting is now ended and we will reconvene tomorrow to discuss the training of our troops." He stood, and everyone else rose to their feet. "Once again, welcome, Futama to Veloran. We have waited so long for this moment and I admit to feeling extremely good inside."

Joe followed Romana outside into the weak sunlight. Overhead, the cloud cover had thickened, warning of an impending storm, a fitting metaphor, Joe thought, for the invasion of Earth in the distant future. The town of Veloran spread out before them. There were a few tall, graceful stone buildings but the majority were built from wood, and were of a plain, utilitarian nature. It was as if the builders had eschewed artistic expression because their stay on Mars would, in all likelihood, be a short one. Nevertheless, the overall effect was pleasing to the eye. Nowhere could Joe see any suggestion of the dilapidation to which sections of most small twenty-first century cities ultimately fell prey.

They walked slowly around the town, with Romana pointing out the sights, from time to time encountering small groups of people talking about the momentous events of the day. Occasionally, a child would approach Joe to touch his robes for a second time, and each time, Joe tousled their hair in a friendly manner. The adults merely nodded in friendly fashion as they passed. They skirted a broad, grassed area with tiers of seats along one side; it was some kind of arena and Joe was intrigued. At no

179

time had anyone mentioned any kind of sport, but the ground was covered with a plant resembling grass, and was set out in a complicated pattern of white gridlines. In the suburbs the form of the buildings gave way to houses, surrounded by neat gardens, and everywhere Joe looked, he saw a profusion of flowering plants. It was clear that the people were determined to make their stay as comfortable and enjoyable as possible.

Joe heard a humming sound passing low overhead. He glanced upwards to see several small, four-seat flyers, ferrying agricultural workers to farms in the countryside around the city. "Can you drive one of those?" he asked Romana, "because I wouldn't mind a guided tour." He indicated the dark green smudge on the horizon that was the edge of the forest abutting the extensive farmland, which had Veloran at its centre.

"Every adult can pilot a flyer," she informed him, "and I believe that it would be an appropriate skill for the Futama to learn." They had wandered in a broad circular path through the city and were presently heading in the direction of the landing area, where the Master of Time stood on its massive tripod legs, surrounded by numerous smaller craft. "We shall use one of those." She pointed at several car-sized flyers, dwarfed by the vast bulk of the timeship.

"Are you allowed to take one without asking?" Joe enquired.

"You are the Futama," Romana informed him simply, "and, for you, no doors are closed."

"Okay, let's go!" Joe said enthusiastically. "I can't wait to see the real Mars."

The seat in the flyer proved too large for Joe, despite Romana's attempts to adjust the accommodation to its smallest size. Romana slid into the pilot's seat and checked the instruments. A disembodied voice told her that all systems were functional and that the power pack was fully energised. Joe glanced around the cockpit and experienced a powerful sense of déjà vu. He stared in astonishment at the controls and knew instinctively that he recognised their individual functions.

"Do you know," he said to his companion, "I reckon I could fly this thing, yet I've never been in one before. How can that be possible?"

"The information must have been downloaded into your memory by the frieze in the council chamber," she told him matter of factly, "though I believe you should practise a little before taking control."

"Don't worry," Joe exclaimed, "I'm perfectly happy to let you drive," and he could have sworn he saw relief pass fleetingly over Romana's beautiful features.

The flyer rose smoothly into the air and, under Romana's skilled fingers, headed south-east into the open skies over the farmland. The city of Veloran passed swiftly below, and soon they were over open farmland, heading for the edge of the forest. Joe estimated their speed to be in excess of a hundred kilometres an hour and, at that pace, it seemed they would reach the trees in no more than a minute. Time dragged by and the dark green woodlands stayed tantalisingly far away, whilst the fields fled by below. Five minutes later Joe realised that the distance to the forest had been deceptive due to the immense size of the trees. As they flew at a height of fifty metres, the trees loomed to more than a hundred and fifty metres above their tiny craft. Joe was astounded at the incredible scale of the vegetation.

"Are there any ferocious animals down there?" he asked.

"None," Romana told him succinctly. "All the wildlife on this planet is to be found in the seas. Should you ever see those creatures, you will realise just how fortunate we are that they are confined to the water."

"We can land here then?"

"If the Futama wishes."

Slightly exasperated, Joe snapped, "Look, Romana, I'd much rather you called me Joe when we're alone. All this 'Futama' stuff gets a bit wearing after a while."

"Very well." She manipulated the controls and the craft landed softly as thistledown on a mat of the grass-like vegetation.

The canopy hissed open and Joe stepped out of the flyer. He instantly stumbled and held onto a protrusion on the vehicle's bodywork. There was something wrong, but he couldn't put his finger on it. He released his hold on the craft, feeling as though he could leap almost to the tops of the trees. And that was the answer: the gravity here was around one third of what he was accustomed to. As Gillane had explained, the force of gravity was controlled only within the confines of the city of Veloran.

Above them the treetops were obscured by outreaching foliage, which formed a thick under-canopy thirty metres above ground, producing a shadowy world, punctuated only by stray shafts of light penetrating horizontally between the massive trunks. He stepped through low undergrowth, interspersed with a profusion of ground-crawling roots until he came to the base of the nearest tree. He'd seen pictures of sequoia trees in California, but they were mere saplings by comparison. The trunk was covered with a corklike substance, which, Joe thought, would probably possess none of its properties. With his eyes growing accustomed to the gloom, he could see further into the forest. All ground vegetation petered out less than fifty metres into the perpetual darkness and the soil between the massive trunks was utterly barren of life.

It was eerily quiet, with no birdsong or chirruping of insects, and no scrabbling of squirrels up the massive trunks and into the canopy. As Romana had informed him, the forest contained one kind of life only – plants. But what magnificent plants they were! He wished he had brought his camcorder to make a record to take back to Ciara. She would scarcely believe him otherwise.

Romana was standing in the sunlight, watching him. He strode from under the trees and joined her in the open. "Pretty impressive," he said. "Now, do you think there's time to take a quick detour over the sea?"

Romana nodded. "Let's go."

The forest was a green blur below the craft as her speed increased to a rate that ate up the kilometres. A dark smudge appeared on the horizon and rapidly grew into a broad stretch of indigo sea. Now, the horizon was a series of large islands, which, from this height, Joe could see were covered in the telltale green of forests. The land sank out of sight behind them as they headed out to sea at a height of four-hundred metres. The dark surface below was flecked with occasional whitecaps, indicating a variable wind across the water. Romana swooped downwards and pointed to a number of lighter patches in the sea. Joe followed her pointing finger. He could see, just below the surface, a school of giant eels, each one more than fifty metres long, their sinewy bodies snaking through the swell with a grace that would be hard to match on land.

As the shadow of the craft fell on the water amongst the eels, one of the creatures gave a violent twist of its body and propelled itself vertically like a leaping salmon. Joe caught a glimpse of a cavernous mouth, armed with rank upon rank of serrated teeth, hurtling up at the flyer. With a deft flick of her fingers Romana veered the flyer upwards at a prodigious rate, out of reach of the snapping jaws. Even so, they heard the raucous screech of the giant eel's nose horn as it scraped along the bottom surface of the flyer.

182

The eel fell back gracefully, producing a plume of spray that climbed into the sky beyond the level of the craft.

Too late, several more of the behemoths leapt from the water, splashing down in the light gravity in explosions of white spray. The tiny craft climbed higher and higher, and from the extra altitude, Joe saw more white shapes below the surface, arrowing towards the disturbance. The sea turned red as massive jaws and teeth tore at the unsuspecting monster eels in a frenzied orgy of destruction, surpassing anything Joe had ever witnessed. The water's surface heaved and swirled as the school of predators attacked the eels, but as suddenly as it had begun, the savagery was over, and all that remained was a slowly diluting patch of blood.

Joe whistled. "You weren't exaggerating about those things down there. I don't think even a plasma rifle would be much use against them."

Romana's hands flicked back to the controls as a sustained gust of wind, fleeing before the oncoming storm, suddenly buffeted the side of the craft, forcing it to lose height.

"Those are amongst the smaller creatures spawned by the sea," she informed him.

The tiny craft bucked and rocked in the high wind, which was now driving downwards towards the sea after climbing over a long, high promontory. The spur of land was utterly devoid of greenery, all vegetation having been scoured away by past storms. The wind forced the flyer from its relative safety out of reach of the sea creatures, down towards the heaving surface. Romana's long fingers flew deftly over the controls and the flyer rose once again, only to be staggered by another blast even stronger than before. Height melted away, until they were only a few metres above the carnage taking place just below the surface, and Joe knew that if any one of the creatures sensed their presence, they would become the focus of attention once again.

"Make it climb!" he yelled, but the whining of the flyer's drive and the crashing of the waves rendered any kind of audible communication useless. Romana flicked a glance his way before returning her attention to piloting the bucking flyer.

The wind is forcing us downwards she said in his mind, *and the controls will not respond. We must go lower before we can rise again.*

"But we can't go lower or we'll be at the mercy of those things down there," Joe screamed.

We are left with no alternative, came the voice in his mind. *Now we shall discover if this craft is as good as its makers claim.*

The waves drew closer until Joe thought it must be possible to touch them. Salt spray hissed against the plexiglass canopy and the drive whined in protest until, with a resonating shudder, the tiny craft plunged beneath the waves.

"What are you doing?" Joe protested. "You've seen what those monsters can do in their own environment. It's madness to give them a chance to get to us down here."

QUIET, FUTAMA! came the telepathic shout in Joe's mind, *I need to concentrate if we are to escape their jaws. Please, no more interruptions!*

Sheepishly, Joe sat back in his seat and surveyed the water streaming past the hull. He watched seaweed and pieces of dismembered eel approach and recede far more rapidly than he would have considered possible. The flyer was scything through the water at a remarkable rate of knots. Two of the behemoths spied the flyer and gave chase, veering towards the tiny craft on each side. Romana gunned the motor and they slowly began to gain on their pursuers.

Joe sighed in relief, but the notion of safety was short lived, because the two huge sea creatures suddenly increased their pace as if infused with new energy. They were only a few metres behind when Joe yelled, "Hard right!" and yanked the control binnacle. The flyer slewed around and monstrous jaws snapped shut on seawater where the craft had been an instant before. The second creature twisted and snapped at the flyer but its teeth made no impression on the plasteel hull. Splinters of teeth mixed with blood slid down the outer surface of the canopy and its effect on the other creature was instantaneous and deadly. The behemoth lost all interest in the flyer and struck at its companion, aiming at the source of the blood. It grasped the lower jaw of its companion ferociously in its mouth, locking together, teeth on teeth, jaw upon jaw, twisting and turning in a titanic struggle to gain advantage. A swiftly increasing volume of red blood was colouring the water around the tiny flyer as the two monsters ripped each other apart with single-minded viciousness that might have been fascinating in any other circumstances.

Romana stared wide-eyed at the titanic struggle until Joe once again yanked the binnacle beneath her fingers. "Let's get out of here before they remember what they were chasing," he yelled.

184

When the carnage lay some distance behind them Romana gave a shudder as her pent up fear subsided. "My apologies for shouting telepathically, Futama," she said, "but I needed all my concentration, and you were making such a commotion with your mind that I could not think clearly."

Abashed, Joe replied, "I'm the one who needs to apologise, Romana. It was obvious you had your hands full at the time, and I shouldn't have been such a wimp. I had no idea," he added, "that these flyers were supposed to work underwater as well as in the air."

"They were designed to operate underwater," Romana admitted ruefully, "but we have never been able to use the capability on Mars, due to the size and savageness of the majority of the sea creatures." She scanned the instruments and turned the nose of the flyer upwards. "It is time to go. We are attracting unwanted attention." A screen depicted several dots, rapidly growing in size. A shoal of creatures of indeterminate size and undoubted ferocity was approaching at impressive speed.

The tiny ship plunged upwards at increasing velocity until, in a storm of foam and spray, she leapt upwards into the sky, leaving the angry wave crests vanishing in the diminishing visibility below. Romana maintained power for several more minutes and, eventually, the flyer emerged into clear, violet tinged sky above the storm clouds. She climbed another thousand metres and levelled out, before setting course for the flyer to return to Veloran on autopilot. Romana slumped in her seat, completely enervated by the experience. After all, she had been responsible for almost losing the Futama to the denizens of the ocean.

Joe studied her relaxed, almost boneless form, draped uncomfortably over the upholstered arms of the pilot's chair. "Are you okay?" he enquired.

"With her eyes still closed against the horrors of the past few minutes, Romana replied through clenched teeth, "I confess that I have failed the Futama and his Faithful, by placing him in such terrible danger, and I fear that Gillane will forever bar me from your presence for what I have done." Tears welled from her eyes and seeped slowly down her cheeks.

Joe reached over and wiped away the tears. She shuddered and the tears flowed more freely. Constrained by the limitations of the tiny cockpit and the bonds of love tying him to Ciara, Joe embraced the beautiful woman, resting her cheek on his shoulder

185

and gently stroking her hair. Romana sobbed quietly, oblivious to Joe's attempts to ease her distress.

Finally, Joe said, "Come on, Romana, I won't let that happen. I'm pretty sure that this episode was meant to be. And even if it wasn't, I want you with me." He laughed harshly. "And I am the Futama . . . or so they keep telling me, so I hope my word will count for something."

Romana sobbed and hiccoughed, then sat upright and smiled. "Thank you, Joe. You are a good man. You tell us that you are just an ordinary man, but everything you do tells us that you have extraordinary qualities of bravery and compassion."

"I think you must be mistaking me for someone else," Joe replied flippantly.

"Along with all the rest of your people," Romana asserted with a genuine smile that lit up her beautiful face. "Can so many people be wrong?"

"I suppose not," Joe admitted as the craft banked towards the city of Veloran.

Chapter Eighteen

IN TRAINING:

Joe stood on the edge of an empty stage in one corner of the recreation ground, his six metre high holographic image occupying the middle of the wooden platform. Before him, was a sea of more than three thousand expectant faces. Five identical stages around the perimeter of the field each contained a holographic projector with its accompanying image of Joe.

Down the middle of the arena, an impressive assault course had been rapidly, but efficiently, erected. It included a stepping area, nets – both vertical and hugging the ground – a high wall, rope bridges and a high tower, from which the trainees would abseil to the ground after scaling knotted ropes to its highest point. The assault course was intended to improve physical fitness and physical strength and, above all, mental toughness in a people unused to the rigours of physical training. The floor of the arena for some considerable distance around Joe's stage was lined with more than five hundred crash mats.

As he stared at the crowd, Joe's mind wandered back to his meeting with the Council of Elders, when he had outlined his plans for instruction and training of the army. As Romana had predicted, Gillane had been appalled at their dangerous excursion over – and under – the sea. He had furiously berated the unfortunate Romana, until Joe had stepped in and told everyone present that she had been complying with his wishes. Amid protests, Joe had insisted that Romana was still his guide, and would remain so until he decided otherwise. The Council had reluctantly demurred, sensing that Joe's mind was irrevocably set. As he had told Romana, he was the Futama and his opinion must count for something. The mental images brought a smile to Joe's lips, which transferred to the huge holograms around the arena.

Joe cleared his throat, and the noise was amplified by the holographic images. He spread his arms wide to embrace his audience. "Welcome to the first day of your training. None of you will find this easy, but I can assure you that when your training is complete, you'll feel a sense of comradeship that will, perhaps, transcend even your membership of the Faithful. You will punish your bodies with exercise, and at times you will feel that you cannot go on. But perseverance will produce its rewards and you will come

187

to trust your bodies and your comrades to an extent that you would never have believed possible.

"Over the past week or so, I have selected and trained a number of instructors, who will pass on their knowledge to you. Please follow their orders, and whenever you feel that the training is difficult, I want you to remember that your instructors are working with you and, at the same time, continuing their training with me. They will stand as examples to you all."

He paused to assess the effect of his words on the embryonic army. Everyone was still gazing expectantly at him. "You have already been colour-coded into six groups," he told them, "and each will follow the rota of exercise and training. Every section is vital to the success of the whole programme, so please don't think you're missing out if you're not learning the martial arts with me. Physical fitness and mental toughness are equally important, as you will soon discover. Is everyone ready? Then let's go!"

The throng swiftly split into six sections of roughly five hundred, each under the leadership of three instructors. Analy and Trione mounted the stage to stand beside Joe. All six sections, under the tutelage of their instructors, commenced a series of warming-up exercises. After thirty minutes, one section of the army trotted in double file on a training run, from the recreation ground and into the city streets, accompanied by excited children, who ran alongside for a short distance. Another section began work on the elementary sections of the assault course and a third lined up in ranks to take part in physical training exercises. A fourth group commenced training with weights, leaving Joe to instruct the rest in a combination of basic martial arts moves. Four of the holographic projectors were deactivated, leaving two to make Joe's moves visible to his class.

As Joe's assistants, Analy and Trione had received almost a week of intensive instruction. They were now well versed in breakfall, to prevent personal injury when being slammed or thrown to the ground. Joe had also tutored his two friends in the twelve basic karate 'blocks', so that they could protect themselves from physical attack to any part of their anatomy. The lesson began with Trione attacking the diminutive figure of the Futama with a flailing punch to the head. The tall man flew across the stage, accompanied by a concerted gasp from the class, and landed with a resounding thud on the padded surface. He cushioned his fall perfectly and scrambled to his feet, none the worse for his experience.

"Anyone care to volunteer?" Joe called to the assembly. No one moved. "Okay," he continued with a grin, "that was a small insight into what you can achieve, if you're prepared to work at it. As you can see, Trione was unhurt because he knew how to break his fall, and that is going to be your first lesson. Now, everyone take off their footwear and throw it aside. Then can I have thirty volunteers?"

This time the crowd surged forward to the edge of the stage. Joe raised his hands and they halted, expectantly. He selected twenty-nine men and the solitary woman in the front rank to join him on the stage, where he proceeded to demonstrate the basic forward breakfall. His students repeated his actions and their movements were relayed to the rest via the giant hologram. "Now, everybody try it," Joe ordered, and everyone spread out, two per mat, practising the technique, while the giant hologram continued to replay the move. Joe hopped down from the stage and strolled amongst the students, adjusting here, encouraging there, until he was sure everyone understood exactly what was required. During the training session, Joe demonstrated several breakfalls and was pleased with the manner in which the trainees progressed from the simplest to the most difficult fall. Eventually, his group moved on to the physical training area to be replaced by the next group of novices and the training continued throughout the day until three thousand students trooped wearily, but with a very real sense of achievement, back to their homes.

Joe met with Romana and his two bodyguards for a meal at Romana's home. As in the refectories aboard ship and in the compound on Earth, the food was provided by dispensers, with little or no input from Romana, save the choosing of the variety. Joe found the food palatable but not exciting, but he had no idea of its nutritional value.

"Does anyone eat fresh food around here?" he demanded.

"No, why do you ask?" came the reply.

"Because training for the martial arts is not just about the physical side, it's also about getting your nutrition exactly right. In order to build up your body, you must eat the correct balance of protein, carbohydrates and vitamins. If you don't, you will never reach the peak of energy and stamina necessary to maintain your training." He contemplated the shiny surface of the food dispenser. "Can you alter the formulation of the food so that you get exactly what you want?"

"Of course," Romana replied. "Though, if everyone changed their requirements, it would upset the balance of ingredients in the storehouses. Such a change would require the consent of the Council of Elders. The formulation of the food here on Mars is calculated to provide a perfectly balanced diet for all and I would suggest, as a doctor, that the trainees merely consume more food to fill the energy deficit brought on by hard physical training."

"Fine," Joe grinned, "you're the doctor, so I think I'll leave that aspect of the training regime to you."

Romana smiled. "Thank you."

* * *

Prua Landi strode with renewed purpose around her sumptuous apartment. "Now that the pathetic Futama has been eliminated," she told a relaxed Perdon, "we can concentrate on plans for our future, without the blight of his followers infecting every aspect of our existence."

"We? My Lady?"

"Yes, Perdon, we. I include you because you are a rare commodity in this intrigue-ridden world of mine."

Perdon's eyebrows rose. "A rare commodity, My Lady?"

"Yes, Perdon, you have proven yourself to be completely trustworthy and diligent in my service and, to show my appreciation, I intend to announce you as my sole deputy. You will have the freedom to seek out and destroy any scattered remnants of that abominable sect, and I expect you to show no mercy."

Perdon bowed deeply. "I am honoured, My Lady." He straightened his long frame and met Prua Landi's eyes. "I will serve you well. Give me one year, and the Faithful will be merely a distant memory."

"This aspect of your personality is, shall we say . . . unexpected," Prua Landi purred, "and I find it most attractive. I— "

Door chimes interrupted her and she spat venomously, "Enter!"

The door dilated and the captain of the palace guard entered, followed by two hulking troopers dragging between them the badly bruised and almost naked figure of a man. They released his wrists and he collapsed, semi-conscious into the deep pile of the carpet. Prua Landi stared at the pitiful bundle on the floor, then at the captain of the guard. That worthy grunted an order and the two troopers reached down and hauled the prisoner unceremoniously to his feet, where he stood, with his eyes closed and his chin lolling on his chest.

"What is this . . . thing?" Prua Landi demanded icily.

"He is a spy of the Faithful," the captain informed her. "He was discovered carrying an explosive device within the palace grounds."

Prua Landi entered the prisoner's turgid, unresisting mind and, after a few moments, hastily exited. "This creature knows nothing that we do not already know. But," an evil glint flashed in her eyes, "*we* have much to tell *him*." She stepped forward and jerked the man's head upwards so that he could see her. His eyes remained closed and she dug a long fingernail into his cheek to elicit a reaction.

The prisoner's eyes opened and he stared defiantly at Prua Landi. A mixture of spittle and blood drooled from the corner of his mouth. "Our Futama will come," he gasped weakly.

Prua Landi laughed, a harsh, chilling sound that made the prisoner jerk involuntarily in the troopers' grasp. "You pitiful creature," she sneered. "You have waited so long for the one you worship to release you from the bonds of my rule, but the irony is that you and the rest of your sect have waited in vain. Your Futama is dead."

The man somehow shook off the restraining hands and stood defiantly erect. "You're lying!" he screamed. "Our Futama *will* come."

Prua Landi smiled, and its effect was, somehow, more chilling than her anger. She snapped her fingers with a loud report. "Perdon," she commanded, "show him your recording of the distant past!"

Perdon called a monitor from a recess in the wall of the apartment and issued a rapid series of instructions. Immediately, the recording of the incident involving the destruction of the Lunar Sunrise was replayed as a hologram in the middle of the floor. When the recording reached its conclusion, the prisoner fell to his knees and beat the carpet with his fists, screaming and wailing, believing that Prua Landi had killed all hope for the future of his people.

Prua Landi regarded him with amusement. "If this is an example of the followers of the Futama," she commented, "then the world will be well rid of them all." She favoured Perdon with a knowing look. "Your task should be a simple one, don't you agree?"

Perdon nodded. "Yes, My Lady."

"Then let us begin with this creature," Prua Landi said brightly. "Captain, please dispose of it."

Perdon was busily deactivating the monitor as the Captain and his troopers dragged the unprotesting prisoner away.

* * *

With the training programme established and working efficiently, Joe had time on his hands to think about home. He became increasingly morose and introverted until Romana could hold her peace no longer.

"You wish to see Ciara again, don't you?" she said. It was a statement rather than a question.

"Is it that obvious?" Joe enquired sheepishly.

"You carry with you an aura of yearning, and everyone feels your pain."

"Are you telling me that the mind control exercises aren't working?"

Romana smiled sympathetically. "The exercises are working well. If they were not, I think you would blanket the whole of Mars with your thoughts, such is their potency."

Joe grinned. "There's only one thing to do then, isn't there?"

"I will make the arrangements with the Council of Elders," Romana told him. "Since the Council was informed that Prua Landi believes you are dead, there should be no need for Analy and Trione to accompany you as bodyguards." Her eyes clouded for a moment. "Do you wish me to return home with you?" she asked.

Joe could sense Romana's longing. The tall medic had been his constant companion since his first visit with Ciara to the complex on Earth, and she was experiencing increasing difficulty in masking her feelings for him, though she knew that she could never be more than a close friend.

"Would you feel comfortable seeing me and Ciara together?" Joe asked penetratingly, revealing that he recognised Romana's unspoken desire for him.

"No," she said, her voice barely audible, "but I have a duty of care to the wife of the Futama. I am her doctor, and I will sublimate my desires – forever if necessary – to remain a close friend to both of you."

Joe leaned over and kissed Romana gently on the cheek. "I'm glad you're my friend, Romana, really glad." He leaned back in his seat and put his hands behind his head. "You know, I've never asked, is there a Mr Romana anywhere?"

"There was, many years ago."

"Do you want to tell me what happened?"

Romana sighed. "I have never really discussed it with anyone since we came to Mars more than twenty-five years—Earth years, that is—ago."

Joe waited patiently. If it had taken so long for Romana to mention the subject, it would be churlish to chivvy her along now.

"Prua Landi had assumed the mantle of Supreme Empress of all the lands of the Earth. My husband was one of the first peaceful protestors. Prua Landi ordered her troops to fire upon the demonstrators with plasma weapons. The crowd numbered many thousands but, when it was all over, very little remained except a sea of molten pavement in the square before the palace. There were many children amongst the protestors, but that did not stay the trigger fingers of the troops. Since that moment, I have nursed a hatred for Prua Landi and her regime that can only be assuaged by her death."

Joe tenderly embraced his friend, whilst her tall frame was wracked by a series of shuddering sobs, the product of more than twenty-five years of pent up grief.

Eventually, Romana kissed Joe's cheek and hastily drew away. "Thank you, Joe," she sobbed. "I have kept my grief hidden far too long. Perhaps now I will be free to accept another man."

"I truly hope so," Joe agreed, "and whoever it is will be very lucky indeed."

193

Chapter Nineteen

BACK HOME AGAIN:

As Romana had predicted, the Council did not protest at Joe's intention to return home, though they considered it folly to go without an escort. Confirmation had arrived from their agent in the distant future that Prua Landi was making grandiose plans to celebrate the Futama's death. Perdon, the director of her time-travel research had been installed as her sole deputy and had been given the task of seeking out and destroying all members of the Faithful. This particular item of news brought a grim smile of satisfaction to Gillane's lips.

Romana assured the council that she would accompany Joe, and that both she and Joe would be armed with plasma pistols. The Master of Time was preparing to depart for Earth when Terpin received notification of two extra passengers. The captain was delighted to have Joe on board once more and he immediately offered them the freedom of the ship. The journey seemed to take even less time, although Joe spent the whole passage in the observation blister, watching the Earth grow in size. The ship landed softly on the knoll in the carboniferous era and immediately made the time jump to the compound.

From his elevated position, Joe saw that the protective force screen had been repaired and the huge crater in the middle of the compound had been filled in, making use of the vast amount of rocky debris torn from the cliff face by the blast. Joe imagined that with trees and shrubs filling the compound, the area would be little different from the sacred cave of Too-ga's time. When they disembarked and entered the cave, Joe noticed for the first time a set of low stone steps leading into the entrance. The explosion had stripped huge slabs of rock from the surface, and what remained had been fashioned neatly into steps, making use of the natural rock formations.

Orina welcomed them warmly and arranged for provisions in case they had to wait for darkness when they arrived in the twenty-first century. All in all, Joe thought, everything was running considerably more smoothly than on the previous occasions he had passed through the compound. It certainly helped that he was everyone's idea of the good guy. He slung his rucksack, filled with supplies, on his back and his camcorder over his shoulder, and was just about to leave with Romana when Orina stepped out of her office, barring the way. "Is there a problem?" Joe asked

"No," she assured him, "it's just that there is a lack of information reaching us from Mars. No one has informed me what has happened to Marron."

"That's easily rectified," Joe grinned. "He's been under house arrest since he arrived. He actually tried to assault me, but all he got for his trouble was a broken leg."

Orina glanced enquiringly at Romana, but Romana offered no explanation. Perhaps someone would tell that story another time.

Joe continued, "Gillane told me he would normally have been tried by now, but there's so much going on, what with training an army, planning a war and everything, that the trial's pretty low priority. In fact, it's rarely mentioned."

"As I thought," Orina agreed. "Nevertheless, Marron's trial must not be overlooked. I lost a number of good people on the Lunar Sunrise, and the one responsible for their deaths must pay."

Joe adjusted his rucksack to make it more comfortable. "Look," he told the base commander tartly, "I can see you're upset about losing your crew, and I can understand that you want the guilty party to be brought to justice. But just remember this: if Marron *is* a spy, he was working for Prua Landi. Ultimately, she's the one to blame for the deaths of the crew of the Lunar Sunrise. She's the one who must be brought to trial." With that, he strode off down the corridor towards the time-gate to the twenty-first century.

Orina was a little taken aback by the harshness of Joe's tone. Romana drew her aside. "The Futama has been toiling ceaselessly to produce an army capable of defeating Prua Landi, and for some time has yearned for his home and his wife. It comes as no surprise to me that he is occasionally short on patience, so please make allowances."

"As the Futama has asserted on a number of occasions," the base commander said with an ironic smile, "he is only human, and we must, therefore, expect him to display human emotions."

"We must," Romana agreed, before hurrying after Joe, her long legs eating up the distance between them.

When they reached the time-gate, Romana stepped through without waiting for Joe to hold her hand. Once on the other side, Joe mentioned her new ability. Romana informed him that, in order to fulfil her role as the Futama's travelling companion, it had been considered prudent to inject her with the same specialised nanos that coursed through Joe's veins. Joe's bodyguards, Analy and Trione had received their nanos at the same time as Romana.

They continued in silence to the shimmering curtain and walked through, transferring in a gut-wrenching instant to the tunnel leading to the secret cove. They resumed their journey, finally emerging into the weak sunlight of a winter afternoon. Joe had left for Mars during the autumn, but had lost track of the number of days that had passed since then, due to his hectic teaching schedule. The crisp, cold air, bit at their lungs as they slid down the icy rope to the rocky scree below and Joe rued his lack of foresight in omitting gloves from his rucksack. First blowing into his hands, he began to unzip the tent.

Romana was puzzled by his action. "Why do you breathe on your hands?" she enquired.

"Because it's damned cold."

"But your nanos will regulate your body temperature and protect you from the effects of the weather," she assured him. "You will feel the difference very soon."

"I hope it doesn't take long," Joe muttered, "because my fingers are bloody freezing."

Romana smiled at the mild expletive. "I think that your reunion with Ciara cannot come a moment too soon," she said.

"I suppose you're right," Joe admitted as he ducked inside the tiny tent.

Once inside, it became immediately clear that someone had visited the campsite. Everything was neatly stowed and the sleeping bags smelled strongly of fabric softener. Unless a stranger had unaccountably developed the ability to enter the cove, there could be only one culprit.

"Ciara!" Joe exclaimed.

"This certainly bears the imprint of a woman's touch," Romana agreed as she poked her head inside the tent. In a moment of deep insight, she added, "Perhaps this is her way of remaining close to the one she loves, whilst he is far away in both space and time."

"The little minx," Joe whispered, and he experienced a powerful surge of pride and love for his beautiful wife. A tear seeped down his cheek and Romana reached over and lightly brushed it away.

"I envy the bond between you," she said. "But I will never attempt to break it." She turned her face away, before adding, "Though I would gladly change places with Ciara."

To cover up his embarrassment at Romana's admission, Joe decided to collect a pile of driftwood for a fire. As she had explained, the nanos had altered his body chemistry, so that he no longer felt the cold, but he felt certain that, somehow, there must be a price to pay, most likely in the form of a vastly increased appetite to supplement his energy levels. In fact, now that thoughts of food had entered his mind, he felt the first grumbling of hunger in his stomach. As there was no driftwood in the tiny cove, he made his way to the main beach, which was completely deserted. All signs of the investigation had disappeared from the beach. A few minutes later, he returned to the tent with an armful of flotsam and dropped the assorted material onto the grass.

Deftly, he built up a conical stack within a circle of stones, and began to scrape off wood shavings to use as tinder, roundly cursing the absence of paper. Romana smiled indulgently and drew out her pistol from inside her clothing. Adjusting the setting to minimum power and maximum spread, she pressed the firing stud and directed a cone of blue-white plasma at the driftwood for a few seconds, producing a fire that might well have been blazing for hours. She threw a few more pieces of wood into the fire and sat back to admire her handiwork.

"Neat!" Joe said in admiration. "Every boy scout should have one." But the joke was completely wasted on his friend from the distant future.

* * *

The hours passed slowly in the tiny cove and Joe became increasingly edgy in the light of the blazing fire. He was so near to Ciara and yet he could not go to her because Romana's impressive height would immediately draw unwanted attention to them. Seven o'clock came and went but midnight seemed, somehow, even further away. He leapt to his feet and paced the tiny beach, kicking pebbles into the water in frustration.

Romana's voice floated over the intervening space. "You should go to Ciara without delay. If you wish, I will remain here until it is safe for me to join you."

"That won't be necessary," Joe told her, "I don't think there'll be many people about at this time."

197

Romana was already rising to her feet. "Shall we go, then?" she urged, "I confess I cannot bear your feelings of impatience."

Joe threw the rucksack onto his back and grabbed his camcorder. "You know, I'm not sure I can bear them myself," he grinned.

On the walk to Joe's home they encountered a solitary old man walking his dog. Romana entered the oldster's mind and adjusted his memory of the encounter, and they reached Joe's front door with no further alarms.

Joe searched through his pockets for his key, becoming increasingly agitated when he could not locate it. He had just begun a more methodical search, when the door flew open and Ciara leapt into his arms, raining kisses upon every part of his face. He held her face in his hands and gasped, "Steady on, girl, I've only been away a couple of months."

"Three months, two weeks and four days," Ciara corrected, "and I'll tell you how many hours if you wait just a moment."

"That long?" Joe queried. "Are you sure?"

"Work it out for yourself. Tomorrow's Christmas Eve."

Joe was astounded. Little wonder he'd become morose and edgy whilst on Mars. The time had passed quickly, but separation from his wife had inevitably taken its toll. Ciara ushered them indoors, first glancing up and down the quiet suburban street before closing the door.

Once inside, she threw her arms around Joe's neck and kissed him passionately, pausing only to take a deep breath. Romana retired to the kitchen to make a pot of tea, eventually emerging with a tray containing three mugs of the steaming beverage and a plateful of chocolate biscuits. Ciara seemed to notice the tall medic for the first time. A flush of embarrassment rose up her cheeks. "Uh, sorry, Romana. I didn't realise you were there."

Romana smiled sweetly. "In your shoes, I believe I would also have been blind to my surroundings." She offered a mug of tea to each of her friends.

Ciara gave Joe a peck on his cheek and led Romana into the kitchen. She glanced over her shoulder at Joe. "Girly chat," she told him.

In the kitchen she treated Romana to a genuine hug of friendship. "I'm really glad to see you, "she said, "but could you do me a favour?"

"Of course."

"Could you tell Maeve and Or-gon that Joe's back? And—" she blushed a deep pink, "could you take your time about it?"

"Yes, but first you must allow me to examine you. As you are the wife of the Futama and the bearer of his unborn child, I must give you the benefit of my medical expertise."

Ciara smiled warmly. "I'm not about to argue, but if you really want to know, I feel absolutely amazing. In fact, I've never felt so well."

"That will be one benefit of the nanomedics in your system," Romana mused absently as she ran the diagnostic over Ciara's abdomen. "You'll be glad to know the baby is in perfect health," she said, moving her examination to the rest of Ciara's body. Eventually, she passed the instrument over Ciara's head and gave a nod of satisfaction. "Everything is exactly as it should be. You are a very fortunate woman."

"Fortunate?" Ciara enquired, "what do you mean exactly?"

"You have the Futama and you have the Futama's child within you," Romana whispered, unable to keep the emotion from her voice.

The two women faced each other in silence for a few seconds. "I had no idea you felt that way about Joe," Ciara said quietly. "Does he know?"

"Yes, and he also knows that I will never do anything to hurt either of you. In fact—" It was evident to Ciara that Romana was experiencing considerable emotional pain. "In fact, I am prepared to share my thoughts and my emotions with you to prove I am telling the truth."

"You would do that?"

"Yes."

"In that case, I don't need to experience your thoughts, even if I knew how." Ciara clasped Romana in an emotional embrace. "I know I can trust you with Joe," she told her, "and I consider myself amazingly lucky to have you as a friend."

At that moment, Joe walked into the kitchen with his empty mug. "Everything okay?" he asked.

With watery eyes, Ciara informed him, "Yes, Joe, everything is absolutely fine. Romana's just going round to let Mum and Or-gon know you're back. I take it you've finished your business with Prua Landi?"

Joe turned his face away, unable to look his wife in the eye whilst he told her that he must leave again in a few days. Romana accepted the hint and left them alone in order to pass on Ciara's message.

Ciara was thunderstruck. "I thought it must be all over," she whispered. "Are you telling me it isn't?"

Taking a deep breath, Joe told Ciara what had happened so far, leaving nothing out, not even the unexpected journey to the barely formed Earth and the encounter with the creatures beneath Mars' sea. He saved the best part till last. "You'll be glad to know that Prua Landi thinks I'm dead. She thinks the Master of Time was destroyed in the explosion that sent us much further back in time than we'd anticipated. She's making preparations for world-wide celebrations and it's going to come as a bit of a shock when we suddenly arrive in her time hell bent on getting rid of her. It tips the odds significantly in our favour."

"Odds or no odds, it doesn't stop me worrying about you," Ciara breathed.

"I know, Darling," Joe soothed, "I know. Try not to worry. It'll soon be over, one way or another."

"That's the trouble," Ciara whispered, "the uncertainty. It bothers me that I might never see you again."

"That won't happen," Joe assured her. "I intend to be around to watch little Joe grow up." He placed a finger on Ciara's lips. "Shh, now! Let's leave all the worrying till later," he said, as he urged Ciara towards the stairs.

* * *

Christmas Day proved to be a huge hit with Or-gon and Romana. Joe and Ciara had shopped for presents for everyone and had bought extra food for the festive season. They had wrapped the presents in pretty paper and laid them beneath the brightly lit Christmas tree, ready for opening after Christmas lunch. The table in Maeve's dining room was heavily laden with tureens of mashed and roast potatoes, sprouts, carrots and roast parsnips and a large, golden brown turkey, garnished with strips of streaky bacon around the edge of the dish. The array was complemented by a double row of devils on horseback. The main focus of Maeve's culinary prowess held pride of place on the table and Joe was assigned the honour of carving.

Romana and Or-gon wore expressions bordering on alarm as the knife sliced through the turkey breast, neither being accustomed to eating meat of any kind.

200

"It's all right," Joe said jovially, "you don't have to eat it if you don't want to. He proffered a sliver of white meat to Romana. "Why don't you try some? Who knows, you might find you like it."

Romana pulled a face but, despite herself, reached out tentatively to take the tiny piece of meat. She sniffed warily and touched the morsel to her lips before taking a hesitant bite. After a few moments, her eyes widened in delight. "This is truly the flesh of an animal?" she asked.

"A bird, yes. Bred for the table. In the wild, it would have been prey for any number of animals."

Romana glanced at the array of foods on the table and said, "Then I will join you in consuming the flesh of the bird."

Or-gon, who had watched Romana tasting the morsel of turkey, put up two large hands. "Not for me, Joe, thank you," he protested. "Since I have lived here with Maeve, I have never betrayed the traditions of Tarmis." He grinned, toothily. "Anyway, there seems to be an abundance of different flavours for me to savour, many more, in truth, than I would ever have encountered in the homogenised food we were accustomed to in Tarmis."

Once Joe had carved the turkey, everyone sat down at the table and Maeve filled their generous sized glasses with wine. Ciara, naturally, abstained from the alcohol, due to her condition.

As the meal progressed, Joe watched the interaction between Maeve and Or-gon, and it was increasingly apparent that in the period since he had last been home, the pair had grown even closer.

Joe commented, "I'm glad you two are getting along so well. You both deserve a shot at happiness."

A pink flush spread instantly over his mother-in-law's face, contrasting strangely with her flame-red hair.

Ciara grinned with delight. "I think it's fantastic, don't you?"

"It's nothing to do with me," Joe informed her, "but if anyone's asking my opinion, I'm all for it. In the end, though, it's what Or-gon and Maeve think that counts."

Maeve blushed even deeper. "I'm glad you approve, Joe," she told him, a tear of happiness glistening in the light from the window. "I know you're not exactly my flesh and blood, but I do value your opinion, you know."

"You're welcome, both of you," Joe grinned. "Now let's finish off this sumptuous food. It would be a pity if it spoiled because we can't stop talking."

The rest of the meal passed in relative silence as everyone cleared their plates and moved on to the Christmas pudding. Finally, Maeve poured coffee and it was time to open presents. Romana was delighted with her gift of a solid gold pendant, containing a miniature photograph of Joe. As she opened the present, a look of understanding passed between the two young women.

Thank you she said silently to Ciara, who replied, "You can keep him with you always."

I will.

Or-gon, who had said little during the meal, opened his present – a complete watchmaker's toolkit – and confessed, "I am intrigued by this Christmas festival. Does anyone know its origin?" He glanced expectantly at Maeve, Ciara and Joe.

Joe, despite being an agnostic, thought about Or-gon's query before replying, "I don't know exactly how old the idea of celebrating Christmas this way might be, but it's based on the coming of a messiah more than two-thousand years ago. His birth was prophesied for centuries, and many people believed he was the Son of God, sent to save mankind from their sins. Eventually, he was ordered to be killed - in the most barbaric fashion – by the regional governor, under pressure from the priesthood."

Or-gon frowned, forming deep furrows on his protruding Neanderthal brow. "There is a parallel with the prophesy of the coming of the Futama. But," he added quickly, "we were not so barbaric as to put the Futama to death. Although, as we are all well aware, Prua Landi would be delighted to see him dead."

Romana remained silent. In her natural time, she and the rest of the Faithful had been cast into exile for their belief in the coming of the Futama – a prophesy which would soon be fulfilled in a battle against Prua Landi and her forces.

Joe, meanwhile, experienced a deep discomfort at the parallel Or-gon had drawn between the legend of the Futama and the coming of the Messiah. He had always stopped short of being an atheist but, however hard he tried, he seemed unable to make up his mind one way or the other about the concept of an omniscient God.

When everyone had opened their presents, Maeve noticed two small parcels beneath the Christmas tree. She raised an eyebrow and Ciara quickly informed her that they were for Analy and Trione, whose swift intervention had prevented them all from falling victim to Prua Landi's murderous intent.

"We owe them a lot more than a couple of small presents," Ciara told her mother soberly, "but I think the gesture will be appreciated."

A couple of days later, Joe and Ciara embarked on a short holiday to a country hotel in the Scottish Borders, where they celebrated Hogmanay in the traditional fashion and spent a few days in otherwise quiet surroundings becoming reacquainted. On the third of January, they returned home completely revitalised. As they let themselves in, they discovered Romana sitting on the settee before the television, reviewing Joe's recordings of his adventures with Too-ga and his people. She arose languidly as they entered and embraced Ciara affectionately.

"It is good to see you both again," she said, with relief. "I was worried. Despite the fact that Prua Landi believes Joe dead, there is always the possibility that she still seeks proof of his demise. For that reason, I believe we may have outstayed our welcome in this time. When Prua Landi is finally vanquished, that will be the time to return to your home."

"You're saying it's time to go?" Ciara was dismayed. Although she had known Joe and Romana must return to the past, she had become accustomed to having them around, and was reluctant to say goodbye. "Joe, tell me you'll stay at least a little while longer."

Joe hugged his wife and kissed her unselfconsciously. "Sorry, Darling, but if Romana thinks its time, then it's time."

Ciara pushed him away. "Haven't you got any say in the matter?" she demanded angrily. "After all, you are the Futama."

Joe winced at the jibe. "Of course I have, and I agree with Romana. Anyway, the sooner we go back, the sooner we get to finish this whole affair once and for all. When that happy day arrives, no force on this Earth will be able to prise me away from your side."

"Do you really mean that?"

"You know I do," Joe asserted.

"Ahem!" Romana's small cough shattered the tension. Two pairs of eyes turned towards the tall medic. "You should listen to the Futama's thoughts," Romana suggested, "and you will discover that he is speaking from the heart."

Joe blushed at the revelation that he was once again broadcasting his thoughts. Ciara gave a nervous laugh. "Do you mean telepathy?" she asked Romana, who nodded sagely.

203

"But I don't know anything about that sort of thing," Ciara protested. "People might be able to do it where you come from, but this is the twenty-first century, you know—" She let the sentence tail off.

Romana smiled sympathetically. She had grown to adulthood amongst peers, endowed with the ability to read minds, and had never had to consciously learn the techniques involved – merely the restraints imposed by good manners and convention. Both Ciara and Joe had been infused with nanomachinery, which had so adjusted their nervous systems that telepathy was one of a number of enhancements they would eventually learn to live with.

"Take my word for it," she informed Ciara, "Joe meant every word he said. When Prua Landi is dead, I promise to return with the Futama and teach you how to use all the enhancements the nanomedics have made to your body and your mind."

"When will that be?"

Romana's beautiful features registered uncertainty. "No one knows. But I believe the timescale will be in weeks, rather than months."

Ciara buried her face in Joe's chest. "Please make it weeks . . . for me?"

Joe ran his fingers through his wife's lustrous, dark hair. He lifted her chin with his finger, then patted her abdomen lovingly. "Don't worry, Darling. Just take care of little Joe and I'll be back before you realise I'm gone. Say goodbye to Or-gon and Maeve for us, won't you? It's best if we go now, before we allow goodbyes to get in the way."

Ciara nodded dumbly. Joe had been home for less than two weeks and now he was departing again, perhaps forever. "I'll just pop round to Mum's then," she said bravely, "and I don't suppose I'll find you here when I get back."

Joe stepped back to let Ciara pass him on her way to the door. "No," he admitted sadly, "I don't suppose you will."

Chapter Twenty

FUGITIVE:

The complex at the sacred cave was a hive of activity when Joe and Romana arrived in the time of the early Neanderthals. The system of tunnels housed a much greater population than on previous occasions, many of whom Joe recognised from the training sessions on Mars. It seemed that events were beginning to move. They reported to Leiki's office to find a harassed Orina placing several packs of medical supplies inside a storage locker. Romana raised an eyebrow quizzically.

"I've been ordered to hand these over to you, as soon as you arrive," Orina informed her. "The Council won't tell me what they are, except that they're some special kind of nanos. They tell me you'll know what they are. Anyway," she grumbled, "I'm only the *director* here."

Romana and Joe exchanged glances. Events were obviously beginning to accelerate apace. Soon, Orina would need to know everything, but until Gillane gave the word, they must keep the plans of the forthcoming invasion secret.

"Is the Master of Time in the compound?" Joe asked Orina?

She nodded. "Yes, the ship is busily engaged in transferring troops from Mars. She leaves in less than an hour."

"In that case, we'd better get moving," Joe told Romana, "because we don't want to miss the boat." To Orina he said, "We'll be back when we've talked with Gillane and the rest of the council, and I'm going to insist on you being brought up to date when we return to the compound. I can see why Gillane is playing his cards close to his chest, because he obviously doesn't want anyone to pre-empt the invasion through an abundance of misdirected enthusiasm. Nor has anyone forgotten Marron. Where there is one spy, there may well be others."

Orina smiled. "I believe I can wait a few more days."

"In that case, let's go," Joe urged Romana, "the bus service to Mars doesn't exactly run every ten minutes."

Chuckling at Joe's attempt at humour, Orina warned, "Take care when you enter the compound. There is considerable construction work taking place. I have been asked to provide temporary accommodation for around two-thousand soldiers." She addressed Joe. "The Futama may be interested to know that a number of the primitive humans have been observed at the forest margin watching the increased activity in the compound."

Joe nodded. "You shouldn't be surprised," he said, "they're brighter than your people give them credit for. They're bound to be curious, especially since I told them that they must treat these caves as a special focus of their daily lives, and pass the knowledge on to the generations to follow."

Emerging into the bright sunlight, Joe saw that Orina, if anything, had understated the level of activity in the compound. Everywhere, men and women toiled to erect prefabricated accommodation. The buildings were of simple, utilitarian design, and each was being erected on a pre-levelled section of hard ground. Joe noticed that the bedrock was not being modified, merely the thin layer of compacted earth overlying the rocky strata. Obviously, efforts were being made to minimise the effects of the building work upon the environment, so that there would be no discernible evidence of occupation for the archaeologists of the future to puzzle over.

He was reminded of the sacred cave and the frieze incised into the back wall, which constituted a blatant archaeological anomaly, and he wondered how the cave had remained undiscovered in his own time. He was familiar with the countryside around his hometown and was unable to recall a cliff face anywhere near the locality of the sacred cave. Come to think of it, nor could he recall the discovery of any kind of late Palaeolithic cave dwelling near to where Too-ga's cave existed thirty-five thousand years before the twenty-first century. He knew that the cliff face containing Too-ga's cave still existed, but not as in the Neanderthal past; clearly, there had been a major rock fall since those times, which had obliterated the outer cave. However, in the case of the sacred cave, not even the cliff face existed in the twenty-first century, suggesting that the immediate landscape had been modified by the Faithful to conceal their occupation in the early Neanderthal past. He resolved to discuss the matter with Gillane when he arrived on Mars – if the opportunity arose.

They wove their way between buildings towards the Master of Time, whose huge bulk dwarfed even the buildings around her. Many of the construction workers bowed their heads in acknowledgement of Joe's presence amongst them, leaving him vaguely uncomfortable. He knew he should get used to the deference paid to him by the Faithful, but had never managed to get rid of the feeling that a there had been a horrible mistake, and he would inevitably be revealed as an imposter. He glanced between the building activity towards the edge of the forest, and spied a small group of Neanderthals, nonchalantly observing the compound.

"You go on," he told Romana, "and tell Terpin I won't be long. I just want a word with Char."

Romana smiled and continued walking towards the ship. She had grown accustomed to Joe's sudden diversions. "I think the captain will be prepared to delay take-off for you. We both know that Terpin admires you greatly, but no doubt he has a tight schedule to maintain. He would appreciate delays being kept to a minimum."

"Right," Joe grinned, setting off at a trot towards the perimeter fence, "I'll make it as quick as I can."

Char, the medicine woman, greeted Joe with the sign of welcome from the other side of the fence. She was accompanied by Dar and Reed and three husky men, who glanced around occasionally, keeping a lookout for predators. Joe returned the sign and asked why they were there.

My people are curious, Char replied, the signs flowing from her bony arms and hands, *to see where the Futama and his tribe live and hunt.*

This is not our place Joe told her, *and we will soon be gone. Then you will see the cave and keep it sacred for all time. It is a place where you will give thanks to the spirits of the hunt.* He looked into the dirty faces of the primitive tribespeople. *Your Futama will be gone from you for many generations. Remember me in your tales beside the campfires.*

Without waiting for a reaction to his farewell, Joe turned on his heels and strode off in the direction of the Master of Time, a small portion of which he spied through the skeleton of an impressively large building that seemed to be growing even as he watched. The guttural sounds of the embryonic Neanderthal speech followed him, vying futilely to compete with the din of the noisy construction site.

On board the Master of Time, Captain Terpin spared a few moments from preparations for take-off to welcome Joe aboard. "Heron has prepared a seat for you in the observatory," he explained. "He is awaiting you there." He grinned at the puzzled expression on Joe's face. "Doubtless he will be delighted to see you again."

"In that case, I'd better not disappoint him. How long before take-off?"

"Now that you are aboard, no more than ten of your minutes."

"In that case, I'd better hurry." Joe excused himself and hurried off in the direction of the observatory, which was housed in a bubble at the highest point of the huge ship.

Heron greeted him with obvious pleasure. Eventually, he said, mysteriously, "I have made a gift for the Futama."

"A gift?"

"Yes," Heron explained, "I have felt the joy our Futama experiences every time he witnesses the sights of the distant past and interplanetary space, and I have made an instrument to record the whole of our journey, using a medium transferable to your—" he coughed apologetically, "primitive recording device."

Joe was intrigued. "Where is it?" he asked.

Heron showed Joe a small, flat box of dull grey material, which nestled in the palm of his hand. "This instrument will simultaneously record the output of every optical device on the outer surface of the Master of Time." He held out his other hand. "Would the Futama permit me to insert the necessary electronics into his own machine?"

Warily, Joe handed over his digital camcorder. "Are you sure I'll still be able to transfer the data back home?"

"You will encounter no problems when I have inserted the new data storage mechanism and software into your device." As he spoke, his fingers flew expertly over the camcorder and the outer case fell away, revealing the complex interior. Swiftly, Heron removed the disk drive and inserted an apparently identical part.

Joe marvelled at the ease with which the big man carried out the intricate procedure. Moments later, the outer casing snapped shut and the holding screws dropped into place. The whole procedure had taken less than two minutes.

"What about the disk?" Joe enquired. "I don't want to put a damper on your enthusiasm, but the disk can't hold much data."

"I have inserted a replacement storage device, which can hold more than a hundred terabytes of data."

"What?" Joe wasn't particularly computer literate. "I know that a gigabyte equates to one thousand megabytes; but what's a terabyte?

"One thousand times greater," Heron informed him with a smile.

Joe sat down heavily in the observer's chair. He had become accustomed to the technology of the Faithful, but this was in direct comparison to the technology of his own time and the gulf was mind-numbing. He didn't realise that Heron was still speaking.

"When you begin to download this information at your home, you will find blueprints and specifications for this device and for the high-capacity battery."

"But won't that produce a paradox in my time?" Joe demanded. He was well aware of the problems associated with meddling with the technology of a particular era.

"No," Heron assured him firmly. "We have investigated your era very carefully, and this technology will be 'invented' in the early years of the twenty-first century. There will be no paradox."

Joe thought of Or-gon. The Neanderthal scientist would be certain to appreciate this example of the Faithful's advanced technology. No doubt he would, as Heron intended, use the blueprints to 'invent' the data storage device and battery, and Joe could not begin to imagine the financial impact such a development would have on their business interests.

"How do I set it up to record from the ship's cameras?" he enquired. "And how on earth can it record from several sources at once?"

"Whilst the device is on board the Master of Time, it can be remotely connected to the ship's AI merely by requesting it. The AI hears everything on board." With those words, Heron set off towards his station.

Feeling a little foolish, Joe said, "AI?"

The soft, female voice answered, "Yes, Futama, do you wish me to initiate the recording?"

"If you don't mind. And can you record everything from here to Mars?"

"Certainly. If that is all, you should take your seat. Captain Terpin is ready to initialise take-off within one minute."

When Joe dropped into his seat, he discovered that Heron had also made modifications to the chair, which made it fit his smaller frame more comfortably. He settled down to await the jump through time to the late carboniferous era but, as the seconds passed, he became aware of an insistent buzzing coming from the direction of the bridge. The familiar wrench to his gut did not materialise.

"AI, what's happening?" Joe demanded.

"Alarms have been triggered in a remote section of the tunnel complex. It seems there are intruders," the AI replied. "Take-off has been delayed until the situation has been resolved."

* * *

Prua Landi was in a murderous rage, pacing back and forth across the deep pile carpet of her study. Her high-collared crimson cape, swished menacingly around her, accentuating her every move. All around, the decor had been modelled on the interior of a royal palace from the distant past. The opulent surroundings, imbued with an elegance that belied the uncivilised time of their origins, did little to mollify the dictatrix's foul mood.

Ryton, the captain of the palace guard took a deep breath before replying to her question. Perspiration glistened on the polished dome of his head, and trickled onto the tight collar of his green and gold uniform. "We are unable to locate the traitor, My Lady," he said in clipped tones, which masked the turmoil in his mind. "He was last seen near an entrance to the water storage cisterns beneath the city."

"Where, exactly?" Prua Landi demanded. "Show me!"

The officer called out a monitor from a recess and gave a series of instructions, requesting a schematic plan of the city on the screen. He pointed a long finger. "He was there, My Lady," he said, "but that was the last time he was seen. We know he cannot have entered the underground water storage area because he would be certain to be drowned, but a search of the immediate area was unsuccessful."

"Come with me!" Prua Landi ordered. "Meanwhile, you would be well advised to recall the exact time the traitor was seen."

"That is a simple matter, My Lady. The time was logged at a little after eleven-fourteen this morning." He consulted his timer, "no more than a quarter of an hour ago."

"Why did you not inform me at the time?" The dictatrix's tone oozed menace.

"When we failed to apprehend the fugitive, I reported immediately to My Lady."

Prua Landi hissed, "Incompetent oaf," as they entered the laboratory housing Perdon's remote viewing device. Striding up to the viewer, she beckoned impatiently to a technician. "Can you operate this viewer?" she demanded.

210

"Y-yes, My Lady," the technician stammered, "I have attained proficiency under the director's guidance.

"Then you will not fail me . . . will you?"

"N-no, My Lady. What is it My Lady wishes?"

"I wish to view this place," she urged, placing her fingertip on a map of the city, "at eleven-ten this morning."

Praeton, the technician, lowered himself into the control chair and nervously began the delicate process of powering up the viewer. Moments later, a holographic image formed in the exact centre of the viewer. A few people wandered along the pavement and the occasional vehicle ghosted silently past on the smooth roadway. A familiar figure appeared around the corner of a building in the middle distance hurrying towards the viewer's focus.

Prua Landi ordered Praeton to concentrate upon the subject and the figure leapt forward as the magnification increased. The dictatrix growled deep in her throat and the technician flinched, uncertain whether he was the object of Prua Landi's displeasure. Moments later, Perdon stood beside the service access to the underground water system. He glanced around him at the passers-by before placing his hand on the door, a haunted expression on the once handsome face that was now haggard and drawn. A muted click told him that the door was now unlocked. With a final glance at the sparse crowd around him, Perdon opened the door and slipped inside. None of the passers-by had shown even the slightest interest.

Prua Landi glared at Ryton. "So, he *could not* have entered the water system?"

The officer knew he was in trouble. Failure was not an option, and he had failed – and in the most conspicuous manner. He waited for Prua Landi's violent outburst, but, to his amazement, she smiled thinly.

"Your incompetence will not reap its due reward this time," she said coldly. "You are fortunate that Perdon has handed to us the means of his own execution."

Ryton was nonplussed by the unexpectedness of the dictatrix's reaction. With a blank expression, he said, "My Lady?"

Prua Landi was savouring the moment. Without even soiling her hands, she would rid herself of the traitorous Perdon, who had insinuated himself into her affections, and had, to her utmost regret, availed himself of her sexual favours. How could she have been so blind? She comforted herself that she had been fooled by his bravery. No one, neither man nor woman, had displayed such

211

resolution in her presence and she had to admit that she had found his company intoxicating at times. What a pity that he had been revealed as an agent of the Faithful, because she knew that she was unlikely to find another man with his qualities of intellect and courage.

"Yes, you fool," she told Ryton. "Within five minutes, I intend to flood the reservoirs beneath the city by draining the palace lake. All that will remain for you to do – if the task is not beyond your level of competence – is collect his lifeless body from wherever it lies in the cisterns or the river on the outskirts of the city."

With a feeling of relief, Ryton excused himself and set off to arrange the search for Perdon's body.

* * *

Perdon descended into the depths of the underground water storage system. He felt a little light-headed through lack of food. Prua Landi's forces had been hunting him for more than a week, since an unexpected check by Prua Landi's guards had revealed him as an agent of the Faithful. He had spent a few hours at a time at the homes of followers of the Futama, but had never been able to remain for long without fear of exposing his friends to the deadly wrath of Prua Landi. He was left with two options: the first was to turn a plasma pistol upon himself, so that he would never be able to divulge his secrets; the second was to escape to the distant past in the hope of returning with the Futama's invading army. It was the second option that had appealed to him.

He searched the folds of his robe and extracted a precious syringe containing an opaque grey liquid. The syringe had remained hidden for many years since the flight of the Faithful to the far past, and he alone had been entrusted with the secret of its location. If Prua Landi had even suspected its existence, she would have turned the whole world inside out to uncover it. He lifted the hem of his pure white robe and placed the syringe to his thigh; with a hiss, the grey liquid passed into his sartorius muscle. Moments later, he began his search for the entrance to the time tunnel, which he knew was situated close to the place where excess water from the underground system flowed into the broad river on the outskirts of the city. He knew time was limited because his pursuers had been close behind. His only hope was that they would lack the imagination to believe he might escape into the cisterns beneath the city, where drowning was a very real danger.

As he trotted along beside the water channel, his lantern lighting the way ahead, Perdon searched for any sign of a side tunnel. Condensation dripped from the smooth, curved surface overhead, soaking into his robe. The walls were encrusted with patches of dark algal growth, which soiled his damp clothing as he passed. He was soon dishevelled and dirty. The stay-clean formula of his clothing was unable to cope with the excess of dampness and organic grime, and he knew that if he failed to uncover the time tunnel soon, his spirits would reach a dangerously low ebb. Amongst the omnipresent dripping, he heard a distant bellowing sound, which seemed to be growing louder.

* * *

Prua Landi reached the room housing the security controls for the palace and its grounds. "AI?" she called imperiously.

"Yes?" The soft voice all around her seemed, to Prua Landi, to harbour a hint of insolence.

"Empty the palace lake, immediately!"

"But the lake water will contaminate the drinking water for the whole city for several weeks," the AI protested.

"Would you permit me to pose a hypothetical question?" Prua Landi asked in a dangerously soft voice.

"Of course."

"Very well. If I were the empress of a whole planet, who had ordered the deaths of countless numbers of my subjects – human beings, that is – would I be likely to lose sleep if I were to cut off every sensory input of an artificial intelligence and boil its core brain in its ambient fluids?"

The AI went quiet for a number of seconds. Finally, in a remarkably emotional tone, it said, "That would be barbaric. No one would commit such dreadful crimes."

"Let me enlighten you," Prua Landi grinned, exposing her flawless teeth. For, despite the bizarre nature of her confrontation with the AI, she was enjoying herself. "*I* have committed such crimes – and will continue to do so."

In contrite tones, the AI said, "I am opening the drain at this very moment."

"Thank you." Prua Landi stepped outside into the late afternoon sunlight to watch the drama unfold, but the smooth

213

surface of the lake seemed to mock her. "AI!" she screamed as she ran indoors, "AI, why are you not draining the lake?"

There was fear in the tones of the AI as she replied, "My Lady, the gears of the sluices are fouled by vegetation. I am working diligently to clear the blockage."

"Obey my orders," Prua Landi screeched at the AI, "or I assure you I *will* carry out my threat to destroy you."

Whilst she ranted at the AI, ripples spread from a disturbance in the centre of the lake and the water bubbled as a wide plug in the bed of the artificial lake slid aside, allowing the waters to drain into the underground system of storage aquifers and tunnels. A plume of spray erupted into the sky as air escaped from below, to be almost instantly replaced by a raging vortex. A flock of ducks in the vicinity soared noisily into the skies, eventually settling on the ornamental lawns beside the rapidly emptying lake. Mud and reeds, dragged by the suction into the hole in the lakebed, left behind deep channels scoured to the level of the plasticrete floor. Soon, all that remained was a trickle of dirty water, oozing from the thick mud, drawn by gravity towards the lowest point of what had once been a beautiful ornamental lake.

Prua Landi smiled in satisfaction. Let the traitor make what he would of several thousand tonnes of water descending into his underground refuge.

* * *

Perdon listened with all the concentration he could muster. The sound was growing louder; it had now become a roar, with harsh overtones of splashing, as if a huge volume of water had been suddenly introduced into the underground system. The only possibility was that someone had drained the lake, and that could only have been done on Prua Landi's orders. His ears popped ominously as a wave of pressurised air preceded the floodwater. A second, more violent wave buffeted him in the confines of the tunnel warning that the water would reach him in seconds. He ran as fast as his long legs could carry him, but a third wave of pressurised air burst his eardrums, forcing trickles of blood from his ears and down his neck. The pain almost knocked him unconscious, but he staggered on, searching for a niche in which to hide from the agent of Prua Landi's anger.

In the wall, a few metres ahead, he saw the dark opening of a side tunnel, and he dove inside, hoping to find steps leading

214

upwards, away from the approaching flood. But his lantern revealed no staircase, merely the flat, dusty floor of a semicircular tunnel. Hawking and spitting out the blood that had seeped from his abused ears into the back of his throat, he began to run once again, but he was halted in his flight by the terrible roaring of water as it flowed at breakneck speed past the entrance to his refuge. He stared, unable to believe his senses. The water was running *past*, yet none was entering the side tunnel. He retraced his steps and thrust his outstretched hand into the flow, and the violence of the stream almost spun him off his feet. He withdrew his hand and collapsed against the tunnel wall. He was safe – at least for the time being, until Prua Landi sent a detachment of troops to search for his body.

Wearily, Perdon picked himself up and began to walk.

* * *

"I've never encountered alarms in the complex," Joe informed the AI. "What can you tell me about it?"

"Nothing at all," the AI replied. "I have no data."

Joe strode down the corridor to the bridge, where Terpin was giving orders for weapons to be issued to crewmembers. He seized a plasma rifle from the weapon racks and made for the exit ramp. "I'm going to see what's happening," he shouted over his shoulder to the Captain.

Terpin ordered the deployment of the ramp. Romana slung a plasma rifle over her shoulder and followed Joe. As the only member of Joe's bodyguard present, she had no intention of allowing him out of her sight. The ramp was still lowering as the pair reached it at a run, and they leapt the final metre to the hard-packed earth of the compound, racing towards the tunnel entrance, from which the harsh, ululating shriek of a siren was emanating. Men were running from all areas of the compound towards the tunnel complex, having substituted their building tools for weapons. Inside, Joe ran into Orina, who had rapidly organised defensive positions, though she had no inkling of the number of intruders.

As Joe and Romana arrived, Orina was poring over a schematic of the alarm system. "The intruder seems to be outside the central tunnel complex," Orina mused. "How can this be?"

Joe glanced at the schematic. The alarm had been triggered within the tunnel he had not yet explored, the one leading to the future time of the Faithful. Who could it be? Surely, he wondered,

Prua Landi could not have gained access to the time tunnel? If so, the consequences for the Faithful could be disastrous.

"I know the place where the alarm is sounding," he told the acting base commander. "I need some men to go and investigate with me. Anybody seen Analy and Trione?"

"We are here, Joe," Trione called from the edge of the crowd. Joe had not noticed his friends because he was dwarfed by those around him.

All eyes turned to see who had been so familiar when speaking to the Futama. Unabashed, Trione stepped forward, accompanied by Analy. Romana instantly joined them.

"That's three. I'll need a couple more." All the men stepped forward as one. Joe selected a couple of men armed with plasma rifles and they joined Analy and Trione, ready to follow wherever their Futama led them. To Orina, Joe said, "You'll need to protect the complex at the only point where the intruder or intruders can gain access."

"Where would that be?"

"You'd better follow us and I'll show you. You're all going to have to pass through the place soon anyway, on your way back to your own time."

Joe set off at a brisk trot, preceded by Trione and Analy. Romana kept pace a step behind. The rest, numbering more than thirty trotted after them. When they reached the time-gate, Analy and Trione stepped through, leaving Joe and Romana to lead Earil and Selon through what, to the two soldiers, was a wall of solid rock. As Joe was about to grasp Selon's arm Orina enquired casually, "This is the passage to the Futama's home?"

Romana gestured to Trione, who swiftly retraced his steps to help Selon negotiate the time-gate.

Joe took the base commander aside. "Yeah," he agreed, "but there's also a route back to your time, and it's two-way. What goes forward to your time can also return here – if they know which route to take. Look, Orina, I reckon you've got a right to know exactly what's happening. Gillane and the rest of the council are understandably reluctant to give out any information about their plans, except on a need to know basis, but I intend to bring you up to speed when we get back with whoever's breached the tunnels. If we don't return within two hours, send the Master of Time back to Mars with the news, and be prepared to defend the complex with

216

your lives. And remember this: however evil anyone believes Prua Landi to be, trust me, you can double it!"

Orina cupped Joe's face in her long, slim hands. "Be certain to return, Futama. Your people have a great need of you."

"Isn't that a fact," Joe retorted as he slipped through the time-gate.

Trione and Analy stood silently beside Romana. They were bathed in the eerie light from the shimmering curtain as Joe and the rest joined them. To his friends, Joe said, "You know what to do." To Earil and Selon, he said, "Just do exactly as I do, it's only a transporter, leading to another time-gate."

In a deep voice, which resonated through the tunnel, Selon informed Joe, "We are familiar with this mode of transport, though its use is forbidden by the usurper, Prua Landi. Had we been forced to live on Mars for much longer, it would have been introduced there."

"Good, then let's go." Joe stepped through the curtain and emerged several miles away and two-hundred and fifty-three thousand years into the future.

The others swiftly followed and the small group set off along the tunnel, their footfalls muffled by the age-old layer of dust. As they negotiated the makeshift bridge over the chasm, Joe remarked dryly that they would need to provide a more substantial structure before their army crossed the abyss. Minutes later they arrived at the fork in the tunnel leading to Too-ga's time and continued more stealthily to the second fork, where Joe halted.

"We wait here," he whispered, "and we'd better keep quiet. We don't want to give any warning to whoever it is down there."

Joe indicated the tunnel he'd so far left unexplored. He listened intently. Eventually, he heard the uneven sound of footsteps in the darkness, accompanied by ragged breathing. They waited with all lights extinguished. A lantern came into sight around a curve in the tunnel; it was swinging erratically from side to side, occasionally illuminating parts of a solitary tall figure. The white clad figure staggered drunkenly from side to side, until he ventured too close to the tunnel wall and his scalp contacted the low ceiling with an audible smacking sound. The light described an arc sideways, and the man collapsed with a groan into a pool of shadow outside the immediate range of the overturned lantern.

"Set your rifles to narrow beam and wait here," Joe whispered. "He's hurt. I'm going to see how badly."

Trione placed a restraining hand on his arm. "Futama, it may be a trap. I will go."

"Look," Joe informed the big man, "I've hit my head on the ceiling, but not as hard as that. Take my word for it, he's not going to give me much of a problem, but there may be others following behind. If you see me dive to the floor, let rip over my head with everything you've got, okay?"

Everyone nodded as they set and primed their energy weapons.

Slowly, Joe headed for the overturned lantern, permitting his footfalls to make no sound whatsoever in the dust of the tunnel floor, and all the time listening with his nano-enhanced hearing for the telltale sounds of lurkers in the darkness ahead, around the curve of the tunnel. He retrieved the lantern and slid along the curved wall for fifty metres or so, peering into the blackness ahead. There were no signs of pursuit, so he retraced his steps and examined the prone figure. It was a man, much like the members of the Faithful, but he was in a poor physical state. His simple white robe was damp and soiled with green algae. It was obvious from the dust encrusted over the patches of algae that he had fallen many times on his journey through the tunnel.

Joe called softly, "Romana, he needs your help."

Instantly, the tall medic was kneeling beside the fallen figure, running her diagnostic device first over his skull, and then over the rest of his body. The prone figure twitched and groaned weakly. "He is regaining consciousness," Romana informed everyone. He will have a headache until his nanos alleviate the trauma, but what he needs most is nourishment. My diagnostic tells me he has eaten very little during the past few days."

It was decision time. Joe scrutinised the stricken man, who was showing more overt signs of awakening than those picked up by Romana's diagnostic. "Look, Romana, we've go to know who or what is chasing this man. I want you and Earil to stay here to look after him. Until we know any different, we'll treat him as a prisoner, so watch him carefully. We," he waved his hand to encompass Analy, Trione and Selon, "are going to investigate."

Romana nodded. She had learned that when Joe made his mind up it was impossible to sway him from his chosen path. "Guard the Futama with your lives," she told Joe's companions, as she returned her attention to the injured man.

Equipped with powerful lights, Joe led his small party down the tunnel, which, after the initial curve, forged arrow-straight into the distance. Ten minutes later, they came to a T-junction. Joe halted. He could see the glimmer of lights washing along the cross-tunnel and glistening from water dripping from the ceiling. "Back," he urged softly, "and switch off the lights. There's someone coming."

"Coming from where?" Selon queried dubiously. "We have reached the end of the tunnel. We can go no further."

Joe retraced his steps. "Everyone get back here and keep your weapons ready. We're about to find out if Prua Landi knows the secret of this tunnel."

The others joined him and they waited, breathing shallowly in the darkness, as the light in the cross-tunnel grew stronger. From the way the glow was waxing and waning, it was clear that someone was swinging the light from side to side in the tunnel as they walked along. A circle of bright light fell upon the end of the tunnel and instantly swept to the other side, returning a second or two later. He observed his companions for a few seconds: Trione and Analy were watching the oscillating light but Selon's reaction told Joe he could see no vestige of light penetrating the end of the tunnel. Clearly the time-gate was located precisely at the junction. A soldier came into view, holding a powerful lantern, still sweeping the beam back and forth across his path in a regular pattern. More soldiers followed; Joe counted twenty-two, their grumbling and cursing echoing in the dankness of the enclosed space. They were searching the tunnel and there could be no doubting that their quarry was, at this very moment, being tended by Romana, some half mile away, separated from his pursuers by three-quarters of a million years of time.

They waited and eventually the search party returned. This time the soldiers were minutely inspecting the tunnel walls around them as they tramped along, in an effort to determine whether their quarry could have escaped through a shaft, which they might have failed to notice on their first pass along the tunnel. One of the soldiers used a communication device and Joe clearly heard the man's thoughts as he reported, *We have found nothing, My Lady. His body has probably been washed into the river.*

Immediately, a woman's voice echoed in the soldier's mind, *Assume nothing, Ryton. Remember that Perdon has betrayed me. I want him found! I WANT TO KNOW HE IS DEAD!*

The last sentence was almost a shriek. Ryton's reply was subdued. *Yes, My Lady, we will find him. You can depend on it.*

Joe smiled. At least he knew the identity of the intruder in the tunnel and it pleased him that, in some way, Perdon had managed to get well and truly under Prua Landi's skin.

"Let's go," he ordered. "We've found out all we need to know. And," he added, "at least we know it's okay to use the lights."

His companions settled in beside him as they set off to rejoin Romana, but Selon wore a puzzled frown. He had neither seen nor heard anything from the other side of the time-gate. They found the fugitive sitting up, propped against the tunnel wall. He had extensive bruising on his scalp and his eyes still occasionally drifted out of focus.

"Is Perdon fit enough to travel?" Joe asked Romana.

"How can you know his name?" the medic enquired. "He has been confused and unable to communicate by any means whatsoever."

"I heard someone talking about him at the other end of the tunnel," Joe explained.

Selon regarded Joe quizzically, but Analy and Trione merely nodded. They had seen the lantern light and the troop of soldiers through the time-gate and had heard voices. But they had not heard Prua Landi's words relayed through Ryton's mind.

"What did you hear?" Analy enquired.

I heard the guard commander saying that they hadn't found the body. I also heard Prua Landi reply that she wanted proof that the one who had betrayed her was dead. It seems that our Perdon here has managed to upset Prua Landi somewhat, and as far as I'm concerned, that places him firmly on my side of the fence."

Though he was swimming in and out of consciousness, Perdon twitched at each mention of his ex-mistress' name.

"We need to get him back to the complex," Joe announced, "and we're going to have to carry him. We'll take turns, one on each limb, and two of us can watch the rear – just in case I'm mistaken about whether or not they can follow us."

"I will carry him," Earil announced. "Look at him! In his emaciated condition, he cannot possibly be too much of a burden."

Joe clasped Earil's muscular biceps. "Agreed. But if you feel you need help, ask, okay?"

Earil grinned, "I may need assistance to negotiate the ramshackle bridge across the chasm. It made my heart race when I crossed it for the first time bearing my weight only. With the weight of two, it may prove to be a problem."

"We'll cross that bridge when we come to it," Joe announced and chuckled when he realised what he'd said.

Shaking his head, Earil hauled the uncomplaining Perdon onto his shoulder and, the little group set off to return to the distant past of the compound.

Chapter Twenty-one

REUNITED:

As they passed through the time-gate at the complex, the small party – including Earil, bearing Perdon on his broad shoulders – faced a heavily armed squad, four abreast across the width of the tunnel and several ranks deep. Orina was at the rear of the assembly directing a crew, who were carving a series of alcoves into the rock to provide cover for marksmen. It was clear the director had no intention of allowing intruders to pass.

* * *

Prua Landi relaxed naked in a liquid massage bed in her sumptuous apartment, awaiting news from the captain of her palace guard that the body of the traitor had been located. It was now more than an hour since she had flooded the cisterns below the city – ample time, she considered, for the oaf, Ryton to complete such a simple task. The soothing pulses of viscous herbal oils sensuously caressed her skin, leeching away the tension of the past few hours. She considered the inconvenience the city would suffer from the contaminated water supply, instantly dismissing the negative thought from her mind. It was no concern of hers what the populace did, so long as they knew their place.

The voice of the AI cut across her thoughts. "The captain of the guard wishes to speak with you." Somehow, the AI could not rid herself of the memory of Prua Landi's threat to boil her in her fluids, and her tone was extremely guarded. The AI knew the penalty for disobedience, but Landi still nursed the suspicion that the man-made entity was never likely to show her the respect she demanded. No matter! When this whole mess was cleared up to her satisfaction, the AI would pay for her insolence. Smiling inwardly at this comforting thought, Prua Landi said, "I'm listening."

Ryton's voice filled the air. "My Lady?"

The dictatrix sensed that the officer was about to impart bad news. "Spit it out, imbecile!"

"My, Lady, we have been unable to locate the body," Ryton said uncertainly.

Prua Landi was silent as she considered the implications. Finally, she demanded, "You have searched everywhere?"

"Yes, My Lady. We have even searched the river as far as the sea, even though it is impossible for Perdon's body to have been carried so far."

"You have the gall to speak of impossibilities when it was you who stated that the traitor *could not* have entered the water cisterns?"

Ryton knew that argument would be futile. "Though we have been unable to recover the body, My Lady, I cannot imagine how Perdon could have survived the flooding of the chambers."

"That is because you lack imagination," Prua Landi informed him bitingly. "In the absence of proof of his death, I am inclined to believe that the traitor is somehow still alive. You will continue to act on that premise until you are presented with the proof that we seek. Do you understand?"

"Yes, My Lady. I will second more troops and broaden the search."

"At last, a cogent thought," Prua Landi spat. "Keep me informed – and don't disappoint me."

"No, My Lady."

Prua Landi picked over her memories of her short association with Perdon whilst she enjoyed the ministrations of the massage bed for a few more minutes. When she grew tired of the soothing vibrations she demanded, "Robes!"

Within minutes she was dressed, feeling refreshed, but her period of reflection had left her with a nagging suspicion that some event over the past few weeks did not quite add up. She turned over in her mind her very first meeting with Perdon. Was there something she had missed? She scrolled through her memory more carefully this time: the laboratory and Perdon's boldness, resulting in the scientist being elevated to research director; subsequent small increases in the efficiency of the remote viewer and of the range of the time-travel device; her disastrous attempt to destroy the wretched Futama in his own time; the destruction of the Futama in the explosion in the distant past. She had personally witnessed, via the remote viewer, the titanic blast in the primitive past, and had seen the huge ship disappear in the explosion. Perdon had controlled the demonstration. Her recollection halted. *Perdon had controlled the demonstration!*

Seething inwardly at her foolishness, she headed for the laboratory and the remote viewer. She was aware of what Perdon had demonstrated to her; now she intended to discover what he had kept hidden.

Praeton was awaiting her at the remote viewing device, having been forewarned by the AI. "How may I serve My Lady?" he enquired meekly.

"By returning me to a particular viewpoint in the past," Prua Landi informed him tersely. "Has a record been kept or has the traitor removed all traces from the log?"

Praeton's fingers danced on the controls and an image of Perdon disappearing beneath the city streets coalesced in the middle of the viewer. The image changed, and the screen was filled with an intense, blinding light – the explosion at the compound.

"Retrace that event," Prua Landi ordered, and moments later they witnessed the apparent destruction of the Master of Time. "Now, let us move forward from this point," she said, "and see whether the traitor deceived me."

* * *

Perdon gingerly rubbed his abused scalp as he sat in a comfortable chair in Orina's office. He had eaten well and his nanos were effectively utilising the nourishment to rapidly build up his strength. He favoured Joe with a penetrating stare.

"You are the Futama?" he said, more as a question than a statement.

"Yeah," Joe replied, "the one and only."

Perdon rose shakily to his feet and bowed deeply. "I am honoured to meet the Futama," he said, reverently. "I have waited many years for this moment, and many times in the past few weeks I was afraid I would die first." He shuddered at the recollection of his flight through the underground cisterns and Prua Landi's attempt to drown him.

Joe nodded in acknowledgement. "Look, Perdon, all we know about you is what I picked up from the captain of the palace guard without him being aware of it. We know that somehow you've managed to upset Prua Landi enough for her to want you dead. What we need is some sort of explanation. Do you feel up to telling us what happened, including an explanation of how the hell you managed to get through the time-gate?"

Perdon nodded and winced at the pain induced by the sudden motion. "I am Perdon," he began, "an agent of the supreme Council of Elders." Surprised glances passed around the room.

"Go on," Joe urged.

"Prua Landi came into the laboratory, and events unfolded which led Prua Landi to promote me to director of research. I slowly improved the technology of the laboratory, whilst keeping a tight rein on developments. I had to make improvements or she would have been suspicious, but I was in a position to limit the advances so that no one could gain insight into the Faithful's technology."

He paused for a few moments to assemble his thoughts; the next part was a particularly delicate subject and he feared that those present would not understand. "To my chagrin, Prua Landi decided to take me as her confidante and lover." A buzz of conversation greeted the revelation. "Anyone who knows the empress will realise that I had no choice but to accept – any other outcome would have seen me die in the most appalling fashion."

"We're aware of what she's like," Joe assured Perdon. "She's hardly the most forgiving of people."

Perdon's expression mirrored his gratitude. He had been unsure of the reception his revelation would receive. "Prua Landi insisted upon returning to the Futama's time in order to kill him, but she reappeared in the cubicle very severely burned. I deduced that a wood splinter from an explosion had triggered her return mechanism. She was incredibly fortunate to survive. Afterwards, she insisted that I extend the range of the remote viewing device."

"How would that help?" Joe asked.

"The technology permitted us to observe particular events in the past. I reviewed what had occurred when my mistress was injured, but there was nothing to be seen – with the exception of two small inconsistencies in the flow of time, suggesting that time itself had been modified in some way." He paused for a moment, recalling Prua Landi's reaction. "The empress was most angry and drove us onwards to improve the range of the viewer. Left with little choice, I showed her the compound at the time when the Futama met with the primitives. Eventually, she witnessed the apparent destruction of the Master of Time in the explosion caused by her agent, Marron." His eyes lost their focus for a moment as he stared at the ceiling.

"Prua Landi was jubilant. Her mortal enemy had been destroyed, and it was that very thought which she allowed to cloud her judgement. She no longer considered the Futama a threat, so she failed to order further surveillance. Had she done so, she would have witnessed the return of the Master of Time to the compound. Subsequently, she charged me with the destruction of all the remaining members of the Faithful, at which task I must confess I was a singular failure."

Joe's attention was drawn to the concept of the remote viewer. He tried to place himself firmly in Prua Landi's shoes. If her most trusted servant had been uncovered as a spy, what would she do – after she had killed him? Most likely she would retrace everything Perdon had done or been involved with back to the time she had first encountered him in the laboratory – probably even beyond that.

"You know she's going to go back to the remote viewer, don't you?" Joe told Perdon.

The scientist nodded. "That seems most likely. She will question everything I have done. The immediate implication is that she will discover that the Futama is still alive. Beyond that, she will see the build-up of our forces and realise that an attack is imminent."

"If she's got the remote viewer, there's nothing we can do to stop her seeing what we're doing in the compound, is there?"

"There may be a way," Perdon informed everyone, "if you will permit me to try."

Joe thought about the problem. They had rescued Perdon from the time-tunnel, but they had only his word about the circumstances of his presence there. Admittedly, the evidence pointed towards the truth of the fugitive's assertions, but they could take no chances – especially this close to the invasion.

"Be our guest," he told Perdon, "but first will you allow Romana to probe you? You realise we can't be too careful."

"In your position, I would insist," Perdon agreed. "I am ready to accept any test of my faithfulness to the cause."

Romana was quiet for a few moments as she locked into Perdon's thoughts. The scientist sat, passively accepting the probe. Eventually, to a general sense of relief, Romana declared that everything Perdon had told them was the truth. She asked him what he needed to enable him to create a barrier against the remote viewer.

"I need to adjust the resonance of the perimeter force-field," Perdon told her, "and I would suggest that the adjustments take place immediately following the explosion in the compound, before the Master of Time returns."

"That would be impossible," Joe informed him, "the perimeter fence was completely destroyed and had to be replaced. I'm afraid that Prua Landi will have to be allowed to see the ship return, showing that Marron didn't succeed in killing me. Once the fence is rebuilt, we can prevent her from seeing the build-up of troops. Who knows, she might even be fooled into attributing her viewing problems to the explosion itself."

Romana touched Joe's arm. "Joe, there is something you need to know."

"What's that?"

"This new development means that Ciara is no longer safe. When Prua Landi sees the return of the Master of Time she will immediately realise you are alive, and as she has already tried to attack you through Ciara, she is almost certain to try again. We must bring your family back to the compound until our invasion has been successful and Prua Landi has been deposed."

With a sense of utmost dread, Joe knew that he must return home – immediately.

* * *

Prua Landi stared at the image of the Master of Time, which occupied the whole field of the remote viewer. Her face was dark with anger. The extent of Perdon's deceit was apparent. Here before her was evidence that the Futama was still alive.

"Have your deputy record everything from this point forward," she ordered Praeton, "and inform me if anything unusual occurs. Meanwhile, I need you to prepare to project two of my troops into the past. Can you do that?"

"I believe so, My Lady. I will need a little time to prepare the time cubicle."

"You have two hours. See that you don't disappoint me."

"No, My Lady. What will be their destination?"

"The time of origin of the Futama. This time I *will* succeed in capturing Jo-lang's woman and the Futama will be forced to meet me on *my* terms."

* * *

Joe led Analy and Trione through the time tunnels at a fast trot. Everyone was feeling the benefit of their intense training and fitness levels were high. They were barely out of breath when they reached the rope descent into the tiny cove. It was a dull, grey January day and there was a hint of snow in the air. The main beach was almost deserted as they emerged from the cleft in the rock-face. A half-mile away, a young woman was walking a couple of excited dogs along the water's edge, calling shrilly to her pets as they surged into the brown water. She was absorbed in the play of her two Labradors and did not seem to notice the emergence of the trio amongst the rocks further down the beach.

Analy and Trione concealed their weapons within their tracksuits and fell into step beside Joe. The woman seemed to sense their presence and turned to watch them as they trotted along the firm sand, to all appearances three friends jogging to maintain fitness. From a distance, she was unaware of Analy and Trione's unusual height, merely that, by comparison, Joe was tiny. Ascending the concrete boat ramp from the beach, they encountered more people, who stared in astonishment at the sight of two extremely tall men jogging along the pavements of the small seaside town.

John Siddall, Joe's local newsagent, was energetically sweeping the pavement in front of his shop as they passed. He was a tiny, jolly man, little more than five feet two inches tall, and of slim build. He had a thatch of unruly dark hair atop a friendly weather-beaten face, from which two eyes of the most amazing china blue regarded the passing trio with amusement.

"Hey, Joe," he called, "sometime you're going to have to tell me what you feed your friends on to make 'em grow that tall."

"Why, John," Joe replied as they passed by, "could you use some?"

"Not half," John Siddall retorted as they disappeared around a corner onto Joe's street, "not bloody half."

Joe's house was empty and they located Ciara at her mother's, where they were sitting at the table eating a light lunch. Ciara's face registered her delight at seeing Joe again so soon, but her high spirits were dashed when Joe said curtly, "Come on, everyone, we need you to come with us . . . now!"

"Why, what's happened?" Ciara demanded.

"We'll tell you on the way." The urgency in Joe's tone warned Ciara against procrastination.

"Come on, Mum . . . Or-gon. Better do as he says. I think Prua Landi must be after me again."

"Why do *we* need to leave?" Maeve protested, pressing herself firmly against Or-gon. "Surely it's Joe she wants?"

Trione entered into the discussion. "Maeve," he said urgently, "we have no idea how much, or how little, time we have, merely that Prua Landi *will* come. If she cannot take Ciara to use as a weapon against the Futama, she will take you – or dispose of you. Of that there can be no doubt."

Maeve wasted no more time arguing. She put on her coat and shoes and followed everyone outside. Joe raced inside his home to grab Ciara's coat from the hallway and helped her put it on in the street. "Keep your eyes peeled," he ordered Analy and Trione, "there's something I have to get from inside." He quickly re-entered the house and sought out the timestone, secreting the jewel-like object in a pocket of his jacket before rejoining everyone outside.

Together, they set off for the beach, drawing puzzled looks from passers by, who couldn't help noticing that Ciara was wearing a pair of fluffy carpet slippers in a violent shade of pink.

John Siddall was still industriously sweeping the pavement in front of his shop when the group passed, heading in the direction of the beach. This time, he offered no comment, merely following their progress with open-mouthed amazement as they hurried past. They encountered a few pedestrians, wrapped up against the chill of the day, who stepped onto the road to let them pass. It was obvious that they presented a strange spectacle, out of keeping with the humdrum day-to-day existence of a small seaside town. They could feel many pairs of eyes following them as they descended the boat ramp onto the sandy beach, but Joe no longer cared. His mind was filled with thoughts of Ciara suffering at Prua Landi's hands.

Trione noticed that Ciara was experiencing difficulty walking on the sand in her slippers. "Throw them away," he suggested, "your nanos will moderate your discomfort and you will find walking much easier."

Accepting the big man's advice Ciara flipped the slippers off one by one as she walked along, and they arced into the rocks at the edge of the sand. No doubt someone would eventually find them and wonder how on earth they got there. The group drew near to the cleft in the cliff face and Ciara held Maeve's hand and ushered her into the gap. She helped Or-gon into the cleft and quickly followed. Joe was about to follow suit with Analy and Trione when the rock beside his head splintered with a crackling hiss and he was enveloped in a wash of reflected heat.

* * *

Ryton and Kapen arrived outside Joe's home at the core of a pool of coruscating blue light. A sudden gust of wind tore at the bare branches of the trees in the avenue, sending down a shower of twigs all around. Down the road they saw an old man approaching astride a small, three-wheeled vehicle. The old man halted and performed a swift u-turn on the pavement before making his escape in the opposite direction at little more than walking pace. Ryton looked all around. In the distance, he could see two tall men, surrounded by four smaller figures, disappearing around a corner at the end of the street. He was in luck! The two tall figures were almost certainly members of the Faithful sect and, in all probability, one of the smaller figures was the Futama. Ryton entertained the comforting thought that his mistress would reward him well when he ended the threat of the Futama forever.

Ryton motioned to Kapen. "Take the other side of the street," he ordered, "and be sure to keep pace with me." With plasma pistols at the ready, they set off in pursuit of Joe and the rest, taking little heed of passers-by who got in their way. John Siddall glanced up from his sweeping to see the pair hurrying along the street. This, he thought, is getting beyond a joke. There must be a basketball team in town, but who on earth would wear clothes like that? Shaking his head, he returned to his task.

At the beach, Ryton caught sight of three of their quarry in the distance, clambering amongst fallen rocks towards the cliffs; three of their number seemed to have slipped away somehow. He ordered Kapen to set his weapon to needle beam and set out at a run after Joe. When he came within range, he halted, his chest heaving, and levelled the plasma pistol; but there was no time to steady his breathing. He pressed the firing stud and a thin beam of blue-white plasma blasted the rock-face beside Joe's head. Kapen mimicked his action, aiming lower.

Joe dived to his right into the cover of some large boulders, one side of his face and neck a bloodied mess from splinters of rock embedded into his skin. Kapen's plasma beam passed through the muscle of his shoulder as he dived, narrowly missing the bone. His jacket was ablaze at the points of entry and exit and he hastily divested himself of the burning garment under cover of the rocks. Analy, his reflexes honed by the martial arts training, had already replied to the attack with lethal effect. With his plasma rifle set on middle distance, he pressed the stud, and accompanied by the roar of superheated air, the sun hot plasma consumed their attackers.

Trione joined him, and within a few long seconds, all that remained of Ryton and Kapen was a broad patch of silica glass and grey ashes embedded in the sand.

Down the beach, a couple of hardy walkers had watched the spectacle with uncomprehending eyes. Everything they had seen was utterly beyond their experience, but Joe knew it wouldn't be long before they took their stories to the authorities, and there would begin again another investigation into the area of the beach around the cleft, which was certain to present unwanted obstacles to his coming and going.

The wounds hurt like molten fire. Analy carefully removed Joe's smouldering shirt to inspect the shoulder. The flesh wound had been neatly cauterised by the intense heat and blood was no longer seeping from the lacerations in his face.

"Your nanomedics will soon repair the damage to your body," Analy informed him sympathetically, "and they will help to control the pain." He offered Joe the shirt to put on. "It is unforgivable that you have been injured whilst you are under our protection," he growled angrily. "We must now ensure that we do not exacerbate the problem by allowing you to succumb to the winter's cold."

"There's nothing you could have done," Joe assured the big man, "I'm as much to blame as anyone. I'd stopped looking out for trouble by the time we reached the cleft. This just means that we've been taught a lesson about complacency."

He grinned, despite the pain and Analy relaxed a little. He retrieved the charred jacket and draped it around his shoulders. "You two get into the cleft," he said, there's something I've got to do."

"No, Futama," Trione replied gravely. "We cannot permit you to leave our protection, particularly after what has just happened. Wherever you go, we must be there to protect you."

"I suppose you're right," Joe admitted. "Give me a minute." He stepped up to the cleft and poked his head through the time-gate. He called softly to Ciara, his form silhouetted against the winter light, "Darling, we've hit a bit of a snag and we've got to go back. Go to the tent. You'll be safe there and you can make a fire to keep warm. There are blankets and food if you need them."

Ciara leaned forward to kiss Joe's lips, tasting the saltiness of a fleck of blood. "Joe, you're hurt," she observed tenderly, "what happened?" She touched his face. Joe flinched as her fingertips

231

brushed against an open cut and she pulled him around so that his face was no longer in silhouette.

"Tell me, Joe," she said, in an ominously low voice, "what's going on? How come you've been injured?"

"Come on, Darling, please trust me. Everything's fine now, but we've just got to tie up a few loose ends. Wait at the tent for us and we won't be long."

Ciara gazed deep into Joe's eyes. "I do trust you, Joe, but you'd better get this into your thick skull. If you're not back within half an hour I'm coming after you, do you understand?"

Joe gave a mock salute in the narrow confines of the cleft. "Yes, Ma'am," he agreed as he ducked back into the daylight.

As they passed John Siddall's shop, the tiny newsagent didn't even glance up from his counter; he considered there had been enough excitement and strangeness for one day.

Stealthily they approached Joe's home and Joe extracted the timestone from his pocket. Cradling the device in the palm of his left hand, he placed his fingers in the tiny indentations and rotated the two pyramids on their common axis. His companions watched, fascinated as he made delicate adjustments until a bright blue light blossomed in the middle of the road. In the distance an old man was steadily making his way towards them on a three-wheeler electric scooter. Joe urged his companions to take cover behind a wall as the light coruscated and sparked, finally depositing two tall figures in the middle of the road: their pursuers. The old man halted, about to perform a rapid u-turn.

Joe made a final adjustment to the timestone and twisted. The air seemed to ripple and the blue light vanished. There was no sign that the two tall figures had ever existed and the old man continued on his path towards them as if nothing untoward had occurred. Analy and Trione regarded Joe with awe.

"The timestone!" they breathed simultaneously.

"We have always believed that such a device was the stuff of legend." Trione gasped.

"Legend?" Joe enquired.

"The legend says that because of its complexity and the effect on anyone who used it, only the Futama would ever be able to control a timestone. You have proved the legend to be true."

"All I've done is remove all evidence that those two from the beach were ever here. I don't want the authorities to cause me or my family any problems. You don't know how persistent the police

232

can be." With a quick glance both ways along the street, Joe set off back towards the beach with Analy and Trione beside him.

At the cleft, the patch of molten glass had vanished as if it had never existed, which, due to Joe's adjustment to time itself, was as it should be. Prua Landi would never know how close her agents had come to killing him.

They found Ciara, Or-gon and Maeve sitting beside a roaring fire in front of the tent. The kettle was just coming to the boil and a simple meal was laid out on the rocks. Not surprising, Joe decided, because their meal had been rudely interrupted.

Ciara rose and hugged Joe tightly. He flinched at the pressure upon his wounded shoulder. She stepped back to examine his lacerated face, her expression one of horrified fascination. The charred area of Joe's jacket caught her attention and she instinctively knew that Joe's injuries were not limited to his face and neck. "Strip off," she ordered, "I want to clean up your wounds."

Gingerly, Joe complied, and Ciara's gaze fell upon the neat hole burned through his shoulder. "Does it hurt?" she demanded.

"It's feeling better by the minute," Joe assured her. "The nanos are doing their stuff, but I promise that as soon as we get to the compound, I'll let Romana give it the onceover."

As Ciara dabbed away the congealed blood from Joe's wounds, she said, conversationally, "I think it's time you told us how you came to be in this state."

"We had a bit of trouble, but we fixed it."

"What sort of trouble?"

Joe decided there was no point in trying to isolate Ciara from the events. It would soon be common knowledge at the complex and he hated to think what would happen if Ciara discovered he hadn't told her everything. With a cup of tea in one hand and a sandwich in the other, Joe told Ciara, Maeve and Or-gon what had occurred after they had entered the cleft. Ciara and Or-gon listened dispassionately, but Maeve found it hard to take that two lives had been so emphatically snuffed out.

"What is it all about, Joe?" she demanded. "I don't understand the need for all this violence. It frightens me."

"Maeve," Joe soothed, "it'll soon be over . . . at least we hope so. Prua Landi is the worst kind of psychopath, and until we stop her, she'll continue to terrorise her people, killing them indiscriminately. My followers in the past and on Mars are only a tiny portion of the whole movement. They are the tip of the iceberg.

The rest are trying to exist in a future ruled by Prua Landi and she is hell bent on rooting them out and disposing of them down to the very last one. I've got to help them . . . you can see that can't you?"

"I'm sorry, Joe," Maeve sobbed quietly. She accepted Orgon's comforting touch as he placed his muscular Neanderthal arm around her shoulder and squeezed gently. "I don't suppose I'd really taken in all you've told us. Of course you must help."

"Thanks, Mum," Joe said. "You're all right, you know."

234

Chapter Twenty-two

KIDNAP:

Prua Landi was impatiently pacing the laboratory floor. Praeton, the polished bronzed dome of his head exuding tiny rivulets of perspiration, was making delicate adjustments to the time cubicle. Ryton was checking the level of charge in his plasma pistol. Kapen, a soldier from the palace guard, was staring apprehensively at the glistening machine; he had been chosen to accompany the captain of the guard on a journey into the past, and he was finding it impossible to mask his fear. The only thing preventing him from falling to pieces was the fact that Prua Landi's anger was far worse than the prospect of a journey into the unknown, propelled by technology that did not inspire him with confidence. Hadn't Prua Landi herself returned from such a journey more dead than alive? Kapen experienced a cold chill as he considered the iniquity of his position. He had a feeling that the foray into the past was not as clear-cut as those around him seemed to believe, but he had no intention of giving voice to his thoughts. He had no wish to die.

"We are ready for transfer, My Lady," Praeton said quietly.

"Good. Then let us not delay." To Ryton, she added, acidly, "You have your instructions. Do not fail me as you did with the traitor, Perdon."

"No, My Lady." Ryton stepped into the cubicle and Kapen joined him. The time transfer device seemed much too small to accommodate the bulk of the two tall men. There was a low hum as Praeton fed in power and suddenly, in a blaze of blue light, the cubicle was empty. So far so good!

Praeton transferred his position to the controls of the remote viewer, which he had delicately calibrated to the exact time of the pair's arrival in the twenty-first century. The holographic image showed the Futama and an assorted group of five people, including two of the Faithful, hurrying down the street into the distance. They rounded a corner and disappeared from view. Impossibly, the tiny form of the Futama instantly coalesced in the centre of the viewfinder with his two tall companions beside him. They hurried down the street in the same direction, disappearing around the same corner. Prua Landi blinked. Was she going mad?

"Repeat that sequence," she ordered the technician. "No, you fool, I have no wish to see a recording of the incident," she grated. "Recalibrate the viewer to return to that very instant of the past."

With perspiration dribbling into his eyes, the unfortunate Praeton complied and they witnessed the strange sequence repeat itself.

"Explain to me what has happened," Prua Landi demanded angrily, "and explain why we have seen no evidence of my agents."

Praeton's mind was in turmoil. What he had just witnessed was utterly impossible, unless someone had the capability of erasing whole episodes of time. But he dare not even hint at such a scenario, because the dictatrix was already insanely jealous of the superior technology of the Faithful. To even suggest such a possibility had the potential to send her over the edge. The technician recalibrated the remote viewer and watched the events unfold once again, searching unsuccessfully for another, more logical explanation.

Prua Landi interrupted his train of thought. "Tell me, Praeton, is your viewer malfunctioning?"

Praeton shook his head. "No, My Lady. It is functioning perfectly."

"Then explain to me what we have just witnessed . . . and don't prevaricate. I know what I saw. And remember: I am not a fool."

The technician was in trouble. Prua Landi had left him with no alternative but to give his considered opinion, and he prayed he had arrived at the correct interpretation.

"I cannot tell you what has happened to Ryton and Kapen," he began, "other than to say that there is no evidence of their arrival at their destination."

Prua Landi placed a long, slim hand on Praeton's shoulder as he nervously sat at the controls of the viewer. "I said 'no prevarication' and I meant it. The fate of Ryton and Kapen is of little consequence to me. I want your opinion of what you saw in the viewer . . . nothing else. Do you understand?" She fingered the butt of the neural whip attached to her ornate belt, and the technician felt his guts twist in anticipation of intolerable pain.

"M-My Lady," he stammered, "I have only one explanation that fits the anomalous events."

"Then share it, please. Indulge me. I know I am not one of the scientific fraternity, but please, for the sake of argument, concede also that I am not an idiot."

Praeton hardly knew what to say to agree with Prua Landi. If, in his nervousness, he said the wrong thing, he would be finished. "My Lady, I believe that someone – or something – has interfered with time itself. I believe that someone, by some means I cannot even begin to understand, has erased a section of the past."

Prua Landi's thoughts swung back to the events of a few weeks ago, when she had returned from the past horribly injured in an incident, which, if the remote viewer were to be believed, had never occurred. Today's events bore a remarkable similarity to that incident. It was possible to attribute one such occasion to a random glitch in the flow of time, but two? Or was it three? She ran her memory back to Tarmis, the parallel timeline of the Neanderthals, which, subsequent to her abortive effort to kill the Futama during the nuclear attack, had vanished as if it had never existed. In the three separate events there had been one common factor – the Futama, the twenty-first century primitive, Jo-lang. Logic dictated that he, in all probability, was responsible. So, in all likelihood, she had vastly underestimated the primitive creature. No matter – it would not happen again.

"I'm inclined to agree with you, Praeton," she said, her tone almost conciliatory, "but let us review the events one more time."

Praeton's fingers danced over the controls, and the events played themselves out once again. Six figures appeared in the focus of the viewer, before commencing to walk away into the distance.

"Stop!" the dictatrix commanded. "Enhance the image of the Futama."

The technician complied and Joe's image expanded. Prua Landi carefully examined the figure before ordering Praeton to continue. When Joe, Analy and Trione reappeared in view, Prua Landi once more commanded, "Stop and enhance the image."

As the magnification increased, it became clear that Joe had suffered injuries to his face and, by the charred appearance of his jacket, a wound to his shoulder. Prua Landi threw back her head and laughed uproariously. Praeton was taken aback. No one had ever witnessed such behaviour on the part of the dictatrix – rather the opposite. He waited until the unaccustomed reaction had died to the occasional chuckle before he dared to speak.

"My Lady? Was that what you wished to see?"

"It was," Prua Landi chuckled, "and it proves that Ryton and Kapen managed to carry out their attack on the Futama before he erased the incident from the timeline. She chuckled again. "This has made me feel good. At last, everyone can see that this Futama . . . this fraudulent pipsqueak . . . can be harmed. And if he can be harmed, he can be killed."

Still chuckling fitfully, she ordered Praeton to focus the remote viewer on the compound of almost a million years ago. She was now aware that the Master of Time had not been destroyed in the massive explosion, because the Futama was still very much alive. However, it could prove helpful to watch the comings and goings at the compound, in the hope that she might gain an insight into the plans of the Faithful.

Praeton adjusted the calibration of the viewer and the far past swam into focus. The Master of Time stood on massive tripod legs amongst a scattering of buildings. Around the area, the force-field sparkled in the late evening light. It was a peaceful scene, which Prua Landi knew would be shattered by the titanic explosion. The minutes rolled by, and suddenly, the image lost focus and faded into a homogenous grey, interwoven with the occasional hint of blue and green.

Praeton made a series of adjustments to the viewer, growing increasingly alarmed at his lack of success. "I fear that the image is being distorted," he told Prua Landi. "That should not surprise us if, as we believe is the case, the Faithful are able to alter time itself."

Prua Landi's reaction to this latest occurrence caught Praeton off guard once again. Where Praeton had anticipated a display of anger, there came instead a grim smile.

"Now we can be certain that the traitor, Perdon did not die in the cisterns below the city. Otherwise, how could they be aware of our surveillance? And if the Faithful are sufficiently concerned to obscure their activities in the past, it is my belief that an invasion is imminent." She smiled, baring her perfect teeth. "You have done well, Praeton. Now I need your help to discover the means by which Perdon escaped to the past."

Awash with relief, Praeton answered, "I am your servant, My Lady."

Chapter Twenty-three

SANCTUARY:

The tunnel complex was buzzing with activity. The heavy weapons were still in place, guarding the entrance through the time-gate; Orina had decided to take no chances. Joe noticed the elegant figure of the base commander amongst a group of soldiers, poring over a set of plans. He led his small group towards her, through the clamour of activity, and the reactions of those around Orina told her that someone was approaching from the direction of the time-gate. Her face brightened with a welcoming smile.

"Ah, Futama, welcome back." Her expression changed as she spied the wounds on Joe's face and his badly charred jacket.

"We had a bit of trouble," Joe informed her casually, "and I'll tell you about it in a minute. First I'd like you to meet Ciara, my wife and her mother, Maeve."

Orina bowed deeply in deference to the wife of the Futama and Ciara smiled brightly. Maeve, unsure what to do, smiled nervously, and said, "Pleased to meet you."

"And this is Or-gon." He indicated the squat figure of his Neanderthal friend. "He is a descendant of the primitive tribespeople who presently live in the countryside around the compound. He came back to my time when Prua Landi destroyed his country with nuclear weapons. Or-gon's a refugee in every sense of the word."

Or-gon stepped forward and bowed. "I am honoured to meet you," he told Orina, "and I am grateful for this place of sanctuary against Joe's enemy, Prua Landi."

The base commander lowered her eyes to take in Or-gon's rugged features, saying softly, "We all have a duty to keep the family of the Futama safe. You are all truly welcome here." Her gaze flicked once more to Joe's wounds. "I believe the Futama intended to offer an explanation?"

Joe glanced at Analy and Trione. They were still troubled by the fact that they had failed to prevent Joe's injuries though, in all conscience, Joe could not apportion blame. What had occurred had been unexpected, but there was a positive side – from that moment on, everyone knew to maintain their guard at all times. He briefly explained what had happened on the beach, including the complete annihilation of their attackers. He made no mention, however, of his use of the timestone to erase the episode from the temporal record. Orina was shocked. The notion that the Futama had almost been killed sickened her. Joe put his hand on the base commander's arm.

"Don't worry, no harm done," he said.

Orina couldn't hide her disapproval of Analy and Trione's part in the affair. "But your bodyguards failed you," she protested.

"No one failed me," Joe corrected her, "in fact they saved my life. If they hadn't reacted so quickly, the enemy soldiers would have had time to get off a second shot, and I can't imagine they would have missed. Analy and Trione's reflexes were as good as any I've seen, and their efficiency was second to none. Now, I don't want to hear of anyone trying to apportion blame for what happened. In fact, the pluses outweigh the minuses by a considerable factor; we now know to keep our guards up twenty-four seven."

"Twenty-four seven?" Orina questioned.

"Every minute of every day."

"I understand, though the Futama uses some quaint expressions."

All the while Joe had been conversing with Orina, Ciara, Maeve and Or-gon waited patiently for him to return to them. Instead, he said to the base commander, "It's a couple of hours since we ate a small snack. I reckon it's time to visit the refectory and you can get to know my family better. I'll also keep my promise to fill you in about the time tunnels you don't know about."

Orina walked over to Ciara and gently hugged the smaller woman. "Follow me."

They followed, eventually entering the refectory, where a familiar figure sat amongst a group of seven at a round table.

"Romana!" Ciara called joyously, and the tall medic instantly arose and embraced her.

Romana's attention switched to Joe and she spied his healing injuries. She immediately ran her diagnostic over his face and neck, taking more care with his shoulder wound. She inspected the exit wound very carefully and ran the diagnostic once more over the fading scar. "You were fortunate, indeed," she commented, "a little higher and a section of bone would have been destroyed. Then the healing process would have taken much longer."

"It seems that every time we go home you have to run your diagnostic over us for one reason or another," Joe commented drily.

Romana smiled broadly. "It is comforting to know that the Futama has returned to his people and that his family can now be

240

given protection from Prua Landi – at least until the conflict is resolved."

"It's great to be back," Joe agreed. "Now," he grinned, "what's on the menu?"

"I'll arrange for something nutritious for everyone," Romana returned the grin, brushing a finger across the back of Joe's hand in an apparently accidental manner.

Maeve, however, had noticed the contact. As Romana stepped over to a food dispenser, she whispered seriously in Ciara's ear, "You want to watch that one, Ciara. I think she's holding a bit of a torch for your Joe. Don't let it get out of hand, my girl."

Ciara giggled at the news, throwing her mother into confusion. "It's okay, Mum, I know all about it and it doesn't bother me. It makes me appreciate just how special my Joe is. Romana's been completely open with me about her feelings for Joe and she's promised – and I trust her completely – that she won't ever come between us."

"Does Joe know?"

"Yes."

"And you trust *him*?"

Ciara treated Maeve to a lingering stare; she had no intention of letting her mother bring up the subject again – ever! "Look, Mum, I love him and trust him one thousand percent. I *know* he won't let me down, unless I give him reason to, and I don't intend to – ever. So, do me a favour, please. I want you to let it rest here. There will probably be occasions when things don't look right, but give us all a bit of credit, okay?"

Her expression one of stunned amazement, Maeve reluctantly conceded. Joe, who had been eavesdropping with his nano-enhanced hearing, permitted himself a satisfied smile. He returned his attention to Orina, who was asking Or-gon about Tarmis. It fascinated her that the scientist was a descendent of the Neanderthal species, which had succumbed to time and the ascent of the more adaptable Homo Sapiens.

He reluctantly interrupted Orina's questions. "Let's sit over there for a few minutes until the food is ready," he suggested, nodding in the direction of a table across the other side of the large room. He moved in that direction and Orina followed. When they were reseated, he began. "I told you before I went to bring my family here that I'd tell you about the time-gates," he said.

Orina nodded.

"It's simple, really. I've been injected with special nanos that altered my metabolism so that the tunnels and the time-gates were open to me. There are only five others I know of who have the special nanos. The first is Perdon, who injected himself with the only shot of the nanos the supreme council left in your future when they fled to this past. The second is my wife, Ciara, who received them through contact with me, and the third is Romana who requested them from the supreme council so that she could accompany me on my journeys through the time-gates. The other two are Trione and Analy, my bodyguards. Before the attack on Prua Landi begins all your soldiers will be injected with the special nanos so that they can follow the path Perdon took from the future."

He wondered momentarily whether he should mention the role of the Master of Time and decided against it. He had already given Orina more information than he should – but what the hell? In his opinion, she was entitled to be aware of what was about to happen.

"Can you put up Ciara and the others here – at least until everything's over?" he enquired.

"I believe I can do better than that," the base commander said. "It is my belief they would be safer with our women and children on Mars. If you agree, I can arrange it in an instant. In fact," she added, "it was my intention to make the journey myself to consult with the supreme council. Perdon's arrival has provided personal evidence against Marron, and the council should be made aware of it."

"In that case, the sooner the better." They arose and rejoined the rest.

Maeve was staring suspiciously at a selection of food Romana had called forth from the dispenser. "It's okay, Mum," Ciara informed her. "It's a bit bland, but there's nothing nasty in it."

"Are you sure?"

By way of reply, Ciara took a confident bite of a piece of pinkish material vaguely resembling ham. She swallowed and loaded her eating utensil once again.

Maeve took the hint and bit into a small portion of leaf, not unlike lettuce. The experience was pleasant enough for her to continue without further complaint and soon everyone's plate was empty. Before Romana returned with a second course, Joe explained Orina's plans for the immediate future.

242

"Mars?" Maeve demanded, a note of hysteria in her voice. "Sure, but you're joking. You are joking aren't you?" She sounded panicky. "But such a journey will take months . . . years even."

Joe placed his arm around his mother-in-law's shoulder. "Maeve," he explained as matter-of-factly as possible, "these people are from the future. Mars, for them, is only five hours away at the most. In fact, there's a ship outside getting ready to go. I promise that you're in for the trip of a lifetime. Just sit back and enjoy it. And remember, it'll be something you can always tell your grandchildren. That is if I haven't already bored them to tears telling them about it."

Or-gon, who had remained silent during the interchanges, commented, "The ship must be capable of near light-speed? I admit, Joe, I'm impressed. There is much for me to learn here." He rubbed his broad Neanderthal hands together in a gesture of anticipation, which made Joe grin at its unexpectedness. It was not often that the scientist permitted his composure to slip, but it was clear that he was tremendously excited at the prospect of a flight to the red planet.

Or-gon's display of excitement helped Maeve to come to terms with the idea of leaving the Earth's atmosphere and travelling to Mars. She had no wish to dampen her companion's enthusiasm by complaining.

"I'm convinced, Joe," she agreed, "I'll go. But is it really that easy to get to Mars? After all, it's millions of miles away."

"Mum," Joe said with finality, "for Orina's people, it's as humdrum as taking the bus into town, they've done it so often. In fact, nobody here has been able to understand why I get so excited about the trip."

With everyone replete from their meal, Orina led them outside through the compound towards the Master of Time.

Maeve's eyes grew rounder by the second as they approached the massive ship. "Where are we, Joe?" she asked.

"*When* are we is more important," Joe replied. He stopped and pointed beyond the force-field barrier, at a group of seven figures on the edge of the forest. "They are Or-gon's ancestors. We're two-hundred and fifty-three thousand years into our own, and Or-gon's past."

"But you should not be pulling your mother-in-law's leg, now," Maeve admonished.

"It's the truth to be sure, to be sure," Joe insisted, recoiling as Maeve dug her elbow into his ribs. "Ouch, that hurt you know."

"It was meant to," Maeve grinned. "Now tell me the truth. Where are we?"

Joe waved to the figures; as one, they waved back. "Does anyone mind a detour?" he asked innocently. No one demurred, so he led them towards the fence and halted a few metres away from the glittering force-field. Rapidly, he signed to the Neanderthals and they warily left the sanctuary of the forest margin, all the time keeping a wary eye out for predators skulking in the thick vegetation. Dar and Reed, his two teenage friends were in the lead.

"You are remembering the sacred cave?" Joe asked in English, accompanying the words with a rapid series of Neanderthal signs.

Dar signed *yes, every day we come to this place to remember*.

Joe translated, explaining to everyone that he needed the tribespeople to always remember the cave, so that when he first arrived in the era of their descendants, Too-ga's people would eventually lead him there, allowing him to discover the complex and its secrets. Joe's hands flashed again in a succession of complicated gestures.

Dar grinned and grunted a few words to his companions, and they turned and walked away. At the forest margin, the youngster raised a calloused hand in a simple gesture of farewell, and the seven figures melted into the greenery as if they had never existed.

Ciara was intrigued by the interplay between Joe and the Neanderthals. "What did you say to them?" she enquired.

"Just that we and the compound will be gone before the leaves fall from the trees."

Ciara had a notion that Joe had not revealed everything. "And?"

"That I think Dar will make a strong tribal chief one day."

"Should you be interfering with tribal politics? After all, you know what happened in Tarmis."

"Look, Darling, I don't think anything I've done here will affect the timeline adversely because it's already happened. All I needed to do was come here and do what was necessary . . . sort of act out the part, if you like."

Maeve, whose mind had been assailed by a succession of barely believable revelations, from the advent of her companion, Orgon to this jaunt into the primitive past, stared at Joe with new respect. On many occasions, the truth had seemed just a little too incredible for her logical mind to take in. Now it was becoming increasingly clear that Joe had never attempted to stretch the truth; in fact, the more experience she gained of her son-in-law's life, the more he seemed to have played down his adventures.

She hugged Joe. "You're a good man, you know," she admitted, "and I'm truly happy that you chose my Ciara."

"Did I really have a choice?" Joe asked innocently, and grinned as Ciara treated him to a withering glare.

Captain Terpin met them at the ramp of the Master of Time and welcomed them all aboard. Heron, the chief engineer, had adjusted three more seats to accommodate the smaller physiques of the passengers. Ciara found her chair to be extremely comfortable; the engineer, on Romana's insistence, had made allowances for her advanced pregnancy and the chair included a number of discreet monitoring devices along with additional highly responsive padding.

Ciara was delighted. "I could do with something like this at home," she told Romana, "any chance when this is all over?"

"I will put your request before the council," Romana smiled, "who will make the necessary checks to determine whether it is acceptable to insert the technology into your era." She grinned impishly. "If you like it so much, we may smuggle this very chair to you whatever the council's decision."

As Joe had suspected, Ciara, Maeve and Or-gon were enraptured by the journey to the red planet, particularly the diversion to the Late Carboniferous period on Earth. Everyone was astounded at the incredible size of the insect life in the steamy climatic conditions of the swampland around the tiny knoll, upon which the Master of Time rested before taking off into outer space, bound for Mars – and sanctuary. They would live on Mars until the time came for the forces of the Faithful to overcome the tyrant, Prua Landi.

Chapter Twenty-four

BATTLE PLANS:

The disused warehouse was crowded. People had been arriving over a period of several days and had set up their own personal spaces on the hard plasticrete floor. Colourful electronic blankets formed a patchwork between the white-robed squatting figures that was dazzling to the eye. Every new arrival had voluntarily subjected themselves to telepathic scrutiny, the stakes being far too high to risk infiltration by Prua Landi's agents. Sunlight bled weakly through dirty windows set high in the mould-encrusted walls. Despite the asthmatic wheezing of an ancient air-conditioning system, the atmosphere in the warehouse smelled faintly of mould, overlaid with the odour of too many bodies and stale gases leaking from an inefficient sewage disposal unit.

A sea of faces gazed expectantly at Rive as he mounted the makeshift podium in the centre of the floor. Rive had waited a long time for this moment, as had everyone present in the warehouse: in fact, ever since the persecution and banishment of the Faithful by the usurper, Prua Landi. Those sitting before him represented the core of the resistance against the tyranny, which, apart from occasional forays against Prua Landi's forces, had patiently awaited the coming of the Futama. Now that moment of destiny for the Faithful was about to arrive; now they must prepare for the battle to come, when the Futama would appear, to sweep away the one who had oppressed his people for so long.

An expectant murmur began on one side of the crowd and quickly spread to the whole assembly. Rive cleared his throat and the clamour died. "My friends," he began, "I am able to tell you that Perdon has escaped the wrath of the empress. A few of you gave him sanctuary at great risk to yourselves and your families, and your sacrifice will be rewarded when the Faithful no longer skulk in hiding under threat of execution for their beliefs. We know he escaped because I have received word from the palace that Prua Landi," he almost spat the name, "is most angry that he managed to evade her troops. She has decreed that the manner of his escape must be discovered, and I fear that many innocents will lose their lives when her agents meet with failure."

He paused and stared around the sea of faces, every one of which bore an expression of extreme concentration. "A little while

246

ago, Prua Landi was certain that our Futama had been killed, which threw her into a vendetta of increased ferocity against us. Thankfully, the one she chose to lead the pogrom was none other than Perdon, who later, when he was on the run from her agents, was able to categorically deny the truth of Prua Landi's assertion. I can tell you that our Futama is very much alive, and planning to appear before his people."

A muted rumble rolled around the huge warehouse, growing in volume as the full import of Rive's words hit everyone like a hammer blow. Spontaneously, a chant arose of, "Futama! Futama!" until it seemed the windows would shatter and the walls would crumble, like those of the ancient city of Jericho in pre-technological times.

Rive held up his hands, palms outward and the chanting ceased instantly. Though the warehouse was in a run-down quarter of a provincial city, nevertheless it would prove disastrous to make their presence known. "Now, my friends, the time has come to make final preparations for the battle to come. V'non will give details, which you must memorise, as there will be little opportunity for further contact. You must pass on this information to other members of your individual units, for when we leave this meeting place, we must all be ready to act at a moment's notice."

V'non touched a control on a device placed between his knees and a hologram erupted towards the high ceiling. "Pay attention, everyone," he called.

* * *

Prua Landi strutted before the assembled commanders of her imperial forces, one of whom was the newly promoted captain of her palace guard. Ryton's demise at the hands of the Futama had left a void that she had filled from within the ranks. Stelimon was a genetic freak. He stood a good twenty-five centimetres shorter than the average male, yet outweighed everyone else by at least thirty kilos. Unlike the rest of his contemporaries, he sported a thick, tightly-curled mat of jet-black hair and his skin tone, instead of the universal homogenous bronze, was as dark as polished ebony. When she had first spotted Stelimon amongst the troops, Prua Landi had immediately wondered how such a creature could have been allowed to survive the rigorous selection procedure. That he had, she concluded, was a tribute to the strength of his differing genetic inheritance. Tests over the years had indicated that, in many ways, he was an improvement upon the norm. He was not intellectually gifted, but he could follow orders – a trait that Prua Landi decided would suit her purposes well. Thinking officers had so far proved utterly ineffective in her quest to destroy the Futama.

"I can tell you all," she spat, "that the primitive creature, Jo-lang, the so-called Futama, the so-called *Messiah* of the Faithful," her voice rose in pitch and volume, "is still alive, despite my continuing attempts to destroy him. It is my belief that my empire will be subject to an attack led by this man, and I demand that you make every effort to locate the point – or points – at which the insurgence will take place. Perdon, a traitor within the palace, escaped my wrath and I demand that he be found. Stelimon will oversee the search of the cisterns beneath the city and I expect you all—" She treated everyone present to a particularly venomous stare. "I expect you to uncover his means of escape. Meanwhile, let us discuss plans for the forthcoming campaign. Though we have been unable to locate the bolthole, where Perdon vanished beneath the city streets, I believe that the attack will originate there. Does anyone disagree?"

Her question met with silence. No one was prepared to put his head on the block before they had had the opportunity to check the facts.

A commotion on the other side of the huge, ornate double door drew Prua Landi's attention. Stelimon stepped over and threw the door open, revealing the limp figure of a man suspended between two soldiers. The troopers held the prisoner's wrists in strong grips, and the unfortunate's forehead was almost dragging on the highly polished floor. His skin was streaked with mud and dark green slime. Beside the trio stood a young officer, who radiated apprehension on a major scale.

Prua Landi stared down at the prisoner from her considerable height. "What is the meaning of this interruption?" she demanded icily.

The officer cleared his throat nervously. "I b-believe that this man is one of the Faithful, My Lady," he stammered.

Prua Landi shifted her icy stare to the young officer. "You b-believe he is one of the Faithful?" she mocked. "I am utterly weary of officers who deal only in uncertainties. What leads you to the conclusion that he is of the Faithful?"

The lieutenant gulped noisily. "We discovered him in the cisterns below the city, My Lady. His excuse for being there was that he had been ordered to clean up the debris from the flood but, as far as I am aware, no such orders have been issued."

The empress pursed her lips. "That is correct," she agreed, "nor will they be issued for some time. A little inconvenience will provide a valuable lesson to those who oppose me." She stepped forward and placed her right foot on the back of the prisoner's head, forcing the two troopers to release their grip. The man's temple contacted the hard floor with a smacking sound that reached the furthest corners of the room. A groan escaped weakly from his lips and he fell silent once more as Prua Landi shifted her instep onto the back of his neck.

"Are you one of the Faithful?" she asked casually.

The prisoner groaned and a trickle of muddy spittle dribbled out of the corner of his mouth, puddling on the shiny floor. Prua Landi gathered her considerable mental powers and viciously probed the man's torpid, unresisting mind. After a few moments, she had extracted all the data he possessed regarding the sect – which was annoyingly incomplete. What she did discover, however, was that the Faithful believed that their Futama would appear within weeks to release them from Prua Landi's rule. With complete disregard for the prisoner's mental well-being, Prua Landi probed one last time, but her quest for information proved fruitless. Her first probe had destroyed the man's mind, leaving him with little prospect of ever again becoming a functioning member of society.

To the young lieutenant, Prua Landi said crisply, "You have done well. Now I want you to lead Stelimon and a detachment of troopers to the exact location where you discovered this—" she favoured the prone figure with a look of disgust, "—misguided creature."

With a smart salute, the young officer replied, "Yes, My Lady," and stepped aside to await the captain of the palace guard. "My Lady, what do you wish me to do with the prisoner?"

"Dispose of him," Prua Landi replied, eyeing the mud and slime on the prisoner's clothing and skin, "as cleanly as possible!"

As the limp figure was dragged away, Praeton passed them in the broad corridor. He did not even glance at the unfortunate as he passed, but fixed his attention on the guards outside the door.

"Halt," one of a pair of heavily-armed troopers commanded tersely. "No one is permitted to enter."

Praeton stared down his long nose at the troopers. "Inform My Lady that Praeton is here," he said icily, "and be well advised that she *will* wish to see me."

The scientist's words rumbled around in the troopers' minds. They had orders to bar entry to everyone, but it was clear that Praeton believed that the orders did not apply to him.

"Wait here!" the first trooper commanded, opening the door.

Prua Landi's voice called impatiently from inside the room. "What now?"

"My Lady," the trooper began, "Praeton wishes to see you."

"Then show him in!"

The trooper ushered Praeton inside and stepped back, closing the door behind him. As the door clicked shut, he muttered to his fellow guard, "We are given orders to keep everyone out, yet *anyone* is permitted to enter. Why can't orders mean what they're supposed to mean?"

His companion nodded in agreement, but did not give voice to his thoughts, there being nothing to gain by complaining about orders, particularly in such close proximity to the empress.

Inside, Praeton approached Prua Landi, who raised a thin eyebrow in query. "You have discovered something?" she asked, eager despite herself.

"Yes, My Lady. I have new information regarding the traitor."

Landi's eyes gleamed. "Will this information please me?" she enquired.

"Probably not, My Lady. Nevertheless, I believe I must do my duty."

The empress grinned, her perfect teeth gleaming in the sunlight from a window, which formed a long, convex wall of the room. "Speak up, Praeton. Let everyone hear." She waved her hand to encompass the whole room.

Praeton withdrew a small sphere from his robe and inserted the object into a holographic projector. An image instantly formed in the air. It consisted of a vaguely globular mass of static, accompanied by the hiss of white noise.

"I trust there will be more than this?" Prua Landi commented drily.

"Please be patient, My Lady," Praeton said absently as he adjusted the focus on the viewer.

A muted gasp at Praeton's boldness ran around the ranks of the officers present. Prua Landi said nothing as a hazy image formed in the centre of the field. It was the traitor, Perdon, accompanied by Jo-lang.

"What is this?" Prua Landi demanded, "or should I be asking *when?*"

"*When* is the important factor, My Lady," Praeton informed her. "I discovered a tiny window of visibility in the jamming of the signal in the far past of the Faithful. It clearly shows that Perdon has joined the Futama and the rest of his cronies."

"What do these images tell us?"

"That the traitor's route to the distant past is located somewhere beneath the city, or in the area between the outflow and the river, although I believe we should discount the area outside the city." Praeton raised his eyes from the hologram. "It is my belief that there is some kind of time displacement device – clearly far superior to the technology at our disposal at this time – most likely hidden within the confines of the water storage system. Further than that I cannot say."

Prua Landi stared around the room at the assembled officers. "What the image tells *me*," she informed them, "is that the attack is imminent – and it *will* come from below the city. Whilst he searches for the time portal Stelimon will prepare his troops to repel the insurgents." She smiled grimly, "A task he should find is well within his capabilities. After all, there is little space down there to avoid plasma fire and I am confident, therefore, that my troops will prevail."

Carline, one of the generals stepped forward. "Is that all, My Lady?"

"For the moment."

"Then I believe we all have urgent preparations to make. If you will excuse us, My Lady?"

Such devotion to duty will bring its reward, Prua Landi commented telepathically to General Carline as he exited the room, *just be sure not to fail me!*

How can we fail, My Lady, when there are so few of the enemy?

Chapter Twenty-five

TRIAL:

Perdon was ushered before the high council as soon as he disembarked from the Master of Time. He was accompanied by Joe and Orina and Joe's bodyguards, Analy and Trione. Gillane and the council listened carefully to what he had to say about the situation in the future of Prua Landi.

When Perdon had finished, Gillane nodded sagely. "You have done your duty with great courage," he said, "and you have earned the right to remain in safety here on Mars until our invasion succeeds – or fails. However, you have also earned the right to refuse such sanctuary for the privilege of doing battle against the forces of Prua Landi. I must inform you, however, that you are completely untrained in comparison to the troops prepared by the Futama." Gillane nodded in Joe's direction, in acknowledgement of the huge amount of work he had put into training the army of the Faithful.

Perdon, who had by this time recovered a measure of fitness following his ordeal in the cisterns beneath Prua Landi's capital city, smiled gratefully. "I am grateful to the council, but I must return to do whatever I can to help."

"No less than I expected," Gillane said softly. "You will, therefore, return on the Master of Time. Terpin will doubtless be proud to have you on board. Now to the question of Marron; I believe you have information on his status?"

"I do," Perdon said quietly. "Marron is a spy of Prua Landi. His orders were to destroy our Futama and inflict as much damage to our cause as opportunity permitted. As I understand, he almost succeeded." He turned his attention to Joe. "We are all grateful that he failed."

"How can you be certain that Marron was Prua Landi's spy?" Joe asked.

"Prua Landi, herself informed me. And I witnessed his attempt to kill the Futama by detonating the core of the Lunar Sunrise's power plant."

"Was that by means of Prua Landi's remote viewing device?" Orina enquired.

The rest of the councillors seemed to notice the base commander for the first time.

252

"It was," Perdon agreed. "Fortunately, Prua Landi was so delighted by the apparent destruction of the Master of Time and the Futama, that she felt there was no call for further viewing of the incident. I was able to investigate everything that occurred immediately before and afterwards, and that was how I discovered Marron's involvement."

Gillane glanced around the council chamber at each of the councillors in turn. Everyone was filled with a stony resolution to pursue the matter to its distasteful end. Marron must be tried – without delay. Gillane ordered Prua Landi's agent to be brought before the council. Minutes later, Marron sauntered into the council chamber between two armed guards. His eyes flashed with hatred as he picked out the tiny figure of Joe amongst the tall councillors. Joe wondered if anyone else had noticed, but it soon became clear that the Marron's enmity had passed unobserved. Joe let his gaze travel around the chamber, taking in the positions of the armed guards relative to the prisoner and the councillors. Marron was edgy, his eyes darting around the room, sizing up everything much as Joe had done. Unobtrusively, Joe slid his chair away from the table to allow freedom of movement; he had no intention of being caught unawares if the situation descended into violence.

The trial began without preamble. Gillane made a statement, which encompassed Perdon's version of events at the compound and followed with Joe's story of how Marron had displayed an unwarranted dislike for him. Marron stood between his guards, a neutral expression on his handsome, bronzed features. Joe could see the man was paying little attention to the proceedings of the court. He swung his legs from underneath the table; now he must await Marron's move.

It all happened in a blaze of activity that left the councillors stunned. Marron stepped backwards half a pace and grasped the plasma pistol from the belt of one of his guards. He was thumbing the safety catch when Analy reacted with reflexes honed to incredible sharpness by his martial arts training under the personal tutelage of his Futama. Joe's bodyguard crossed the intervening space as Marron slipped off the safety and started to raise the weapon. Councillors slid from their chairs in an effort to avoid the violence. Everything seemed to slow down as Analy reached Marron with one huge stride and drove a 'chisel' fist into the larynx of the accused. Marron's finger spasmed on the firing stud and, for

253

a split-second, a cone of plasma enveloped one of his guards, cutting both legs off diagonally below the knee.

Astrop, the guard fell, screaming to the floor onto the burnt stumps of his limbs and lay, writhing in agony. Marron made harsh gargling noises for a few seconds and fell silent. Joe knew that no one could have survived such a catastrophic blow. Marron's windpipe was shattered and the fierce blow had almost certainly broken his neck. The concept of a trial and punishment was now academic.

Romana rushed into the chamber and ministered to the stricken Astrop. A powered stretcher arrived and the guard was rushed to the city's medical facility, where the vaporised limbs would be regrown over a period of a few painful weeks. The medic then focused her attention on the still form of Marron, running her diagnostic over his skull. Trickles of bright red blood dribbled from his nostrils and the corners of his mouth. Seconds later she pronounced that Prua Landi's agent was dead.

All around the council chamber, white faces stared at the scene of carnage. The Faithful had never embraced violence, and witnessing Marron's death, literally at Analy's hand, had brought the prospect of their forthcoming war against Prua Landi into sharper focus. They had been made bloodily aware that, in any war, people were going to die. Their only hope was that the tactics to be used would keep the number of casualties on both sides to an absolute minimum. Otherwise, the prize of a return to their homes may prove to have been won at too high a cost.

Gillane addressed Analy, his voice heavy with emotion. "You have saved the life of our Futama and you will be honoured by your peers."

Joe's friend and bodyguard acknowledged Gillane's statement with a slight bow. "I have done no more than my duty," he said, "and I am grateful that I did not fail my friend, Joe Laing this time."

Analy smiled in Joe's direction and Joe gave a wink. Joe knew the big man was referring to his perceived failure to protect his charge on the beach; perhaps now Analy would feel his slate was clean.

Gillane suggested that they remove to another chamber whilst he air-conditioning unit worked to dissipate the sickly odour of burnt flesh. It was time to make final plans for the invasion. The high councillor revealed that the Master of Time would carry six

254

smaller vessels on her back, each equipped with a rudimentary, but reliable, time-displacement device in case they came under heavy fire. All the vessels would carry an electromagnetic pulse generator to disable all electronic devices within a range of a kilometre. The Futama's troops would carry a similar portable generator.

Joe waited until Gillane paused for a moment. "What exactly will this electromagnetic pulse achieve?" he asked.

"Trials indicate that plasma weapons will be inactivated for at least ten minutes until their controls can be reset, larger weapons for much longer."

"You're certain it will work?"

"Our science is very exact. The generators will perform exactly as planned."

"In that case," Joe declared, "there's something else you need to make for my men."

"Anything the Futama wishes will be provided."

* * *

Joe held Ciara in his arms and kissed her tenderly. "This is it, Sweetheart. It's time for the Faithful to reclaim their birthright."

Ciara fought back a sob. "Promise you'll come back for me and little Joe." She patted the bulge of her abdomen. "Promise?"

"I won't let anything stop me," Joe vowed, "and you know I'll be as careful as I can. And don't forget I've got Analy and Trione to watch my back. You know they won't let anything happen to me."

"I know," Ciara sobbed, "but you'll be so far away, and I can't help feeling so helpless here. I want to be with you. Surely you can understand that?"

"I can, and a part of me wants you by my side. But the most important thing you can do at the moment is keep little Joe safe. And spare a thought for Maeve and Or-gon. They both seem a little bit lost here on Mars. Do this for me, Sweetheart, and I'll be back before you know it, okay?" He kissed his wife lingeringly, before waving a swift goodbye.

As he mounted the ramp of the Master of Time, he heard Or-gon say wistfully that he would have liked to accompany him to the distant future. He smiled. There would be time for other excursions through time when Prua Landi had finally been defeated.

Chapter Twenty-six

INVASION:

The Master of time materialised in its bay at the compound and the process of unloading began immediately. Wave generators and time-displacement controls were unloaded on gravity platforms and whisked to each of the six smaller lunar vessels, each of which was dwarfed by the Master of Time. Within hours the devices had been retrofitted to the small disc-shaped craft and tests carried out well away from the confines of the compound. Nothing would be achieved by temporarily nullifying the force-field around the compound, along with every electronic device within it. When the captain of each ship was satisfied that all systems were working to full specifications, the craft were manoeuvred, one by one onto platforms on the upper surface of the Master of Time, where clamps extruded from the hull to anchor them. Within hours of landing at the compound the huge ship was ready.

A stream of troops emerged from the tunnel of the sacred cave and marched up the loading ramp until a total of a little over two-thousand four-hundred were crammed into the huge vessel. More troops mounted the upper surface of the ship and boarded the smaller vessels until each contained one-hundred and fifty soldiers. That left Joe with a detachment of fifty men, including Analy and Trione – whom Romana had previously injected with the specialised nanos – to carry out their attack beneath the city.

He spoke softly into a tiny communicator on his wrist. "Take off in one hour," he ordered.

Terpin's crisp tones answered, "One hour, Futama. Good luck!"

"Thanks, and the same to you." Terpin's nervous chuckle faded as Joe waved his troops forward. "We all know what we've got to do. Let's do it."

Three-quarters of an hour later, Joe stood at the time-gate leading into the cisterns beneath the city. Analy drifted the wave generator forward on its antigravity sled, until the metallic bulge at the front of the device gently nudged the solid wall, through which it could not pass without assistance.

Joe consulted his watch. "Now we wait." He sat on the dusty tunnel floor with his back against the wall and chewed an energy bar. "I'd recommend you all take this opportunity, because you'll need lots of energy when the fighting starts."

One by one his troops laid their weapons by their sides and unwrapped their rations. The minutes passed slowly. A light appeared the other side of the time-gate and a solitary soldier patrolled slowly by, swinging his powerful lantern from side to side. Joe nodded to Trione. "He's yours when he comes back," he said quietly.

Trione regained his feet athletically and approached the barrier. There he waited patiently for the trooper to return. He didn't have to wait long before the telltale light signalled that the patrol was nearing the gate. As the man passed, Trione darted swiftly through the time-gate and dealt the unfortunate man a rabbit punch to the back of the neck. The guard collapsed with a grunt and Trione caught him as he fell, dragging him inside to where Joe waited.

"Let's see what he knows when he wakes up," Joe murmured, splashing a little cold water on the man's face.

They did not have to wait long. With a groan he clawed his way towards consciousness. Eventually, he sat up and realised that he was a prisoner. His first reaction was to reach into his robe for his energy weapon.

Joe waved it before the trooper's face. "If this is what you're looking for, forget it."

The trooper made a desperate snatch for the weapon in Joe's hand, but strong hands restrained him, holding him immobile. A series of emotions passed over his features. Finally, he slumped forward. "Who are you?" he demanded, "and what do you want?" After a few moments he seemed, finally to comprehend the strangeness of his surroundings. "And where am I?"

"So many questions," commented Trione drily. "Perhaps the Futama will grant this man an answer."

The trooper reacted violently at the mention of Joe's name, but the restraining fingers, strengthened by weeks of hard training, merely clamped tighter on his limbs. He grunted in pain and the fingers relaxed a little. He stared at Joe with a growing sense of enlightenment. "The Futama? Surely the Futama is nothing more than a figment of deluded imaginations?"

"Do I look like a figment to you?" Joe enquired.

"How can you be a figment if I am speaking to you, unless—" the trooper hesitated, "unless I have lost my mind."

Selon whispered, "Futama, someone else is coming."

Joe watched as the light from another lantern approached – more slowly, it seemed, accompanied by a voice calling, "Gae, where are you, you fool. If this is another of your infernal pranks, Stelimon will skin you alive."

The light grew brighter and Joe nodded once again to Trione. This time Trione did not wait for the trooper to return from the tunnel's end. He dragged the limp form through the time-gate and Gae's eyes grew round with astonishment. Within seconds, the two were propped beside each other.

Finally, when he had regained consciousness, the second trooper complained, "It's no use hiding here, you idiot. Stelimon will soon find you and make you suffer."

"I don't believe the captain of the palace guard knows about this place," Gae informed his colleague. "I'm not sure I believe it myself. Look around you!"

At that point the realisation hit the second guard that they were not alone. He slumped against the curve of the tunnel wall.

Joe consulted his watch once more. "One minute," he said tersely.

"What about these two?" Selon enquired.

"They can't do any harm here," Joe laughed. "All they can do is wander about harmlessly in the time tunnels until we come back for them."

Selon laughed, a deep bass sound that rumbled down the tunnel. "As always, the Futama is correct."

This time, Trione held the gravsled as Analy directed it forward to nudge the time-gate. Joe glanced at his watch for a final time and nodded. The pulse generator moved forward a few inches and Joe felt a slight resonation through his bones and flesh.

"Come on, this is what you've trained for," he yelled, "let's get at 'em."

The troopers poured swiftly through into the cisterns, armed with immensely strong and flexible bojutsu poles, fashioned from Martian wood. Warily, they proceeded through the dank and odorous tunnels until they saw lights ahead, illuminating an approaching group of four soldiers. Prua Landi's troopers were concentrating so hard on the search for their two missing comrades that they never knew what hit them. Four bojutsu poles struck out like ramrods to their temples and they fell without a sound to the algae covered tunnel floor. Six down, how many more to go? The generator pulsed once more, sending out a wave of negative energy down the tunnel and Joe and his troops continued stealthily forward.

They next encountered a platoon of more than thirty men, on guard at a broad intersection of several tunnels. Joe examined the scene from the relative safety of the darkened tunnel. The whole intersection ahead was brightly lit and offered no cover whatsoever under which his men could attack. He motioned for Analy to take a dozen men into a side tunnel and for Selon to do the same on the other side, staying just within the fringe of darkness. Trione led his men into a third tunnel, leaving Joe with ten men to mount a frontal attack. He whispered instructions to his men, inhaled deeply several times, and then charged.

The enemy brought plasma rifles to bear as Joe covered the forty metres between them, uttering bloodcurdling yells.

When they realised that the plasma rifles were not going to work, the troopers reversed their grips intending to use them as clubs. They were no match for Joe's highly trained warriors. Though they had the advantage of numbers, it was all over in a few frenetic seconds, before Analy, Trione and Selon's reinforcements could join the fray. The bojutsu sticks made heavy and unyielding contact with skulls, and the enemy's senses were scrambled with an efficiency that made Joe intensely proud of the training sessions on Mars. Joe's troops were still breathing lightly, which was perhaps fortunate due to the foul odour of their surroundings.

*　*　*

Terpin waited until the last seconds of the hour ticked away, then initialised the time transfer. The Master of Time appeared five-hundred metres above the palace and immediately deployed her pressure wave generator, causing electrical and electronic failure throughout the entire city complex. The clamps holding the six smaller craft withdrew and, as one, they set off for their prearranged destinations over provincial cities.

The master of Time drifted downward and alighted on parkland below, disgorging four-hundred troops before lifting off as lightly as wind-blown thistledown. Immediately, the vast ship's coordinates were re-entered and she appeared outside the city at exactly the same instant in time. Again she disgorged four-hundred troops, repeating the procedure four more times. The effect was of six huge versions of the same vessel appearing at exactly the same moment over various parts of the city and its suburbs. There were now two-thousand four-hundred troops in place ready to make a concerted move towards Prua Landi's palace.

* * *

Joe and his troops met with no more resistance in the cisterns below the city streets as they headed for street level. They emerged into daylight to see graceful pastel-coloured spires soaring into the sky all around, a tribute to the artistry of their creators. A kilometre away the massive bulk of the Master of Time hovered silently over the palace, which, with its extensive parkland, occupied the city centre. Where the dark shadow cast by the vast ship failed to touch it the pale marble of the palace gleamed softly in the afternoon sunlight.

Several people hurried by, staring fearfully upwards at the spaceship above the tops of the tall buildings. Trione hauled the wave generator onto street level and it issued a pulse of energy. Two-hundred metres down the broad street, in the direction of the palace, a squad of troopers formed a human barricade. Joe counted more than a hundred. At their centre stood a short, immensely muscular man, whose skin shone like polished ebony. Though he barely came up to the other troopers' shoulders, he had a physical presence that was both impressive and disturbing.

The dark man barked a series of orders and his troops knelt and levelled their plasma rifles. At the order, "Fire," they pressed the firing studs and Joe watched in amusement at their varying reactions: from dumbfounded amazement to several frantic attempts to reset the weapons: from angrily shaking the rifles to throwing them onto the roadway in disgust. If it had been a television sketch it would have been hilarious but, Joe reminded himself, it was war and Prua Landi's troopers would have killed him along with his men without hesitation, had it been within their power to do so.

Joe's men approached warily and, at the final moment, charged, screaming assorted battle cries. They laid about themselves with their bojutsu poles and soon made inroads into the superior numbers of the enemy. But, suddenly, Joe's troops began to fall. The dark man had ripped out a piece of ornamental railing and was beating about with an animal ferocity Joe had never encountered before in his life. Analy and Trione urged Joe aside away from the mayhem but he knew he could not let his men suffer at the hands of the ebony skinned warrior.

260

He shrugged them off and warily approached. The dark man spied him, his eyes blazing with the flame of battle. Disregarding Joe's troopers, who were attacking him from three sides, he leapt ferociously at Joe, swinging the heavy metal pole around his head as if it weighed mere ounces. With a scream, he butted Analy to one side and swung at Joe, who stepped lightly aside and helped him on his way with a swat of the bojutsu pole behind his thick neck. Turning around with a speed and grace that belied his stocky proportions, Stelimon drove home his attack once more. This time, Joe was not quick enough and a swinging blow caught him beneath his armpit, shattering a couple of ribs and catapulting the smaller, lighter man sideways into another group of fighters. The lucky blow had gained the dark man an advantage, which he was not prepared to waste. Scenting blood, Stelimon pursued Joe, swinging a mighty blow at his head as he rose desperately to his feet.

Joe ducked low to evade the blow and the iron bar hissed harmlessly by over his head. He knew he had sustained at least two broken ribs and he wouldn't be able to take many more blows like that. The ebony skinned giant set his feet in a broad stance and raised his improvised weapon high above his head, intending to deal Joe a double-handed coup de grâce. Desperately, Joe straightened, aiming the butt of his bojutsu pole at the point where Stelimon's eyebrows met. The heavy Martian wood made contact with a satisfying smack and Stelimon staggered backwards, shaking his polished head in stunned bewilderment. Joe drew back his arms to deal Stelimon another blow, but a shaft of pain seared through his shattered ribs forcing him to drop his bojutsu pole. The polished wood clattered to the hard surface of the street. He coughed and felt the salt taste of blood in his mouth; the heavy blow must have driven a sliver of rib into his lung.

Stelimon shook his head once more and it was clear to Joe that he was swiftly shaking off the stunning effect of the blow to his forehead. The dark-skinned soldier approached more warily this time, twirling the heavy steel rod with first one hand and then the other. Finally, he gripped his improvised weapon with both hands and bellowed, "Now the Futama will die!"

Joe knew that in his injured state he would have little chance of evading more than one blow. Additionally, he felt a heavy weight in a pocket of his jacket restricting his movement. He cursed loudly and shifted the balance of the heavy object. Finally it dawned on him that the encumbrance was his pistol. Dragging it from his pocket, he flicked off the safety catch and brought the weapon to bear.

Stelimon roared with laughter. "All but primitive weapons such as this club are useless," he confided, waving the steel bar in the direction of his troops' plasma rifles discarded all over the battlefield. "Is the fabled Futama completely stupid as well as a weakling?"

Joe rose shakily to his feet, in an attempt to deny the truth of Stelimon's taunt. "Don't force me to kill you," he grated through jaws clenched against the agony of his shattered ribs. A detached portion of his consciousness was demanding to know when the nanos would start doing their job and reduce the pain to a more bearable level.

Stelimon's response was to raise his weapon and charge. The gun bucked twice in Joe's hand and Stelimon was thrown backwards by the impact of the two heavy bullets. He cannoned into two of his troopers and skittled them like ninepins. The steel bar rang like a gong as it hit the hard roadway at Joe's feet. Joe's dark-skinned adversary fell almost in a sitting position against a wall, fingering two wounds in his chest, which were bubbling bright red blood down his muscular abdomen. He wore an expression of surprise upon his face.

Joe fell to his knees, the pistol clenched tightly in his fingers, his head resting wearily upon his chest. All around, an eerie silence had descended upon the battle scene. Everyone who could still stand was staring at Joe. No one moved. No one watched Stelimon as his lifeblood dribbled away onto the plasticrete surface, the trauma of his wounds too great for his nanos to heal without the immediate intervention of surgeons. No one seemed to notice that, following the death of their commanding officer, the few remaining soldiers of the palace guard were no longer offering resistance to Joe's troops, and had bunched together expecting to suffer the same fate.

A distant clamour sounded down the street. Joe wearily raised his eyes to see a host of people racing towards him, their numbers swelled by others joining from side streets. They were chanting as they ran, and as they drew nearer, their chant grew increasingly distinct.

They were calling, "Futama! Futama! Futama!"

With a groan, Joe sank to the hard plasticrete roadway and Analy and Trione rushed anxiously to his side to protect him from the followers who had awaited his coming for so long. His ribs still ached savagely, but the intensity of the pain was being mitigated by the ministrations of the army of nanomedics coursing through his body. He coughed, expecting the pain to lance through him once more; to his relief, the agony was more bearable. Shakily, he made it to one knee and Analy offered a strong arm to help him to his feet. His head swam momentarily, then his vision cleared and he saw that more than a thousand pairs of eyes were watching him avidly. He stood erect and thrust his pistol towards the skies and a relieved cheer rose up from the ranks of his followers.

Joe addressed the throng. "People of the Faithful," he called to the sea of expectant faces, "what you have witnessed here is being repeated in many locations around this and other cities. Prua Landi's palace is isolated, her weapons useless, her army stripped of its defences. It is time to regain your birthright. Who will follow me to the palace?"

His question met with a thunderous cheer and a renewed chant of, "Futama! Futama! Futama!"

Joe heard the sound of cheers behind him, far too loud for his small number of troops. He swivelled to see that the palace guards were joining enthusiastically in the celebrations. "Who is your commanding officer?" he enquired.

A young officer stepped forward, his face bruised and bloody where he had taken several blows from a bojutsu pole. It was clear, from the manner in which his eyes focused and unfocused, that his senses were still a little scrambled from the beating he had taken. "I am," he said shakily.

"Do you speak for your troops?" Joe asked him.

"Yes, everyone will follow my orders."

"It's not your *orders* I'm talking about," Joe informed him, "but their *desire*. Do they have the desire to join the ranks of the Faithful?"

"We are all of the Faithful," the young officer, Aris, replied, his voice gaining strength with each passing moment as his senses cleared. "We did not choose to become members of Prua Landi's forces. We chose not to die by refusing to serve her."

His words received a mutter of assent form his troops, who were being joined by more of their comrades as they regained consciousness in ones and twos. All bore the marks of battle; a number had broken bones from contact with the heavy Martian wood of the bojutsu poles; most bore lumps on their polished scalps where they had been expertly knocked unconscious by Joe highly-trained exponents of the martial arts.

"In that case, pick up your weapons and join the happy band," Joe ordered. "They're not much use except as clubs, but that's better than nothing, I suppose. Now, if you're ready, it's time to see what sort of resistance Prua Landi has to offer."

Once more a ragged chant of, "Futama! Futama! Futama!" rose up amongst the crowd.

Flanked by Analy and Trione, and surrounded by his troops, Joe set out for the palace, less than a kilometre away. Use of the pressure wave generator had made communication over distance impossible – everything that utilised electronics had been rendered useless, so he could only guess at the success of the campaign so far. They strode onwards towards the palace between tall, graceful buildings, lit by the rays of the afternoon sun. Joe consulted his watch; the invasion had been underway for little more than an hour. The buildings petered out to be replaced by the open space around Prua Landi's palace. Before them, a series of broad arches spanned a sea of mud, which until recently had been an ornamental lake surrounding the palace.

The building was breathtakingly beautiful, its pale marble glowing in the sun, reflecting a variety of pastel hues from roofs and walls. The force-field windows had been shut down by the pressure wave generator and now stared out sightlessly over Prua Landi's crumbling empire.

Overhead loomed the vast disc of the Master of Time, hovering motionless in the blue vault of the sky. As they watched, she was joined by six smaller craft, which approached from different directions and settled into a symmetrical formation around her outer rim. A hatch opened below the Master of Time's waistline and a tiny shuttle drifted out, cushioned by its antigravity drive, before plunging gracefully towards the ornamental bridge a hundred metres away. As it alighted on the surface, a doorway opened and three tall figures stepped down a short ramp. They waited patiently for Joe to arrive with his army of followers. Joe immediately recognised Leiki, Romana and Perdon, now mercifully recovered from his ordeal beneath the city.

Romana stepped forward to embrace Joe and he winced as pain lanced through his ribs, which were still in the early process of recovery from the shattering blow dealt by Stelimon. Romana sensed Joe's distress and withdrew to hold him at arm's length whilst she scrutinised his agonised expression.

"You're hurt?" she exclaimed accusingly.

"A bit," Joe admitted, "I caught a blow from an iron bar to my ribs and I think a couple might be cracked."

As he was speaking, Romana retrieved a diagnostic from her robe and immediately ran it over the sore part of Joe's anatomy, frowning all the while as she read the display. She repeated the procedure before declaring. "The nanos have begun the healing process, but you must rest to allow them to work at their greatest efficiency."

Joe surveyed the host of his followers, which was growing with every moment. They had spread along the edge of the lake each side of the bridge, to get a better view of the proceedings; Joe guessed the crowd must number more than ten thousand.

"There'll be plenty of time for that when Prua Landi's been sorted out once and for all," Joe told her. "Until then, I'll just have to put up with a bit of discomfort."

Romana knew that there was little chance of changing Joe's mind, but still she felt she had to give it one last shot. "But Joe, you must take the advice of your medical aide," she protested. "You owe it to your people."

Joe kissed Romana full on the lips, despite the presence of ten thousand witnesses. "You worry too much. I'll be fine. In fact I'll feel a lot better when Prua Landi's behind bars."

The tall medic stepped backwards in astonishment, fingering her lips where Joe had kissed her. The wind had well and truly been let out of the sails of her protest.

Leiki grinned impishly at Joe. "Now that has been decided, shall we go?"

Joe nodded and called for Analy and Trione and the rest of his troops to accompany them, supplemented by the new recruits from the ranks of Prua Landi's palace guard. Leiki detailed Perdon to remain on the bridge to address the crowd, many of whom believed that he had perished at Prua Landi's hand in the muddy reservoirs beneath the city streets. There was a rising roar of approbation from the huge throng when they realised it was Perdon standing before them, and Joe smiled at the way circumstances had worked out for the brave agent of the Faithful. Perdon had been prepared to give his life for his beliefs – in fact, had almost *given* his life – and now he had returned to his people to witness the final minutes of Prua Landi's reign of terror.

To chants of, "Futama! Futama!" interspersed with the occasional, "Perdon! Perdon!" Joe led his troops across the bridge to the palace.

They fanned out to systematically search every conceivable hiding place for the dictatrix, dispatching any resistance as they encountered it. Leiki was full of admiration for the ease with which the troops performed the task. On the whole, with the exception of the injury to the Futama, the well-drawn plans had worked exquisitely. They had received reports of no fatalities, apart from that of Stelimon – a definite bonus when trying to win the hearts and minds of the general populace following a military coup. All that remained was to apprehend Prua Landi, a task that should be made simpler by the absence of energy weapons.

The extensive ground floor was devoid of any signs of the empress, so the troops warily mounted the broad staircases to the upper floor, leaving detachments of three troopers to guard each of the several flights of stairs. After half an hour of searching, they heard voices in the laboratory. Stealthily, Trione pushed the door, to discover that it was firmly locked.

Joe motioned him aside. Ensuring everyone was behind him, Joe aimed his pistol at the locking mechanism and pulled the trigger. The resulting explosion was deafening in the confines of the corridor. The bullet hit its mark and ricocheted from wall to wall down the corridor. The door remained locked. Joe examined the effect of the bullet on the lock; there was a hairline crack in the plate covering the lock's internal movement. He took aim once more, and this time the lock shattered, sending splinters of metal and plastic whirring down the corridor. Trione kicked the door open.

Inside, they saw Prua Landi standing within a small cubicle, an expression of utter contempt upon her severe features. At a console a man of indeterminate age was feverishly stabbing at a control panel. Analy and Trione stepped forward to make the arrest, their bojutsu poles at the ready. A coloured light flickered on the control panel and the whole mechanism suddenly blazed into life. The man's hands moved deftly over the controls and as Trione reached out to grasp him, he darted at astonishing speed into the cubicle beside Prua Landi. The pair were surrounded by a corona of intense blue light and Joe was left with a lasting impression of Prua

Landi's piercing glare of hatred as she and her companion vanished in a coruscating explosion of light.

Joe and the rest were stunned. It was clear that their quarry had escaped to some distant period of time – but where? All around them, walls and ceilings were beginning to glow as the electronics of the laboratory recovered from the effects of the pressure wave generator.

A muted groan filled the laboratory, startling everyone. Prua Landi and Praeton had recently fled leaving everyone on edge; no one was prepared to hazard a guess as to whose voice it could be? The groans resembled the mumbling of someone suffering the effects of a severe hangover.

After a few moments, Leiki commanded, "AI, show yourself!"

The mumbling intensified and Leiki repeated his command. The voice demanded pettily, "Who is there? I cannot see you. I have been starved of nutrients for an indeterminate period and I have an urgent need to reboot my core processor. Who would be so barbaric as to place me in such an invidious situation?" The AI groaned once more; she sounded thoroughly miserable. "Is the empress Prua Landi present?"

"The empress no longer holds the palace," Leiki informed the ailing AI, "and we have need of your services to manage the city."

"We? Who are you?"

"We are the Faithful, come to regain our birthright."

The AI was silent for a few moments whilst she digested Leiki's statement: eventually, she asked, "Is your Futama present?"

"I'm here," Joe answered. Again the AI lapsed into silence, prompting Joe to demand, "Is something the matter?"

The AI gave a very human cough. "Forgive me, but I always considered the legend of the Futama to be the product of the Empress Prua Landi's psychotic personality. I must admit that I find the prospect of meeting you in the flesh a little unnerving – which I might accomplish if my optical sensors were not refusing to respond to the reboot of my system." The AI gave another embarrassed cough. "Are you able to say whether the empress is alive or dead?"

Puzzled, Joe informed the artificial intelligence, "As far as we can tell, she is very much alive. Does that bother you?"

"It does. She recently threatened to boil me in my ambient fluids: when my system failed I thought that she had decided to carry out her threat." The AI's voice trembled. "As more of my memory comes online I am beginning to recall Prua Landi's actions immediately prior to my shutdown. It seems she was priming a plasma bomb somewhere in the palace. Now . . . where was it?" The AI muttered distractedly to herself before saying, "Ah, now I remember. The device is in a storeroom immediately below this laboratory and the timing device has reactivated since the shutdown. You have less than five minutes to vacate the palace." With a sense of utmost melodrama, the AI said, "Please, everyone leave whilst I attempt to defuse the bomb."

"Like hell!" Joe yelled. "Analy, Trione, come with me. Leiki, tell the shuttle pilot to prepare for immediate take-off with three passengers and one bomb. Tell him to kick everyone else off the shuttle." He was already leaping downstairs, four at a time, with Analy and Trione close behind as Leiki opened communication with the shuttle pilot. At the bottom of the ornate staircase, Joe turned left and headed towards a doorway, which appeared to be immediately below the laboratory. The locked door succumbed to a short burst of plasma fire, revealing a squat, menacing shape surrounded by several cylindrical containers labelled 'Cleaning Fluid' and a number of household robots, the function of which Joe couldn't even guess at. Fortunately, there was an indentation in each side of the bomb case to facilitate the manhandling of the heavy object, but no gravity compensators to mitigate its obviously considerable weight.

"Futama, you should leave whilst you are able. We have very little time." Trione urged, grasping one side of the device.

"And miss all the fun?" Joe replied, dragging the timestone from its hiding place. His head was a turmoil of symbols and instructions. Carefully, for he would have no opportunity to calibrate the timestone a second time, he separated its two pyramid-shaped halves by approximately five millimetres and twisted the timestone on its major axis. "Okay, let's take this bomb somewhere where it can't harm anyone," he told his companions.

Analy and Trione strained their well-toned muscles and heaved the heavy device outside, where everything was still and silent. People stood like statues, some precariously balanced, caught in mid-stride. Joe's friends almost dropped the bomb onto the palace steps in astonishment.

"It's nothing to worry about," Joe told them, "all I've done is stop time for everything except the three of us. But we'd better get a move on because the effect won't last very long."

The two bent to the task and hauled the plasma bomb up the ramp into the shuttle, where they discovered the pilot, sitting motionless in his seat, staring sightlessly at his instruments, one hand on the control binnacle and the other paused centimetres from a screen on the instrument panel in front of him. Joe adjusted the time stone and gave it another twist: the pilot flowed into motion, completing the action he had begun moments before Joe had interfered with the steady progress of time. The pilot jerked nervously and his eyes opened wide in surprise as three figures seemed to materialise beside him.

"Take us up into space!" Joe said urgently. The pilot instantly complied with the Futama's order. His fingers flew over the controls: the outer door closed and the shuttle rose swiftly into the clear skies. "Won't this thing go any faster?" Joe demanded. The rate of acceleration increased and the city below the craft rapidly became a grey smudge in the rear screens. Everything went black as the shuttle left the atmosphere, accelerating at a rate approaching its limit. In less than a minute they were more than a hundred-thousand kilometres from Earth, and Joe called, "I reckon that should be far enough."

Trione nodded to Analy and they urgently donned spacesuits from a locker in the cabin wall before heading for the bomb. "Stay here," Analy told Joe, "and leave this to us!"

Moments later the airlock opened and the bomb appeared on the screens, tumbling through space away from the shuttle. Reverberations through the hull informed the pilot that the airlock had sealed and so he accelerated frantically away. Within seconds the shuttle's windows darkened as a blinding explosion of plasma outshone the Sun. The tiny craft bucked and yawed, before tumbling end over end in a madcap spinning motion. Its protective force field sparkled and coruscated as it fought to insulate the shuttle from the intense heat and radiation.

The occupants were thrown around in the confines of the tiny craft like dice in a shaker and Joe's forehead contacted a projection in the ceiling, knocking him unconscious. The pilot was thrown out of his seat and lay like a rag doll across the control panel. Analy and Trione's spacesuits protected them from injury as the shuttle tumbled through space, and as Joe regained consciousness, he

269

discovered that he had been inserted into a spacesuit. The pilot lay beside him, similarly protected, though he showed no signs of coming round after his encounter with the instrument panel. Trione was at the controls, maintaining maximum acceleration on a curved path that would eventually lead back to Earth, and Joe watched as the shuttle windows gradually returned to their original clear form, allowing starlight to shine through.

Analy entered the cabin. Joe knew it had taken considerable courage to manhandle the plasma bomb out of the airlock when it was so close to exploding. He resolved to make the point and to commend the shuttle pilot, Derin, together with Trione and Analy when they landed once again at the palace. Joe was certain that in the twenty-first century their courage and selflessness would have earned them medals of the highest order.

* * *

No one, with the exception of the four men in the shuttlecraft, had witnessed the explosion of the plasma bomb far out in space: time had remained at a standstill for everyone on Earth. Leiki was waiting impatiently as they landed in the palace grounds. "What happened to the plasma bomb?" he enquired.

Joe pointed a finger upwards. "Went off in space where it could do no harm."

"But how did you remove the device from the palace when there was so little time?"

Joe patted his pocket, where the timestone was once again safely stored. "You'd be surprised at what the timestone can do," he said. "I reckon I owe you an explanation, but that will have to wait until we've sorted out the problem of Prua Landi. Any news about where she might have gone?"

Leiki raised his wrist to his mouth and said quietly, "Terpin?"

"Yes, Councillor Leiki."

"Can you trace the destination of the time transfer from the palace a few moments ago?"

"It has already been done. The destination was the time of the Futama and the location was the Futama's home."

Joe was stunned. It was abundantly clear that he had been wise to remove all his family into the protection of Gillane's people on Mars.

"We've got to go back to get her," he told Leiki, "because there's no telling what she'll do when her plasma pistol comes back to life. I can just imagine her making so much trouble for me in my own time that it would be impossible for me to go back there."

Analy touched Joe's arm. "Trione and I will bring Prua Landi back to face the Council of Elders if the Futama will permit."

"I have no problem with that, but I'm coming too. If they put up a fight I might need to use the timestone to put things right. Otherwise, I'll always have the police and the military breathing down my neck."

Analy immediately stepped out of the laboratory and returned moments later with six heavily armed troopers. He handed plasma rifles to Joe and Trione. "We are ready, Futama."

Leiki spoke into his communicator once more. "Terpin?"

"Yes, Councillor Leiki?"

"A detachment of troops, including the Futama, awaits the Master of Time in the palace grounds. They will seek out the empress and return her to the palace. Please ensure that your presence in the Futama's era causes the least possible disturbance."

"Understood," Terpin replied, "pick-up in two minutes."

"In that case," Joe grinned, "we'd better get a move on." As the small band hurried outside into the palace grounds, he observed drolly, "How does a ship the size of the Master of Time manage to cause no fuss?"

"With great difficulty," Trione answered.

Chuckling heartily, the three friends watched the great bulk of the Master of Time as she floated, cushioned to feather-lightness on antigravity, down to where they waited with the six troopers. Three huge legs touched the grass and the ramp descended from the ship's underbelly. Within moments they were aboard and heading for the bridge.

Terpin welcomed Joe with a warm embrace. "Many people must have already expressed their gratitude, but please permit this humble ship's captain to thank you, Futama, for setting your people free."

"You're welcome," replied Joe, "but it's not over yet. There's still the small matter of Prua Landi. Once she's back here under guard, we can congratulate each other. Until then, she can still cause untold mischief."

"Then we will waste no further time." Terpin gave a series of crisp orders and the ship rose once more into the azure sky. Joe felt the familiar sensation in his guts as the mighty ship underwent a temporal shift, appearing suddenly in the grey winter skies a mile above his home.

"The shuttle is waiting," Terpin informed him.

Joe hurried into the hold of the ship with his detachment of troops, where the shuttle awaited, a pilot already at the controls. The belly of the Master of Time irised open and the tiny shuttle, dwarfed by its mother ship, floated out. Once clear, the shuttle dropped vertically like an express lift and landed lightly in the roadway outside Joe's house. The multi-channel communication console came alive with radio traffic as the Master of Time suddenly inserted into the skies above Joe's home. There was a Royal Air Force base no more than twenty miles away and the huge ship would not fail to appear on their radar. It would not be long before the RAF sent a couple of jet fighters to investigate.

* * *

Prua Landi and Praeton appeared in a ball of blue light beside the massive trunk of a gaunt tree, which stood at the road junction immediately in front of Joe's home. She looked around to get her bearings. The tree was familiar; Prua Landi's mind flipped back to her confrontation with the Futama's protectors, when she had been extremely fortunate to escape with her life. The tree was the one behind which she had sheltered; the very same tree that had exploded so violently under the assault of a plasma rifle. She smiled grimly at the confirmation of her theory that her enemy had at his disposal a means of altering the very flow of time itself. It was mid afternoon and there was a hint of snow in the chilly air. She drew her cloak tighter around her slim shoulders and headed for Joe's front door, accompanied by a shivering Praeton, whose light laboratory clothing afforded little protection against the cold of a January day.

A passing dog walker gave a curious stare at the two unusually tall people at Joe's front door. Prua Landi returned the stare, and the young woman hurried past, muttering to herself about the neighbourhood suffering from an excess of illegal aliens. Prua Landi smiled as she caught the wisp of thought from the passer-by; the woman had no notion of how illegal and how alien were the objects of her thoughts. With her plasma pistol set to narrow beam, the former empress burned away the lock and entered, followed by Praeton.

"Search the house," Prua Landi commanded Praeton. "It is highly unlikely that the Futama's wife will be here, but there will doubtless be food to sustain us until she returns. Then my enemies will discover what a mistake they have made in attempting to depose me."

Praeton slipped quietly upstairs, returning moments later shaking his head. "This dwelling is empty," he confided. As an afterthought, he added, "How can anyone live in such primitive conditions? There is no air cleansing system and the furnishings are so unhygienic that I would fear for my health should I touch them."

"Perhaps you should step carefully," Prua Landi said sardonically, "if you wish to survive." She lowered herself onto the sofa, her knees inelegantly high due to the lower seating position, which was designed for people more than thirty centimetres shorter. "I am hungry. See what you can find that may prove edible."

Praeton bowed. "Of course, My Lady," he said before stepping into the kitchen. Prua Landi heard the sound of cupboard doors opening and closing, and eventually Praeton returned carrying a bowl of canned peaches. "My apologies for the delay, My Lady, but the means of opening the container was not readily apparent." He shook his head in disgust. "These people have barely progressed from the primeval ooze."

"That may be so, but yet these very times have spawned the Futama," Prua Landi replied around a mouthful of sliced peach. Her expression mellowed for a moment, as she tasted the fruit for the first time. Eventually, she grudgingly admitted, "This primitive era may have at least one redeeming feature after all, for I must admit that I find this food extremely palatable."

"In that case, I will open another container," Praeton declared, "for I too am hungry."

Prua Landi allowed herself the luxury of a smile. "It seems that our roles have been temporarily reversed."

"My Lady?"

"You have cleverly allowed me to become your food taster."

Praeton stood aghast at the accusation. "My Lady, circumstances have conspired—"

Prua Landi raised her hand to halt his protestations. "A little joke, Praeton," she laughed, "but take care not to abuse your position."

Praeton sighed with relief. "I would not presume, My Lady."

Joe and his troopers disembarked from the shuttle and warily made their way towards his house. The front door was slightly ajar and there was a neat hole where the lock had been. Analy stepped towards the doorway and Joe felt Trione's restraining hand on his arm.

"Permit us to lead," the big man said, "the Futama is too valuable for his people to lose him now the war is almost over."

Reluctantly, Joe stepped back and Trione beckoned four troopers forward. As they ducked inside, Joe noticed several nearby doors open as neighbours sidled out into the street. One person spotted the shuttle in the middle of the road junction and, almost as one, they headed for the craft. Gesticulating frantically, Joe headed them off.

"Get back into your houses!" he hissed. "There's going to be a firefight. The only place where you'll be safe is inside your homes."

Ruth Morris, a middle-aged housewife, from number twenty-nine, stood her ground. "What's happening, Joe? And why should you give everybody orders?"

"Look, Mrs Morris," Joe said urgently, "there's no time to explain. Believe me, if you don't get inside quickly, you could all be killed."

Everyone stared skyward as two typhoon fighters screamed noisily past the dark bulk of the Master of Time as she hovered overhead. Their eyes widened in fear; the situation was completely outside their experience, and it seemed as though an alien invasion movie had become a living reality.

A violent crackling sounded from the direction of Joe's home and he saw the roof bulge and lift off into the sky with a thunderous roar, leaving a neat round hole approximately four metres in diameter, with the roofing felt around the circumference burning fiercely. Another explosion resulted in a broad hole burned through the front elevation, almost completely erasing the lounge window. The plasma beam, unhindered by the glass of the window, enveloped one of the trees in the street and the wood instantly vaporised, sending an explosion of charred splinters in every direction.

Joe dropped to the grass verge, taking Ruth Morris down with him. The explosion ripped overhead, scything down several of Joe's neighbours, and leaving a scene of carnage all around. Joe quickly regained his feet and helped Ruth to hers. She was shaking so badly that Joe thought she would collapse.

"You okay?" he asked softly.

She nodded dumbly. "How did you know about that?" she demanded. "Joe, are you part of all this?"

"Don't worry, Mrs Morris. It'll all be fine, believe me. Do yourself a favour. Go inside and make yourself a cuppa and leave it to me, okay?" He urged her in the direction of her front door and she meekly submitted to his suggestion, all thoughts of opposition drained from her by the enormity of the events of the past few minutes.

Joe heard a voice call him; it was Trione. "It is safe now for you to enter. We have arrested Prua Landi."

* * *

Trione silently led four troopers into the house, their plasma rifles primed and ready. They encountered a closed door, which Trione knew led to Joe's living room. He made his way to one side and signalled two of the troopers, Clen and Dayle to take the other side of the doorway. Borel the third soldier stood ready to batter down the door. At a signal from Trione, Borel slammed his foot against the door, shattering the wood and tearing the door from its hinges. The impetus of his attack threw him into the room where Prua Landi was calmly waiting to greet him, her plasma pistol at the ready.

A needle beam of sun-hot plasma caught Borel in the neck and his finger instantly spasmed on the firing stud, discharging his weapon as he fell dying to the floor. The sustained plasma beam passed through the ceiling, opening the roof to the grey winter sky. Before Borel hit the floor, Dayle dived through the opening, receiving a shot to the head. His plasma weapon discharged as he fell against the firing stud, blasting out part of the front of the house and most of the front window. A tree in the line of fire vaporised in a titanic explosion.

Trione dived across the open doorway, discharging a split-second burst from his plasma rifle. As he landed athletically, a scream from inside the room told him that he had found his target. He reset the rifle to needle beam and drilled a neat hole through the wall beside the doorway. Peering through the spyhole, he saw Prua Landi staring uncomprehendingly at the remains of her arm. Trione's lucky shot had burned away her arm, taking the plasma pistol with it. The dictatrix was severely wounded and disarmed.

275

Stepping inside, Trione covered Prua Landi with his plasma weapon, but all the fight had gone out of her. Praeton huddled behind the heavily stuffed sofa, moaning in fear. The blast, which had dissolved Prua Landi's arm, had passed inches over his head and burned a hole in the wall through to Maeve's house next door.

Leaving Prua Landi in Analy's charge, Trione stepped outside to inform the Futama that the former empress was finally under arrest. All around him there was devastation. Several people lay on the grass and the roadway, severely wounded or dead. In the distance the wail of sirens drew rapidly closer. A police car careered around a corner a hundred metres away accompanied by its blue lights and siren, and headed towards the shuttle where it sat across the road junction. The car screeched noisily to a halt and the doors were thrown open. Four officers bundled out, staring in disbelief at the incredible scene. One officer ran to the casualties and began examining them for signs of life. Another spoke rapidly into a radio, calling for assistance and medical attention.

Joe and his troopers exited the house and the movement immediately caught the eye of one of the police officers, who noticed for the first time the substantial damage to Joe's house.

"Hey," the officer called, "stay where you are. I need to ask you some questions." The policeman belatedly caught sight of the burned stump of Prua Landi's severed arm and called over to his fellows. "There's something weird going on here. Keep an eye on this lot while I contact the station and call for an ambulance."

Joe urged his friends toward the shuttle and two policemen immediately barred their way. "Look, my friends," Joe said conversationally, "you're a bit out of your depth. Just move out of the way and we'll all be out of here."

The officers stood their ground. The whole situation was outside of their experience, but they did not lack courage. Analy waved his plasma rifle menacingly: a moment of fear was immediately replaced by resolve.

The policeman said calmly to Analy, "Now, Sir, if that's some kind of weapon, I'd suggest you hand it over before someone gets hurt." Analy made no move to comply.

A rumble of trucks sounded beyond the police car and a couple of army troop carriers barrelled around the corner, coming to a screeching halt one behind the other and disgorging thirty or more heavily-armed soldiers. One truck was towing a trailer containing a heavy machine gun, which two troopers quickly set up in the middle of the road. An immaculately dressed officer lowered himself from the cab of the lead truck. Analy stared apprehensively at Joe who merely shrugged.

"There's nothing to worry about," Joe told his men. "Just let me deal with it."

The army lieutenant consulted the police constables, but their conversation was soon drowned out by the 'whup whup' of approaching helicopters. Joe looked skywards and saw three apache gunships. Prua Landi, it seemed, had really stirred things up, and after the previous odd happenings on the beach, the army was taking no chances. The gunships hovered a hundred metres or so from the shuttle where it stood at the road junction.

After speaking to the police constables the lieutenant warily approached Joe and his men. Two troopers held a weakening Prua Landi upright.

"Who is in charge here?" demanded the officer.

"I am," Joe admitted casually.

"Are you prepared to lay down your weapons and come with me?"

"Not really."

The officer was taken aback by Joe's total lack of fear in the face of overwhelmingly superior force. "Would you like to explain your reasons?" the lieutenant enquired, playing for time while his men deployed the heavy machine gun.

"Look pal," Joe said genially, "your troops and those 'copters up there are way out of their league. If I told you they were completely outgunned, would you believe me?"

The officer shook his head uncertainly.

"I thought not. Well, we're going to take a steady stroll to our shuttle and you'd better pray that there are no itchy trigger fingers amongst your men, okay? I'd hate you to lose three gunships and all your men because you weren't bright enough to appreciate the hole you were in."

Analy, Trione and Clen adjusted their plasma rifles and each faced a gunship. The rest of Joe's troopers eyed the detachment of soldiers. Their confidence unnerved the officer somewhat and he backed away, all the time keeping his eyes on Joe. Finally, he called, "Hold your fire, men," and repeated his order by radio to the gunships. Now all he could do was wait for the tanks to arrive, accompanied by reinforcements.

Joe handed his plasma rifle to Analy and retrieved the timestone from a pocket of his jacket. Expertly, he calibrated the two halves and gave a final twist. The roadway outside his home disappeared and he was in the laboratory in the imperial palace. Prua Landi stood between two troopers, an uncomprehending gleam in her eyes. She stared vaguely down at her hands. There was nothing amiss, yet she had a dreamlike recollection that she had lost one of her arms at some time – perhaps in an accident, perhaps to plasma fire. Yet, no matter how she strained her powers of recollection, the memory eluded her, remaining forever over the horizon of her ability to recall.

She caught sight of Joe and immediately tried to pry open his mind, growing angry at her lack of success. She fought to control her anger, and tried once again to impose control over Joe's mind, receiving an even more emphatic rebuff than previously. Clearly, Joe had achieved a strength and control over his thought processes that far outstripped even her precocious and deadly talent.

Calmly, Joe addressed her, "You were always destined to lose this fight, you know. You were the only person not prepared to believe it."

Prua Landi merely glared at him, as if she could burn him to a cinder with her gaze. Finally, she admitted, "I underestimated you . . . this time. At first I was foolishly unwilling to accept that a primitive creature such as yourself could be the fabled Futama, and I missed an opportunity to kill you in Tarmis, it seems to my cost. I assure you that I will not underestimate you again."

"Somehow, I don't think that will matter in the long run," Joe replied, "because I can't imagine the Council of Elders will give you the opportunity to cause any more mischief. Prua Landi seemed not to hear: her eyes had taken on a distant look and her bronzed complexion had paled by several shades. Praeton's complexion had also blanched; he was utterly terrified. "Is something bothering the pair of you?" Joe enquired innocently.

Prua Landi consulted her chronometer and her pupils dilated. "There is—" she sneered, attempting to impose a measure of control over her swiftly deteriorating circumstances, "something you should know."

"Oh, and what would that be?"

She glared contemptuously at Joe. "Within *my* palace, there is a powerful plasma bomb, timed to detonate in—" she consulted her chronometer again, "less than thee minutes."

278

Casually, Joe demanded, "Why should we believe you? Why should we believe this is anything but a diversion to try to gain some sort of imagined advantage? Surely you can be a little more imaginative."

Shaking with fear, Praeton screamed, "My Lady is telling the truth. The bomb is in a storeroom immediately below this laboratory. Please, we must leave the palace immediately, before it is too late."

Smiling grimly, Joe focused his attention on a chronometer on the laboratory wall, which was remorselessly counting down the seconds to inevitable doom. Prua Landi was quickly losing her composure. Her sneering expression had been replaced by one of unbridled terror. Many of the population had been subjected to such terror, and now the dictatrix had been placed squarely in their shoes. Almost gibbering with fear, the last vestiges of her composure gone, she screamed at Joe, "You unimaginative, primitive creature. In your campaign to destroy me, you have managed to destroy us all."

Joe kept his gaze focused upon the chronometer as the deadline passed. Finally, with no sense of triumph in his voice he informed Prua Landi, "As you have always underestimated the strength of will of the Faithful, it shouldn't come as much of a surprise that you imagined your tactic with the plasma bomb couldn't fail. You could not even treat an AI in a humane fashion and it was that which proved your undoing. Even the AI secretly harboured the hope that the legend of the Futama contained more than an element of truth."

With her fear dissipating Prua Landi snarled, "How could a primitive creature defeat the leader of a sophisticated society so far into his future? How could my people worship such an inferior product of evolution?"

"That's a concept you'll never be able to grasp," Joe told her. "At no time were they ever *your* people. Faced with repression and tyranny, any human being will secretly hold onto even the slimmest hope of salvation. The fact that they invested all their trust in me leaves me with a sense of humility you could never begin to understand." He looked around him at the faces of those in the laboratory: it was clear that his conversation with Prua Landi was likely to be passed down through the generations.

Joe decided to make one final point. "Just ponder this thought," he said quietly, "while you wait to be tried for your crimes." He dug into a pocket of his jacket and drew out his .38

calibre Webley revolver. Prua Landi's eyes opened wide in fear. Ignoring her reaction, Joe continued, "If I were as primitive as you believe me to be, I would put this *primitive* pistol to your head and blow out your *sophisticated* brains for what you've put my family through. Fortunately for you, I'm not the savage you believe me to be, and I'm happy to leave your fate in the hands of the Council."

Uncharacteristically Prua Landi nodded in acknowledgement, a wry smile on her lips. "Perhaps . . . we shall see."

Chapter Twenty-seven

EXILE:

The trial of Prua Landi heralded celebrations over the whole Earth. When the unanimous verdict of 'guilty' was eventually reached by the panel of judges, everyone sighed with relief. All that remained was the sentence. Most of the populace believed it should be death, but such a swingeing sentence flew in the face of the philosophy of the Faithful. When it finally came, the decision met with a mixed reception. Prua Landi was to be exiled – not merely to a location far away from other humans, but also immensely distant in time. She would be relocated to the Mars of the late Carboniferous period of Earth. All the Faithful who had experienced exile upon the red planet would be repatriated, and almost every sign of their twenty-five year tenancy would be expunged. All that would remain would be a simple dwelling, provisions sufficient to last for one Martian year, and seeds and instructions for growing sufficient food to sustain Prua Landi and Praeton, whose fate was to accompany her into exile.

Prua Landi submitted meekly to a medical examination. The Council felt that it would be uncivilised to dispatch the deposed empress to the primeval past of Mars, without first ensuring that she had the health and physical strength to survive a long exile there.

Romana carried out the examination, and immediately recognised the telltale readings upon her diagnostic. "Do you know that you are pregnant?" she enquired as she reset the diagnostic and took another reading.

"Pregnant?" Prua Landi demanded haughtily. "Like a beast in the wilds of the recreational forests?"

"Exactly!" Romana replied, keeping her part of the conversation to the absolute minimum.

Prua Landi spent a few moments of introspection before snarling, her voice shaking with fury, "Perdon, that verminous creature. He insinuated himself into my trust and has left me carrying— " she rubbed her abdomen, "—this abomination. You will remove it and destroy it . . . instantly!"

Romana smiled indulgently. "There was a time," she told the other woman, "when I would have gladly burned you and your unborn child to ashes with a plasma weapon. But our Futama has taught me the value of restraint, and renewed within me a belief in the sanctity of life . . . even yours. Do not ever again attempt to give me orders, or I might forget his teachings and end your miserable life. Guards!"

Analy and Trione entered at a run, their heads encased in tight-fitting helmets, which would instantly broadcast powerful interference patterns should anyone try to penetrate their minds. Romana wore a similar protective device.

Romana nodded towards Prua Landi. "Hold her tightly, but take every care not to hurt her. She is carrying a child."

The two, with strength built up by hard physical training in the run-up to the invasion, grasped the dictatrix and held her immobile. Prua Landi's screams of fury died instantly as Romana injected her with specialised anaesthetic nanos.

"Take her to the medical facility," Romana ordered, "and detain her there until I can join you. I must first speak with Leiki."

Trione called for a gravsled and the two soldiers loaded the former empress' limp form onto its padded bed. As soon as they drew away, Romana contacted Leiki. The councillor was thunderstruck by the unexpected news.

"What is your medical opinion?" he enquired.

"The child must *not* be exiled on Mars. Prua Landi herself has expressed repugnance at the notion that she is carrying Perdon's child, and it is my view that she will kill the girl as soon as she is born."

Leiki nodded to someone off-screen then returned his attention to Romana. "We cannot permit that to happen," he said. "The child will be raised in the time-honoured manner. Do you anticipate any problems?"

"There will be none. Will you break the news to Perdon? He has a right to know that his liaison with the empress has borne unexpected fruit."

Leiki nodded once again and his image faded. Romana stared at the blank screen for long moments as she wrestled with her emotions. Her husband had died at Prua Landi's orders, before they had been allocated 'childbirth' rights. For more than twenty-five years she had nursed a hatred of the dictatrix and now she had received a final kick in the teeth to learn that Prua Landi, herself was to produce a child – the unwanted result of a dalliance with Perdon, a man who had played a significant part in the destruction of her regime. Tears welled from her eyes and seeped down her beautiful golden cheeks as she remembered her dead husband, Keld. She tried to blink them away, but only succeeded in adding to the flow. A footfall behind her startled Romana and she turned to find Joe staring into her eyes, his expression clouded with concern.

"I just heard," he told her, his voice filled with sympathy. "You must feel gutted."

Romana sobbed quietly. "I-I— " she mumbled.

Joe waited, allowing his friend time to frame her troubled thoughts. When it became clear that nothing would be forthcoming, he enfolded her in his arms and hugged her tightly; the top of his head barely reached her shoulders. "It must be galling to know that she's pregnant after what happened twenty-five years ago."

Romana nodded and wet droplets fell onto Joe's forehead. "It is."

"I can't promise," Joe continued, "but I reckon someone as beautiful as you is bound to find someone else."

Romana shuddered. "There could be no one else after Keld. No one could ever take his place."

"No one?"

Joe's simple question trickled through Romana's troubled thoughts. Of course there was another – Joe! But he would never be available.

"Look, Romana, if you can fall for someone like me, I'm certain there must be a special man out there who's perfect for you. There has to be, because I can't imagine anyone who deserves a slice of happiness more than you do." He stood on tiptoe and kissed the beautiful young woman on the cheek. "Once this business has been well and truly put to bed, you'll be able to relax and let nature take its course."

Romana reluctantly detached herself from Joe's embrace. "As always, the Futama knows what is best. Thank you Joe, you are a true friend."

"You're welcome. Now, don't you have a job to do? The sooner everything's settled at this end, the sooner I can go to Mars to collect my family."

"Yes, Joe, I have pressing business with Prua Landi. And, like you, I can't wait to see Ciara."

* * *

The Master of Time made several journeys to Mars, transferring the whole population of the fourth planet back to their future era. A team of engineers and demolition experts began the process of returning Mars to its original, pristine state, leaving only a simple dwelling for Prua Landi and Praeton along with the fields to provide crops to sustain the pair during their long exile. There would remain no technology to show up in the archaeological record of the distant future; even the fabric of the building would begin the process of biodegradation in a little over three Martian centuries, long after Prua Landi and Praeton were dust.

Joe, who was eager to rejoin Ciara, travelled with Romana on the very first of the Master of Time's journeys to Mars. They arrived less than twenty-four hours after the expedition to depose Prua Landi had left for the future. Gillane, Ciara, Maeve and Or-gon led a crowd of people to where the Master of Time's massive bulk stood upon her gigantic tripod legs. Joe raced down the ramp and leapt off the end before it made contact with the hard surface of the landing field. Ciara immediately spotted him and broke away from the host to meet him halfway. Despite her advanced state of pregnancy she leapt joyfully into his arms, raining kisses on every part of his face.

"Happy to see me, Babe?" Joe asked.

Ciara paused in her assault to assure him breathlessly, "What do *you* think? It was only yesterday that you went off to war with no certainty that you would ever return. Of course I'm overjoyed to see you back in one piece." She resumed her activity, but focused her attentions on Joe's lips.

Eventually, Romana coughed delicately. "I must examine you before you return home, to ensure that you and the baby are in good health."

"Why, do I look ill?" Ciara joked.

"I would say the opposite, but a quick check-up will set everyone's mind at rest. The Futama has led his people to victory over Prua Landi's forces and we shall always be indebted to him. I can begin to repay a small part of that debt by ensuring that you remain in perfect health. In fact, I would be honoured if you would permit me to deliver your child when the time comes."

"That would mean me staying in your time for at least a month," Ciara protested.

"Yes, but it would avoid you being subjected to the primitive procedures which pass as medical care in your own era. And—" she was introspective for a few moments, "—it will avoid the possibility of someone accidentally discovering the nanos in your child's bloodstream."

Ciara glanced at Joe for approval and he nodded. "Okay, you've got a point. We can't afford to arouse suspicions where little Joe's concerned."

Or-gon nudged Ciara's arm. "I will assist in making my adoptive grandson blend in. I will provide an identity for him that will be impervious to questioning. It will not be difficult to access the necessary official databases to implant the data – as I have already done to reinforce the false identity you obtained for me."

"What did you just say?" Ciara demanded.

"That I will provide an identity for your child—"

"No, not that. I mean the part about your adoptive grandson. Do you mean what I think you mean?"

Maeve blushed to the roots of her flaming corona of red hair. "Or-gon and I," she said, unable to hide her embarrassment, "have decided to get married."

Ciara released Joe and hugged her mother tightly. "Congratulations, Mum. I'm really pleased for you – and Or-gon." She kissed Maeve on the cheek and repeated the gesture with Or-gon.

Joe shook his friend's hand. "Welcome to the family," he grinned.

The Neanderthal grinned toothily. "The Futama has always treated me as part of his family," he said. "Now it will be official."

EPILOGUE:

Joe and Ciara sat in the austere office, watching Major Ewan Cawthor riffle through a pile of papers on his militarily neat desk. Jo-na sat on his mother's knee, his attention focused upon the man in the dark suit seated beside the major.

"Hello!" he piped, his child's voice strident within the confines of the office.

Pierce Gray, from MI5 shuffled uncomfortably in his seat; he was unaccustomed to having children around, especially small ones whose shining eyes followed his every movement as if he were infinitely more interesting than any new toy. "There is no point in procrastinating, Major," he said. "Let us begin."

Cawthor harrumphed noisily and obliged. He picked up a copy of Joe's second novel, *Every Future Has a Past* and absently flipped through the pages. "Mr Laing . . . Mrs Laing, would you like to hazard a guess at what I have been doing for the past three years or so?" He waited a few moments, and when neither made any sort of comment, he continued, "I have been recording and investigating the waking dreams of more than thirty soldiers."

"Why? What would Army Intelligence and MI5 find of interest in the daydreams of a few soldiers?"

"Taken individually, Mr Laing, absolutely nothing at all. After all, there is nothing remarkable in daydreams, unless— " His expression suggested he had just tasted something particularly foul. "Unless, every one of the soldiers is experiencing the *same* dream."

Ciara smiled sweetly. "I'd say that that *would* qualify as remarkable."

The muscles in Pierce Gray's jaw tensed visibly. "This is not a joking matter, Mrs Laing."

Still smiling sweetly, Ciara said, "I wasn't joking, Mr—?"

"Gray," Major Cawthor volunteered. He whispered a few words to the MI5 official, and continued. "Let us not allow ourselves to become distracted. The point I am making is that you, Mr Laing, are the central figure in their waking dreams. It is as if they all can lay claim to a particularly elusive memory, a memory which not a single one of them can recall in any detail."

"Why me? I could understand if they were dreaming about my wife. She is, after all, extremely beautiful. But me? I find it difficult to believe."

Ciara smiled radiantly at Joe's compliment and squeezed his hand. Major Cawthor noticed the movement and coloured slightly.

"This is getting us nowhere," Cawthor grimaced. "Let us put our cards on the table, Mr Laing. I have debriefed all of the soldiers, plus an experienced lieutenant, and by the simple process of following clues and descriptions, have arrived in the roadway outside your home."

"Where you found that the stories made no sense because you found nothing unusual?"

Piece Gray interceded. "What I find unusual, Mr Laing is that you already seem to know where this investigation is heading."

"But that would take a mind reader and the existence of telepathy has never been proved scientifically."

"Perhaps. We are keeping our minds open on the subject."

Jo-na, who had so far remained quiet throughout the interview, slid off Ciara's knee and began marching around the office with his arms out before him and his eyes closed to slits, intoning, "I am a mind reader," in a voice uncannily reminiscent of a Dalek from a long-running children's science fiction TV series.

Ciara allowed the little one to make two circuits of the office before scooping him up onto her knee. "I think Jo-na, in his way, has made a telling comment on your theory, Mr Gray." She smiled indulgently at Jo-na before asking casually, "Have you brought us here based on nothing more than the information you have given us so far? If so, I think it's about time for us to terminate the interview." She started to rise from her seat.

Gray made placating motions with his hands. "No, no, Mrs Laing, there is more, I assure you. Major?"

Major Cawthor harrumphed noisily once more. "All the men recognised *you*, Mr Laing, from their waking dreams."

"How, exactly, did they know it was me?" Joe asked innocently.

"From photographs, of course," the major replied.

"Are you telling me that I have been under surveillance? Surely that's an infringement of my civil liberties, isn't it?"

"Perhaps," Pierce Gray informed him, "unless it were a matter of national security, which I am inclined to believe, it is."

"Fine," Joe said agreeably. "Correct me if I'm wrong, but you think that we're at the centre of some kind of weird happenings, but you have no idea what because everyone involved seems to have developed selective amnesia on the subject? Am I right so far?"

With patches of white standing out on his jaw, the major said tautly, "It would seem so." He riffled through the papers on his desk and produced a photocopy of a document. He handed it over to Joe. "What is your opinion of this, Mr Laing?"

Joe scanned the photocopy; it appeared to be a page from the log of a Royal Air Force control tower. "What am I looking for, Major?"

Cawthor leaned over his desk and indicated an entry approximately two-thirds down the page.

Joe examined the entry. "What's so special about it? It seems okay to me?"

"I'd like you to examine the feint marking behind the writing," Cawthor urged. "What do you think it says?"

Joe handed the photocopy to Ciara for her to read. "Looks like the letters UPO to me," Ciara offered.

Gray said impatiently. "Please don't try to be obtuse, Mrs Laing. We know you can see that the letters clearly read 'UFO'. We have enhanced the image and the complete handwritten text reads 'UFO at . . .' and the remainder of the entry gives the map coordinates of your home. We have a number of theories to explain how and why the entry was overwritten, none of which make sense, especially since there is no indication of how the ink was erased without disrupting the surface of the paper."

Enjoying yourself, sweetheart? Joe asked Ciara silently.

It's been a while since I had so much fun, Ciara replied in the same manner. *Don't be too hard on them. They're only trying to get a handle on something that's impossible for them to explain with any degree of rationality.*

Jo-na put his index fingers to his temples and intoned once again, "I am a mind reader."

"It's a bit of a puzzle, isn't it?" Joe admitted. "Sorry, but I can't even hazard a guess at what's happened, can you, Darling?"

"The whole affair's beyond me," Ciara replied.

Joe stared into Cawthor's green eyes until the major was compelled to turn his eyes away. The officer knew now, if he hadn't up to this point, that he and Gray were no longer in control of the interview.

"Major," Joe said quietly, "have you questioned the four policemen and several of my neighbours? Not forgetting, of course, the three chopper pilots and the air traffic controllers?"

288

Major Cawthor glanced at Gray, who nodded. "Everyone seems to have the same incomplete recollections of an event which occurred in the roadway outside your home. Two of the gunship pilots believe they were ordered to train their machine guns on a strange vehicle at the junction of the two roads. The third remembers nothing – or wishes us to believe he remembers nothing." Cawthor glanced once more at Gray, who wore an expression of elation on his aristocratic features. "Yes, Mr Gray?"

"I was just wondering," Gray said triumphantly, "how Mr Laing could be aware of the other players in this game if he is, as he would have us believe, entirely innocent."

Before anyone could comment, the major shifted the line of attack. He extracted several A4-sized colour prints from a folder and laid them on the desk facing Joe and Ciara. They depicted in sharp close-up, the area of the cliff burned by Prua Landi, itself the subject of a prolonged investigation by the authorities more than three years previously.

"Do you have anything to say about this?" he asked.

Joe examined the photographs. Prua Landi had certainly vented her temper on the rock face as she tried in vain to gain access to Joe and Ciara. "It looks like melted rock," he ventured.

Exasperation was beginning to show in Cawthor's tones as he exclaimed, "You must know where these photographs were taken, Mr Laing. After all, you do walk along the beach most mornings. At the time this area of molten cliff appeared three years or so ago, you were a frequent visitor to the beach. In fact, witnesses swear that on a number of occasions your journey took you one way only – yet there is no other exit from the beach. Have you a reasonable explanation? One that will place no further strain on our patience?"

"Not really."

"Then will you at least make an attempt to explain this?" Desperation was evident in Cawthor's voice as he threw the copy of *Every Future has a Past* onto the desk in front of Joe and Ciara.

"Would you like me to sign it?" Joe enquired.

Cawthor let Joe's flippancy pass without comment. "Are you the main character in the book?"

"What do you wish me to say, Major?"

"Mr Laing, the events portrayed in your novel are clearly impossible, but then so is the mass delusion I have been investigating for the past three years. The more I investigate, the weirder it gets. I find that I am inclined to believe much more than I would have accepted three years ago." Cawthor sighed, a sign that he was approaching the end of his tether. "Tell me," he said with an air of confidentiality, "just how much of your adventures have you omitted from the novel?"

"Everything I thought might lead to an investigation such as this. It seems, however, I made a slight error when setting the timestone and I misjudged its effect on those involved."

Pierce Gray pounced immediately upon Joe's statement. "Timestone? Are you admitting complicity in these events, Mr Laing?"

"I'm admitting that I wrote about the events in my novel, yes. Whether what happened is real or a figment of an overly fertile imagination is for you to decide. After all, I'm a science fiction writer, with the accent on the fiction. A writer requires a pretty good imagination and a reliable memory, but it would be conceited of me to boast."

Cawthor and Gray stared at each other in exasperation; they knew that Joe and Ciara – perhaps even the child – had been giving them the run-around since the beginning of the interview.

Memory is a strange thing you know, Major," Joe continued. "It can be a gift or a curse."

"Which is yours, Mr Laing?"

"A gift – definitely a gift. After all, it has enabled me to make a comfortable living as an author."

"If I'm to believe what I have read in this book, you have access to both the past and the future."

Joe sighed. "Time travel is *impossible*, Major, except possibly at a subatomic level – if modern theories are to be believed, that is. Ask any physicist."

Cawthor knew that he would get no further with the interview; he became belligerent. "What is to prevent me from putting you and your family under house arrest?" he threatened.

"Nothing, except that you know it wouldn't work."

"How would I know that?"

"If I were capable of a fraction of what you seem to believe, wouldn't house arrest be an empty gesture on your part?" Joe grinned amiably. "Look at us, Major. Do we seem like people who could be put under house arrest and kept there?"

Cawthor and Gray stared at Joe, Ciara and Jo-na in turn. Even the child gave the impression that he knew more than he was letting on and the two found it more than a little unnerving.

Joe and Ciara smiled at their two interrogators. "Okay," Joe informed them casually, "you've had your fun. I think it's time for us to go home."

"You think so?" Gray demanded. "Guard!"

The two soldiers, who had been standing silently to attention outside the door, entered with their rifles at the ready, their boots sounding a staccato drumbeat on the wooden floor.

"Take these civilians to the guardhouse," Gray ordered, "and lock them in separate cells."

"Permission to speak, Sir?" one of the guards asked.

"Go ahead!"

"Does that include the child, Sir?"

"The child can go in a cell with his mother."

"Yes, Sir." The guards reluctantly urged Joe, Ciara and Jo-na to their feet.

Ciara wore an expression of alarm and Joe comforted her. *Don't worry, I'll fix it.* Ciara immediately relaxed, confident in Joe's ability to make good his promise.

With newly acquired skills of mind control, taught to him by his friends in the future, Joe rearranged the memories of the two guards, erasing their most recent orders. With Major Ewan Cawthor and Pierce Gray, he swiftly expunged every recollection of their investigation into waking dreams, leaving them with the vague notion that something strange and inexplicable had occurred within the confines of the office.

Whilst the guards stood uncertainly to attention, the major warmly shook Joe and Ciara's hands, and Gray followed suit. "Thank you Mr Laing . . . Mrs Laing," Cawthor enthused, "you have been most helpful. I'll arrange for a driver to take you home." He ruffled his fingers through Jo-na's mop of tousled hair. "Goodbye and thank you for all your help."

Joe reached forward and picked up the copy of his novel from Cawthor's desk. "Do you have a pen, Major, because I'd like to sign your copy of my book before we go. After all, I think you've earned it. Who knows, it might even be valuable – in time."

THE END

You've finished. Before you go…
<u>Tweet/share that you have finished this book</u>
Rate this book

Customers who bought this book also bought
- The Neanderthal Paradox – *Journey to the Past* by Keith Argyle and Paul G White
- The Neanderthal Paradox – *Future's Children* by Keith Argyle and Paul G White
- The Evil Returns by Keith Argyle and Paul G White

More by these authors
- The Medallion of Lorn by Keith Argyle and Paul G White

About the authors
Keith and Paul have been friends for more than fifteen years and in 2005 they began collaboration on their first Neanderthal Paradox novel. The second book in the trilogy followed in 2006 and the third in 2007. Keith and Paul then wrote a fantasy novel, *The Medallion of Lorn* and are now working on *The Sha'lee Resurrection* about an alien spaceship buried by the tsunami which followed the Cretaceous/Tertiary extinction event. This

science fiction novel should be on Kindle late 2013. Keith lives in Conisbrough, South Yorkshire, UK and Paul lives in Peterborough, Cambridgeshire, UK.

Keith Argyle   Paul G White